D1430985

INFERNO

Benito Pérez Galdós

INFERNO

Translated and edited by Abigail Lee Six

PHOENIX HOUSE
London

First published in Great Britain in 1998
by Phoenix House

Typeset in Sabon by SetSystems Ltd, Saffron Walden, Essex
Printed in Great Britain by
Clays Ltd, St Ives plc

British Library Cataloguing-in-Publication Data
is available upon request.

ISBN 1 861591 07 1 (Cased)
1 861591 08 X (Paperback)

Phoenix House
An imprint of the Weidenfeld & Nicolson division of
The Orion Publishing Group
Orion House
5 Upper St Martin's Lane
London WC2H 9EA

CONTENTS

FOREWORD

In spite of his relative obscurity in the English-speaking world, in Spain Benito Pérez Galdós enjoys a status analogous to that of Dickens here or Balzac in France. Born in Las Palmas, in the Canary Islands in 1843, he went to Madrid to study law in his early twenties. He failed to complete his degree, for he was sidetracked into the writing career to which he would devote the rest of his life. His literary apprenticeship was enhanced by a trip to Paris in 1867, where he was exposed to the French writers of his time, notably Balzac, whom he greatly admired. The following year, he used a French translation of *The Pickwick Papers* to produce a Spanish version, demonstrating his love also for Dickens. By this time he had begun to work as a journalist, a lifelong profession which he successfully combined with his literary work. In 1886, he became a member of parliament. Political controversy delayed his election to the prestigious Spanish Royal Academy until 1889. By the time of his death in 1920, he had been blind for almost a decade.

A prolific writer, Galdós produced a total of 78 novels and 21 plays, in addition to his journalistic work. Although his other writing is now beginning to receive more critical attention, it remains true that Galdós's fame is mostly attributable to the group of fictional works to which *Inferno* belongs, called by some critics the 'Social Novels' and all written between 1870 and 1915. Despite their fictional status, however, these narratives are inextricably bound up with the sociopolitical climate of their author's lifetime and ingeniously weave historical events and personages into their fabric. The remainder of Galdós's full-length prose works are called collectively 'National Episodes' and, as this suggests, are historical works in a stricter sense of the term.

Inferno was published in 1884. This places it near the zenith of the author's production, just before the creation of his masterpiece, *Fortunata and Jacinta* (1886–87). However, *Inferno*'s setting backtracks 17 years to cover the period of November 1867 to February 1868. This was a time of political turmoil which would culminate in September 1868 in the so-called Glorious Revolution, when Queen Isabella II (1833–68) was dethroned. For this reason it is worthwhile to consider briefly the sociopolitical climate in Madrid in the 1860s, in order to give some background to the atmosphere of *Inferno*.

For decades already, the nobility had been losing its hold over the country and a new bourgeoisie making inroads into the power structure. Thus, blue blood was no longer the single entry requirement for the upper echelons of Spanish society; now the wealthy business and banking class had acquired social standing too. It is this class, together with a broad spectrum of civil servants that Galdós places in the centre of many of his social novels. Here in *Inferno*, we have Francisco de Bringas offering a glimpse into the civil service and Agustín Caballero, with his friends, providing insight into the world of banking and commerce.

The key political groupings in the years leading up to the Revolution were the Liberal Union, and the Progressives and Democrats. The Liberal Union took power in 1858 and held it until 1863. A broad coalition that aimed for stability through reconciliation of opposing political forces, it was helped by a general disenchantment with politicking in the country, a successful military campaign in North Africa, and also the economic boost provided by the rise of the railways in Spain. The Progressive and Democratic Parties, which joined forces in 1866, both sought to unseat Queen Isabella, but with the difference that the Democrats contained a strongly republican element. Power shifted unstably between these political groups in the period immediately preceding the Revolution. Some of the key political figures of the times mentioned in *Inferno* are three army generals: Juan Prim, Ramón María Narváez, and Leopoldo O'Donnell. Prim (1814–70) was the principal leader of the 1868 Revolution and became premier afterwards. Narváez (1800–68) led the Moderate Party from 1844 until his death in the April just prior to the Revolution. In spite of the term 'moderate', this was an authoritarian conservative. O'Donnell (1809–67), had founded the Liberal Union in 1856 and headed three governments in the years leading up to the Revolution.

The press in the mid-1860s was an important political weapon. *La Correspondencia*, which Francisco de Bringas reads, was a right-wing publication, supporting the Liberal Union and a favourite with the politically moderate, stability-seeking bourgeoisie. That it should be Don Francisco's preferred paper confirms the centre-right impression of him and may have been effective shorthand for the reader contemporary with Galdós to pigeon-hole him politically. Rosalía, on the other hand, positions herself to the political right of her husband, notably in the scene of the portrait hanging in Chapter 3.

One of the joys of reading Galdós is undoubtedly his masterful use of irony. *Inferno* is no exception in this respect. Whilst proper names often contain quite simple irony, the plotting of this novel exploits a more complex variety based on the dialogue Galdós conducts with two cousins of his own realist genre: the melodramatic serial represented by Ido's creative talents on the one hand, and on the other, the theatre where Rosalía loves going so much, with the associated notions of theatricality, role-playing, and stage management. In Chapter 12 for example, Amparo gives up trying to write to Agustín to thank him for the money he has sent because her efforts sound as artificial as if they had come from a character of Ido's. And when she attempts suicide, this is portrayed as highly theatrical even if we do not doubt the veracity of her desperation. She carefully chooses the backdrop and costume most appropriate for her grand exit and visualizes the drama of the next scene when Agustín finds her dead. Her failure to pull this turn of the plot off is in keeping with the way in which the novel distances itself from such melodramatic forms.

Thus, *Inferno* continually draws attention to its own status as fiction and quality fiction at that. Indeed, one might regard it as a demonstratioin by Galdós that the elements of a pot-boiler or a melodrama – for the triangle formed by Amparo, Agustín, and Polo surely could be the makings of such products of popular culture – can have realist life breathed into them, so that they transcend those genres for which they seem so well suited and acquire an altogether grander status in terms of depth and subtlety. One of the key strategies employed within the novel to make this point is Ido and his clichéd, impoverished version of almost identical material. Along with the theatrical references throughout, Galdós thus creates an extra dimension to the novel that enriches the reading experience beyond the delights – undiminished for all that – of well-wrought realist narrative.

Notes on reading Inferno in translation

The present translation is based on the first edition of *Tormento*, edited by Eamonn Rodgers (Oxford: Pergamon, 1977). His notes and personal advice were an invaluable resource in the preparation of this English version. The earlier translation, *Torment*, by J. M. Cohen (London: Weidenfeld & Nicolson, 1952) was consulted for comparative purposes, but in no way served as a basis for this version, which is my own.

Living conditions

One of the major differences between urban living in Britain and Spain, in the nineteenth century as well as the twentieth, is that whereas the norm in Spanish cities has been to live in a flat, however large or wealthy the family, a house would be more usual in Britain. Even the opulent Agustín does not occupy the whole building that he owns, but as is typical, has the grand first floor for himself; a family like the Bringases, whose English equivalent would almost certainly have been living in a house, has the first floor of the building where they live too, but in contrast to Agustín's residence, their street is narrow, their rooms dark and small, and they are tenants instead of owner-occupiers. Amparo, the poorest of the main characters, is in a garret, a more easily recognizable social statement for the English reader and Ido lives one floor down from her, suggesting his marginally better financial position. The Spanish term used casually for all of these very different types of abode – as well as for the whole building containing them – is *casa*, usually translated as 'house'. I have rendered it variously as 'abode', 'home', 'building', and occasionally 'house' too, because 'flat' and 'block of flats' carry inappropriate connotations, but the image to retain for the reader is of central, old Madrid, its streets lined with large buildings, often with commercial premises on the ground floor, the first floor having the most spacious accommodation and therefore occupied by the richest household, and then with each storey up the building, poorer and poorer occupants in more and more cramped conditions.

Thus, in the heart of Madrid, the street address alone would not necessarily betray very much about social standing and this may be one reason why Rosalía expresses horror at the thought of moving out to the newly built Salamanca district, where there was class segregation by neighbourhood. There, she would be less able to camouflage the social position of her family.

Names

A note on Spanish surnames may be useful to the English reader. In this respect, nineteenth-century practice does not differ from present-day convention. Spanish people have two surnames, the first their father's, the second their mother's (which is to say, their maternal grandfather's). Except when the first surname is one of the most common ones (such as Sánchez in the case of Amparo), they are usually known casually by their first surname, but use the second as well for any official business. It is therefore normal for Spanish people to know the two surnames of their friends rather as in the English-speaking world one is likely to be aware of the middle initial of one's acquaintances. When women marry, they usually retain their maiden names for official purposes, but are also known by their husband's surname. They often adopt a formula of using their maiden first surname (that is, their father's) and their husband's, while dropping their mother's surname, although all three names may well remain in circulation, as is the case with Rosalía, who uses *Bringas* (her husband's), *Pipaón* (her father's), and then instead of *Calderón* (her mother's), prefers the entirely bogus *de la Barca*, inspired by the great Spanish seventeenth-century dramatist's name, Pedro Calderón de la Barca (1600–81).

Forms of address

Another problem with the rendering of any Spanish text into English is our lack of distinct polite and familiar forms of address. These carry tremendous emotional weight that it is all too easy for Anglophones to underestimate. It is more than a social convention in Spanish and subtler than the use of first-name versus title-and-surname in English. Fernando Díaz-Plaja claims that a lady of the 1860s in Spain would find a kiss less compromising than the use of the familiar form and points out that gaining permission to switch from polite to familiar form constituted a major victory in a man's campaign to win a lady's favours (p. 111). The social status of characters, what they think of their own standing relative to that of others, the different degrees of intimacy they will allow or are trying to obtain with others are just some examples of what may be evoked by these forms.

For instance, Felipe, Agustín's servant, uses the polite form to

Amparo and she uses the familiar to him. This suggests that he is respectful towards her and looks up to her socially; her use of the familiar expresses, amongst other things, her somewhat maternal warmth towards him as well as her self-image as his social superior and his acceptance of this. I have inserted 'Miss' in his speech to her to try to reflect this social inequality, but it is certainly less subtle than the Spanish.

A more striking example comes from Agustín and Amparo's developing relationship. His use of the polite form to her at first is respectful, shy and, in contrast to her use of the same form to him, it is optional; he could have used the familiar as she is beneath him socially and younger; the fact that he does not is already suggestive in Spanish. The turning-point represented by the switch from formal to familiar form of address in Chapter 20 has an emotional depth that simply has no equivalent in English. Amparo's flattered bewilderment is matched in the Spanish text by Agustín's repeated slips into the polite form and self-corrections back into the familiar, which are impossible to render into standard English. The amorous intimacy that all of this evokes on the emotional level is then also inflected by the social equalization suggested by Agustín's wish for Amparo to use the familiar form to him. The atmosphere of embarrassment that pervades this scene is attributable to a combination of these two elements that cannot easily be teased apart.

On the other hand, by clinging to the polite form with Polo, Amparo clearly conveys that she does not wish to return to their earlier intimacy, whereas he stubbornly uses the familiar to her as he tries to resuscitate their relationship.

Galdós also uses a wealth of subtly different ways to refer to his characters in the third person. The use of the definite article with surname gives a colloquial feel to the narrator's style and can be affectionate and/or derogatory. I have adopted the form 'our dear Mrs Bringas' for 'La de Bringas', reflecting the affectionate connotation but with a sarcastic edge. 'La Empera-dora' for Amparo has been rendered as 'our Emperine', to reflect the non-standard feminine form, as well as the irony of drawing attention in this way to the meaning of her second surname.

ABIGAIL LEE SIX

INFERNO

CHAPTER I

Descalzas corner. Two figures, their faces concealed by mufflers, come onstage from opposite sides and bump into one another. It is night time.

FIRST MUFFLED FIGURE: Idiot!
SECOND MUFFLED FIGURE: *I'm* not the idiot.
FIRST: Can't you see the road?
SECOND: And you, haven't you eyes in your head? ... You almost knocked me over.
FIRST: I was just walking along.
SECOND: So was I.
FIRST: Be off and to hell with you. [*Continuing on his way towards stage right.*]
SECOND: What a temper!
FIRST: If I catch you, my lad ... [*Stopping threateningly.*] I'll teach you how to speak to your elders. [*He peers at the second muffled figure.*] But I know that face. Gadzooks! ... Isn't it you?
SECOND: And I know you too, sir. That face, if it isn't that of the Devil himself, is Don José Ido del Sagrario's.
FIRST: My dear Felipe! [*Letting his muffler slip off and opening his arms.*] Who on earth would have recognised you so wrapped up? Why, if it isn't Aristotle himself. Embrace me, my dear fellow ... and again!
SECOND: Well, what a fortunate encounter! Believe me, Don José; I'm happier to see you than if I'd found a sack of money.
FIRST: But where have you been hiding, lad? What have you been up to?
SECOND: It's a long story. And what about you, sir?
FIRST: Oh! Let me catch my breath. Are you in a hurry?
SECOND: Not much.
FIRST: Well let's have a chat, then. It's a chilly night, and there's

no need for us to hold a conversation in this windswept little square. Let's go to the Lepanto café; it isn't far. I'll treat you.

SECOND: I'll treat *you*.

FIRST: I say, I say, evidently someone's feeling flush.

SECOND: Well, things aren't bad. What about you, sir?

FIRST: Me? Well, if I tell you that, frankly, I'm doing better than I have ever done, perhaps you won't believe me.

SECOND: That's good, Mr de Ido. I asked after you several times, and as no one ever gave me any news, I used to wonder: 'What can have become of that dear soul?'·

[*They go into the Lepanto café, a poor, sad, dilapidated establishment in Santo Domingo Square, which has now closed down, leaving no shadow or trace of its former glory. They sit at a table and order coffee and drinks.*]

IDO DEL SAGRARIO [*solemnly, placing his two elbows on the table as though they were objects that would have been in the way elsewhere*]: We're both so eager to tell of our troubles and fill each other in on all our doings and our good fortune, that I don't know whether to take the lead myself or let you begin.

ARISTO [*removing his cape and putting it, neatly folded, on a stool near his own*]: As you prefer, sir.

IDO: I see you have a good cape . . . And a tie with a pin like a gentleman . . . And very decent clothes. My good man . . . you have come into a fortune. Whom are you mixing with? Has some uncle turned up from the Indies?

ARISTO: The fact is – let it be said once and for all – that I have at present the best master in the world. There can be no better under the sun now or ever.

IDO: Good! Bravo! A round of applause for this model master. But is he as messy as that Don Alejandro Miquis?

ARISTO: Quite the reverse.

IDO: A student?

ARISTO [*proudly*]: A capitalist!

IDO: My dear man . . . I'm open-mouthed. Is he very rich?

ARISTO: He has . . . [*expressing immensity with his voice and gesture*] an incalculable amount.

IDO: Well I never! Didn't I tell you that God would remember you eventually . . . And now tell me frankly: how do I look?

ARISTO [*with unconcealed mirth*]: Well sir, I find you . . .

IDO [*jubilant and dribbling transparent saliva from his lower lip*]: Out with it, man, out with it.

ARISTO: Well, I find you . . . corpulent.

IDO [*with ineffable delight*]: Yes, yes, others have said so too. Nicanora maintains that I put on two pounds per month . . . Why, the felicitous change in my position, in my career, in my lifestyle is bound to express itself in this wretched flesh. I am no longer a child-tamer; I am no longer engaged in turning beasts into men, which is the same as manufacturing ungrateful wretches. Didn't I tell you that I was planning to change from that miserable job to a more honourable and lucrative one? . . . A serial-writer took me on as his clerk. He dictated, I wrote . . . My hand a flash of lightning . . . The man delighted . . . An onza each instalment. My author falls ill and says: 'Ido, finish that chapter.' I take up my pen and bang! I finish it and dash off another, and another. My good man, I shocked even myself. My master says: 'Co-writer Ido . . .' We began three novels at the same time. He dictated the openings: then I took up the thread, and off we went chapter after chapter. It is all stuff about Philip II, you know: muffled figures, bailiffs, dashing gentlemen, and ladies, my good man, more delicate than glass, more easily inflamed than tinderwood . . .; the Escorial, the Citadel of Madrid, Jews, Moors, renegades, bad old Antonio Pérez, who for intrigue was more than enough on his own, and the oh so villainous princess of Eboli, who can see more with one eye than four people with two; Cardinal Granvela, the Inquisition, Prince Carlos, lots of rustling skirts, lots of friars' habits, lots of throwing bags of money around for any little service, underground passages, madcap nuns, intrigue and trickery, bastard children at every turn, and King Philip thick with ointments . . . To be brief, my dear fellow, reams and reams go by in that way . . . Share the earnings; half him, half me . . . New cape, well-fed children, Nicanora cured . . . [*Pausing, breathless.*] Me, with a full belly and as happy as can be, working harder than the bishop and making a mint.

ARISTO: A lovely profession!

IDO [*getting his breath back*]: Don't you believe it! It takes brains, for it's the devil of a fuss and bother. The publisher says: 'Ido, explosive imagination: three heads in one.' And it's true. When I go to bed, lad, I feel my brain bubbling like a pot on the fire . . . and in the street, when I go out for diversion, I keep thinking about my scenes and my characters. Every church becomes the Escorial, every night watchman a tipstaff and every

cape a pelerine. When I lose my temper, I come out with
forsooths without meaning to, and instead of a 'Good Lord',
what slips from my lips is that 'Gadzooks!'. I am likely to call
my Nicanora Doña Sol or Doña Mencía. I sleep late; I wake up
laughing and say: 'Now, now I see how the one who fell into
the trap is going to escape.' [*Excitedly, which puts Felipe on his
guard.*] Because you should know, my friend, that there is a very
long underground passage, dug by the Moors, which joins up
the Platero house, where Antonio Pérez lives, with the Calced
Carmelite nuns' convent of the Santísima Pasión de Pinto.
ARISTO: Well! It certainly is long ... [*Smothering his mirth.*]
What a business! You've obviously got yourself into quite a
tangle! But the important thing is to be earning money.
IDO: Cash! As much of it as I want. Now I'm making eight
duros per instalment. I can polish off my part in two days. Soon
I'll be working on my own, once we've finished the new job
we've been commissioned to do now. The publisher's a man
who knows his stuff and he says: 'I want lots of sentiment in it,
so it makes people cry, and plenty of moral content too.' When
I hear him say that my brain at once catches fire. My companion
consults me ... my answer is to read him the first chapter that I
drafted the night before at home ... the man delighted! Frankly,
the thing is going well. I imagine that rooting around among
some ruins I find a chest. I open it carefully, and what do you
think I find? A manuscript. I read and what is it? The most
moving of stories, a book of memoirs, a diary. Because either
one has the spark or one hasn't ... With us both hard at it,
we've already done fourteen instalments and the thing won't be
finished until the publisher says: 'That's it, lads, kill it!' [*Draining his glass of brandy.*] This liquor is marvellously invigorating.
ARISTO [*looking at the café clock*]: It's getting late, and though
my master's very good, I don't want him to scold me for dilly-
dallying when I'm on an errand.
IDO [*very over-excited and not listening to what Felipe is
saying*]: As I was saying, I've put in the story two pretty girls,
poor, you understand, very poor, who are scarcely scraping
along the whole time. But they're as pure as the Paschal Lamb.
That's where the moral content comes in, there, for these
orphaned lambkins, solicited by so many greedy wolves, val-
iantly resist and are so hostile to anything smacking of sin that
they act as an example to the other lasses of the day. My

heroines wear their fingers to the bone sewing, and the hungrier they are the more they cling to their virtue. The tiny room where they live is as clean as a new pin. Fresh and artificial flowers, because one of them waters the pots of Sweet William and the other goes in for making silk carnations. In the morning, when they open the little window that gives on to the roof ... I'd like to read it to you ... It says: 'It was a beautiful morning in the month of May. It seemed as though Nature ...' [*Rambling.*] At this point there's a knock at the door. It's a lackey with a letter full of banknotes. The two pretty little girls are furious at this and write to the Marquess on perfumed paper ... and I have them give him a piece of their mind. In short, they want to triumph in virtue more than they want money. Oh! I forgot to tell you that there's a duchess, as wicked as wicked can be, who wants to lead the girls to perdition because she's so envious of their beauty ... There's also a banker who stops at nothing. He thinks that money by the fistful will put anything to rights. Fiddlesticks! I take my inspiration from real life. Where is integrity to be found? In the poor man, in the labourer, in the beggar. Where roguery? In the rich man, in the nobleman, in the minister, in the general, in the courtier ... The former work, the latter spend. The former pay, the latter suck. We cry and they feed off us. The world ought to ... But what are you doing, Felipe? Are you falling asleep?

ARISTO [*rousing and shaking himself*]: Sorry sir, dear Don José. It isn't lack of respect; it's just that even with the little I drank of that accursed brandy, I feel as though my head's full of stones.

IDO [*with growing feverish malaise, the last dam to his loquaciousness now down*]: Ah, this is life-giving ... for with this warmth running through me, the muse will be with me for the whole night, and now I'm going home and shall dispatch sixty pages at a stroke ... [*Jumping up.*] You're a veritable milksop. Drink some more.

ARISTO [*rubbing his eyes*]: On no account. I should keel over in the street. Come on, Don José.

IDO: Wait, man. Don't be so energetic. What's the hurry?

ARISTO [*putting his hand into his breast pocket*]: I'm off to deliver this letter.

IDO: To whom?

ARISTO: To two young ladies who live alone.

IDO [*thunderstruck*]: Felipe! ... To two pretty, virtuous little girls, alone in the world! Undoubtedly a letter full of money. Your master is a banker, a cad who wants to dishonour them.

ARISTO: Slow down ... You've had too much to drink, sir.

IDO: You see, you see? [*His eyes popping out of his head.*] You see how fantasy may invent all it will, but reality invents much more? Appetising orphan girls, temptation, letter, millions, virtue triumphant. [*Gesticulating emphatically with his right arm.*] Mark my words. What do you bet they slam the door in your face? What do you bet you'll go tumbling down the stairs? Chapter: 'How the Marquess's emissary takes the measure of the stairway.'

ARISTO: But my master is no marquess ... My master is Don Agustín Caballero, whom you probably know.

IDO [*penetratingly*]: Whatever he may be, inside the letter you're carrying there lies an instrument of immorality, of corruption. There are notes in that letter.

ARISTO: Musical ones maybe, for they are theatre tickets, for tomorrow's Sunday afternoon performance. You see, my master's cousins, Mr and Mrs Bringas, can't go, because one of their children is ill.

IDO: Bringas, Bringas! ... [*Remembering.*] Aristotle, my friend, let me see the envelope.

ARISTO: Here. look.

IDO [*reading the envelope, he utters a formidable monosyllable of astonishment and puts his hands to his head*]: 'The Misses Amparo and Refugio.' But they're my neighbours, they're the two little orphan girls of Sánchez Emperador ...

ARISTO: Do you know them?

IDO: But we live in the same building at 4 Beartas Street, me on the third floor, them on the fourth! It's from that pair that I take my inspiration for my writing ... You see, you see? Real life pursues us. I write marvels, real life plagiarises me.

ARISTO: They're good, pretty girls.

IDO: I'll tell you ... [*Meditative.*] They give no grounds for talk in the neighbourhood, but ...

ARISTO: But what? ...

IDO [*with great mystery*]: Real life occasionally imitates those of us who know more than she does, but she also invents things that even someone like I, with the imagination of three men, would not dare to dream of.

ARISTO: Well, put those things in your novels.

IDO: No, because they have no poetry. [*Frowning.*] You don't understand art. Some stupendous things that happen can't go near the covers of a book, because people would be shocked . . . horrible, ill-fated, prosaic things, things that will always be banished from our honourable republic of the arts! I mean, if I told you about . . .

ARISTO: Tell me!

IDO: If you could keep a little secret!

ARISTO: I can, I can!

IDO: Really?

ARISTO: Come out with it, Don José.

IDO: Well . . . [*After looking all around, he puts his lips to Felipe's ear and speaks quietly to him for a short while.*]

ARISTO [*listening saddened*]: I see . . . What a business!

IDO: This mustn't be talked about.

ARISTO: No, it mustn't.

IDO: Nor must it be written down. What base prose it would make!

ARISTO [*reflecting*]: Unless you, with your imagination of three men, could turn it to poetry.

IDO [*vehemently shaking his head*]: You don't understand about art. [*Trying to bore a hole in his forehead with his index finger.*] I quarry my poetry in here.

ARISTO: Come along, Don José.

IDO: Come on; and since you and I are taking the same direction towards where I live . . . we shall speak . . . way. When you have carried out . . . errand, you will call in. Nicanora will be so pleased to see you. Handshake . . . chat, memories, explanations . . . [*His language becoming more and more incoherent and slurred.*] I . . . speak to you Emperines . . . you . . . of this illustrious master . . . distinguished . . . opulently wealthy . . .

CHAPTER 2

In 1867, Don Francisco de Bringas y Caballero, second in command at the Royal Commission of Holy Places, was a fine fellow who admitted to being fifty. He is still alive, God preserve him. But he is no longer that agile, strong man, with that sociable temperament, that amenable turn of phrase, that generous nature, that helpful, gentlemanly disposition. Those of us who had dealings with him then scarcely recognise him today when we see him in the street, leaning upon a manservant, dragging his feet, bent double, with half his face hidden under a muffler, almost blind, shaky, dribbling and as clumsy in his speech as in his gait. A pitiable gentleman! Sixteen years ago he boasted the best health of his time; he fulfilled his professional duties in our offices with unheard-of conscientiousness, and ran his domestic affairs with impeccable order, second to none in meeting his obligations at home and in society. He did not know the meaning of debt; he had two religions, that of God and that of thrift, and in order that all in such a blessed soul should be perfect, he devoted much of his free time to a variety of household duties of indubitable benefit, demonstrating in this way the sharpness of his intelligence as well as the dexterity of his hands.

From his earliest years he was a civil servant, as were his father and grandfathers before him, and it is even believed that his great-grandfathers and their ancestors served in the Administration of both old and new worlds. There is no connection between this gentleman and the well-known Madrilenian commercial family of the same name which passed it on to some famed shopping arcades. The Bringases of our very dear friend Don Francisco, hailed from La Mancha, and the second surname came from those Caballeros of Cadiz, an opulent family last century, which lost its entire fortune after the war. Our good friend Don Francisco made slow but steady progress in his career, in sections that were then seldom touched by the inconstancy and tumult of politics. Staying well under the wing of the best birds of his time, Bringas never saw the pale face of redundancy and was certainly the most fortunate of Spanish civil servants.

His position on the payroll was as safe as that of an oyster lying on the deepest sandbank where the fishermen cannot reach; a rare piece of luck in the Madrilenian bureaucracy which, buffeted constantly by politics, ambition, envy, idleness and vice, is a world of infinite suffering.

Bringas was no politician, nor had he ever been one, although he had his ideas, like any Spaniard, moderate though they were, let it be said. He was not ambitious and did not even smoke, so lacking in vices was he. He was so hard-working that he quite effortlessly and gaily did his own job and that of his extremely lazy superior. At home he wasted no time and his mechanical skills were so numerous that it will be difficult to number them all. Nature had bestowed upon him useful and varied talents, enabling him to repair all sorts of broken objects. Any damaged chair that fell into his hands was soon as good as new and his fingers had a miraculous touch for gluing a piece of fine porcelain that had been smashed. He even dared to tackle clocks and watches that refused to go and mechanical toys that had stopped working in the children's hands. He restored books whose bindings had deteriorated, and varnished furniture that had lost its shine through time and wear. He could give a new lease of life to a kidskin fan, or a tortoiseshell hair-comb, or the lowliest kitchen utensil. He made cribs from cork for Christmas decorations and little wooden toothpicks for all the year round. In his home there was never any need to call a carpenter. Bringas knew better than anyone how to nail, to join, to upholster, to mend a lock; and iron and wood, ivory inlay, shoe leather, gum and paste, screws and nails, sandpaper and emery boards obeyed his every command. He had tools of all kinds, and a myriad of provisions and equipment; and if it fell to him to wield a tapestry needle to join pieces of carpet, he could do that too. He was a master at using old material from a disused, stripped piece of furniture to re-upholster another. At the same time, Bringas was a man who was not too proud to polish the silver in his shirtsleeves on a difficult day when there were guests. He made coffee in the kitchen like a true gourmet and if pressed, could be persuaded to make a paella that surpassed the best work of his noble wife and the house cook.

Our dear Mr Bringas was an excellent, even an outstanding father. His wife, Doña Rosalía Pipaón, had given him three children. The firstborn, aged fifteen, had already finished school, passed his leaving examinations with flying colours, and was very proud of his learning; he was to read law, in order to follow – but even more gloriously – in his venerable father's bureaucratic footsteps. The rest of the family consisted of a little girl of ten and a boy of nine, both of whom had inherited their mother's graces; because Mrs Bringas was a handsome woman, far younger than her husband, who was a good decade and a half her senior. Her weak point was a certain obsession with the aristocracy, for although the Pipaóns did not descend from Iñigo Arista, on Rosalía's maternal side, the surname was Calderón, which authorised her up to a point, to cultivate – if only in fantasy – a luxuriant family tree. Careful observation gives us to understand that that Rosalía did not lack the credentials to affiliate herself, via the maternal line, to that poor, servile branch of the nobility which has shone in court duties of minor importance. When she showed off her noble descent, it was not glorious acts in politics or combat that she recalled, but those lowlier ones, gained in the obscurity of personal service to the Royal Person. Her mother had been a lady-in-waiting, her uncle a halberdier in the royal escort, her grandfather a palace steward, more and less distant cousins of her mother had been equerries, pages, messengers, beaters, keepers of the livestock at Aranjuez, etc. etc.

There would be an explanation for Rosalía's adding *de la Barca* to her second surname; but all the heraldic learning in the world will not account for the topsy-turvy combination that she used to make the name sonorous and well-rounded, calling herself Rosalía Pipaón de la Barca. She would pronounce this flaring her pretty little nostrils emphatically, a physical feature which, with infallible precision, marked either a surge of ancestral vanity, or one of those resolutions made by her inexorable will.

For this lady there were two things divine: Heaven, or the abode of the chosen, and what we know in the world by the laconic noun, *Palace*. In the Palace lay her history and also her ideal, for she aspired to an elevated post in the administration of the national heritage for Bringas and to a home on the second floor of the regal dwelling-place. Any little word, phrase, or thought which ran counter to the total and permanent superiority of the Royal Household over all of God's and man's creation, made the good lady so furious that even her beauty seemed to be eclipsed and overshadowed, such was the dilation of her pretty nostrils, such the discomposure that wrath gave her red lips. Rosalía was, to say it once and for all, one of those plump beauties, with a babyface and the small, well-shaped, graceful features that prevail over time and the hardships of life. Her sound health, defending her against ageing, gave her a freshness that would be the envy of other women who, at the age of twenty-five and after having a single child, look as though they have given birth to an entire regiment. She had so often heard herself compared with a Rubens figure, that, by a strange phenomenon of habit and assimilation, whenever the illustrious Fleming was named, she felt as though a family member had been mentioned . . . the family being, let it be clear, the Pipaón de la Barcas.

At the beginning of November, Bringas was obliged, owing to the family's pressing need for more space, to move house from Silva Street, where they had lived for sixteen years, to another in the narrowest section of Los Angeles Hill. There was no shortage of difficulties and breakages in a removal which contained such diverse objects, some of value, two or three good paintings, bronzes, mirrors, lampshades, and some extremely rich curtaining, cast-offs from Palace decoration. How right Bringas was to keep repeating Franklin's apt phrase: 'Three removes are as bad as a fire.' And he became very irritable and cross seeing how much had been broken, how much had been scraped, how much and how many things had been damaged. Luckily he was there to repair everything. The removal carts were transporting goods from six in the morning until very late at night. The clumsy fumbling brutes who do the job treated the furniture ruthlessly and it was all shouting, heaving, rough words and actions. While everything was being checked, Bringas carried out on his own the august functions appropriate to an industrious and intelligent master of the household. Helped by two people he trusted completely, he put mats and carpets down all over the house, because he had no faith in professional carpet-layers, who ruin so much and only want to get out of a tight corner and finish the job any old how. Once the carpets were properly laid (an occupation which has the unfortunate consequence of placing this venerable personage before us in the undignified posture of crawling around on all fours), he decided to put all the furniture in its proper place, assemble the iron bedsteads, hang everything that was meant to be on the walls, fix everything of practical use in place, spread the decorative items around with artistry and grace, all single-handed. This tiring and exasperating job can never be finished in two nor yet three days, for even when it seems completed, there are minor matters left over which are the torment of the inhabitant on the following days: at the end of the party, there is always something that cannot be fitted into life.

It is perhaps a great pity that the first time we come across this interesting couple, it should be on such a tumultuous occasion as a removal day, amidst the mess of a household before it is settled and in the heart of a choking cloud of dust. It is not our fault that the highly respectable Don Francisco Bringas should look somewhat comical as we meet him in a worn old jacket, with an even older cap pulled down over his ears, his physiognomy besmirched by the dust, his feet in baggy slippers; at times crawling across the carpets to measure, trim, adjust; at times nimbly climbing on a chair, hammer in hand; now running along the corridors in search of a nail, now shouting down to hold the ladder steady.

Bringas wore gold-rimmed glasses and was clean shaven. A happy coincidence spares us the need to describe him, for two words suffice for all who read this to have an image of him as bright, palpable and large as life as if he stood before them. He was the very image of Thiers, the great French historian and politician. What an extraordinary resemblance! It was the same round face, the same hooked nose and thick, grey hair with the pear-shaped tuft on top, the same good, broad forehead, the same ironical expression, coming one knows not whether from the mouth or the eyes or the tuft, the identical profile suggesting Roman ancestry. It was also the whole physique, the strong, stocky build. All Bringas lacked was the deep look in the eyes and all that is peculiar to the physiognomy of the spirit; he lacked that which distinguishes the superior man who can make history and write it, from the common man who was born to mend a lock and nail down a carpet.

CHAPTER 3

Rosalía, for her part, rivalled her matchless husband in productive activity that day. With a scarf tied round her head, her body swathed in an ancient housecoat, she worked without respite, helped by a friend and the maid of the house. The three women furiously pursued the dust with implacable determination, and whilst one attacked the floor with a broom, the other lashed the furniture with a duster. The cloud enveloped and blinded them as gunpowder smoke envelops the heroes in a battle; but the women, with indomitable bravura, were not cowed by the enemy that entered their lungs, and were determined not to flag until the villain was expelled from the house. After that, what one who liked such expressions might wish to call the artillery of cleaning – water – came into action, and against this the suffocating enemy had no defence. The maid turned the kitchen into a lake, and the sight of Rosalía was quite something wading through it, her skirts picked up, and wearing some old boots of her husband's. The skivvy, kneeling down, was washing the tiles, mopping up the muddy, viscous water with various rags and squeezing them out into a bucket, while the other two scrubbed the pots and pans, providing with their clattering a musical accompaniment to this bitter fight. The lady of the house was up to her shoulder in the pitcher, so as to clean its dark inside perfectly, and the friend was polishing the brass and copper with quicklime powder and a scourer. The greatest pleasure of it for the three females was to see how, from the general background of dirt, one piece after another was coming up shining and beautified by its cleanliness. Their success inflamed them and had them working with even greater determination and excited faith in their achievements. The black water in the bucket carried everything away to the depths. Thus, dust returns to the earth after having impinged upon the empire of light in the air; but, alas, the earth sends it back again, challenging the power and energy of its persecutors, and this alternation between infection and purification is an emblem of the human combat against evil and the invasive advance of matter upon man, the eternal and elemental battle in which the spirit succumbs without dying or triumphs without killing off its enemy.

Owing to an inveterate habit of giving orders, Rosalía's tongue never stopped wagging throughout the work, even though the other two women were working hard enough to have no need of any kind of stimulus. The diligent friend who was helping heard her name every thirty seconds.

'Amparo, what on earth are you doing? I've already told you not to start one thing before you've finished another. Harder, dear, harder. Have you no spirit . . .? Come along, pull yourself together . . . I wish everyone had my temperament . . . But what in Heaven's name are you doing, child? Are you blind?'

The maid, a wiry, muscular woman, did not have a moment's peace either.

'For goodness' sake, Prudencia, you're not pulling your weight . . . This is so tiresome! . . . It's enough to drive one to despair . . . Why must I always be surrounded by people like this?'

Meanwhile, the great Thiers . . . I mean, Bringas, over in another region of the dismantled household, was not stopping nor silent for a single instant.

'Felipe, the hammer . . . Come on, man, you're standing there like a fool looking at the portraits instead of listening to what I say . . . Give me the wing-nut . . . look, there it is. You keep losing everything, forgetting everything . . . What kind of a brain did the good Lord give you, lad? I shall tell your master all of this, and maybe he'll box your ears and wake you up that way . . . What are you doing, staring at that chest? Have you lost something? Oh, the porcelain figurines . . . Come along, lad, pay attention. Hold the ladder now . . . Hey! Bring me the pliers, boy, the screwdriver . . . Get a move on.'

An old man, a protégé of the household, was helping too; but he was not allowed to touch anything, except for lifting very heavy items, for he was extremely maladroit and left a fearful trail behind him bearing witness to his destructive clumsiness.

One of the couple very often needed the other to pass judgement and authorise the positioning of some object, and all along the corridor, one would then hear shouting and calling for help as if a very life depended upon it. 'Bringas, come, come here. We cannot place this hatstand.' Or else Amparo would come into the drawing room in great dismay and say:

'Don Francisco, the points of these nails have bent.'

'I've only got one pair of hands, dear. Wait a moment.'

In spite of Bringas's superior decorative judgement, he did not trust himself and wanted to consult his wife when there was a tricky problem.

'Rosalía . . . come here, dear . . . Where do you think I should hang these pictures? In my view, the one of Christ with the crown of thorns should go in the middle.'

'Not so fast; the middle is for the portrait of Her Majesty . . .'

'That's true. Let's put it up.'

'Her Majesty looks very low. Raise her a little, a couple of inches.'

'Like this?'

'Fine.'

'Where shall I put O'Donnell?'

'I'd put *him* somewhere else . . . for indecency.'

'Honestly . . .!'

'Put him wherever you wish.'

'Now we'll hang Narváez . . . The portrait of Don Juan de Pipaón will go on this side. Felipe! . . . Where has that wretched boy got to?'

A moment later:

'Bringas, Bringas, come here.'

'What's the matter?'

'The hatstand's falling on top of us!'

'I'm on my way.'

'Bringas, we can't manage the marble slab for the washstand on our own.'

'Send Mr Canencia. Careful, careful . . . Canencia, give them a hand over there . . . There'll be hell to pay if you break my slab . . .!'

Faced with these difficulties, Bringas kept saying, as Napoleon had done when he learnt that the Battle of Trafalgar had been lost: 'I can't be everywhere at once.'

Felipe Centeno, a servant to one of Don Francisco's relations, was lent to them that day to help out in their monumental task. Not a moment's breathing-space did he have from that exceedingly active gentleman nor from that lady, who was a veritable tornado. Had he had three bodies, they would not have sufficed to see to everything: 'Felipe, take that vase very carefully and put it on the *chiffonier*. Now let's put the lampshades in place ... Felipe, go to the kitchen and bring some water ... Hey, troublemaker, come here. Take the ladder to the bedroom; we're going to tackle the frame for the drapery over the bed.'

Exhausting! But at the same time, victory! ... At nightfall, husband and wife, satisfied and proud of their work, sat down, absolutely worn out, and looked at it, flattering each other with appreciative compliments. 'The drawing room has turned out very well. Pity there was no room for the Pipaóns' family tree and the Saint Thomas the Apostle, the Mengs copy ... The lamp isn't a bit high, is it? ... We'll have to put the finishing touches tomorrow. The fact is, dear, that we have a magnificent abode. What a splendid small parlour. From here, with the door wide open, there's something regal about it. You could almost believe you were looking at the Gasparini Room at the Palace, don't you think? It must be an illusion, but one could swear that your grandfather looks more handsome and grand in his halberdier's uniform, with the red of Christ's blanket matching it. The carpet is just right. I joined up the piece they gave you two years ago at the Palace with the one you managed to get a month ago so well, and I lined up the pieces so carefully, you can't see the difference in the design ... They might have given you both of the pair of bronze candlesticks ... but in that household everything is in such complete disorder ... The coloured candles inside the shades have a magical effect. If they were lit, it would look like something out of the *Thousand and One Nights*.'

As the day was so full of hustle and bustle, food was brought from the nearest eating-house, and the children, who had spent the whole day at Caballero's house, came back at night time, to go to bed. They larked about so much, what with the novelty of the whole place and of their rooms, that Rosalía had to give more than one hiding to bring them to their senses and in this way a day of so much satisfaction did not end without tears.

On the following days, the pleasure, pride and vanity of the Bringases for the assets of their new home, manifested themselves as they welcomed and showed round the friends who visited them. Don Francisco and his wife took their visitors all round the place, showing it off room by room, with none omitted, and extolling the comfort, spaciousness, and good use to which they were putting each one.

'It's the finest abode in Madrid,' Rosalía would say, her nostrils dilated, as she conducted Mrs García Grande, her bosom friend, through the labyrinthine passages. 'I do declare that if we had built it ourselves we couldn't have had a better lay-out of all the rooms.'

Husband and wife alternately took the words out of each other's mouth to praise their home, which was unique and unrivalled, in the opinion of both; for in this couple, and particularly in her, a belief had taken root that what they had themselves was always far superior to what other unfortunate mortals enjoyed.

'Just look at the bedroom, Cándida . . . What a beautiful room and so cosy! There are no draughts whatsoever.'

'Notice the stucco . . . one rarely sees it better applied.'

'This little room is where I wash. Isn't it sweet? It is tiny, but there's ample space.'

'Indeed there is. Notice these corridors. It's like a bull ring here it's so spacious and airy . . . It must be a yard and a half wide at least.'

'You could gallop horses down here. This room is where I do my sewing, and it's here that Amparo and I shall be all day long. Next comes Paquito's room, overlooking the courtyard. That's where he keeps his books, all in apple-pie order; there's his desk for writing up his class notes; there's his bed, and his clothes stand.'

'Take note, Cándida, of the magnificent light in here. In summer, you can see to read until four in the afternoon.'

'Now just look at the dining room and see how spacious it is. The table for eight fits perfectly. In the other place, space was so tight that we felt as though the dresser was about to come down on our heads, and Bringas had to stand up to let the maid pass with the dishes.'

'Take note, Cándida, of this imitation oak panelling wallpaper. Those foreigners invent prettier things every day . . .'

'In this other little room, which also overlooks the courtyard, Bringas keeps all his tools . . . It's a real workshop. You have to see the kitchen too. It's possibly . . .'

'No need for a possibly: it *is* the most beautiful kitchen in Madrid . . . Now comes our daughter's room . . . A bit dark, I know, but what does she need light for?'

Returning to the drawing room after this triumphal and

eulogistic excursion, her ladyship, never sick of praising her home and congratulating herself on it, could not restrain herself.

'Because as far as I'm concerned, Cándida dear, wild horses couldn't drag me from this neighbourhood. Anywhere outside this little patch, doesn't feel like Madrid to me. I was born in Plazuela de Navalón, and we lived in Silva Street for many years. If two days go by and I haven't seen Oriente Square, the Senate Building, and Santo Domingo el Real and La Encarnación, I feel as though I haven't lived. I do believe that when I hear mass elsewhere than at Santa Catalina de los Donados, the Royal Chapel, or Buena Dicha, it does me no good. It's true that this part of Los Angeles Hill is somewhat narrow, but I like it this way. I feel as though we have more company when I can see the neighbour opposite so close by that one could shake hands. I want neighbours on all sides. I like to hear the man who lives above us going upstairs at night; I enjoy feeling people above and below us living and breathing. Solitude terrifies me and I shudder when I hear about the families who have gone to live in that cemetery of a neighbourhood that Salamanca's building way out on the other side of the bull ring. Lord above, how frightening! . . . And besides, this place is a beehive: so lively! People are going by at all hours. All night long you can hear passers-by talking and you can even make out what they're saying. Believe you me, it's good company. As our quarters are on the first floor, we feel as though we're in the street. And besides, everything is so handy . . . The butcher downstairs, the grocer next door; a fish stall virtually on the doorstep; chemist, confectioner, chocolate shop, dairy, draper, ironmonger, all in the little square; in short, if I say that everything . . . We can't complain. We're so centrally located that we hardly have to walk to go wherever we want. We live close to the Palace, close to the Ministry of State, close to Bringas's office, close to the Royal Chapel, close to the stables, close to the Armoury, close to Oriente Square . . . close to you, close to the Pez girls, my cousin Agustín . . .'

Just as she mentioned this person, the doorbell rang; someone came in.

'It's him,' said Bringas; 'but he has crept in so as not to be heard.'

'He's realised we have company,' observed Rosalía laughing, 'and no power on earth will make him come into the drawing room. He's so odd . . .'

CHAPTER 4

It is difficult to determine the social station held in the Bringas household by Amparo, our Amparo, Amparito, Miss Amparo, for all four of these manners of address were used on her. She was to be found at that point where friendly relations and ones of servitude are blurred, and it was impossible to say if she was subjugated by a dear friend or if a tyrannical mistress showed favouritism towards her. This girl's household duties were so numerous and the affection she received in return was so meanly rationed that one may be sure that her status was that of poor and bothersome relation. That is the most distant kinship known, and we had better make it clear that blood relationships, between the families of Sánchez Emperador and Pipaón, were of the kind one would have to be quick off the mark to grasp. Amparo's mother was a Calderón, like Rosalía's mother, but they came from branches far apart from one another; their common ancestor might have been found (if some idle soul had sought it) in a Palace beater who went into the service of María Teresa de Vallabriga and Prince Don Luis.

Bringas had few dealings with Sánchez Emperador; but he had received an invaluable service from Rosalía's father in days gone by, and he showed constancy in his gratitude. Shortly before his death, the unfortunate concierge of the School of Pharmacy called Don Francisco and said to him: 'I've spent all my savings on my illness. I'm leaving my poor daughters without a penny to their name. If you'll promise me to do all you can for them, I shall end my days in peace.' Bringas, who was a good-hearted man, promised to protect them within his modest means and he did keep his promise.

After they had buried their father, the two orphaned girls moved into the smallest and cheapest home they could find, and took that heroic oath known as *living by their labour*. That oath, taken by a lone woman, unmarried and virtuous, was and is like vowing perpetual hunger; but those well-bred girls had faith, and the first disillusionments did not make them lose heart. They would have had an exceedingly hard time without Bringas's overt protection, and the more or less covert help they received from other friends of Sánchez Emperador and those indebted to him.

The social position of Rosalía Pipaón de la Barca de Bringas was not, in spite of her contact with the Palace and people of standing, best suited to high-flown aristocratic pretensions; but she had an affectation of petty pride that often inspired her to proclaim with dilated nostrils the merits and breeding of her ancestors. She was likewise fond of mentioning titles, describing palace livery and exaggerating about her friends in high places. In a society like that one, or like this one, for the changes in sixteen years have not been very great; in this society, I say, not invigorated by work, and where family, personal recommendations, nepotism and friendships, have more value than elsewhere, individual initiative is replaced by faith in connections. Those with good connections expect all the good they desire to come from the relation whom they flatter or from the political leader whom they serve, and they rarely expect anything of themselves. In this matter of having *good connections*, Mrs Bringas was second to no one on earth, and from this solid foundation she soared to the lofty heights of her petty Spanish pride, a vice based on an inveterate laziness of the spirit, the idleness of many generations and the lack of moral or intellectual education. And if that society which preceded the 1868 Revolution differed at all from our own, the difference resided in its more trivial and lymphatic character, in its even greater vanity and laziness, in its greater fear of political change, and in its civil-servicitis; it was a society which revolved entirely around half a dozen poorly paid posts, a society in which a certain stupid scorn could be discerned towards anyone who did not figure high on the Government payroll or was not at the Palace, in however lowly a capacity.

That is why Rosalía could not forgive the Emperador daughters for being branches of such a humble shrub as the concierge of a teaching establishment, a mere doorman! Moreover, Sánchez Emperador had been placed at the School of Pharmacy by Don Martín de los Heros, and his progressive credentials sufficed for Rosalía to create in her mind a yawning abyss between the livery of the State and that of the Palace.

When Amparo and Refugio sat down at Rosalía's table, something which occurred three or four times each month, she missed no opportunity pointedly to display her own superiority. But she did not know how to do this with the delicacy and fine tact of people who carry the stamp of nobility in both their blood and their breeding; or how to do it without wounding her inferior; she did it in an affected way which ill concealed the vulgarity of her intentions. At the same time Rosalía used to show a thoughtless cruelty, which sprang from her heart like weeds in a wasteland. This detail characterises Mrs Bringas and gives a clear idea of her limited intelligence as well as her perverse moral education, an age-old vice of pure-bred Spain which is not eliminated nor even concealed by the veneer of urbanity sported for purposes of superficial relations by the vast majority of fine gentlemen in frock-coats and ladies in mantillas. Furthermore, the struggle for survival is rougher here than elsewhere; in the distribution of political favours it can be positively ferocious; and in life's everyday sphere, it expresses itself in the form of the manifold varieties and extraordinary manifestations of envy. Strange to say, one comes across superiors envying inferiors, and it happens that those with ample food may fight furiously and zealously over a miserable crust. All of this, which is generally true, can serve as a basis for an exact understanding of the humiliations to which that lady subjected her protégées, and of the meanness of her way of playing Lady Bountiful to them.

Bringas was not like this. When Amparo would arrive there, half-dead with exhaustion, and Lady Pipaón would say in desultory fashion: 'Amparo, go to Concepción Jerónima Street right away and collect the children's pinnies that I've had put aside for me'; when she made her cover enormous distances, and then sent her to the kitchen, and for any trivial matter scolded her harshly, good Don Francisco would stand up for the orphan, asking tolerance and kindness of his wife.

'Let her work', Rosalía would remark. 'So what? She has to live from her work after all. Do you think she's going to come into money? Let her grow accustomed to being pampered and then see what she lives from when we're not here for any reason. These girls have got into very bad ways ... Everyone, Bringas, must cut their coat according to their cloth.'

Refugio, the younger of the two, soon tired of her vain

relation's protection. She had a somewhat defiant character and she held her independence dear. The tone and manner of her protector, as well as the work she made her do, irritated her so much that she renounced her claim to support from the family and took her leave one day, never to return. Amparo, who was of the utmost humility and had a weak character, went on being subjugated to that burdensome protection. She had enough good sense, moreover, to understand that liberty was more miserable and dangerous than bondage in this particular case.

When she retired to her abode at night time, after having run exhausting errands, some quite inappropriate to a young lady, after having sewed until her head spun, and having run to and fro countless times doing everything Madam ordered, the latter might give her some pockmarked nuts, or some raisins on the point of fermenting, old meat, bits of salami and marzipan, two or three pears, and some home-made pudding that had gone off. With used clothing Rosalía was hardly ever generous, for she wrung so much wear out of her clothes that when she gave them up they were well nigh useless. But she did relinquish the occasional surplus shred, some bit of frayed sash or grubby corduroy, the remnant from a dress-length, ends of ribbon, or old buttons. Bringas, for his part, was not grudging with his protégée and let her benefit from his generous dexterity; he was always willing to mend her umbrella, put a new nail in her fan, or new hinges on her little sewing-box. Aside from this (let it be writ large, so that the audience may be well aware of it), Amparo received a weekly sum from her protector in cash, which varied according to the fluctuations of that thrifty and supremely economical man's personal exchequer. Bringas kept in the right-hand drawer of his desk (which was of the pedestal variety), various little piles of coins. This was where the necessary for all the different household expenses came from, paid with a promptness and scrupulous order that we only wish the state Exchequer would imitate. There was no such thing as surplus there until every debt had been settled. Bringas was inexorable about this, and thanks to such healthy rigour, not a farthing nor a penny piece (Thiers's own expression) was owing to anyone. The remainder after the necessities were paid, was recorded weekly in the ledger and was transferred to the surplus kitty, and there was even another space for the leftover from the surplus, which was, as can plainly be seen, a quintessence of cash, and the last word in domestic order. It was from this third category of capital that the complex stipend of Amparo proceeded, generally taking the suitable form of the most worn peseta notes and cuarto coins. All of it was recorded by Don Francisco in his book, which he had made himself out of office paper and sewn very well with red thread. The dear man had the meritorious weakness of deceiving his wife when she called him to account over these weekly extravagances, and if he had given fourteen, he would say in a soothing tone as he put the book away:

'Don't worry, dear. All I've given her is nine reals . . . I cannot begin to imagine how the poor soul will manage to pay for her lodgings this month, because her good-for-nothing sister will give her no help . . . But we can do no more for her. And it seems miraculous that we can stay afloat with so many expenses. This month, the children's footwear has unbalanced our accounts somewhat. I hope that Agustín remembers what he promised concerning Isabelita's piano lessons and the school fees. If he does, we're doing fine. If not, I'll give up the idea of having a new overcoat this winter. And the same applies to your hat, my dear . . . My fool of a cousin could buy you an expensive one, you see; but he doesn't understand about real necessities, and it wouldn't be right to let him know that we depend on his generosity. Plenty of tact is what's called for with him, for these anti-social characters usually are extraordinarily suspicious and perspicacious.'

CHAPTER 5

If she did not have much in the way of chores, or any well-paid casual work, which very seldom came her way, Amparo never failed to go along to that first-floor abode in Los Angeles Hill. There we behold her, reliable, always the same, in a changeless mood and temperament that was impossible to upset, serious without becoming despondent, quiet, long-suffering, the living image of patience, if this, as it seems, is a beautiful image; hard-working, willing, economical – indeed, almost miserly – with words, a faint smile upon her lips if Rosalía was cheerful, engulfed in the deepest sadness if Madam was unhappy or angry.

Let us listen in on the daily refrain:

'Amparo, have you brought the green silk? No? Well leave your sewing and put your cloak on; off you go right away to fetch it. Stop off at the ironmonger's and bring back some knotweed leaves. Oh! I was forgetting; bring me two stoppers, the ones for a cuarto each . . . Are you back already? Good; give me the change from the peseta. Now, take yourself down to the kitchen and see what Prudencia is up to. If she's very busy, help her wash the clothes. Then come back to finish off this collar for me.'

And full of the spirit of protection, on other occasions she would soar to the heights of patronisation, as a balloon filled with gas rises heavenwards. Thus she declared, in extremely cordial tones:

'Amparo, under our wing you can find, if you're a good girl, a stable position, because we have good connections and . . . Ah! You know what occurs to me as I speak? A brilliant idea. Why, you should simply take the veil. With your character and your lack of interest in having sweethearts, you're not the marrying type, and above all, you're not going to make a good marriage. So give it some thought; it's just the thing for you. I'll take care of obtaining the dowry. I think that if Her Majesty were told about you, she would give it. She's so charitable, that if it were up to her, she'd spend all the nation's money (which isn't much, believe you me), on charity.'

And another day, she is reputed to have said:

'Listen here ... I've had another good idea ... I'm on form today. If you decide to go for the nunnery, I don't think we need to trouble *Ma'am*, for she receives more than enough requests and petitions from the needy every day, and the poor dear distresses herself because she can't help everyone. You know who'll give you the dowry? Can't you think? You're not getting it? ... Cousin Agustín, who's always pondering on how to use the fortune he brought back from America. I must put it to him cleverly, to see how he takes it. He's the very model of a good man; but as he is somewhat odd, one has to know how to deal with him. Even though he's so open-handed, one can't ask for something in straightforward fashion. He's distrustful like all recluses and is likely to come out with some childish naïvety or other. One has to know how to deal with him, one has to have – as I do – a knack for handling people in order to make the most of him ... Just yesterday, look, he gave me a magnificent hat ... All because he saw me toiling away at fixing up the old one and heard me despairing of my limited funds ... With a bit of help from you, you'll have the dowry ... I think that's him ringing ... He arranged to bring me tickets for the Príncipe Theatre today ... And that hopeless Prudencia can't hear the door ... Prudencia! You'll have to go ... No, that mule of a maid is on her way ... It's him ... Didn't I tell you? Good morning, Agustín; come in, go round that way. Kick that basket of clothes out of the way. Now slam the door. Draw up the empty trunk. Move that shawl that's on the chair ... Don't take your hat off, it's not hot in here.'

This was taking place in the small sewing room, which was also Rosalía's dressing room and was full of cupboards and clothes stands, with calico drapery to protect the piles of skirts and dresses from the dust. Enormous trunks took up the rest of the space, leaving so little room for people that when they went out and came in, they had to plan a route and often could not find one.

'And what have you been up to?' asked Rosalía. 'Have you already had your horse-ride? ... Look, straighten your tie, for at the rate you're going, it will soon be hanging down your back

... Oh! You're so dishevelled! If you let yourself be ruled, you would be another man in no time. You wouldn't recognise yourself.'

'I'm too old now to be reformed,' Caballero countered, smiling. 'Let me stay as I am. Is the tie all right like this? What a fuss. You'll be amazed to hear that I've lived for the last fifteen years without seeing a mirror, or at least, without seeing my own face and without knowing what I look like, which comes to the same thing.'

'Lord above! You really are something! ... And one day you finally looked at yourself and said, like the man from Caspe: "That's not God, but I know that face..." Do you hear, Amparo?'

The two women laughed.

Agustín Caballero was past his boyhood; but fatigue and the labours of a difficult life had doubtless played a larger part than the passing years in the physical decay that his face portrayed. In his black beard, threads of silver gleamed, unevenly distributed, for the part below his temples was almost entirely grey, whilst the moustache and all that grew beneath his lower lip was black. His hair, close cropped, also displayed a capricious distribution of those infallible signs of fatigue with life: frost at the temples, and the rest a dense black, lightly sprinkled with silvery streaks. The colour of his face was very poor indeed, the colour of America, the glow of fever and fatigue in the intense, humid heat of the Mexican Gulf, the mark or insignia of the colonising apostle who builds the powerful civilisations of the future Hispano-American world from the lives and health of so many noble labourers.

I always saw in Caballero a robust physical constitution, half defeated in harsh combat with Nature and mankind, good health undermined by a thousand trials, beauty tanned by the sun. That head and that body, well cared-for by hairdressers and tailors, would have been more handsome than the average. But social reclusion and Herculean labour stole forever all the elegance and refinement of both, and even the possibility of acquiring them. This is why Caballero, very sensibly, had realised that it was worse to pretend to be something that he was not than to present himself just as he was to the vulgar appreciation of the effeminate society in which be lived. Truth to tell, that man who had lent positive, if not brilliant service to the civilisation of America, was rough-mannered and clumsy, and seemed extremely out of place in a bureaucratic capital where there are people who have made brilliant careers out of knowing how to knot their tie. This is not the first time that the raw Yankee, transplanted over here, has had to flee from pure boredom, with no desire ever to return. Caballero remained longer than others, and challenged what we might call his unpopularity. He had made many people smile with petty malice; he was clumsy in his greetings and incapable of sustaining a light and pleasant conversation. Amidst happiness and relaxation, he remained taciturn and deadly serious. Whilst the basic formulas of life in society were not foreign to him, he was a layman in many of the more advanced type, which are the product of refined custom and continual regulatory innovations.

His lack of concern was not so great that he could be completely indifferent to the ridicule which he sometimes attracted, and to avoid it, concerned to maintain his dignity, which he valued highly, he fled from the company of convivial people. He lived an exceedingly retiring life, and only maintained constant contact with his cousins the Bringases and two or three friends in the world of Madrid banking and business, whom we shall meet presently.

In October that year, tired of the tedium of his life in Madrid, Agustín left for Bordeaux, where he had some business to conduct. But he returned unexpectedly soon and without explanation. All he said to Bringas was: 'I was more bored there. But I intend to return, God willing, if a plan I have works out.'

Whenever Rosalía enjoined him with lively exhortations to stay on after dinner, and almost forced him to join the modest company gathered in her drawing room, he would spend the whole evening in a corner, as quiet as if he were at church, or else tolerating the verbosity of some elderly gentleman or middle-aged lady of the kind that talk non-stop. As far as his fortune was concerned, nobody knew the truth. Some imagined it to be colossal, some moderate and very wisely invested; but it was the very mystery in which this matter was shrouded that made him most interesting in the eyes of many, and there was one family in the Bringases' circle, which used warlike zeal and every social strategy to win him over. But he, revealing subtle cunning, more appropriate to the savage than the courtesan, put up such a brave resistance to his besiegers that they were forced to retreat and were not tempted to make a second assault. Needless to say, the notion everyone had of his immeasurable wealth and his noble and lofty character provided him with much special dispensation. The truth is that had he wished to yield to so many friendly onslaughts, his coarseness would have passed for wit and his abruptness for the most perfect elegance.

Do smoke if you wish,' said Rosalía. 'Tobacco smoke doesn't bother me or Amparo. Tell us again about that mirror so we can laugh some more. Fifteen years without seeing your face!'

'It's true . . . And for two and a half years a friend and I were in the Sierra Madre mountains without the displeasure of seeing another soul.'

'You've no need to swear to that to make me believe you. We know you well enough. And when you did see a human being you took to your heels, didn't you? You've kept those habits, cousin. The other afternoon, when you were in the drawing room and the Pez girls came in, you jumped out of your skin and couldn't get away fast enough. I thought you'd throw yourself over the balcony. Why are you like that, why are you afraid of people? You're so wrong. I expect you think people don't like you, that they laugh at you. Not so, you fool. Everyone respects you and praises you. I know you're not unpleasant, far from it. People like you, Agustín, they like you, I'm telling you. Plenty of women I know think you charming, and if you weren't so retiring . . .'

'I don't trust this, I don't trust it,' murmured Caballero, like someone waiting for the catch.

'You're so shy! And at forty-five years old, mind you . . . Do I miscalculate?'

'Thereabouts . . .'

'At forty-five years old, not to know . . . not to enjoy the pleasures of society . . .'

'Every man,' declared Agustin, 'is the product of his own life. A man is born, and then Nature and life make him what he is. This society has the same right to say to me: "Why aren't you the same as I am?" as I have to say to it: "Why aren't you like me?" Work, solitude, fever, constancy, setbacks, fear and daring, horses and ledgers, the mountains of Monterrey, the Rio Grande and the putrid Matamoros coast, have made me what I am. Ah! When one's character has set like bones, when one's past history has been engraved on one's face, it's impossible to turn back. This is how I am; and the truth is, I have no desire whatsoever to be otherwise.'

Point taken, yes . . . But we're not asking you to be a young dandy; all we're asking is . . .'

Rosalía, who liked nothing better than to delve into the depths of this juicy subject, because of the authority and clear-sightedness she showed in the field, kept having to interrupt her observations crossly in order to attend to domestic matters. Five minutes did not go by without Prudencia coming in with a message as annoying as it was important.

'Madam, the honey seller.'

'None today.'

'Madam, the syrup man . . . Madam, the charcoal merchant . . . Madam, the baker. How much shall I take? . . . Madam, please would you take the soup off . . . Madam, the vintner . . . Madam, a message from the Pez ladies asking if you're going to the theatre tonight . . . Madam, soap . . . Madam, shall I go for coal?'

And the tormented lady answered without growing muddled, and she had to go out and in, and take money out, and give orders, and go to look in the larder, and to and fro, and again, and back and forth . . . But she never lost hold, amidst the household labyrinth, of the thread of her subject, and continued with a sigh, thus:

'All we ask of you is that you be amiable, polite . . . and that you don't run away when visitors arrive . . .'

'Enough, cousin,' said Caballero, tired by now of the lecture . . . 'Let's speak of other things. Here are the tickets for tonight's performance at the Príncipe, stalls.'

'Oh! Thank you . . . For generosity you're unbeatable, that much is true. But, what's this? You've brought three? . . . Are you coming yourself?'

'I don't think so . . . the third one is for . . .'

He gestured at Amparo, for his shyness was such that he sometimes dared not call those before him by name.

'Her? . . . Heavens above, Agustín. But she doesn't, wouldn't, can't go; she doesn't even like it,' declared Rosalía, dilating her nostrils as much as she could.

The very idea of appearing at the theatre with the Sánchez girl, whose humble wardrobe was incompatible with any sort of social display, put Mrs Bringas in a state of the most extreme irritation. She could not understand how such an absurdity could even have occurred to her cousin. Putting to one side all his other departures from good taste, this one was enough to crown Caballero king of social ignorance.

Amparo was laughing, but saying nothing, looking at Caballero with indulgent disapproval, rather as one looks at a child who deserves to be forgiven for his silly behaviour, typical of his age, because of his good character.

'You're second to none for good timing,' said Mrs Pipaón with some malice towards her cousin. 'That's a fine thing to suggest to her. You offend her . . . without meaning to, of course . . . Suggesting she go to the theatre is a slap in the face. What do you think the two of us were talking about just now, and not only just now, but on other occasions? What is the inclination and desire of this unfortunate girl? Don't you know? But how should you know, with your head forever in the clouds? You lack perception. Anyone else would have realised that Amparo yearns to become a nun . . . That goes without saying, because she can't, she mustn't, she really is in no position to aspire to . . . Why, we speak of nothing else at home . . .'

'Hold on there, dear lady,' Caballero pointed out, smiling. 'Nobody has said anything to me.'

'But that's something one gathers, something one guesses,' she rejoined with the vehemence that she always used to express her opinions on the most absurd matters. 'In society, a man picks up ideas even as they swiftly flit by. But you see nothing unless things are placed before you, right under your nose, like this.'

'Let's have done with it.'

'Another man would have understood the difficulty involved in realising this thought, the difficulty with the dowry . . . That goes without saying. Amparo is poor. As for us, we're rich in goodwill, nothing else. It's true that we have good connections, and that good connections smooth the worst paths. We do have many friends, including some powerful ones. Are we to be so unfortunate as to be unable to find some rich bachelor or other who in a sudden burst of generosity will say: "I'll give the dowry for this young lady to become a nun"?'

Rosalía turned to her cousin with a look that revealed her certainty that she would obtain a categorically favourable response to the indirect question she had just put to him. Agustín, wounded in his sensitive heart, would infallibly reply:

'Here is your man'. But our dear Mrs Bringas saw her cunning plan fail this time, for the cousin, not showing whether he had understood, suddenly rose to his feet and said:

'Well, cousin, I have to go.'

With ill-concealed rancour, Rosalía could not help exclaiming:

'That's right ... as dim-witted as ever ... Off you go, dear, God bless and regards to everyone at home.'

CHAPTER 6

Caballero took a step towards the door. But at that moment Rosalía's two small children came in, home from school. They both ran to embrace their mother and then Amparo.

'A little kiss for your cousin.'

'Come here, my pretty one,' said Caballero, who adored children.

'Tea time, Mama,' they both clamoured simultaneously.

'Tea time, Mama,' repeated Caballero, taking each by the hand and heading towards the dining room with them.

Isabelita, a red scarf on her head and embroidered slippers on her feet, hopped along, hanging from Agustín's arm. The little boy, swathed in a kind of greatcoat which trailed along, and displaying a running nose, reddened by the cold, walked like an old man, lame and hunched. But he suddenly began to leap about and pull so hard on his uncle's arm, that the latter could not help complaining.

'Be sensible, children, do.'

A moment later, each of the Bringases of the future was furiously tackling a piece of dry bread. Caballero sat on a chair next to the dining table, and watched them, entranced, dwelling on and envying that tremendous appetite, that happiness with which they overflowed, like a fountain's bowl brimming over with babbling water. Alfonsito, who had been to Price's Circus with his uncle the previous Sunday, devoted all his free time to performing acrobatic tricks. Yearning to become a clown, he sought to imitate the splendid turns that he had seen. Without removing the greatcoat that was strangling him, he was turning difficult somersaults over the chair-backs.

'You will fall, child ... this little monkey is going to kill himself one fine day ... If you take him back to the Circus, you shall see,' his mother was saying, running after him.

Isabelita, sitting on her uncle's lap, and taking the bread in her left hand, was showing him a well-thumbed booklet in her right hand, containing various transfers.

Her Ladyship, having taken off Alfonsito's overcoat, breeches and shoes, so that his furious acrobatic obsession should not destroy his clothes, returned to her daughter and cousin.

'Would you like anything to eat or drink, Agustín? How about a drop of manzanilla? It's the one you gave us. So you'll be drinking your own.'

'Nothing for me, thank you.'

'I trust you're not being backward . . .'

From the other side of the table, the lady stared silently for some time at the fine pair the savage and the little girl made and was struck by a thought peculiar to her, peculiar to the circumstances, and which had become commonplace and almost second nature to her. It was a cause of affliction which had come to torment and persecute the good lady, and as such it crossed her mind many times every day. Here it is:

'If I had the power to take ten years off my cousin and give them to my little girl . . . what a wedding, gracious me, what a wedding and what a catch. I should see to everything being the best possible, and I'd tame the boor, who under his shell conceals the best heart in the world. Oh! Isabelita, my child, what you're missing for not being born sooner . . . And you so innocent on that savage's knee, oblivious to your misfortune! . . . So innocent on that pile of gold, not realising what you're missing! Ah! If you had been born nine months after I married Bringas, you would be sixteen by now. Poor daughter of mine, now it's too late! When you reach marriageable age, poor Agustín will be bent double . . . The things that God does! Oh, Bringas, Bringas . . . Why didn't we have our daughter in the autumn of '51? An income of a cool twenty or thirty thousand duros. It makes my head spin . . . Enough to be one of the wealthiest households in Madrid . . . And now, where will that brute of a man's fortune come to rest? . . .'

This thought was so vivid, so strong, that the ambitious lady would see it outside herself just as if it had taken bodily form and substance. Evening was falling, the dining room was dark. The thought fluttered around the top of the sombre room, bumping into walls and ceiling, like a bewildered bat that cannot find the way out. Lady Pipaón, owing to the gathering darkness, could no longer see the pair. All she could hear were the kisses Caballero was giving the little girl, and her peals of laughter and squeals when the savage bit her lightly on her neck and cheeks.

Another thought, distinct from the above mentioned, although related to it, sometimes surged out of the brain of Bringas's wife, only discernible on the outside by the very slightest frown and the indispensable dilation of the nostrils. This thought crouched so low in the last, most remote brain cell, that Rosalía herself was scarcely aware of it with any clarity. Here it is, extracted with the point of a scalpel finer than any other thought, as one could extract a grain of sand from a tear-duct with the surgical power of a stare:

'If the Lord, in His infinite wisdom, were to take Bringas . . . and the very thought horrifies me, because he is my beloved husband . . . but supposing God wished to call this angel to His side . . . I should be very sorry; my grief would be so great, so very great, that words cannot express it . . . But a year and a half or two years later, I'd marry this brute . . . I should refine him, I should polish him, so my children, Bringas's children, would be splendidly placed, and I believe, I do . . . I say it with faith and sincerity, I believe that their father would bless me from Heaven.'

'Light, light,' said a strong voice at this point.

It was Bringas, who was returning from his evening walk. Every afternoon, when he left the office, he would go to the Exchequer, where he would meet Don Ramón Pez and the chief clerk of the Treasury. The three of them would take a stroll down the Paseo de la Castellana or in the Retiro Park and then return directly to their respective abodes at six or half past six.

'Hello . . . Are you here?' asked Don Francisco, bumping into Caballero.

'Do you know we're going to the theatre tonight? Agustín has brought us seats in the stalls.'

'I'm sorry,' apologised Bringas; 'I intended to work tonight . . . Ah! Light is being brought, thank goodness . . . Look, all of you, at these pretty hinges that I've bought to repair the Marchioness of Tellería's chest. It'll be as good as new . . . But listen here; if we're going to the theatre, we must eat early. It's a quarter to seven, dear.'

Rosalía, intent on expediting the meal, went off in search of Amparo, and with that affection with which she found herself brimming whenever she was getting ready to dress up for a night out, she said:

'My dear, stop working now . . . Put this light on my dressing table, for I'm going to start getting ready, and look in on the kitchen to see if that feckless Prudencia has made the meal . . . You had better set the table yourself . . . What dress do you think I should wear?'

'Wear the caramel-coloured one, madam.'

'That's it, the caramel-coloured one.'

Amparo went through to the kitchen.

'Light in my room,' repeated Bringas.

The young master, who was in his room studying with Joaquinito Pez, also asked for light. So that his assiduous son should not be left in the dark, Don Francisco gave up lighting his room and with paternal self-sacrifice spoke thus:

'I shall dress in the dark . . . Agustín, why don't you stay and eat with us? More shall eat so less shall we eat.'

Rosalía, who at that moment was passing by with a large jug on her way to the kitchen in search of water, gave her husband a discreet jab in the arm. Bringas instantly understood that wordless language which meant 'Don't go and invite anyone today.'

'Ladies and gentlemen,' said Amparo, smiling, 'clear the way. I'm going to set the table.'

And while she was spreading the cloth, Caballero, watching her, answered mechanically:

'I can't today. I'll stay another day.'

At that moment, a faint oratorical murmur was heard coming from the next-door room in which Bringas's studious son and the no less sharp Pez boy were shut up. Both had begun a law degree, and were practising verbal fisticuffs, spurred on from such an early age by that pure Spanish trivial ambition to stand out in court and Parliament. Paquito Bringas knew no Grammar, nor Arithmetic, nor Geometry. One day, talking to his uncle Agustín, he let himself say that Mexico had a border with Patagonia and that the Canaries were in the Caribbean. And yet, this luminary wrote essays on the *Social Question*, which left his little friends stunned. This infant thought he had a flair for Parliament, and as Joaquinito Pez was not to be left behind, they both imagined themselves practising the art of making speeches, for which they instituted an infantile academy in Paquito's room, rather as they might have set up a Nativity scene or a little altar. They whiled away the hours of the afternoon giving perorations, and whilst one played the orator, the other played the Speaker and the audience. Sometimes other friends came to join in the game, Cimarra's boy, Tellería's, and then the parts were better distributed, and there was no need for the same person to be calling for order and applauding.

Agustín and Don Francisco walked across to the door and heard these high-flown words coming from Joaquinito's own lips: 'Gentlemen, let us turn our gaze back to Rome; let us turn our gaze back to Rome, gentlemen, and what shall we see? We shall see personal property and the liberty of the individual enshrined for the first time . . .'

'Boys today are in league with the devil . . .' said the father, his delight unconcealed. 'At fifteen they know more than we do when we reach old age . . . And this one, he's going to make a career for himself. Pez has promised me that as soon as the lad has graduated, he'll give him a position in the treasure-trove tax division . . . If he goes on practising like this, he'll be a better speaker than many Members of Parliament . . .'

'These confounded lads,' observed Agustín, 'seem to have been brought into the world by the goddess, the fairy or the witch of chatter . . .'

'And in the matter of bringing them up, my dear Agustín,' Bringas remarked, rubbing his hands, 'I'm not of your opinion. What you've told me so often about sending him to stay in Buenos Aires or Veracruz with good letters of recommendation would be to ruin his brilliant bureaucratic or political future . . . Hey, boys,' he added opening the door of the room. 'Your little sitting is adjourned. Bring that light . . .'

Joaquinito, emerging from the room with a pile of books under his arm, said goodbye to Don Francisco, and Bringas's firstborn handed the light over to his father, who then made his way to his study. This room had a small kind of alcove which served as both a workshop and dressing room for the good gentleman. Here were his tools, his washstand, and his clothes.

'Come here, Agustín,' he was saying, light in hand, as he marched solemnly towards his room.

With the light falling full upon that visage, which also belonged to one of the most illustrious personalities of the century, our Don Francisco looked like the spotlight of history illuminating events. When they arrived and had put the smoky oil-lamp upon the table, Thiers said to his cousin:

'Paquito will be a clever civil servant and after that . . . Lord knows what. Now what's worrying me most is how to bring up Isabelita, who'll be a grown woman in a few years. We must find a piano teacher for her . . . a French tutor. Music and languages are essential in good society.'

Caballero must have been in the clouds, because he made no answer at all.

Meanwhile, Rosalía was calling Amparo to help her dress and simultaneously sending her to the kitchen to ensure that the meal was not delayed. Not having two selves, she was having difficulty attending to such diverse duties. The lady, having finished her hair, had thoroughly rubbed her neck and shoulders with a wet towel, and then carefully began to make up her face, which actually did not need much art to be beautiful.

'For goodness' sake, dear, go and check down there . . . No, first pass me that blue bow. Go on, run along. They can serve the soup now. You will eat with us; then you can put the children to bed before you go.'

Shortly afterwards Prudencia was placing the steaming tureen on the dining table, and the younger children were running round calling everyone to eat. They were the first to be seated, with much fuss; then came Don Francisco, now dressed and very clean, but with his smoking jacket on instead of his frock-coat; he was followed by Paquito, reading some book or other, and lastly, Rosalía appeared.

'You look beautiful, Mama!'

'Quiet . . . I'll give you a hiding.'

'Your skin is snow-white, Mama . . . absolutely lovely!'

And it was true. Rosalía all dressed up in her most elegant attire, did not seem the same person as that shabbily clad one we were used to seeing every day, devoted to her domestic chores, sometimes wearing a useless housecoat in shreds, sometimes in old boots of Bringas's, almost always uncorseted, and her hair looking as if it had been combed by the pet cat. But on theatre nights she would transform herself with a little water, not much, with the contents of the little bottles on her dressing table, and with the frills and furbelows that she had a talent for positioning artistically on her graceful self. At such times, her skin was whiter, her eyes became somewhat languid, and she showed off her pretty, full neck. Tightly laced into a good corset, her body, commonly flaccid and sagging, was also transfigured,

acquiring the smooth firmness of a figurine. This was a torture
for a few hours, but a delightful one, if one may put it like that.
She made her appearance in the dining room with her dressing
gown on looking like a surplice, and all that was missing was
her caramel-coloured dress, for her to rival a duchess.

'Will we be late? . . .' she said, hurriedly serving small portions
to her children and Amparo.

'I think we'll be there halfway through the first act. They're
playing *Dar tiempo al tiempo*.'

'By Pipaón de la Barca . . . I mean, by Calderón. My head is
in a whirl! Quickly, quickly, eat up . . . And Agustín?'

'He left . . . We were talking about finding a piano teacher for
Isabelita, when he suddenly said, without looking at me: "I'll
buy your daughter a piano and pay the teacher," and without
saying good night he was off like a shot. I think Agustín isn't
right in the head.'

The food was scarce, badly made, and the eating of it rushed
and unpleasant. Before it was finished, Rosalía left the table to
put the finishing touches, and after her ran Amparo, who had
hardly eaten anything at all. The lady examined herself minutely
in the mirror on her dressing table, wielding her powder puff
with nervous, rapid strokes. Then she put on her dress, and
when that difficult operation was over, there was the inevitable,
endless epilogue of pins and bows.

'Now,' she said to Amparo, 'you can put the children to bed
and then go home. Don't stay late . . . Oh! Tomorrow you must
bring me two bunches of scarlet braid, and don't forget the cold
cream from Tresviña's . . . Also bring four quarters of lily root
and then go past the poultry butcher and buy me half a dozen
eggs. That will be all.'

The children were still fooling around in the dining room.

'What's that noise? Paco, tell them that if I go in there . . .
Let's see; coat, gloves, fan. Bringas, are you ready?'

'Yes, I am now,' said the father of the family, who had just
slipped on a coffee-coloured topcoat . . . 'Will we need an
umbrella? We'll take it just in case.'

'Come on, let's be going . . . Look how late it is! Have we
forgotten anything?'

'She turned round at the door and hurried back.

'Lord above! I was leaving my opera glasses behind . . . Come
along . . . see you anon . . .'

CHAPTER 7

They were walking, because expenditure on a carriage would have upset the balance of Don Francisco's absolutely rigorous budget, for it was thanks to his plodding, methodical ways that his salary of twenty thousand reals allowed them to cover so much. Rosalía was very happy at the theatre, enjoying, more than the performance, seeing who was coming into the boxes and who was leaving them, if there was a large crowd, if the X or Y ladies were there and what dresses and accessories they were wearing, whether it was the Marchioness or the Countess's turn to use the seat. In the intervals Bringas read the *Correspon-dencia* and then went up to this or that box to say hello to such and such lady, while Rosalía, from her seat in the stalls, exchanged smiles with her lady friends. She had good looks, without however ranking amongst the celebrated beauties; she was simply *our dear Mrs Bringas,* an extremely well-known person, somewhere between vulgar and distinguished, who had never been the victim of malicious gossip. Although it is not small, Madrid sometimes seems so (and then it seemed more so), due to the small turnover of people in the avenues and theatres. It's always the same faces, and anyone who attends the venues for public entertainment with any regularity soon comes to know everybody.

What Rosalía liked, above all else, was to figure, to be seen amongst the titled or persons notable for their political position and real or apparent wealth; to go where there was hubbub, animation, false, genteel conversation, bragging about material comfort, even if, as in her own case, such bragging was an effort to conceal the shameful wretchedness of our bureaucratic classes. She was beautiful and she liked to be admired. She was virtuous and she liked this to be known too.

It is worth noting the heroism of the Bringases in showing themselves in theatre society with that display of social position and that air of contentment, like people who are only on this earth to enjoy themselves. The whole salary of the second in command at the Royal Commission for Holy Places would not have sufficed to cover that extravagance of the seats in the stalls, had these been bought at the box office. Over and above the fact that Don Francisco was a man of impeccable integrity, the nature of his post would not have permitted him to wangle a bonus for himself, as the Pezes and other civil servants of their breed are reputed to have done. No, the Bringases went to the theatre – let us be clear about this – on charity. Those slaves of saintly poverty did not permit themselves such luxuries except when this or that lady-friend of Rosalía's sent them their tickets because they could not go that night; when Mr Pez or some other employee of his ilk let them have their small but well-placed box. But the fortunate family had so many and such good connections, that these kindnesses were oft repeated. Then the generosity of their cousin Caballero increased this theatrical gallivanting.

The striking imbalance to be observed today between the lavish appearances of many families and their official budget, perhaps emanates from an economic system that is less innocent than the angelic Thiers's talent of thrift and Rosalía's skill in exploiting their connections. Social parasitism today has a different character and more harmful and shameful causes. Examples like Bringas still exist, but they are in the minority. Let us not try to prove that such miracles are worked by much economising and a little flattery, because no one will believe it. When some foreigner, unfamiliar with our public and private customs, goes to the theatre and wonders at so many people with their elevated social position written on their disdainful faces, at so many ladies extravagantly adorned; when he hears that the majority of these families' only income is a miserable and shabby salary, an economic principle exclusive to ourselves is established, which will soon surely have to be given a purely Spanish label, like the word *pronunciamento*, which is going round the world and has already found its way to the antipodes.

This has no bearing on the poor, unfortunate Bringases, who were familiar with making very painful domestic sacrifices in order not to lower their social standing by one iota. In the summer of '65, soon after the opening of the Northern railway line, the family did not consider it decorous to miss going to San Sebastián. For this purpose, Don Francisco cut out the first course at all meals for three months, and the trip took place in August, using free tickets of course. In order not to have to keep two maids, our good man blacked his own boots every morning and he is even reputed to have mended them now and again, demonstrating in this way his obsession with thrift as well as his knowledge in all sorts of crafts. Rosalía swept and tidied their room. When Amparo started going there, she did Rosalía's hair, and beforehand the lady used to do it herself, for Bringas had declared death and destruction to hairdressers' expenses. Meals were generally of soup-kitchen scarcity, which is why the children were so pale and puny. Upon seeing a cork or a nail in good condition in the street, Don Francisco was a man who would bend down and pick it up, if he was on his own. He habitually used the blank sheets in the letters he received for writing his own. He had a drawer which was a branch of the Rastro flea market: there was no old and useful item which was not to be found there. He subscribed to no newspaper, and had never bought a book in his life, for when Rosalía wished to read some novel or other, there was no shortage of people to lend it to her. And the same economic rule was equally well applied to the use of time: Bringas was never too rushed to brush his clothes and take the mud off his trousers. When Prudencia was very busy with the cooking and laundry, the head of household, going to the kitchen in his shirt sleeves, was not too proud to prepare the oil-lamps or make the salad; and on cleaning days, he lined the kitchen shelves with scalloped paper himself. The narrator indiscreetly brings these little things out into the light of day so that one may see that if the couple knew how to exploit society, they did not fail to make themselves worthy, thanks to their sublime management, of the bargains that they enjoyed.

CHAPTER 8

Three nights later, the cousin repeated the gift of the theatre seats; but Rosalía hesitated to accept them, because her little boy had caught a terrible cough and seemed to have something of a temperature. The lady asked everyone who called round: 'What do you think, is he slightly feverish?' And she ceaselessly asked her husband: 'What shall we do?. Shall we go to the theatre or not?' A love for ostentatiousness did not exclude maternal sentiment in the descendant of the Pipaóns and this is why, after much vacilation, she resolved not to go out that night. But after six o'clock, the little lad was so lively that the opposite opinion gained ground, and with ingenious reasoning, Rosalía made it prevail in the end.

'All right, we shall go, although I'm in no mood to leave the house,' she said, preparing her finery. 'But you, Amparo, will stay here tonight. I don't trust Miss Feckless. If you stay, I shall have peace of mind while I'm out. A bed will be made up for you on the dining-room sofa, where you shall sleep beautifully, like those nights – remember? – when Isabelita had her tonsillitis. Pay attention to what I'm telling you. You're to give him the syrup before he goes to sleep and if he wakens, another teaspoonful.'

Let us not omit to mention, since we are on the subject of medicines, a rather valuable detail that may be added to the innumerable examples of the Bringases' worldly wisdom. That fortunate family received its medicaments free from the Palace apothecary, thanks to the inexhaustible munificence of the Queen. For the sole cost of a well-fattened turkey at Christmas time, one of the salaried doctors in the service of the royal household visited them when they were indisposed.

The children went to sleep after much boisterous larking about, and at half past nine the house was all silent and peaceful. Tired from work that day, Amparo sat down next to the dining table, where the lamp remained alight, and passed the time by looking through a voluminous book. It was the Bible, the Gaspar and Roig illustrated edition. It had been a present given to Don Francisco by a friend who went to Cuba, and it consitituted, together with the Madoz dictionary, the entire bibliographical wealth of the household, apart from Paquito the orator's books. The tired young woman paid more attention to the colour plates than the text; she idly turned the pages one after the other, and in this way some time went by until the doorbell announced the arrival of a visitor ... Amparo was wondering who it could be when Caballero walked in and bade her good evening most cordially.

'Did they go to the theatre?' he asked with surprise either studied or genuine: there is no real knowing just which. 'This afternoon I found them inclined not to go. That's why I came. And the little lad?'

'He's still fine; there's nothing wrong with him ... I stayed here so that Rosalía could go out with peace of mind.'

'So much the better. Good Lord ...' mumbled Agustín, putting down his cape and hat. 'This dining room is cosy and warm. What are you reading?'

Amparo held out the book, smiling.

'Ah ... good ... I have a better edition ... Let me see that illustration? An angel between two columns surrounded by light ... What does it say? *And there was a man, whose appearance was like the appearance of brass.* Good, that's good.'

The savage's physiognomy was usually difficult for an observer to penetrate; but in that instance and at that moment one might have ventured to give to the expression on that face the following interpretation: 'I knew well enough that those fools were at the theatre and that I'd find you all on your own.'

'Good Lord ...'

And he could not find his way beyond this, even though he had a great hunger to talk, to say something. Standing alone before her, without fear of indiscreet witnesses, the shyest man in the world was going to be loquacious and communicative. But the bubbles of eloquence burst silently on his red lips, and ...

'Let me see that illustration ... It says *Who is this that cometh from Edom?* ... Good Lord ...'

The problem in such situations is to find a good beginning, to hit upon the key and formula of the exordium. Aha! Now he had found it. Caballero's black eyes flashed for a moment, like those of an artist or orator about to be inspired. Now he had the first syllable on his lips, when Amparo, with frank and natural language that he would not have been able to imitate in those circumstances, killed his inspiration for him.

'Tell me, Don Agustín: for how many years were you in America?'

'Thirty,' replied the person of that name, resting from his efforts to take a verbal initiative, because it is soothing for a man of few words to answer and follow the easy course of a conversation imposed upon him from without. 'I went when I was fifteen, poorer than poverty itself. My uncle was settled in the state of Tamaulipas, near the border with Texas. First I spent ten years on an estate where horses and a few Indians were all there were. Then I based myself in Nuevo León and made several journeys to the Pacific coast, crossing the Sierra Madre. When my uncle died, I settled in Brownsville, beside the Rio Grande, and I set up a trading post with my cousins the Bustamanteses, who have now been left on their own with the business. I came to Europe because of poor health and because of sadness . . . Oh! It's a long story, very long, and if you were patient . . .'

'Well of course I shall be . . . You must have toiled a great deal and also had many terrible frights, for I've heard there are poisonous snakes and other fearful animals, tigers, elephants . . .'

'Not elephants.'

'Leopards, dragons or what have you, and especially snakes yards long that wind round you and squeeze and squeeze . . . Lord above, how horrible! . . . And do you intend to go back there?' she continued, without giving Caballero time to explain about the actual fauna of those countries.

'That doesn't depend upon me,' answered the man from the Indies, looking at the oilcloth covering the table.

'Well, who can it depend on, Don Agustín?' observed Amparo with perhaps excessive familiarity. 'Are you not free?'

Caballero looked at her for a moment, but the look he gave her was quite something. It seemed as though he was burning right through her with his eyes and lifting her clean out of her seat. Then he repeated the *it doesn't depend upon me*, visibly uneasy, and he spoke so quietly and inarticulately that his words were felt more than said.

'Is it true that you're going to take the veil?' he asked next.

'So says Rosalía,' she replied humorously. 'She'll say it so much that in the end maybe it will come true. Oh Don Agustín! Lucky is the man who is his own master, like yourself. We women without parents nor any means to earn a living, nor a family to protect us, nor any certainty about anything save that in the end, the very end, there will be a hole to bury us in, we women are in such a sorry position . . . The nunnery business, well, what can I say, at first I didn't like it; but it's gradually sinking into my mind and I shall end by deciding to do it . . .'

A tumult of ideas surged up, teeming in the brain of that shy man; words by the thousand came tumbling to his dry lips. He was going to say admirable, vehement things, yes he would say them . . . Either he said them or he would explode like a bomb. But his nerves bucked at this point; that damned brake which his inner self invariably put on his speech suddenly crushed him with supreme force, and out of his lips, like the foam sputtering from those of an epileptic, sputtered these two words:

'Well, well.'

Amparo, with her naturally perceptive nature, realised that Agustín had something more than such a cold, colourless and such a dull *well, well* inside him, and ventured to stimulate him thus:

'And you, what do you advise me to do?'

Before the all too familiar brake could operate, spontaneity, racing ahead of everything in Caballero's soul, dictated this reply:

'In my opinion it's a nonsense for you to become a nun. What a pity! Indeed, we shan't allow it . . .'

Once this daring concept was out, Agustín began to feel that – strange to say! – his scorched, dry face was blushing. It was like a dead tree that miraculously fills with potent sap and then puts forth a brief flower on its topmost bough. His heart pounded and behind those words came these:

'Become a nun! That belongs in dead countries. Beggars, priests, civil servants; regimented, institutionalised poverty! . . . But no; you're called to a finer destiny, you have many merits.'

'Don Agustín!'

'Yes, that's what I say and I'll say it again . . . You're poor, but of great, of the greatest qualities.'

'Don Agustín, you're upsetting yourself a great deal,' she murmured, leafing through the book.

'And so pretty! . . .' exclaimed Caballero in a kind of ecstasy, as though the words had uttered themselves on their own, with no intervention from his volition.

'Lord above!'

'Yes, indeed, yes.'

'Thank you, thank you. If you insist; it's not something we should fight over. You're very kind.'

'No, no,' said the coward, becoming bolder. 'I'm not kind, I'm not refined, I'm not gallant. I'm a rough, coarse man who's spent years and more years turned in upon myself, at the foot of enormous volcanoes, beside rivers the size of seas, working as people do work in America. I'm a stranger to social lies, because I haven't had the time to learn them. So, when I speak, I tell the pure truth.'

Amparo, while still pretending to be mildly interested in the illustrations of the Bible, seemed now to wish to change the subject, for she said:

'I shouldn't go to those lands for all the world.'

'Really? . . . Who knows! One misses a great deal when one's alone, but one also gains a great deal. The harshness of that primitive life blunts a man's manners; but it polishes him on the inside.'

'Oh no! Don't talk to me about that life. What I like is tranquillity, order, staying at home nice and quietly, seeing few people, having a family to love and that loves me; living in relative ease and not going through all those terrible frights to pursue a fortune which is found in the end, but rather too late and when one can no longer enjoy it.'

What good sense! Caballero was enchanted. The concordance of Amparo's ideas with his own must have encouraged him suddenly to open the mysterious treasure chest of his secrets. The supreme moment was approaching.

'Good Lord . . .' he mumbled, collecting his ideas and seeking help from his memory.

Because, when he came to the house, he had already prepared his declaration; he had a magnificent plan with apt sentences and reasoning. The mute are usually wonderfully eloquent when they say things to themselves.

CHAPTER 9

What Caballero had thought was this:

'I'll get there, and as my cousins will have gone to the theatre, I'll find her on her own. A better opportunity I'll never have. I must be brave and override that damned brake. I'll go in, greet her, sit down opposite her in the dining room. First we'll talk about matters of no importance. She'll be sewing. I'll say why does she work so hard. She'll answer, I can just hear her saying it, that she likes working and she grows bored when she does nothing. Then I'll say that that is most worthy and that ... Right, on we go: I'll spring this on her: "Amparo, you must aspire to a better position, you're not all right where you are, in this ill-concealed servitude; you have merit, you ..." And she, I can just hear her saying it, all modesty and good grace, will start to laugh and she'll answer: "Don Agustín, don't say such things." Then I'll talk about work again, that it's a necessity for me, and I'll say that unoccupied in Madrid and bored stiff, I went to Bordeaux to set up the banking business. When she hears this, it's indubitable, it's infallible, I can just see it, she'll start laughing again and looking at me very directly, she'll say: "But Don Agustín, why did you come back to Madrid to be even more bored and do nothing after one month in Bordeaux?"

'Once I hear that question, I'll have the ground prepared. The answer is so easy, that all I'll have to do is open my mouth and let the words come out, without fear choking me or shortness stopping my voice. Line by line, the sentences will flow quickly from my lips and I'll say: "Since you speak in this way, I shall give you a frank answer, uncovering all that lies within me. You shall understand me ... The tedium of Madrid followed me to Bordeaux, and my spirit there was as incapable of putting a business in order as it had been here. You won't comprehend, so I'll explain. I spent the best part of my life working as people do work in America, in a world that's taking shape. Solitude was my companion and my sadness fed off my solitude at the same rate as the cold pile of my fortune grew. Few friends, no family. Ah! My child, you don't know what it's like to live for so many years, the best of one's life, deprived of the warmth of man's most necessary sentiments, inhabiting an empty house, seeing all those around us as strange, not feeling any other affection than that which a drawerful of money inspires, with no other closeness than that of the weapons we use to defend ourselves from thieves, sleeping with a rifle, awakening to the sound of the creaking carts they use for fetching and carrying . . . To be brief: I came to Europe secure that I had enough capital to spend my life here and on the journey I said to myself: 'But have you lived during all this time? Have you been a man or a machine made of human flesh that mints money?'"

'When I'm saying that, she'll listen to me with all her heart, her beautiful eyes staring at me. I'll grow braver and now quite without fear, I'll go on in this way: "I mustn't conceal anything that lies locked in my sad, sad heart, disconsolate in its virginity. I haven't lived in Mexico City, where I'd have been bound to meet women who'd have interested me. That nightmare city, that Brownsville, that's neither Mexican nor English; where one hears the two languages mingling to form a horrible jargon, and where one lives only to do business; a cosmopolitan town, a promiscuity of races; that city of fever and fight couldn't offer me what I needed. The local customs were corrupt, as is to be expected in a town where things are changing at a furious rate, making family life impossible. The great fortunes that were being improvised on that benighted soil originated in the cruel War of Secession, the provisioning of the troops from the south and the contraband in military effects. Because of the vicissitudes of the war, which made business change direction every day, we speculators couldn't have a fixed abode. We could be in Matamoros one minute and Brownsville the next. Sometimes we had to load our supplies hurriedly and sail north up the Rio Grande to near Laredo. And it was such a confusion of conflicting interests, such a social and moral mess! Americans, French, Indians, Mexicans, men and women of all castes, jumbled and muddled together, hating one another for the most part, very rarely respecting one another . . . It was hell. Living in sin, polygamy and polyandry were the order of the day there. There was no religion, nor moral law, nor family, nor untainted affection there: all there was was commerce, fraud in goods and feelings . . . How to find in that kind of life what I yearned for so much? Once I saw I was rich, I said: 'Good luck to them,' and set sail for Europe. During the crossing, I thought in these terms: 'Now in old Spain, poor and orderly, I'll find what I'm lacking, I'll find how to round off my existence, building for myself a quiet and happy life for my old age . . .' I reached Spain. There was nobody left in Cadiz from what was at one time a large Caballero family. I decided I wanted to see Bringas, my mother's brother. I came to Madrid, and I liked Madrid, believe me. This town where parading up and down is an occupation in itself was pleasing to me, I who had desiccated my soul and my life in work similar to the labours of heroes and knights, if one strips them of their poetry and dresses them up in the robes of selfishness. Relationships between people are smooth and easy here. Pretty, graceful, and refined women are to be seen everywhere. Where there is such an abundance of goods (forgive the commercial term), it's easy to find stuff of quality. A few days after arriving here, I saw a woman . . ."

'On reaching this exceedingly delicate point, I'll have to muster all the force of my spirit not to say something foolish. On we go . . . "I saw a woman who seemed to combine all the qualities that during my former solitary life, I used to attribute to the dream woman, that great, beautiful, select, unique woman who shone within my soul by her absence and lived within me as part of my life. When what one's thought about for a long time appears outside oneself, in human flesh, the time has come to believe in Providence and to find that life is justified. My joy was great when I saw this woman, and from the very first moment I liked her so much, so much . . . I'll say it clearly, with all the plainness of my character. Now listen, I saw her on a Saturday and I'd have married her on the Sunday. I felt as though I'd seen her and known her and had dealings with her for many years, almost since she was this size and scarcely able to reach up and put her hands on this table. It seemed to me that I possessed all her secrets and that no detail of her life was unknown to me. I don't know why, her looks and her eyes were her soul, her life history, and they were admirably – almost miraculously – diaphanous. A strange thing, isn't it? Everything I needed to know about her I knew just by looking at her. Suspected deceit, duplicity, lying . . . oh! There was no room for any of this as soon as I looked at her. Love and trust were a single sentiment just as in other cases love and mistrust are. I had no need to search for information about her past in order to know that she was virtuous, prudent, modest, simple, wise, just as I had no need of another pair of eyes to know that she was beautiful. And believe me, the fact that she came from a humble background was more to my liking; the fact that she was poor, even more, much more so. I abhor those girls who are so vain and pretentious that it contrasts with their parents' no better than average position; I abhor affected women, women who dress up, fashion-mad, the ones whose frivolity spells out the ruin of their future husbands..." Well, on we go ... "I wanted to tell her what I felt, and I had no opportunity nor suitable place to do so. My shyness prevented me from looking for that opportunity and getting rid of witnesses ... I'm not a great talker; I have no gift for it, or to put it more precisely, I lack initiative in conversation. My heart is startled by the sound of my voice and shrinks in alarm from the efforts of my voice to drag it out into the open and public shame. I thought of writing a long letter, but that seemed ridiculous to me. No, no; I had to make an effort and confront her and put the matter to her in these brief but emphatic terms: *I want to marry you. Give me a yes or no quickly*. I made up my mind to this in Bordeaux, and without further delay, I hastened back here. I was sadder there than here, and every day that passed without realising that dream made my life more intolerable. The beloved image never left my imagination. I could see her so clearly, so clearly that it was as if she stood before me, with her beautiful, beautiful eyes, light and dark of my life, her chestnut hair, her sweet sad expression, and that gracious acceptance of her state of poverty, which ennobles her so much to my mind ... On the train I was thinking: 'I get there, I tell her, she accepts, I marry and we go to Bordeaux to live out the rest of our lives.' But I got here, I saw her ... – that devil of a brake! – and I said nothing to her."

'By the time I get to here, Amparo will have understood perfectly. She'll hear my words with bewilderment, not knowing what to say. I'll hardly need to add another word, nor pronounce the time-honoured cliché "I love you", which is only used in novels now. I'll end with these pithy words: "If I'm not pleasing to you, tell me so frankly. I'll add one detail which I don't think is out of place. I'm rich, and if you do want to marry me, we shall set up house wherever you like. In Bordeaux? Fine, in Bordeaux.

In Mecca? So be it. You want to live in Madrid? It's all the same to me. I leave to you the choice of country, because as things stand today I consider myself in exile . . . What have I said? Ah! When the mute start to speak, it's terrible. The rest falls to you." '

This was Caballero's studied declaration; this was the speech that he was carrying in his memory, *mutatis mutandis*, like an orator who goes to the Chamber, ready to take his parliamentary turn. But when the moment to begin arrived, our good man from the Indies found it so difficult to find the opening words, that all the sections and concepts of his well-structured oration became muddled in his brain, and he knew not where to break in. All of it, words and ideas, evaporated, leaving him only with a profound sense of grief and the terrible awareness of his own silence. Time, there is no knowing how much, slipped by between those two wordless figures, and whilst Caballero looked at the lamp as if he would extract from its light the remedy to such a great confusion, Amparo idly let her gaze fall upon the lines of the book and she read sentences like this one from the Psalms: *I sink in deep mire, where there is no standing: I am come into deep waters, where the floods overflow me.*

She closed the book abruptly and as if picking up an interrupted conversation she said:

'And do you intend to return to Bordeaux?'

God of the mute, what a lucky opportunity! The reply was so natural, so easy, so human, that if Agustín did not speak up he deserved to lose his tongue for the rest of his life. A flash of lightning shot through his brain. It was a brief, ingenious, and transparent answer. When he felt it in his mind, his whole being was moved, jabbed by a superhuman stimulus. Like a telephone articulating words transmitted from a distant organ, our dear Caballero let this courageous reply be heard:

'Yes . . . I intend to retire to Bordeaux when I lose all hope . . . when you become a nun.'

Amparo heard this with shock; she turned very pale, then flushed deeply. She did not know what to say . . . And he was so calm, like someone who has completed an act of titanic magnitude with one sudden effort. Now launched, he would undoubtedly say more concrete things. And what would she answer? . . . But suddenly they heard a metallic and jarring sound . . .

Dingaling! . . . the doorbell. Bringas and his consort were back from the theatre.

CHAPTER 10

It caused no surprise to Rosalía to find her cousin at home at such an unlikely time. He had gone to see how the little one was getting on. What could be more natural? Agustín loved the children so much that when the little dears were ill, he was as upset as if they were his own children and he flapped about and wanted to call every doctor in Madrid. What a capital father he would be if he married! ... Too apprehensive and meticulous perhaps, for one should not take the little coughs and fevers and other minor ailments that were a normal part of childhood so much to heart.

On the Saturday of that week, when Amparo and Rosalía found themselves in the sewing room, the lady spoke to her protégée in these words:

'You know what Agustín told us today? That we mustn't worry, for he'll provide your dowry ... he'll provide your dowry. Do you hear? Now, make up your mind to it.'

Amparito said nothing, and her silence perturbed the august lady's spirit so much that she could not help becoming slightly cross.

'You seem to be rather lukewarm to the news. Now look, it's for your own good. I've known foolish and irresolute women; but no one comes close to you. Unless a Marquess turns up and carries you off ... And frankly, that's hardly likely to happen the way things are going.'

Amparito, wishing to set her protector's mind at ease, said she would think it over.

'Yes, you can spend your whole life thinking it over. In the meanwhile, Heaven knows what may happen ... Madrid is full of traps. Let yourself go, let yourself go, and you'll see ...'

When it was time for her to leave, Amparo gathered up her sewing, put on her veil and said goodbye:

'Here,' said Rosalía, coming out of the larder and with a magnanimous flourish handing her two Astorga buns which were so infested with ants they looked as if they would walk away on their own. 'They're very tasty . . . Oh! Wait. You can take these old boots of Paquito's to the cobbler where you live so he can renew the vamp on them. Bundle them up in the large kerchief. Don't forget to go by the milliner on Monday. Then you can go to the hairdresser and bring me the crepine and the hair, so Bringas can make me the switches, and he'll also make one for you.'

Amparo stopped a little while longer, wandering around trying not to be noticed. She was waiting for Bringas to give her the small quantity that he was accustomed to put in her hand every Saturday; but to her great surprise and affliction she saw that Don Francisco gave her no more that night than an affectionate 'Goodbye, dear', spoken from the door of his study. As she very discreetly expressed the suspicion that her worthy employer had overlooked something, Bringas found himself in the difficult situation, which grieved him greatly, of having to formulate a categorically negative answer, saying as one says to beggars in the streets:

'There's nothing for today, dear. Another time.'

Don Francisco adjusted his glasses with his right hand and with his left, held back the curtain of his study door. Through the small gap which was created, Amparo saw Mr Caballero as she was leaving, seated in an armchair and paying more attention to the scene just described than to the newspaper in his hand.

That day Agustín was invited to eat there, and it goes without saying that whenever he accepted their invitations his grateful cousins would go to extraordinary lengths to treat him and wait upon him. Distressing sacrifices, achieved ingloriously at home, *sub judice*, led to that result; and in those sacrifices lay the explanation for Bringas's inability that Saturday to be as charitable as he had been on others. Yes; the addition of a plate of fish or a skinny bird to the daily meal, made a horrible mess of the family budget and forced Don Francisco to make transfers from one column to another, until the arithmetical problem was resolved by punishing the last column, which was charity.

While the happy family was sitting down at the well-provisioned table, amidst the children's cheerful din, Amparito was slowly mounting the stairs to her home, weighed down with sadness (if this isn't sentimental, tell me what is). Her sister opened the door, in garb and appearance that proclaimed she was busy dressing to go out, that is: in petticoats, her shoulders bare, well laced into an old corset, with her comb in one hand and the light in the other.

The little parlour they entered, small and far from elegant, contained a part of the furniture of the late Sánchez Emperador: a sofa which vomited its wool stuffing from several mouths, two rheumatic armchairs and a mirror whose silvering was damaged and pockmarked everywhere. The dressing table occupied the place of honour in the parlour, since there was no better place for it anywhere else, and on its marble top, Refugio placed the ancient oil-lamp in order to continue her creative enterprise. She was making herself curls and little ringlets, and every so often would dip her comb in bandoline, like a pen in an inkwell, to write upon her brow those characters in hair that were not without charm.

Opposite the dressing table was the portrait, a large photograph, of the above-mentioned girls' Papa, with his braided cap and the most kindly appearance one could ever see. Paying court to him were other portraits of graduates of the University in medallions combined within a fringe that must have been made of medicinal herbs and chemist's materials. Over the chest of drawers an outsized plaster angel bore down holding something or other in its right hand, although its only job now was to hold the shade of the oil-lamp when it was not in its proper place.

Amparo took a seat on one of those armchairs dating from 1840, whose velvet was what had been left over when the deans' benches were made; and breathing hard, from the fatigue of climbing so many stairs, she did not take her eyes off her sister. The latter, raising her arms, continued her hair styling with total dedication of body and soul to the masterpiece. Her hair was her best point, a mass of gentle shadow which set off her face, as white as it was tiny. A missing tooth on the upper gum was the jarring note in that face; but even this discord gave her a certain piquant attraction, resembling, in another order of sensations, the stimulation pepper gives to the palate. Her saucy eyes had a look of scornful vivacity, and her slightly flat nose gave her the prettiest, jolliest kind of ugliness imaginable. When she laughed, all the little imps from malice's inferno wriggled on her face with a trembling like that of infusoria in liquid. Black sideburns descended from her temples and disappeared as they were shaded into her white skin, and her upper lip boasted an inch of moustache stronger than what true aesthetic law provides for a woman. But the most appealing feature in this girl was her very ample bosom, out of proportion with her height and stature. Her scanty clothing on that occasion revealed other disproportions of supreme interest for sculpture, similar to those that gave their name to the Callipygian Venus.

With such charms, Refugio still could not stand comparison with her sister, whose grave beauty, both classical and romantic in style, full of melancholy and sweetness, could have inspired the most extravagant odes, the tenderest idylls, the most pathetic dramas, whilst the other was a charming subject for Bacchic verse or picaresque inventions. Doña Nicanora, the wife of their neighbour José Ido, used to say with reference to Amparito, that if some good dressmakers took her on, if they dressed her up from head to toe and presented her at a society gathering, neither duchesses nor princesses would surpass her.

'And what a perfect figure!' Mrs Ido would add, rolling her eyes as was her wont. 'I had the chance to see her when we were going to the Jerónimos baths together ... The statues in the museum are laughable by comparison.'

Refugio was the first to speak, saying:

'How much have you brought home today?'

'Nothing,' replied Amparo without rancour.

'Off you go to our relations' house ... Be their servant. I tell you and you take no notice. You actually like being a maid; I don't. There's your reward for you.'

She turned towards her sister, and articulating her words poorly because she had two pins between her lips, she continued her tirade:

'Humiliate yourself more, be their servant, drag yourself along at the feet of the stuck-up dragon, wipe up the children's dribbling. What are you waiting for? You fool, you dimwit, all there is in that house is wretchedness, wretchedness with a poor veneer ... They seem like high society and what are they? Just poor souls like ourselves. Take that varnish off them, take away their connections, and what have they got left? Hunger and pretentiousness. They go to the theatre on charity, they pick up scraps of material they're throwing away at the Palace, they beg with good manners ... No, I for one don't praise them. My lady Doña Rosalía isn't going to browbeat me, with her

Marchioness's airs and graces. That's why I gave her a piece of my mind that day and I haven't been back, nor do I intend to ... She can't stand the sight of me, and neither can that simpleton of a gutless husband. I know he slanders me ... the maid told me so ... Oh! ... Look now, I've got so cross talking about those people that ... I very nearly swallowed a pin.'

Amparo made no reply.

'What have you got there?' Refugio went on, looking through the bundle that Amparo was still holding in her right hand. 'A gold mine at the very least. Let's see. Half a bread roll, two Astorga buns, three bits of ribbon ... Shall we throw all this out onto the roof?'

Amparo made a defensive move as if to protect her bundle.

'Now you see what you get out of clinging to those paupers ... Look at yourself and look at me. You look as though you've just come out of hospital; I go around without luxuries, but managing quite nicely; you're wearing boots with holes in them and ... Look at these that I'm christening today.'

She lifted up a foot so that her sister could examine the pretty boots she was wearing.

'What money did you buy them with?' said Amparo, taking the boot and turning it over as if it had no foot inside it.

Refugio took a long time before she replied.

'You're hurting me ... Well, well,' she said at length, turning back to her dressing table.

'How much did they cost you? Where did you get the money from?'

After a while, Refugio gave this answer:

'I sold that satin skirt ... you know? ... besides, I had a bit of money of my own ...'

'You? ... How long is it since you sewed one stitch? Have you been back to the shop? Have they given you work?'

'There isn't any at the moment. Things are bad in Madrid,' rejoined the girl, seeking to avoid the subject. 'As people are talking of nothing but revolution, Cordero says there's not a peseta coming in ...'

Amparo removed her veil and folded it carefully to put it away in the chest of drawers. Her sister was washing her arms with furious vigour.

'If you like, we'll eat now.'

Amparo went out along the corridor and into the kitchen. After a short while, she returned angrily saying:

'Every time I come home, my heart sinks. What a mess! This looks like a pigsty. Nothing's in its proper place. You're hopeless . . . Heavens above, the state of the kitchen! All you think about is dressing up. What have you got for supper?'

'Oh! Don't worry . . . the same old stew as always. Ah! . . . Doña Nicanora lent me three eggs.'

'And I can see there have been some changes here. You're always moving things to and fro. Where have you put the irons?'

'The irons? . . .' stammered Refugio, somewhat embarrassed. 'I'll tell you . . . there's only one left. I've sold the other two. What did we need them for? You know the coalman came yesterday in the devil of a fury. And the landlord was here today . . . Don't be angry, sister dear,' she added, stroking her face sweetly,' 'but I've had to pawn your shawl . . .'

Amparo became really cross; but her sister found no better reasoning to placate her than this:

'To avoid it, my dear, all you have to do is bring many thousands from Mr and Mrs Bringas's house . . . Open your pretty little rosebud mouth and beg, beg . . . they would want the money for themselves . . . Tell me something, if I hadn't done what I did do, what should we eat today? Would we keep going on your Astorga buns and your yard and a half of ribbon?'

Amparo, silent and overwhelmed with misery, had spread a tablecloth on the oilcloth of a skirted table. On this she put some chipped plates, spoons with broken handles and two forks whose bone handles looked like keys wrenched from an old piano. A little while later, Refugio appeared with a steaming pot, whose base, covered with ash, still had a few embers on it that were rapidly going out. She emptied it onto a serving dish and took it away forthwith.

She was soon back and sitting down. She took several pieces of bread out, of a basket, and as she put them on the table one by one, she said scornfully, '*Pâté de foie gras* . . . sweet-cured ham . . . stuffed turkey in aspic.'

With this silliness, even the elder sister, who was in no mood for jokes, smiled for a moment and said:

'You always have to be silly.'

'Well, if we get sad . . .'

Amparo ate little of that poor, insubstantial and colourless stew. Refugio, who had been in the street almost all day and done a great deal of exercise, had a good appetite.

'Not all days are the same,' said the younger sister. 'When we're least expecting it, a fortune may walk through the door ... Ah! Wait till you hear about the dream I had last night ... First, I'll tell you that yesterday evening I spent more than an hour at Ido's. That good sir, all enthusiastic and with his hair on end, insisted on reading me a little of the novel he's writing. It's really funny! ... What a lot of nonsense ... I don't understand it; but I think ... I was saying to him: "Don José, you're wiser than Solomon" and he was so proud. He says that his heroines are us, two poor orphans, poor and virtuous, you understand ... It turns out that we're the daughters of a very fine gentleman ... and we sew away to make our living ... Oh! And we make flowers. You, who are the more romantic and speak in a refined way saying high-falotin things, spend your nights writing your memoirs ... It's really funny! And you put down in your diary what happens to you and all your opinions and everything that occurs to you. He imagines that he's copying paragraphs from your journal ... I've never laughed more ... The man made my head swell ... At night time, since my mind was full of all that rubbish, I dreamt some daft things ... What things, dearest! I dreamt you'd landed yourself a millionaire of a sweetheart ...'

Amparo, who was listening to the tale indifferently, suddenly gave the most spontaneous smile, when Refugio reached the part about the dream. That smile came from the bottom of her soul. Her sister expressed her good humour with loud guffaws.

'It's late ...' said she, rising impatiently. 'I'll finish dressing right away.'

'Where are you going?'

'What do you mean, where am I going?' Refugio rejoined, not knowing what to answer and giving herself time to fabricate a reply. 'I told you already ... Didn't I tell you? ... Well, I thought I'd told you.'

'Are you going to the theatre?'

'Just so. The Rufete girls have invited me. Then we're going to the café, where there's a fool who'll treat us to hot chocolate.'

'Which theatre are you going to?'

'The Zarzuela ... We're going on the stage. One of the Rufete girls is in the chorus.'

'I don't like that crowd,' Amparo observed in extremely bad temper. 'I'm always resolving not to let you go anywhere, and especially not at night. But I have no strength of character . . . I'm so terribly weak.'

Refugio already had her skirt on and was donning the bodice, using her arms and hands energetically to stretch the cloth so as to be able to fasten the hooks. In this way, it was such a close and tight-fitting bodice that it looked as if it had been moulded on her.

'To tie me down,' said she of the missing tooth with a certain haughtiness of tone, 'you would have to meet my needs. You can live on birdseed like a canary and dress in the rags that your darling Rosalía gives you, but I . . . frankly, naturally, as Ido says . . .'

She twisted her body, as if she had a pivot at her waist, to see her shoulders and part of her back. The dress was pretty, new, elegantly cut and somewhat showy in its shape and adornments. With pins in her mouth again, she said to her sister:

'And if you want me to tell you straight, I don't like you ordering me around as if I were a child. Am I wicked? No. You ask me how I bought the boots and fixed myself up with this dress. Well I'll tell you. I'm working as a model for three painters . . . a dressed model, you understand. I earn my money honourably . . .'

'You'd be better off sewing and staying at home. Oh, sister, you're going to come to a bad end . . .'

'Well, you . . . You know what I say. You'll end up running a boarding-house . . . I'm not going down that road. I'm behaving myself.'

'You're not behaving yourself; I shall have to straighten you out,' said Amparo, overcoming her weakness and showing determination.

'And with what authority? . . .'

'With an elder sister's.'

'There's a fine piece of nonsense! . . . It would be fair enough if you were any better than I am,' observed the stubborn Refugio, provocatively turning round, irritated, brandishing her argument as if it were a sword, before her sister's defenceless breast; 'but since you're not . . .'

And then dipping the point of her weapon in the poison of irony, she went on to say:

'Make way for the virtuous young lady, the angel of the house
. . . Oh! I don't want to – speak out – I don't want to shame
you; but let it known that I'm no hypocrite, dear, respected
sister. Even though we're alone, I don't want to say more . . . I
don't want to make your face turn the colour of the velvet on
that armchair . . . I'm off.'

Amparo froze with shock and Refugio departed. She looked
so smart and well turned out that she was a pleasure to behold.
Her religion was her own person, the pride she took in making
herself look pretty and being seen and admired. Doña Nicanora
always commented scornfully: 'She who spends so long washing
herself must be up to no good . . . Whatever they say, a virtuous
woman doesn't need so much water.'

Amparo was left alone, sitting in the armchair, her arm resting on the side-table and her cheek in the palm of her hand. She let time slowly pass in this position, and her meditations were like drowsiness for her. Things from the present and the past, some agreeable, others terrible, hideous, flowed through her mind and went round in a changeless sequence as surely as the hours on a clock-face. Every idea and every image chased those before it and was pursued by those behind. The colour and the sense of them varied, but the inexorable circle was not broken. At certain intervals a black shadow appeared, and then the thinker opened her eyes as if in terror, looking for the light. And the brightness had its effect; the shadow took flight, but made a deceptive retreat, because the solemn and awesome circular movement kept bringing it back. Amparo would open her eyes and shake her head a little. There are occasions when one can come to imagine that ideas escape through one's hair as if they were a current akin to electricity. This is why the human race has an instinctive head movement which means: 'Be off, memory; slip away, thought.'

The thinker could not properly appreciate the passage of time. Every so often, she just had a vague awareness that it must be very late. And sleep was so far from her that in the depths of her brain, behind the knitted brow, a strange feeling was burning into her . . . the conviction that she would never sleep again.

She suddenly jumped and her heart missed a beat. The doorbell had sounded. Who could it be at such a late hour? Because it had already struck ten and perhaps half past ten. She felt afraid, a fear that could be compared with nothing else, and she wondered if it would be . . . Oh! If it were, she would throw herself out of the window down to the street. Uncertain as to whether to open the door, she listened hard for a short while, wondering whose hand had taken hold of the green bell pull, grubby as it was, indeed. The bell pull was in such a state that whenever she rang it she used to wrap her handkerchief round her fingers. The bell sounded again . . . She decided to look out through the little window with its two crossed bars.

'Oh! . . . It's you, Felipe.'

'Good evening. I've come to bring you a letter from my master,' said the lad, when the door was opened wide to him and he saw standing before him the beautiful figure of our Emperine, always a delight to him.

'Do come in, Felipe,' she mumbled, her voice failing her as it does when one has the feeling that one's heart is leaping up into one's throat.

'How are things with you, miss?'

'Fine . . . and you?'

'We're getting on all right. Here.'

'Won't you sit down?'

She took the letter. She could not manage to open it and her heart told her that it did not contain, as on other occasions, theatre tickets. And then, the envelope was so well stuck down, that she had to put her fingernail under one of the corners to get a start and then tear it open . . . Lord above! . . . But she could not manage to take out what was inside either . . . Such clumsy fingers! . . . At length a sheet of the finest blue paper emerged, and inside that sheet, other bits of paper peeped out, green and red and somewhat grubby. They were notes of the Bank of Spain. Amparo saw the word *escudos*, nymphs with industrial and commercial emblems, many little numbers. She was stricken with such stupidity that she knew not what to do nor say. The idea came to her of putting it all back inside the envelope and returning it. But would he be angry . . .? She put the letter and its enclosures on the table and rested her arm on it all. She was so excited that she needed some time to decide on the best line to take.

'Sit down, do . . . Let's see, tell me how life is treating you.'

If she concentrated on talking, maybe, she could re-establish some order in her whirling head.

'Tell me, how's it going with your master?'

'So well that I don't know what's come over me. I must be dreaming, that's all I can say.'

'He's that good, is he?'

'Good? No, miss; he's more than good: he's a saint,' affirmed Centeno enthusiastically.

'I know, I know. We're all well aware that you're doing well for yourself. You look like a young gentleman. New clothes, nice new hat.'

'He's a saint, a saint from heaven,' repeated the sage, almost in ecstasy.

'And are you studying?'

'I certainly am ... I have little work and I go to school ... I'm telling you that God has smiled upon me.'

'I'm so glad!'

Amparo's mind wandered for a moment from its interest in what she was hearing in order to have this thought:

'How much can it be? I'm embarrassed to look now in front of the boy.'

While she was thinking this, Centeno entertained himself by feasting his eyes on our Emperine's perfect face, her matchless hands, and arms. Felipe was one of her most fervent admirers, and would have looked at her unblinkingly for three weeks together.

'But tell me, how were you lucky enough to meet the gentleman?'

'Ah! ... You see ... I was having a dog's life in the job I had last year.'

'Yes, playing the horn for the petrol merchant.'

'Then I went into the shop in Calle Ancha, you know, number seventeen, where it says: *Hipólito Cipérez's Grocery*. I wasn't badly off there. Don Agustín was a friend of my master; he had met him in America ... When they got talking, there was no stopping them. Don Agustín would go round the whole shop, and as he is so well versed in commerce, he would ask: "What's rail-transported rice going for in Valencia? How do you retail sugar here? How much do English biscuits come out at? Are tinned goods from Rioja a good business?" And Cipérez would tell him all. They often ate together in the backroom, and whenever my master sent a message to Don Agustín, I took it over. I liked the gentleman a great deal and he used to say that he'd taken to me. This is the best part: listen to this. One day, Don Agustín came into the shop and said: "My word, I'm so bored that I'm going to do one of three things: either I blow my brains out, or I marry, or I start working, which is to say one of three things: either I kill myself, or I please myself, or I brutalise myself so I don't feel anything ... The first is a sin, the second

is difficult; let's have the third. I feel like doing something; let
me help you." And stripping down to his shirtsleeves, off he
went to the stockroom and, funny as it may sound, he began
weighing sacks, sorting out crates of raisins and comparing
invoices to work out prices. The other lad and I couldn't help
bursting into laughter; but Don Agustín didn't get angry. Two
days later, which was a Sunday, he gave us money to go to the
theatre. One night, talking to Cipérez about his own household,
he said he needed a manservant and that he liked me, and I went
back with him. I said: "This is mine" and I showed him my
books and I asked him to let me have some free hours to go
back my education. He was very pleased by this: "Of course,
of course . . ." I have little work to do, because there are two
maids. One of them, the one who's in charge, a sister of
Cipérez's wife, is a very good lady, a very good lady. And what
you see there is abundance, but not what you could call
wastefulness. The house is a palace. You can't imagine, miss . . .
Silk curtains, carpets and silver candlesticks . . . In the kitchen
there's a machine for making ice-cream and in the dining room
a set of egg cups which is a hen with chickens, all in silver. You
take the lid off the hen and that's where you put the boiled eggs.
The heads of the chickens lift off and those are the eggcups, and
in the beaks you put the salt. Oh! If you could see . . .! In one of
the rooms there's a marble washstand with two taps, one for
cold water, one for hot. It's a pleasure just to see all that . . .
The stove is made of iron, with a great many doors, pipes,
hotplates and oven and the devil knows what else . . . What a
fortune my master must have spent doing up the house! It's his;
of course it would be. He bought it for so many thousands and
thousands of duros. We live on the first floor. If you only saw it,
miss! The master has a big, a very big bed. They say he wants to
marry . . . and then there are lots and lots of bedrooms, which,
according to Doña Marta, will be for the children . . . There's a
cupboard with three mirrors for ladies' clothes. It's empty. I put
my head inside to smell the cedar-wood; it has a lovely smell . . .
Then there's another cupboard, full of mountains of linen,
which Sir brought back from Paris. We're not to touch that.
There's table linen and other beautiful things, but really beautiful; material with lots of lace, you know? . . . It's not the sort of
thing hands should touch. Then we also have a drawer of silver
cutlery that's never used and china still packed in its straw.

Doña Marta says there's provision there for a family of forty. And every day new things are delivered. As he has nothing to do, Don Agustín passes the time going to the shops and buying things. The other day they brought a big metal lamp. It looks like gold and silver, and has no end of figures and hooks for lights. Ah! If you saw the decanter set: it's a sailing ship, and it's laden with stem glasses ... well, it's just charming. In the room which will be for the lady of the house, there are absolutely masses of funny-looking porcelain figurines. Not a day goes past without the master bringing something new back; and he puts it all there with such care ... And the sofa, the chairs upholstered in silk that he's put in that room! What we say is: "It'll have to be an empress coming here ..." Oh! Another thing in the lady's room is a cage of birds, not real ones, with music, and when you press the button underneath, *tweedletweet* ... toccatas inside begin to play and the birds flap their wings and open their beaks ...'

Centeno was laughing; Amparo started laughing too and at the same time her eyes filled with tears.

'And what does your master do? ... How does he occupy himself?'

'He rises very early, writes his letters to America, and then goes out for a ride on his horse. He rides very well. Have you seen him? He has an excellent seat. After he returns from his walk, he reads his post ... In the afternoon, he usually goes to the Bringases'. Some days he gets miserable and doesn't leave the house. He spends the whole blessed day pacing up and down in his office and in the lady's room.'

'And is he bad-tempered?'

'What are you saying, miss? Bad-tempered? As I say, either my master's a saint or I don't believe in any saints at all. He jokes with me. The nearest he gets to scolding me is to say: "What's this, my good man, what's this?" Other times he comes and says: "Felipe, be serious." Full stop ... I behave myself, even though it's not for me to say. When I'm studying in my room, because I have my little room, he has a habit of suddenly walking in and taking my books and reading them ... As he was working for so many years, he doesn't know much, apart from matters of trade, I mean; he hasn't had time to read. From time to time he asks me something or other and if I know the answer, I tell him; but as often as not I'm stuck too, and the two of us are left staring at each other.'

'Do many friends go to the house?'

'You're joking! Not likely. The only regulars are three gentlemen: Mr Arnáiz, Mr Trujillo, and Mr Mompous. They have coffee and play billiards with the master. They're good people. What there is never a shortage of there, at all hours, is people looking for hand-outs, because Sir is very charitable. The number of comings and goings, you wouldn't believe! Some come clutching letters full of names and others appear in tears. Widows, orphans, people who have been made redundant, the sick. This one is asking for it for himself, that one for some snotty-nosed children. Doña Marta says the house resembles a vale of tears. And the master is such a kind soul that he gives more or less all of them something. Nuns come . . . flocking. Some of them are begging for the old, others for children, this lot for the incurably ill, that lot for the insane, for the blind, for the crippled, for the wretched and for women who have repented of a life of sin. Artists who've lost the use of a hand turn up, then there are the dancers who've dislocated a foot; singers who've gone hoarse and builders who've fallen off scaffolding. The parish clergy come begging for poor nuns and ladies collecting for disabled clerics. Some come begging with the silly pretext of a raffle, and carry a ship in its bell glass, embroidered quilts or a wickerwork cathedral. Certain characters clamour for generosity to a poor actor or to redeem an upright young man from military service. There are women begging for a mass they paid for or for a sick friend who has been prescribed sea air. Street musicians are always playing at the front door and in short, my master, as Doña Marta says, is the second God of the needy . . . And as he's so rich . . . ! Because you don't really know how rich my master is. He has millions and millions . . .' (By this point, Felipe had got so carried away with enthusiasm that he stood up and gesticulated like an orator.) 'What do you think of this? The Bank owes him a great deal, and when he wants money, he puts his signature on a slip of paper and gives it to Arnáiz's collector, who then brings him a sack of notes . . .'

They both laughed with frank, unaffected delight.

'I think, friend Felipe, that you are greatly exaggerating.'

'What are you saying? . . . He's more than a millionaire, you know. He's lent loads of money to the Government, no less. In

London, in Bordeaux, and in America, he has ... it's incalculable.'

With an indescribable gesture, Centeno expressed his inability to appreciate by means of arithmetic the fabulous fortune of his master.

Great as Amparo's interest was in hearing about the wonders recounted by Felipe, her curiosity to examine in privacy the contents of the letter and see if that dear man had written something in it was greater. Consumed with impatience, she said to the lad:

'Look, Felipe, it's late. Won't your master scold you if you dilly-dally? I think you ought to leave.'

'A quarter to nine,' said the doctor, taking a pretty American *remontoir* watch from his pocket with some affectation.

'Well I never! You have a watch? Now that's something!'

'And silver. The master gave it to me on Saint Augustine's day ... The young lady is right. I must go. Don José Ido told me to call in at his room on my way down to chat for a while; but it's late ...'

'Yes, you'd better go home,' observed Amparo, afraid that Ido and his wife, who were great gossips, would find out about the message Felipe had brought. 'Behave yourself with your master and don't give him cause for any upset, dilly-dallying out of doors. You won't find another protector like him. You should treat him with kid gloves; you should hold him dear ...'

'In my very heartstrings, miss ... So ...'

'Goodbye, dear boy.'

'I hope all goes well for you, miss ... God preserve you ... Always so good ...'

'Goodbye, then.'

'And so pretty,' added the doctor, who was now starting to learn to be gallant.

CHAPTER 12

As soon as Amparo was left alone, she wasted no time in examining what she had received. The paper around the bank-notes was blank, but, oh, miracle! They represented a total two hundred times greater than what Bringas was in the habit of giving her every Saturday ... She looked at the blue paper believing she might find some sign there, some cipher expressing the magnanimity of that saintly, angelic, unique man; but there was nothing, not even one stroke of the pen. Such laconicism surpassed the best paragraphs in eloquence. With a great effort of the spirit, Amparo conjured him up in her memory until she could believe she was seeing him, through the door of the study, sitting with a newspaper in his hand, while Bringas was saying those harsh words: 'Another time, dear!'

She was much exercised as to what she should do with the money. To return it was an act of pride that would offend the donor. And truly, she needed it so much, so very, very much ...! The landlord was hounding her and equally fierce creditors were giving her no peace. Yes, yes, the best she could do was humiliate herself before the majesty of that great heart and accept the aid to meet her distressing needs. He wasn't doing it out of a rich man's vanity; he was doing it out of love and charity's pure yearning. How could she snub those two sentiments which, according to religion, are one and the same?

This conclusion took her thoughts off on another track. What Agustín had said to her a few nights ago was of great value. Before hearing that pithy sentence, she had already realised, with a woman's perceptiveness, that Mr Caballero didn't look upon her the way we look upon people who don't matter to us. She'd been able to interpret with absolute certainty that stony coldness, that grave silence, finding in these a terribly expressive meaning. Then he'd unexpectedly said: 'I shall return to Bordeaux when I lose hope, when you ...' Oh! No, no; it could not be; such a happy circumstance overstepped the just limits of human ambition ... But what did that gift signify then? For if at first sight it seemed indelicate, it revealed noble frankness and a desire to attenuate the situation. And given that she was poor, so very poor, why shouldn't she receive help from the man who aspired no less to...? Dream, delirium; this could not be ... And yet, a secret instinct told her it could. Those black eyes had spoken clearly enough. And the aid under discussion should be interpreted as an attempt to put her in a position to be his equal ... Another confusion: indubitable as it was that Caballero loved and wanted her for himself, in what conditions would this be? He wanted to make her his wife or his ... He had said several times that he wished to marry. Furthermore, that phrase he had used to Rosalía, *I shall provide her dowry*, contained an entirely matrimonial meaning.

Amparo grew even more confused when she thought about what she should say to her protector when she saw him at the Bringases'. Would she thank him in the same way as if she had been given a seat at the theatre or a box of chocolates? No ... Would she keep silent? No, not that either. Would she answer with a long and well-rehearsed speech? Even less so. It was not the time to say: 'Bless my soul! Don Agustín, the things you do!' The response to the gracious gift was so difficult and complex, that it would be best to commit it to paper. A letter! A bright idea. Amparo took paper and pen ... But the difficulties were such right from the first word that she threw down the pen, convinced of her inability to perform such a delicate task. Everything that occurred to her sounded pale, dull and affected, as if a character out of Don José Ido's novels was speaking for her. Putting it in writing wouldn't do at all. Style is falsehood. Truth looks on in silence.

The things buzzing in her head, the nonsensical thoughts, the plans she made, the bouts of faintness that suddenly came over her, put her in such a state of over-excitement, that if it was not lunacy itself, it had not far to go to become so. Added to all these reasons for frenzy were the marvels recounted by Felipe that night, which seemed nothing less than the *Thousand and One Nights* recast in everyday style. In the buzzing that she had in her head, Amparo saw the taps of the bath, the stove with all its doors and hotplates, the piles of linen and china, the porcelain figurines and the birds in the musical box. By turns she walked around the room to give air and space to that whole torrent of

vain thoughts, then sat down to stare intently at the light, then
wandered from room to room. One o'clock chimed on the
University clock and she had no thought of asking sleep to give
her rest.

Refugio came in. Surprised to see her sister up, she shuddered,
expecting to be reprimanded for coming back so late. Her face
was flushed and her eyes sparkled with fever or happiness.

'What's up?' asked Refugio, before taking off the shawl in
which she was wrapped.

Selfishness ruled so little in the soul of the elder of the
Emperines, that she did then – as on many other occasions –
something which ran quite counter to her personal interests. She
was so weak! Letting her generous disposition carry her along,
she showed the banknotes.

Refugio opened her eyes wide, showed her teeth in a mad
laugh and said at the top of her voice, which had become
somewhat hoarse from the coldness of the night:

'Dear! Dear!'

'Ah! Take it easy,' said Amparo, putting the money away in
her bosom with a swift movement. 'This came for me. That I as
a good sister may share it with you, doesn't mean that you have
any right.'

'But who . . .?'

'That I cannot tell you . . . You shall know in the future . . .
But I swear that it's the most honest money in the world. All the
debts will be paid. And if you behave yourself, if you do
whatever I order, if you promise me to work and not go out at
night, I'll give you something . . . Go to bed; you must be tired.'

Wordlessly, Refugio went into the bedroom. From the sitting
room she could be seen hanging her clothes up.

Amparo went to bed too. In the darkness, from bed to bed,
the two sisters talked.

'You have to behave yourself; is that understood? . . . Do
everything I order. Your decorum is my decorum; and if you're
wicked, my good name will suffer just as much as yours.'

'The fact is, sister, that if I'm to be good,' countered the other
from between her sheets, 'the first thing you have to do is cut
out the lectures. Don't preach, for that leads nowhere. Why is a
woman wicked? Out of poverty . . . You said "If you work . . ."
Haven't I worked enough then? What are my fingers made of?
They're stiff as wood from all the sewing. And what have I

earned? Wretchedness and more wretchedness . . . Ensure I have food, clothes, and you'll have no more to say to me. What's a woman to do if she's alone, orphaned, with no help from anywhere, no relations and she's been raised with some delicacy? Is she going to go and marry a porter? What decent man will come near us, seeing us so poor? . . . And you know yourself, once they see a girl who's broke and alone, they don't come with honourable intentions . . . Sewing, what's the use of it? You just kill yourself that way . . . That money: did you earn it making shirts, embroidering or fitting hatbands? . . . Don't make me laugh! Did the Bringases give it to you? Very likely! So where did you get it from? Is there anyone under the sun who gives money away for the sake of it, to be kind, out of pure charity? . . . No, dear; don't come to me with hypocrisy . . . Can it happen that banknotes rain down? . . . That doesn't occur either. So, speak out then . . . I need thirty duros, dearest, but I need them tomorrow, no later. You see I owe them, dear, I owe them, and I'm very punctilious. If you give me them . . .'

Refugio's words gradually faltered. She was so tired that the mental excitement, caused by seeing that inexplicable treasure trove, was defeated by exhaustion. She fell into a deep sleep, as was her wont, with the tranquillity of the unjust, resulting from her easy conscience.

In the morning, Amparo, who was awake, heard her sister slowly rising, trying not to make any noise, and stealthily, carefully slipping her hand between the pillows . . .

'Don't be naughty,' said the elder Emperine, giving her a gentle thump. 'I'm awake, dearest. I haven't slept all night. Are you looking for the money? Yes, it was for you anyway . . .'

Refugio went back to bed laughing. They spent the whole morning arguing, once they were up, at times in jest, at times in earnest. Amparo refused to give any money to her sister if she did not promise to change her ways, and Refugio, to achieve her objective without giving up her liberty, used all sorts of flattery and cajolery, or else, from time to time, threats, packaging them in very well-spun lies. She was heavily committed to the Rufete girls, and when she was paid by the painters for whom she was acting as a model, she would return the amount her sister had advanced her. From this yarn she progressed to another and then to another, until Amparo, tired of listening, ordered her to be quiet, for which the younger sister, irritated, let herself lose her temper, and with a voice that shook with rage, she upbraided her sister thus:

'Keep your money, you great hypocrite . . . I don't want it . . . It would stain my hands. It's Church money.'

These words had such an effect on the other sister's state of mind, that she was on the verge of falling to the floor in a faint. Making no reply, she ran to the bedroom and lying on the bed, burst into tears. In the little parlour, Refugio, her tongue quite loosened, continued in this way:

'It was some time since Old Nick's lottery money last appeared round here . . .'

After a lugubrious pause, Refugio saw that between the bedroom drapery, her sister's arm was emerging. The hand on the end of that arm threw two notes into the middle of the room.

'Take it: you're beyond redemption,' said a voice, strangled by sobs.

Refugio took the money. She knew how to get what she wanted from her sister by operating an ingenious mechanism composed of shame and terror. Amparo had not found how to escape this appalling tyranny.

Her fury placated by the possession of what she desired, the younger sister began to feel the twinges of remorse in her soul. Her character was quick-tempered and, as it were, explosive, and she rose to the heights of anger as easily as she fell defeated to the depths of compassion. She had offended her sister, she had given her a terrible blow right in the bloody and painful wound; and afflicted at the memory of this wicked action, she waited for the victim of it to come out so that she could say something conciliatory. But she was not coming out; no doubt she did not want to see her, and in the end, vanquished by impatience more than by consideration towards her sister, Refugio went out into the street.

That day being Sunday, Amparo did not go to the Bringases'. She spent her time tidying up at home, sewing her clothes, and after a brief outing to buy several small things she needed very badly, she went back to her housework with real enthusiasm. She made up her mind to tidy and clean their cramped home really thoroughly. But alas, with that lunatic sister of hers, tidiness was impossible. 'What do I get out of buying anything,' she thought, 'if one fine day she sells it or pawns it all for me?'

She ate alone, because the wanderer did not come home all day. She came in when it was already very late; but the two sisters did not exchange a single word. Amparo was in very grave humour, Refugio seemed sheepish and wishing to be forgiven. Seeing that her sister was not giving way, she went down to Don José's and chatted away to him all night. These long conversations her little sister had at the neighbours' greatly displeased Amparo.

CHAPTER 13

The following day, Monday, Amparo reported for duty to Rosalía, after doing various errands that the latter had entrusted to her. One of the first conversations that Rosalía had with her was horribly unpleasant for Amparo, so much so that she would have gladly gagged the mouth of her illustrious protector.

'I was at San Marcos today,' said Rosalía, 'and I came across Doña Marcelina Polo ... She has certainly gone downhill, the poor lady! It must be because of all the upset she's had with her brother, who, they say, is a wolf in priest's clothing ... She asked after you and I told her you were well, that you might enter a convent. Do you know what her response was?'

Amparo waited, her heart in her mouth.

'Well, she said nothing; all she did was cross herself. She went into the sacristy and I heard my mass.'

At the time when Caballero was accustomed to come, the young woman knew not if it was fear or the desire to see him that was weighing on her spirits ... But the generous man did not come that day, strange to say, and Amparo could find no explanation for that absence except to suppose that he was feeling somewhat as she was, fearful, diffident, shy. He was also weak, especially in affairs of the heart, and did not know how to cope in embarrassing situations. Instead of Caballero, a gentleman came that day, a friend of the family and the most annoying man whom Amparo recalled having seen in her whole life. He was vain, thinking himself a perfect model of good looks and elegance, and he fancied himself quite a wag, a wit and a great connoisseur of women. Whilst he was there he never took his eyes – very large, in the style of hardboiled eggs and wearing the expression of a moribund ram – off Amparo. The proximity of an absolutely minute nose lent outsized proportions to those eyes which, in the opinion of the individual himself, their owner, were the most terrible weapons in amorous conquests. Two spots of crimson on his cheeks contributed to the havoc that such weapons could wreak. A smile with pretensions to irony always accompanied the volley of looks that the gentleman hurled at the girl; and his facial expressions were as tedious, irritating, and stupid as his way of staring. His name was Torres and he was a redundant civil servant who made his living goodness knows how. The impression that this individual and his staring made on the orphan would be conveyed by saying, in colloquial style, that he made her sick to the stomach.

Apart from this torture of ogling and foolish words, nothing worthy of mention happened that day; but when the girl went back home, after nightfall, she received a letter from the concierge's wife. It had been brought in her absence and when she saw the writing on the envelope, she felt fear, wrath, rage; she crumpled it up and when she went up to her abode, she tore it into little pieces, without opening it. The bits of the letter, some inside pieces of the envelope and others loose, lay on the floor for a while, and each time Amparo passed near them, they seemed to demand her attention. One might even suspect that a supernatural hand had disposed them on the mat in such a way that they conveyed something and were a sign of some mute but eloquent demand. She would look at them and pass by, treading on them; but the little scraps of white paper seemed to be clamouring, 'For goodness' sake, read us.' In order to erase all trace of the ill-fated epistle, Amparo brought a broom, emblem of cleanliness and also of scorn. But at the first strokes, curiosity got the better of disdain. She bent down and from among the dust took a piece of paper that said: *moribund*. Then she saw another that read: *sin*. A third had written on it: *to forget is to murder*. She swept harder and very soon all had disappeared.

Yet, the sweeping over, our Emperine's uneasiness was so great that she could not eat calmly. Halfway through her meal, she rose from the rickety chair; she could find no repose; her nerves were fit to snap like strings drawn too tight. She cleared the table; she put on her boots, her veil, and made her way to the door; but when she reached the stairway, she retreated as if she had taken fright and took her boots off again and put the veil away. Even though she was alone and could speak to no one, the power of her thought was such that she hurled at the face of the prevailing sadness and penumbra in the house these extravagant words: 'No, I'm not going . . . Let him die.'

Later on, the intention to go out must have been reborn in her spirit. Every sigh she heaved would have made anyone present tremble with compassion. Then she cried. It was from rage, from pity, from what . . .? At length she went to bed and slept fitfully, her slumber disturbed by horrific, black nightmares. Half asleep, half awake, in the cramped room, cries of pain and pitiful groans were heard, as though the unfortunate girl was in an infernal torture chamber and having her bones broken, her flesh torn, that flesh and those bones that constituted, according to Doña Nicanora, the most perfect living statue that the divine chisel had wrought. Awake before daybreak, in her brain, like a light hanging from a vaulted ceiling, this word shone out: 'Go.' And the oscillation and swinging back and forth of this illuminated word was like this: 'I must go; my conscience tells me to go, and it suits me too, so as to avoid greater evils. I'm going as if to the scaffold.'

The first thing she had to do was invent an explanation for her absence from the Bringases'. If she did not plan them in advance, she would make a mess of these fibs and at the crucial moment she would blunder, giving away that she was hiding the truth. Once the excuse was invented, she prepared to go out, but only did so after her sister had left. Ten o'clock it must have been when she took to the streets, to put it in revolutionary terms, and so fearful was she, that she felt watched and even followed by all the passers-by.

'It seems as though everyone knows where I'm going,' she thought, walking faster than fast to cover the distressing route as quickly as possible. 'The shame of it!'

And the idea that she might meet someone she knew made her cross roads abruptly and take the quietest streets. To make the journey happily, she would have wished to don a mask, and if those had been Carnival days, she certainly would have done so. She crossed the whole of Madrid from north to south. Eleven o'clock it must have been when she turned into Fe Street, which leads to San Lorenzo parish church, and she spotted from the distance the house where she was going by a wire grille hung beside a door, like the insignia of the rag and bone trade. *Rags, wool, stale bread and furniture bought*, said a grubby little poster hung on the wall. The doorway bore no number. Amparo, who had not been there more than once, four months before, could not distinguish it from the other doorways but for that emblem of the wire grille and the sign. Now so close to her

journey's end, she hesitated; but at length, passing a professional
letter-writer's screen, she entered an exceedingly ugly courtyard,
along one side of which a stream of green water flowed, joining
up later on with a brook running with red liquid. It was the
waste from the workshop of a dyer of straw for chair-making
established on the ground floor of the building.

The girl hurried diagonally across the courtyard. She greatly
feared that one of the women standing there would make an
insolent remark; but there was none of this. In the corner of the
yard there was a door to the stairway, which had a masonry
bannister. Walls, steps, and handrail must have last been white-
washed in Calomarde's time; but by now all was dirt and grime
polished by the passage of so many bodies and skirts going up.
A dismal silence reigned on the staircase, which resembled a
reservoir-tank turned upside down. One climbed it to reach the
depths, because the higher one went the darker it became. In the
end Amparo reached the place where a hemp bell rope hung. It
was less clean than the one at her house, for which reason she
also had to hold it with her handkerchief. She rang very gently
and the door, painted with blue distemper, was opened without
delay, revealing the colossal figure of an elderly woman, whose
shiny brown, weatherbeaten face resembled an old walnut
carving. Her hair, the colour of uncarded flax, could be seen
under a black headscarf, and her dress was also black, with a
sheen like flies' wings that betrayed an earlier incarnation as a
soutane. The woman's cracked voice uttered these words,
accompanied by a little laugh, similar to the sound of a rattle:

'Thank God! Let the church bells peal ... He won't half be
pleased.'

'Is anyone here, Celedonia? Any visitors?' asked Amparo with
utmost apprehension.

No one comes here, dear ... He's alone and given up to the
devil. When he sees you, miss ... Come in. There's nothing
wrong with him, you know, nothing but loneliness and sadness.
I tell you to come in and you won't ... Come in, come in, what
are you frightened of? Now he has company, I'm going to the
dyer's.'

Amparo entered a parlour that was not very big with both
windows overlooking the courtyard. This room contained the
furniture of another that had been larger, which gave it the look
of a marine store. Dust reigned absolutely supreme, clothing all

objects in its nasty gauze. It resembled an abode whose owners
had gone away, leaving it in the care of the spiders and the mice.
In the corner opposite the door, behind a small baroque table
with turned legs, positioned beside the window, there was an
armchair covered in torn black oilcloth. In the armchair was a
man, not so much sitting in it as sunk down into it, covered
from the waist down by a blanket.

Upon seeing him, our Emperine went lightly towards him.
The sick man's countenance was all physical pain, anxiety,
bewilderment. She, equally bewildered, held out her hand to
him, and he held it between both of his while he said:

'God be praised ... So many months without an appearance
here! I should have died ... I wanted to die. Oh, Inferno,
Inferno! Abandoning me like this, as one would a dog; letting
me perish in this loneliness ...!'

'I shouldn't have come ... I'd made up my mind not to come
any more ... A horrible sin that can't be pardoned.'

Saying this, she seemed to be choking. She burst into tears
and what tears they were! ... She was crying old tears, tears
belonging to other days and which had not been shed at the
right time. That is why they were terribly salty and horribly
bitter when she tasted them. Her back turned on the sick man,
she stood motionless like one of those pretty images which, clad
in velvet, their face varnished and with a handkerchief in their
hand, represent with their eternal weeping, salvation through
repentance.

He looked at her with a grim and yet frightened gaze. Maybe
he was also crying, but within. His face was like a mask cast in
bronze with verdigris and the white of his eyes was yellowed
like old ivory. In an attempt to take control of the situation, the
sick man cast off the sadness and mourning of the situation with
a violent effort. Listen to what he says in an impatient tone:

'Sweet Inferno, leave that for now. I'm very poorly and rather
emotional. The joy of seeing you after so long overrides everything else. Sit down.'

'Yes,' said she whom the invalid called by such a strange
name and she turned round. 'I've come to perform an act of
charity; I've come to visit a sick friend and no more. Those
follies are over for ever.'

'All right, all right; they're over. But calm yourself now and
sit down.'

Inferno looked all around her in a swift but thorough examination. She blinked her sparkling eyes and her handkerchief
had not quite dried her burning cheeks. A slightly scornful smile
brought her lips to life and she spoke thus:

'I should sit down ... Where, pray? Everything's covered in
dust. It looks as if the place hasn't been swept for three months.
This is dreadful.'

I have permitted no sweeping, nor allowed anything to be
touched ...' replied the misanthrope, 'until you came.'

'Until I came ... Lord above!'

'So that if you don't come ... I let myself die in this neglect.
Now you see how much I need you.'

Inferno looked for something with which to clean a chair, and
having done so, sat down on it opposite the sick man.

'And what does the doctor say?'

'The doctor! ... Celedonia has wanted to bring one several
times, but I always said to her that if she did bring one, I'd
throw him out of the window. I have another doctor; my
medicine is for a person I know to look at me, come to see me,
not to forget me.'

He said this like a querulous child, whose illness entitles him
to be indulged.

'That's enough, that's enough ... It's all in the past,' said
Inferno, struggling to cast off the weight burdening her soul.

'Don't scold me ...'

'I shall simply leave.'

'No, don't do that. I'll be good. But it's quite true what I told
you, that you're my illness when you go away and my health
when you return and that today, just seeing you makes me seem
well and I feel my strength returning. The days I've spent! I've
hardly eaten for a month. Whole weeks go by without my
sleeping ... Celedonia says it's to do with my liver, and I tell
her: "Let her be brought to me ... and you shall see how I am
resuscitated." ... And you're so inhuman, so oblivious ...!
How many letters did I write you three months ago? I quite lost
count. When you didn't reply nor visit me, I resigned myself.
But some days ago, believing I was dying, I could hold on no
longer, and I sent you a few lines.'

'For goodness' sake! ...' exclaimed Inferno, lacking the
strength to stand up to her conscience, 'don't make me regret I
came. That's in the past, it's wiped out, it's as though it never

happened . . . And a whole life dedicated to repentance, will it suffice, I ask, will it suffice for God to forgive? . . .'

Her horror forced her to say all this in an impersonal way, for the words *I, you, we*, would have burnt her lips.

'If suffering purifies, if pain heals,' the sick man declared, hitting himself hard on the head with the palm of his hand, 'if pain heals the soul, I'm purer than an angel . . . Now, if it's essential to wish to drown deeply rooted feelings, if it's not enough to act as though one didn't want them there and if it's necessary really to stop loving, then there's no remission for me. I cannot, nor do I want to be saved.'

Sweet Inferno had no strength to say anything against this. Her weak character succumbed before such categorical determination. She lowered her eyes, bowing her head. The weight of it became so great that she could not bear it.

A minute later, in the simplest and most pedestrian tone in the world, the man spoke thus:

'Do you know? I've started to feel so well since I saw you, that I'd be glad to have something for lunch.'

'But what do you mean . . . Isn't there . . .?'

'Oh, I'm so poor, dear, so very poor . . . I live, if this is living, on charity. All my funds ran out a few days ago. I recovered some of the amount that Pizarro the photographer owed me, do you remember? I spent part of it giving succour to that unfortunate chairmaker's family upstairs; and the rest I've been gradually spending. I still have over three thousand reals owing to me from Juárez and I'll also have whatever the sale of the furniture and equipment from the school produces. The town hall has taken it off my hands; but so far they haven't given me a farthing. If it weren't for Father Nones, I'd have already been taken to the workhouse.'

Amparo went off inside the house and returned shortly afterwards saying:

'But there's nothing here, not even charcoal.'

'Nothing, nothing, not even charcoal,' he repeated, crossing his arms.

Inferno disappeared again. The sick man could hear her clattering in the kitchen and hear the kind voice saying: 'This is shocking.'

'What are you doing?'

'Cleaning a bit,' she answered from the distance, her voice mixed with the sound of pots and pans.

A little later she bustled into the parlour. She had removed her veil and shawl and was every inch the housekeeper.

'But where has that Celedonia got to?' she asked impatiently.

'Celedonia? She's hopeless . . . If she's found someone to chat to . . . What do you want her for?'

'To send her shopping, to call the charcoal-man, the water-man. I can't bear to see the house in this state, nor can I – if I am able to do something about it – watch someone go hungry . . .'

'Who loves you so much. You have spoken like the gospel . . . No, don't regret it.'

'A person who came to the aid of me and my sister in days of wretchedness . . .'

'Bah! . . . Don't count on Celedonia. The poor woman is very good to me, but only serves to eat what little food I have. When she has one of her rheumatic attacks and takes to her bed and starts, her with her shouting, while for my part I'm moaning, and neither of us able to console nor help the other, this house is purgatory. Look, dear, you'd better go yourself and buy what you want to give me. From your hands I'd eat boiled stones. Off you go . . .'

'And if they recognise me?' she said nervously.

She thought for a moment. Then changing her mind and throwing her shawl over her shoulders and, on her head, a scarf that she had been wearing round her neck, she picked up the shopping basket and prepared to go out.

'I'll dare it,' she affirmed, smiling sadly . . . 'This is another act of charity I'm performing and God will protect me.'

'Divine and witty!' thought the miserable gentleman as he watched her go out . . . 'She reminds me of the seraphic wenches who enjoy a place in heaven . . . I mean on the ceiling of San Antonio de la Florida.'

And the sigh he heaved was such that it must have resounded in Rome.

CHAPTER 14

What became of the brilliant position of Don Pedro Polo under the auspices of the esteemed nuns of San Fernando? What became of his famous school, where all the boys of that neighbourhood were licked into shape? Where did his ecclesiastical and civil connections, the profits from his pompous sermons, his beautiful house and fine table go to? It all disappeared; in the brief space of one year, debt carried it all off, leaving only pitiful ruins of so much grandeur. A great and sad lesson which those who have risen swiftly to fortune's catafalque ought to take fully into account! Because if that gentleman's elevation was rapid, more rapid still was his fall. Almost all at once, that whole wobbly edifice came tumbling down and all too soon not a trace, nor a sound, nor even dust from it remained. Especially notable was that the catastrophe was not due to what common people foolishly call *bad luck*, but to the flaws in the very character of the fallen man, to his haughtiness, to his unbridled passions, absolutely incompatible with his status. He perished like Samson among the ruins of an edifice whose columns he had knocked down himself with his stupid strength.

The school is known to have begun to lose its prestige before Doña Claudia's death. The contingent of boys diminished week by week. Alarmed by the harsh treatment meted out to them, the parents were removing their precious darlings from the class and putting them in another where the regime was more benign. And another school-master who set up an establishment in the same street, disseminated absurd rumours about the horrors of Polo and his boys, how he dislocated their arms, split their heads open, tore off their ears and flayed them alive. Later on, people going along the street saw a child come flying out of one of the lower windows like a projectile fired by a catapult. Other equally frightful things were recounted; but not all of what was said deserves to be credited. Passers-by told that on some days the master was like a maniac, shouting and uttering oaths and other words that were unsuitable coming from the mouth of a gentleman of the cloth.

Doña Claudia's death, which was unexpected, was like an extension of that terribly heavy sleep that always came over her after lunch and dinner. This was talked about more than normal. The innkeeper opposite seems to have been upset by the dowager's end because of the good custom he lost. After the misfortune occurred, the *ladies* and Don Pedro began to clash like two substances that refuse to mix. Every day, there were arguments, friction, importunate messages, upset here and there, the ladies very stiff, him even more rigid. The convent messenger, a woman of great loquacity, worthy to be taken to a Parliament, tells that one day the ladies and Don Pedro had a *coram vobis* in the parlour which ended, after much mutual incrimination, in the chaplain telling the nuns to go to ... (to hell, it must have been), right under the nose of the mother abbess. What with this and other things, Don Pedro was obliged to move out of the house and leave the chaplaincy to another cleric of more docile temperament. He had been born to tame savages, to command adventurers, and maybe, maybe to conquer an empire like his countryman Cortés. How could he be any good at such a lost labour, for this and nothing more than this was what that silly job consisted of? ... He left gladly, grumbling about the nuns, whom he portrayed as rotten to the core.

He established himself in his own home, down by Leganitos Street, and there the incompatibility of his character with that of his sister began to be such that living under one roof became difficult. Marcelina Polo, who had been very patient and self-deprecating while her mother was alive, had realised that since she could earn her place in heaven by prayer, there was no need to win it by martyrdom. The maid that they had around this time, an astute gossip of a woman from Segovia, tells that the discovery of some papers or other, allowed Doña Marcelina to discover serious weaknesses of her brother's, and that this brought them into a bitter dispute, which culminated in a split. 'I put up with everything,' she used to say, 'I put up with him throwing plates at my head; I put up with him swearing at me; but a sin as sacrilegious and atrocious as that, I certainly will not put up with.' And she went off to live with a certain Doña Teófila, an elderly lady, who resembled her as one pea in a pod resembles another. A short time later they beguiled Doña Isabel Godoy (who had lost her faithful maid), into going to live with them, establishing themselves in a little house that they took on in Estrella Street. Each of the three had her own special madness; dear Isabel Godoy devoted all of her time to the practice of frenetic cleaning; Doña Teófila's lunacy was usury, and Marcelina's was contemplative devotion, plus a more than mild obsession with playing the lottery, that she had inherited from her mother.

This lady's relations with her brother were from then on extremely cold. She rarely visited him to ask after his health, and she provided no domestic services whatever, nor cared for him in his illnesses. She believed, no doubt, that by praying for him here and there and asking God to lead him away from paths of evil, her conscience could be clear. She spent nearly all day in churches, assimilating their dust, impregnating herself with their smell of incense and wax, which led Don Pedro, when he had a visit from her, to grimace and say: 'Sister, you smell of the sacristy. Do be good enough to stand back a little.'

After falling out with his sister, Polo went to live in the southern neighbourhoods. His decadence was now so visible that he was unable to camouflage it. There was no longer a parish or a brotherhood that would ask him to give one miserable sermon, which was just as well, since he no longer felt like preaching anyway, because the few theological ideas that he had once extracted coldly and unenthusiastically from the mine of his books, had left his head, where they seemed to have been, as it were, in exile and returned to the pages whence they came. Polo, truth to tell, neither missed them nor made any attempt to get them back. His mind, eager for primitive rusticity and simplicity, had lost its disposition for those puffed up and vacuous discourses, and he had even forgotten the theatrical gestures of the pulpit. He was a man who could prolong the falsification of his being no longer and who was heading straight towards a reconstitution of himself in his natural form and meaning, to the re-establishment of his own self-mastery, to revolution within himself, to the destruction and overthrow of all that he found artificial and inauthentic within himself.

It is reported that in the sacristies of the churches where he used to go to celebrate mass, he would start quarrels with the other priests, and that one day he and another character not of a long-suffering disposition had rather too many words and almost came to blows. He put forward ideas so inappropriate to those holy places that on one occasion, they say, even the dumb and unfeeling images blushed to hear him. The rector of San Pedro de Naturales told him not to set foot there again. For some time he wandered from sacristy to sacristy, falling out with the whole of clerical society and giving grounds for malicious rumours. His capital, which was already suffering considerable shrinkage, entered a phase of real strangulation. Poverty showed its sad face, heralding wretchedness, sadder still, on its heels. He might still have found his salvation; but his soul lacked the fortitude to uproot the cause of such a serious and deep-seated disorder. The great energies that his soul had in store and which would have served to earn him epic honours in another age, place and circumstance, were useless against his form of madness. All weapons bounced off the hardness of that petrified life and blood that protected his passion like an immortal breastplate proof to moral and social reason.

Then he was overtaken by feelings that left him disheartened, uneasy, indifferent, and invincibly lazy. He would rise late; he fled in fear from the Church which he believed he profaned by his mere presence; he would spend weeks on end shut indoors like a criminal who had sentenced himself to life imprisonment. At other times he would go out, avoiding his few friends, and spend the day alone, roaming around the city outskirts, poorly dressed in mufti and with a manner that would have made one think him a jailbird just out of prison. Amongst clerics, he retained only one friend, Father Nones, who gently exhorted him to mend his ways and re-establish a normal life. His affection for this good priest led him to live in the humble building in Fe Street and for some time he made timorous efforts to regularise his habits. Then he was stripped of his authorisation to minister and once the weak tie that still strapped his will to the robust body of the Church was broken, he estranged himself completely from it and fell into an abyss of perdition, ruin and wretchedness. He lived in straitened circumstances, stretching the few pennies he had, trying to recover the amounts that some people owed him from his prosperous times. Delivering little letters and messages he gradually, slowly recovered niggardly sums from his debtors. He agreed the sale of school equipment, which was his, with the town hall; but if they made haste to take possession of what they had bought, they were not in any hurry to pay for it.

Just to be unfortunate in everything, Don Pedro also was so in the choice of the housekeeper in his service, an old woman, kindly and without malice, but who did not know how to run either her own or anyone else's household. She was a mother of sacristans, and aunt and grandmother of altar boys, and had been on the door at San Lorenzo rectory for many a long year. She knew the liturgy better than many priests, and had the ecclesiastical almanac at her fingertips. She knew how to ring the bells for a fire, a funeral, and the changes for high mass and was an authority of considerable weight in religious affairs. But with so much knowledge, she did not know how to make a cup of coffee, nor care for someone sick, nor season the most ordinary dishes. Her taste was for loitering in the streets and going to the neighbours' for a chat.

These facts and circumstances – Polo's straying from the path of righteousness, his lack of money, Celedonia's domestic incompetence – led the said household to the last degree of misery and mess. But on a certain day someone who seemed an emissary from heaven walked unexpectedly through the door, and those dead and gloomy premises took on life and light. Soon that smile worn by objects which announces the action of an intelligent and good housekeeper's touch was seen to appear, and the one who rose most jubilantly from the dust to enjoy that sweet caress was the pained, shivering, broken and battered Don Pedro Polo . . .

... whose soul leapt inside his body when he saw Inferno come in with the shopping basket well filled with provisions.

'What abundance!' he exclaimed, his eyes sparkling happily. 'The good times seem to be returning ... God's blessing seems to have entered my humble dwelling in the figure of a saint ...'

He stopped there, severing the thread of that image which came from his soul. Inferno said nothing and went within. Soon Celedonia's tired footsteps and then those of the charcoal- and water-men were heard. Movement and life, the delightful bustle of domestic comings and goings reigned in what had been that lugubrious abode just before. It was agreeable to hear the sound of water pouring, the pestle and mortar grinding, oil sizzling in the frying pan. This was followed by the din of general cleaning, pots and pans clattering, the whip of the duster and the beating away of dust. The girl came into the parlour unexpectedly with a scarf tied round her head, covered by an apron and broom in hand. She ordered the invalid to go into the next room, which he very willingly did, and the windows of the parlour being thrown wide open, the dirt of so many days was seen leaving in a choking cloud shot through with sunbeams. Tireless, Inferno did not allow Celedonia to help her; the latter had limped in to offer her feeble cooperation.

'There's no need,' she told her. 'You go into the kitchen and take care of the lunch.'

'There's a place for all things,' the old woman rejoined. 'I'm going to take him some warm water and see if he wants to shave. He hasn't done so for two weeks, and he's looking like the Good Thief.'

When the parlour was clean and tidy, Inferno returned to the kitchen and then the tumult of water swirling in the sink amongst piles of dishes could be heard. Her arms bare almost to the shoulders, the girl carried out that lowly job, taking pleasure in the coldness of the water and the shine on the wet crockery.

Not resting for a moment, she was into everything and did not open her mouth except to scold Celedonia for her sluggishness. The rheumatic mother of sacristans was more of a hindrance than a help. Then Inferno went to set the table in the parlour. The sun streamed into the room, making the freshly washed wine glasses sparkle. The plates would have shone like new if they had not been chipped at the edges and worn the scars all over of their wretched life in Celedonia's hands.

Don Pedro, well shaven and dressed in clean clothes, returned to his armchair and laughed and laughed, bursting with a nervous contentment that made him seem another man than the one who had shortly before occupied the same place.

'I think,' he said, drumming on the table with his fingers, 'that I've suddenly got back the appetite I had in those old times . . . The power of God! What a day of joy! My soul thinks it's Sunday.'

Inferno came and went without respite. She spoke little and took no part in good old Polo's happiness. There was still much to be done in the kitchen, due to the state of neglect in which she had found everything. So it was then, that lunch, which could have been ready by eleven still took another three quarters of an hour. Don Pedro put his head in at the kitchen door from time to time, to make jokes and hurry things up, and there could be no contrast harder and stranger than his rough, sallow look, the colour of bile, the colour of drama, and his laugh of comedy and the puerile jubilation of his spirits. His innocent jokes went like this:

'But is there no lunch in this house? Madam innkeeper, what are you thinking of, letting your guests starve?'

And then he would burst into frivolous guffaws, echoed only by Celedonia in her candidness. Once the preparations for lunch were completed, Inferno took the scarf off her head and removed her apron, saying:

'Come on, it's ready now.'

When he began to have his lunch, Polo looked the same man as in his best days, with the difference of his worse colour and weight loss. But his discreetly jovial spirits, his somewhat clipped, Castilian-style courtesy, his expressive gaze and his appetite reproduced the happy bygone days. Inferno ate at the other end of the table, and was now a table companion, now a servant, attending to her plate some of the time, serving her friend at other times, for which she kept getting up, going out and coming in diligently. Incapable of lending any help, all Celedonia did was chat about the religious function of the day, the service in honour of the Virgin which was being prepared for the following day and about how badly Father Nones sang, imitating him rather faithfully. Don Pedro sent her to the kitchen several times, but was not obeyed.

Polo wanted to engage the girl in a long conversation; but she defended herself against this resolve, cutting off the misanthrope's words by abruptly getting up to go and fetch something or other. Under no circumstances did she wish to be drawn into a subject of substance; she considered herself a visitor, someone foreign to the household, who had come in with intentions of a similar order to those of the charity workers who made house calls. In her mind she battled to convince herself that she had come to give succour to a sick man, to console a sad man, to feed a hungry man, and sharing in the spirit that dictated the Works of Charity, she dared to create a new one: *Thou shalt dust and sweep the home of those in need* ... She had found there so much wretchedness, so much rubbish, that she could not look upon it with indifference. She added to these ideas, in order to salve her conscience completely for the time being, the intention that this visit would be the last, and a definitive, absolute farewell to the ill-fated friendship that was her greatest mistake and the only stain on her life.

Inferno knew very well how to make coffee. She had learnt this difficult art from her aunt Saturna, Morales's wife, and that day she took great pains over it. When Polo looked at the cup of black, steaming liquor in front of him, the girl, remembering something very important, took a little package out of the pocket of her outfit:

'Ah! I've brought cigars too. I forgot to take them out. They may have broken. A peseta's worth of selected ... This speckled one looks good.'

When she showed the open wrapping paper with the cigars inside, Don Pedro, his heart pierced by a dart of ineffable gratitude, did not know what to say. If he were a man capable of crying real tears, he would have shed them before that model of thoughtfulness, sweetness, and delicacy. He turned his thoughts back to Providence, of which he had formerly said so many good things from the pulpit; but not liking to associate any religious idea to the order of ideas currently reigning in his spirit, he found it more appropriate to recall the fairies, nymphs or invisible beings that had the power to conjure up enchanted palaces in a flash, and to improvise succulent meals, such as he had read about in profane books.

With enormous sadness he saw, when he had not yet finished draining his cup, that Inferno was rising, taking her shawl and her veil, preparing to leave. So it is that nymphs engendered by fantasy or fever vanish into thin air and dream.

'Hey!... What's this?... Already?' he stammered anxiously.

'I'm going. I've nothing more to do here. I'm needed at home.'

'At home! And where is your home?' he mumbled grimly, not daring to say, 'Your home is here.'

'For goodness' sake! That's not the best way to thank me for coming.'

'Sit down,' the misanthrope ordered imperiously, speaking in a tone in keeping with his character.

'I'm going.'

'You're going? It's early. Half past one. If you persist, I'll come out with you. There!... You're going up the street? I'll be behind you. If you're going down, I'll be behind you ... I shan't leave you rain or shine.'

Extremely alarmed, Inferno lacked the strength to protest at such persecution. The burden she felt upon her soul must have been great enough to weigh upon her body too, for she collapsed onto the chair, her arms limp, her head swimming.

'Don't think you're going to do whatever you feel like doing,' Polo observed, half cheerful, half brutal. 'I'm the master here.'

'There are people on whom good intentions are wasted ...', she rejoined, trying to show spunk. 'I received a letter that said "moribund" and I came ... I wanted to console a sick man, and what I've done is resuscitate a dead man who now persecutes me and wants to bury me with him ... What happened to me happened because I'm weak. Weakness like this can never be cured. This very day, when I wanted to come, a voice inside me said, "Don't go, don't go." Lucky are they who were born cruel, because they'll know how to get out of all difficulties ... God punishes people when they're wicked, and also when they're foolish, and He's punishing me for both, yes, for being wicked and for being stupid ... How many crimes are there which, on closer examination, are one folly after another! To have come here: what's that but folly? . . . I suspect God is going to punish me much more yet. I'm living amidst the greatest grief. My life is continual trembling, nervousness, fright, and when I see a fly I feel as though that fly is coming and saying to me . . .'

She could not go on. Tears choked her once more.

'Don't cry, don't cry,' said Polo, somewhat perplexed, looking at the tablecloth. 'When I see you so afflicted, I don't know what comes over me. There truly is a curse hanging over us . . .'

And heaving a sigh from his chest so great that it sounded like a lion's snort, he thought for a short while, his head resting on his hand, so heavily did an idea he had weigh upon him.

CHAPTER 16

'I have an idea, Inferno,' he mumbled in a voice akin to a groan. 'I'll tell you what it is and don't laugh at it. It's an idea born in my loneliness, nurtured in my sadness, so it'll strike you as somewhat savage . . . You see, as there's no hope for me in this society, as I'm less strong than my passions and I've taken such a tremendous aversion to my status, it's come to my mind to get away, but really right away from this country; it's occurred to me to take myself off to the end of the earth, to an island in Asia, or else California, or some English colony . . . There are beautiful lands out there, lands which are a paradise, where it is all innocent customs and true equality; lands without history, Inferno, where nobody is asked what he thinks; fertile fields, where there are wondrous harvests; tribal lands, societies just beginning and which resemble those we see depicted in the Bible. I dream of breaking away from everything and going there, forgetting what I've been and eradicating root and branch the great error of my life, which is to have gone where I wasn't called and deceived society and God, donning a mask to play the bogy-man.'

On hearing this, a ray of happiness flashed in Inferno's eyes, for in that intention to emigrate she saw an easy solution to the terrible problem that was hampering her life and future. But her happiness soon turned to revulsion, when Polo added this:

'Yes, that's my idea . . . to go over there; but taking you with me . . . What? You take fright at that? Coward! You set too much store by things close by and are scared of a mere fly. The world's very big, and God's bigger than the world. Will you come?'

'I!' exclaimed the girl, struggling to conceal her horror and shaking her head.

'Give me one reason why not.'

'No.'

'But one reason . . .'

'No.'

'I'll answer you with a thousand arguments that are bound to convince you. I've given this so much thought! ... I've seen so clearly the pettiness surrounding us! ... Institutions that seem so enormous, so terrible, so universal to us, become grains of sand when we let our thoughts wander across this globe and we go where it's nightfall right now. The planet's big, mark you, and on it there's such a variety of things, of people! ... Just think ...'

Inferno did not just think anything, and if she did think something, she would not tell what it was. Silently she looked at her own hands folded in her lap.

'Give me some reason,' Polo repeated; 'tell me something that's occurred to you. Haven't *you* got an idea? ... What is it?'

'Repentance ...'

'Yes, but ... nothing else?'

'Repentance,' said our Emperine again, without looking at him or moving.

'But tell me something; doesn't this society bother you, doesn't this atmosphere suffocate you, doesn't the very sky oppress you, don't you feel like breathing freely?'

'What suffocates me is something else ...'

'Your conscience, yes ... But one's conscience ... let me tell you ... also broadens when one looks at life in a larger perspective.'

'Mine doesn't.'

'I think,' said Don Pedro in a fit of bad temper approaching rage, 'I think you're rather selfish.'

'Who's more so, pray?'

'All right, I'm selfish ... and you have a heart of stone,' he observed, becoming excited. 'Yes, stone, a lump of ice. It's better to be a criminal than insensitive; and for my own part I can tell you I'd rather go to hell than limbo.'

The girl was debating ways of taking the conversation onto different ground. Her spirit was divided between regretting having made the visit (blaming this wrong step on her weakness of kindliness) and her intention to say to Polo: 'Yes, off you go, Sir, off you go and good luck to you on that island in Africa and leave me in peace.' But her very lack of character prevented her being so cruel and explicit ... Hers was an insoluble problem, given the tenacious and vehement disposition of that man! ...

Amparito's feelings towards him had come to be the most contrary to the incomprehensible frailty from which her misery came; they were feelings of horror towards the person, strangely mixed with a certain respect for his unhappiness; they were pity mingled with repugnance.

The unfortunate girl had as large a dose of repentance in her heart as in her conscience, and she could not find a good explanation for the error of her feelings nor the delirium that had swept her along to sin with a person who soon afterwards was so abhorrent to her ... But she dared not express these ideas for fear of the consequences of such frankness; indeed it is worth noting that if charity played some part in her visit, a large one was also played by that very fear, that suspicion that coldness from her might anger her enemy and propel him down the path of advertisement and scandal. Over and above all other considerations, she placed her interest in concealing her terrible secret. But since these motivations had taken her into that ill-fated house, it was urgent that she think how to get out of it.

'I've left provisions in the house,' she said, 'for many days.'

'You're so kind!' replied Polo, becoming benign and humble once more, as if his illness had attacked him anew. 'You leave and I'm already dying. One fine day, if I don't emigrate, you'll see me begging for charity in these streets. My poverty, dear, is mounting up with compound interest ... I'll be lucky if I die first.'

Amparo already had this observation on her lips: 'Why not mend your ways and try to win back the bishop's authorisation to minister so as to make your living within the Church?' But the idea of introducing any religious idea into that profoundly sad order of ideas repelled her so much, that she swallowed her words. Any recollection of things clerical, any allusion or reference to them made her tremble and shudder, as if a hair-shirt made of ice were being put on her. That was when her conscience rose up more, when her blood boiled and when her heart seemed to come up into her mouth, stopping her breathing. Dismissing those ideas, she spoke thus:

'You mustn't see things so black. And now I remember ... you ...'

Until then she had spoken in an impersonal form; but obliged to use a pronoun, she would have cut out her tongue before addressing him in the familiar form:

'You have debtors . . .'

'Yes . . . and I'm gradually getting them to pay. But that mine is beginning to be depleted now.'

'I know a debtor who could rescue you, by returning to you a fraction of the profits received . . .'

She said it in such a way, that Polo understood at once.

'Don't be silly. I'll get angry with you . . .'

'The fact is . . .,' said Inferno groping with her hand in the hollow of her muff. 'I'd thought coming here . . . This isn't paying a debt, for if I were to pay . . .'

The unfortunate girl could not find the formula, which she wanted to make as delicate as possible, and precisely because she wanted to use the most subtle and discreet form of words, the most stupid of all came out, for she said, putting a banknote on the table:

'If I had more, I'd give more.'

'Goodness me, that's so silly of you! . . .'

'Come on, you haven't exactly got a surplus of funds . . . And I'll get really angry if you insist on being quixotic.'

Don Pedro found it repugnant to receive charity; but the fact that this was a mark of their intimacy, calmed his scruples.

'If I could be as generous as I wished,' she observed, heaving a great sigh and remembering, with renewed anxiety, whence that money had come, 'I shouldn't allow anyone who had been good to me in my own hard times to go without anything. When my father died, who came to our aid? Who paid for the funeral? And afterwards, when we were in such dire straits, who sold his clothes so that we shouldn't go hungry?'

'Hush, silly; that's beside the point. When I'm lucky enough to do a good deed I don't want to be reminded of it again. I don't want it mentioned to me and just see how I am: I'd like the person who benefitted to forget it. That's the way I am.'

Whilst he was saying this, she felt overwhelmed by a myriad of horrible worries, doubts and scruples. Her charitable feelings could not manifest themselves in a calm way, for she was afraid they would betray something highly respectable that had come to take a preferential position in her mind.

The Spirit can indeed have unlikely sympathies! As fire can spread from one combustible body to another nearby, so the soul's anxieties can catch and easily propagate if they find matter on which to feed the flames, matter suitably prepared.

Thus, the worry that stirred our Emperine's spirit spread, like a swiftly moving blaze, to Don Pedro's, who suddenly found himself assailed by jabbing suspicions. He turned a colour that no paintbrush could reproduce, unless it dipped deep into the livid ink of a lightning flash; and chewing something bitter, he slowly uttered this phrase:

'Very rich, aren't you? . . .'

She knew only too well how to interpret the irony sometimes used by the ex-chaplain to express his ideas. She understood his suspicion, she had no difficulty reading that electric-light colouring and that inquisitorial look in his eyes, and she feigned preoccupation, pretending to pick up and dust off the muff which had fallen on the floor. She held the truth so dear that she would have given several days of her life to be able to speak it openly; but how to do it, dear God? And the truth stirred affectionately inside her, saying: *tell me* . . . but how and with what words? That truth would not come out of her mouth for all the world. And even though lies were so abhorrent to her, she had no choice but to tell one and a great big one at that. Polo made the deception easy for her by saying: 'Do you have much work, the two of you?'

'Yes, yes . . . We did a piece of work . . . I've been saving and putting away as much as I can for the last month, hiding the money, because Refugio, if she takes it, she spends it all for me.'

And she rose, determined to leave, less because she wanted to go than to avoid speaking of the matter any more.

Another lie. She said that Rosalía de Bringas had instructed her to take the children for a walk that afternoon without fail. That lady wouldn't half be furious . . . with that temper of hers! . . .

His efforts to detain her were futile. She escaped at last. Going downstairs a sense of great relief and repose came over her, as when one wakens from a feverish dream.

'My name is no longer Inferno, I've recovered my name,' she said to herself, walking very quickly. 'I shan't return ever again even if the sky falls in. I'll try not to be weak again; yes, weak, because that's my greatest fault, to be good and very fearful . . . This is over. Come what may, I shall never see him again . . . But if he gets upset and writes me letters and pursues me and discovers me . . . Lord, Lord, let him go to that island in the antipodes, or else take me away from this world!'

Once he was on his own, Don Pedro gave himself up to meditation appropriate to his sedentary sadness, with all the abandon of a man in poor health and with nothing to do. He imagined himself someone different, with another station in life, or at least someone who led a life quite distinct from his own. This work of the imagination – reconstructing himself, preserving his own being, like a metal that is melted down to find a new form in a new mould – took up three quarters of Polo's solitary days and sleepless nights, and the truth is, it toned up his spirit and did his body some good too, because it activated his vital functions. Even though that life was forced and artificial, it was a life nevertheless.

Huddled in his armchair, his hands supporting his head, as if he were shading his eyes, the latter closed, he would let himself go, go . . . from idea to illusion, from illusion to hallucination . . . He was no longer that hapless gentleman, ill and sad, but another who looked quite different, although in substance he was the same. He was on horseback, wore a beard, had a sword in his hand; he was, in sum, a brave and fortunate leader. Of whom and of what? This was one thing that he did not dwell on investigating; but he suspected he was conquering a huge empire. Everything was easy for him; he won formidable battles with a handful of men, and what battles! He could certainly rub shoulders with Hernán Cortés and Napoleon.

Then he would see himself fêted, applauded, acclaimed, and elevated to the highest pinnacle of fame. His fiery eyes instilled fear in the enemy, respect and enthusiasm in the crowds, and another, sweeter sentiment in the ladies. He was, in short, the most significant man of his age. Truth to tell, he did not know if the costume he wore was a coat of metal armour or the modern uniform with brass buttons. On this important point, there was insurmountable confusion surrounding the image he held in his thoughts. What he did know for sure was that his body was not swathed in that horrible black sheath, more loathsome to him than the sackcloth robe of a condemned man.

And letting himself be carried away entirely, his fantasy took him elsewhere. This was a quick change reminiscent of the theatre. Now he was no longer the tremendous warrior who rode his horse over ravines and rough ground, spurring solders on to battle; now, on the contrary, he was a very peaceful gentleman who lived on his estate lands, marshalling troops of reapers and grape-pickers, visiting his threshing floors, busying himself in his wine cellars, seeing his sheep being sheared, and worrying greatly over whether a cow would calf in April or May. That countrified face brimmed with so much contentment that he began to doubt whether it was really him or a false image. He enjoyed hearing his own hearty laughter resounding in that rustic sitting-room, with its enormous log fire, the ceiling hung with salamis and blood sausages and seeing a lovely fresh-faced lady coming and going very busily . . . Those features were not to be confused, oh no, with those of another. And how she preserved her looks, improving with age instead of declining! With each bonny baby she brought into the world, increasing with happy fertility the human family, it seemed as though Heaven enthusiastically and gratefully conceded an increase in her beauty. She was a goddess, an earth mother, the everlasting maternal ideal in all her everlasting loveliness. Because our visionary saw himself surrounded by such a boisterous swarm of children that sometimes they gave him no time to devote to his work and he spent the day larking around with them . . .

'What are you thinking about?' said Celedonia suddenly as she appeared before the table with her hands on her hips. Her piercing, cold words seemed to drill into his ears. 'What are you thinking about, poor sir? Can't you see you're driving yourself demented? Why don't you go for a walk, for you're hale and hearty and your only ailment is all that brooding? . . .'

The dreamer looked at her, startled.

'What? . . . Were you asleep? Don't you see that if you sleep in the day, you'll be awake in the night? Get out into the street, and go anywhere at all, for the love of God; amuse yourself, even if that means going on a roundabout, eating snails, dancing with servant girls or playing pitch-and-toss. You're like a child, so you have to be treated like one.'

Don Pedro looked at her with loathing. Evening was

approaching. The sunbeam that was coming into the room at midday, had now described its accustomed circle around the table and had withdrawn, slipping along the wall of the court-yard until it disappeared over the rooftops. The room was growing dark and cold. Celedonia stood out like the parody of an apparition in a tragedy; so vulgar was she in appearance.

'Will you go to the devil for good and all and leave me in peace, you horrible old hag?' said Polo with all his heart.

'Fine manners you have,' rejoined the sacristans' mother, laughing half scornfully, half in earnest. 'What a way to treat a lady! . . . What you see here was once sweet and twenty, I'll have you know . . .'

'You . . . when?'

'That's my affair . . . Now, let's see. What do you want me to bring you? Do you want dinner? Shall I bring you the newspaper?'

Once these questions had been asked and received no reply, the apparition slowly went out, limping and groaning with pain at every step she took. Don Pedro threw himself back into the green crystalline lake at the bottom of which such beautiful things were to be seen. Diving down two or three times sufficed to transfigure him. . . . Behold him transformed into a gentleman strolling in strange places, his hands in his pockets. This was town and country at the same time, a land of immense work-shops and huge plains furrowed by steam driven ploughs; a land so distant from our own that at twelve midday, the good man said: 'It'll be twelve midnight now in that nasty old Madrid.' Then, seated around a little table with jolly friends, he would be drinking frothy beer; he would take a newspaper as large as a bed-sheet . . . What language was it written in? It must be English. Whether it was English or not, he understood it perfectly, reading this: 'Great revolution in Spain; fall of the monarchy; abolition of the official state Church; freedom of religious belief . . .'

'The newspaper, the newspaper,' bellowed the spectral Cele-donia, putting before him a damp paper, with an extremely acrid smell of printer's ink.

'What a coincidence!' he exclaimed, his face glowing, because the light that Celedonia placed upon the table glared brightly in his eyes.

'But can't you see that you're going to waste away in that

armchair?' observed the housekeeper. 'Wouldn't you be better off going to a café, maybe even one of those places with music too? Wouldn't you be better off if you had a few dances? The main thing is to live a little. Have a spree and enjoy yourself, for there'll be time enough to settle affairs with your soul. Foolish, empty-headed man, God might have given you my rheumatism to teach you to count your blessings.'

The said person began reading his newspaper with great attention. Unfortunately for him, the press, gagged by prior censorship, could give no alarming news to the public, nor speak of the bands of irregular soldiers in Aragón, marshalled by Prim, nor give warning of the coming upheavals. But that newspaper knew how to put all the revolutionary ardour that was consuming the country between the lines, and Polo knew how to read it and was delighted with the idea of a cataclysm that would turn things upside down. If he could lend a hand in such a great enterprise, he would do so with the greatest of pleasure!

He spent the night better than on other occasions and the following day, instead of staying glued to his armchair, he paced up and down the room in readiness, like a man nursing the sweet plan to take to the streets, in the pacific sense of the phrase. Soon after noon, his best friend, Don Juan Manuel Nones, a priest and the most kindly of men, now very old, visited him. A few words need to be said about him.

This gentleman was a blood uncle of our friend the notary Muñoz y Nones, through whom we met him in more recent times. At the time when this story is set, he was temporarily acting as parish priest of San Lorenzo and lived, if our memory does not deceive us, in Primavera Street, along with a lay brother and two nieces, one of whom was married. Dead now (not the niece but Father Nones), I believe he is, although I am not sure. I have a clear picture of the cleric's face; I often saw him walking around the Ronda de Valencia with his niece's children, and sometimes weighed down by a voluminous and heavy rain-cape in I cannot recall which processions. He was lean, skinny, like a carob bean, his face so wizened and his cheeks so hollow that when he inhaled the smoke of a cigar, it seemed as though his flaccid lips were sucked in back to his larynx, his squirrel's eyes, protuberant and terribly lively, his exceedingly tall stature, his great physical energy, agile and ready for anything; jovial and straightforward in his way of dealing with people, and as pure in his habits as an angel. He knew a great many stories and anecdotes galore, real or invented, witty sayings of friars, soldiers, nuns, hunters and sailors, and used to pepper his conversation with them, not shying away from the saucy variety as long as this did not go too far. He could play the guitar, but very seldom took the profane instrument in his blessed hands, except in a bout of innocent high spirits, to please his nieces when they had close friends over. This man who was so good, generally clothed his conversation and his manners in such bizarre attire that many people could not distinguish between his true self and his eccentricities and took him to be less perfect than he really was. *A dotty saint* is what his nephew used to call him.

He was from Extremadura. His father had been a pastrycook and he had been a soldier in his youth. He was at a garrison in Seville when Riego's uprising took place and he would tell the story of it in gruesome detail. Then he was in the firing squad when they shot Torrijos. He had also been something of a madcap, until God touched his heart, whereupon he took to abhorring the things of this world and, convinced that all is vanity and illusion, was ordained. He never had any ambition in his clerical career, and when the Marquess of Gerona was Minister of Grace and Justice, turned down the archdeaconry of Orihuela. Seasoned by human misfortunes, he could stolidly witness the most atrocious of these and gave succour to condemned men, accompanying them to the scaffold. Father Merino, the coalmen of Calle de la Esperancilla, la Bernaola, Montero, Vicenta Sobrino and other criminals passed from his hands to those of the executioner. He had been a great hunter in his time but all he had left of that now was his compass. In sum, Nones had seen much, he knew the great book of life from memory, had off by heart all the philosophy of experience and (how often he said so!) was shocked at nothing.

He had such an influence over Polo that he was perhaps the only man who could put him in his place, as the following will show. Nones had been a friend of his father; Pedro he had known since he was knee-high to a grasshopper and he allowed himself to use the familiar form of address to him and reprimand him harshly, which the unfortunate ex-chaplain would respectfully listen to. When he saw him that day and they had shaken hands with Extremaduran cordiality, a tremendous flood of anxiety swept over the misanthrope, a sudden, compelling and overwhelming desire to pour out once and for all all the grief in his soul upon the breast of a good friend. This yearning was something Polo had never felt; but that day, without knowing why, it assailed him so powerfully that he neither would nor could help satisfying it at once. And he did not make his confession to the priest; he trusted his friend enough to ask him not for absolution, but a salutary and life-saving piece of advice . . .

'Don Juan, are you busy? . . . No? Well I'm going to keep you all afternoon, because I want to tell you something . . . something long . . .'

He said this with unshakeable resolve. His wish to open his heart was stronger than he was himself. There was something in his soul which was overflowing.

'Let's go to it, then,' replied Nones, sitting down and taking out his tobacco pouch. 'Let's start by having a smoke.'

Polo told all with absolute sincerity, hiding nothing that would reflect badly on him; he spoke simply, telling the naked truth, as one speaks to one's own conscience. Nones listened calmly and grimly, paying close attention, without making any fuss, without showing surprise, like someone whose job it is to hear and forgive the greatest sins, and when the other had uttered his last word, supported by an anguished sigh, Nones took his tobacco pouch out again and said with inalterable calm:

'Right, now it's my turn to speak. Another smoke.'

CHAPTER 18

The priest took a fair amount of time to light up, to inhale, to blow the ash away . . . Then, not looking at his friend, he began to give ample expression to his thoughts with these words:

'The truest thing that has been said in the world is this: *Nihil novum sub sole*. There's nothing new under the sun, by which it's conveyed that no human aberration is without precedent. Man is always the same and there are no more sins today than there were yesterday. Perversity is not very inventive, my son, and if we had the entry book of hell to hand, we'd be bored reading it, so monotonous is it. Someone like I who have been dealing with the consciences of criminals and lost lambs for so many years is shocked at nothing. And having said that, let's look to the remedy.

'I see two evils in you: the enormous sin and the illness of the spirit which you've contracted because of it. The one harms the conscience, the other the health. Strong simple medicine is needed to attack both. Yes, Perico, yes (*loud, strong voice*), it's essential to make a clean break, look for the root of the harm and bang! . . . cast it out. If not, there's no hope for you. It'll be terribly painful? (*Mellifluous, soft voice.*) Well, you have no choice but to suffer it. Then the days will come when your wound will become a scar, the days, yes, for one by one, with their gentle, loving caress, each one will take away a little pain, until your wound closes. If you're afraid and instead of making a clean break you want to cure yourself with poultices, the evil will defeat you and you'll eventually be transformed into a beast and be the scandal of society and our class.

'Because look here (*ingratiating voice*), these things, if you think about it, are child's play for someone with a little willpower who can learn to control himself. To succumb to a whirlwind like that is shameful for anyone, and even more for someone wearing seven yards of black merino wool. And (*loud, high-pitched voice*) there's to be no putting your hands to your head and saying "My God, how unfortunate I am! What a mistake I made with my vocation! . . ." You should have thought of that before, because we know only too well (*very familiar voice*) that with this status of ours, we mustn't think foolish thoughts. Where would it all end if the Sacrament could be broken whenever some swell felt so inclined, and back to the things of this world, and here we go with a *say mass today and marry tomorrow*! . . . Not at all, not at all; once you've drawn the short straw, you have to put up with it. It's just the same as when someone who's married the wrong person starts to bemoan their lot. "Well, my friend, what can you expect . . . you should have thought of it beforehand . . ." And what about those who choose a profession and then find it doesn't suit them? The world's full of mistakes. For if we always got it right, we'd be angels. As I say: once you've drawn the short straw (*extremely familiar down-to-earth voice*), you have no choice but to grin and bear it. So, my friend, hard lines, resign yourself and hard lines again and resign yourself to it'.

He said this emphatically, accompanying his words with gestures. Then, taking inspiration from another couple of puffs, he continued his sermon:

'Here we are, two friends face to face. Let's talk man to man first. There are things which seem tricky and ticklish when one doesn't look closely, sacrifices that seem impossible when one doesn't try to make them. But when a resolute will squares up to them, it becomes clear that they're not impossible mountains to climb. My friend (*awesome voice*), bloodier, more frightful battles than the one I'm commending to you have been won by others. How? With patience, nothing more than patience. This is a virtue that has to be cultivated, like all the others, with the help of faith and reason. And you can turn against yourself and say: "Hey there, I'm falling short, gravely short. I must look out for my decorum, my health, my salvation; I'm not a baby." Believe me that once you make up your mind to win the battle with yourself, calling on God to come to your aid and helping yourself with your own intelligence, you'll start to feel you have the strength for the great enterprise and your strength will burgeon. In this, as in the opposite case, my dear son, it's all a matter of making a start. Once you say "I'm putting a stop to this" (*formidable voice*), if you say it with valiant intentions, you'll see how every day a new tie is born in your soul to strap yourself down with, and you'll gradually restrain the innumerable excesses of the beast stampeding around inside you. And I'm not telling you to chastise yourself pitilessly and draw your own blood, no. That's foolish. Trust in faith, willpower and time.

'Ah! Time! (*pathetic voice*). You've no idea what miracles that little gentleman works! And to those he catches full-grown like you, he gives his best and most radical cures. Because don't come here claiming you're a young dandy (*jovial voice . . .*). You have no grey hair; but one day when you're least expecting it, you'll be all grey and then the aches and pains will come one after the other; today a tooth falls out, tomorrow half your hair; today it's rheumatism, tomorrow your stomach . . . And these, dear friend, are the pharmaceuticals used by the great doctor. The ailments of the body are the medicines for the ills of youth in the spirit. I'm telling you and I've seen a lot of the world and bigger, more horrific storms than yours and choppier seas. To sum up my advice, Perico, my friend, listen to my prescription: first make a clean break, total sacrifice, weed out the evil at its source; then hours, days, months, the warm water of time, dear friend. When some years go by, it'll be all over and you'll find that God's blessing has descended upon you, that white rain, that snowfall that blankets everything, an emblem of oblivion and peace.'

Polo, saying nothing at all, let his gaze extend to Nones's venerable head, completely white and pure like the fleece of the Paschal Lamb.

'And now that we've talked man to man,' the priest continued in sterner tones, 'I'm going to speak my mind to you as a priest. But before I start, do be good enough to ask that harpy Caledonia to bring a drop of wine; that is, if you have any, and if not, some water to refresh my preaching faculties.'

The wine was brought and with it Don Juan Manuel fortified his spirits in order to proceed with his talk:

'The ignominious role you're playing to the world – for the priests despise you for being lost to vice and those lost to vice despise you for being a priest – the injury to your health and other temporal damage are trifles compared with the offence you're giving to God, whom you have sought to sell down the river as if He were a coolie . . . forgive the vulgar expression. You're in a state of mortal sin and if you died now you'd go straight to hell every bit as fast as this wine I've just drunk went to my stomach. There's no escape from that, my son, none whatsoever; in that there's no give and take, none whatsoever; in that there's no picking and choosing, none whatsoever. It's the conclusive, brutal, clear-cut answer. You understand that only too well. Now then, poor old Periquillo (*affectionate voice*); talking to you as a friend, as a priest, as an ex-hunter, as an Extremaduran, as whatever you will, I ask you: do you want to save yourself from dishonour, death and eternal hellfire?'

'Yes.'

'Is that a sincere answer?'

'Yes.'

'Well, if you want to cure and save yourself, the first thing you have to do is put yourself at my disposal, abdicate your will to mine and do absolutely everything I tell you.'

'I agree.'

'Right. Well you're going to start by leaving Madrid. My nephew-in-law, the husband of my eldest niece, Felisa, has bought a large estate in the province of Toledo, between El Castañar and Menasalvas. That's where he is; he wants me to go, but my old bones aren't up to being rattled any more. You're the one who's going to dispatch yourself there, today rather than tomorrow. I order you, as the first treatment, to the wilderness; but what a delightful wilderness! There's arable land, livestock, a bit of a vineyard, and so nothing should be missing; there's also a forest that they're clearing in part now. You'll help them, because wielding the axe is the best antidote to any shilly-shallying you might invent. On that estate, in that paradise you will stay until you receive further orders from me. And mind you don't try sneaking off (*familiar, expressive voice; admonishing with his index finger*); mind you don't try writing letters. You must make up your mind that such a person doesn't exist, that God has taken her to Himself ... And I'm not ordering you there to stand with your arms folded looking at the stars, for idleness and sin are two words that express the same idea. You will do all the penance you can, and pay attention to the plan of mortification I'm imposing upon you: rise very early, hunt anything you find, walk here, there, and everywhere, over plains, rough ground and scrub; eat as much as you can, the leaner the meat the better; drink good wine from Yepes; help Suárez in his work; take the plough when necessary or the hoe and the axe; take the flocks to the hills and shoulder a bundle of firewood if required; in short, work, take nourish-

ment, strengthen that sickly, flabby body. I want you to start by putting yourself into a savage state; and if you follow my plan, you'll be so much so that after you've been there for a little while, if they take a stick to you, acorns will fall ... Once you achieve that happy state, you'll be another man, and if that doesn't wipe out all that moping of the spirit, you can cut my right hand off. When a certain amount of time passes, I'll come and see you or you'll write telling me how you are. I'll examine you and if you're well rid of fever, your authorisation to minister will be returned to you and then (*very affectionate voice*), here comes the second part of my curative plan. Pay attention. Whilst you're there ... *civilising yourself*, I'll be dealing with your case in Madrid, and through my friend Don Ramón Pez, I'll get you a curacy in the Phillipines.

Don Pedro started, surprised.

'What? ... You balk at that? Well, I don't vouch for your complete salvation if we don't put much ground and much water between you. Old Nick is no fool and my convalescent might happen to ... Relapses are always lethal, my son. One last word. If you don't accept my complete plan, I abandon you to your miserable fate. What do you say? Are you hesitating?'

The sick man was indeed hesitating, letting his lack of resolution show on his face. Then Don Juan Manuel got abruptly to his feet, wrapped his cloak around him, picked up his shovel hat decisively, and putting it on with a flourish as a soldier would don his tricorn, he spoke thus:

'Bah ... We've talked enough. Keep all your demons and don't count on me for anything.'

Raising his voice, which had turned from affectionate to severe, he shook Polo by the arm saying to him:

'No one makes a fool of me ... you know I have a bad temper and if you push me, I'm still man enough to take you by the arm and make you meet your obligations, like it or not, you idiot, you wicked man, you good-for-nothing priest!'

The latter trembled to hear such angry words, and held his friend back, grabbing him by his cloak. In this way, he wanted to appeal to him to sit down again and go on talking. This the celebrated Nones did, and such humble things did the penitent say and so full of compunction was he, that the old man was placated and both celebrated their agreement with another smoke.

The following day, Don Pedro went to El Castañar.

CHAPTER 19

By the time Amparo got home, it was so late that she decided not to go to the Bringases'. She tried to recall the pretext that she had devised to use the next day to explain her absence; but the ill-prepared excuse had gone out of her head. Another one needed to be thought up and she devoted to this the brief periods during the night that were not taken up by her deliberations on a graver matter. 'Today,' she thought as she went to bed, 'he's bound to have gone over, just when I was missing. He'll be back tomorrow.'

So it was. Agustín had arrived at his cousins' house very early, at that hour of the morning when the living image of Thiers was in the corridors in his shirtsleeves with the wash-basin in his hands, transporting to his little room the water he would use for washing; at that hour when Rosalía, only just risen from the indolence of her feather bed, was devoting herself to duties and jobs unsuitable for one who had been at the Tellería gathering the night before, dressed up to the nines and sniffing defensively through her dilated nostrils. Since everyone knows everyone in Madrid and there were no strangers at the do, it occurred to nobody to say: 'But this lady with her airs and graces, so frightfully elegant and so high and mighty, must be married to a terribly important man or else some rich business-man.' In the eternal Hispano-Madrilenian masquerade, there is no hope of deception and even the mask has become almost unnecessary.

Our dear Mrs Bringas was such a sight that morning, that one might have taken her for a landlady of the humblest boarding-house. How tired she looked and what rags she wore! The maid was out shopping and the lady, after going round the kitchen many times, was getting the children ready for school.

'Hello, Agustín ... Over here so early?' she said to her cousin, when he came into the dining room. 'Last night at Tellería's, someone, I don't recall who, spoke about you ... It was said that you were waking up, and that you only look as though butter wouldn't melt in your mouth. If you're up to something out there . . . We still have to find you a sweetheart, indeed we have, and one fine day, we'll marry you off.'

As she spoke, Rosalía looked sadly at her little girl, while she tied her little pinafore and put on her hat. That ambitious Mama would have wished to stretch Isabelita miraculously by virtue merely of her loving gaze and make her marriageable before Agustín grew old.

'I do declare, cousin,' she said to him in a variation on the same theme as her thoughts: 'not to flatter you, but you look younger and more handsome every day . . . Even if you waited another five or six years, it would be no loss.'

'No, Rosalía. If I marry, it's to be next year.'

'Really?'

'I mean it might be so. I don't guarantee it.'

Bringas called his cousin to make him read a news report in the paper that had just arrived.

'This is going badly, very badly,' Don Francisco observed sadly, as he applied himself assiduously to the task of polishing his boots. 'Bands of irregulars in upper Aragon again . . . The poor queen . . .'

Amparo came in; the charcoal-man, the baker, the maid, the Alcarrian nut-seller came in; and the cramped abode, with the morning traffic, made one want to flee. Don Francisco, having made his boots shine so one could see one's face in them by dint of breathing on them and then buffing, put them on.

'What a hard life!' he said to his cousin, whilst he took the niggardly housekeeping money out of the little drawer. 'And now we have a major commitment. We're to go to the Palace ball, and a Palace ball will unbalance the budget for three months. But Her Majesty insists that we go, and try getting that out of Rosalía's head. We have to go. He whose living comes from the state payroll can't snub the figure of supreme power.'

What Caballero said to this is not known; but he must undoubtedly have made some observations about the unfortunate position of the middle class in Spain. After Bringas had eaten, the two cousins went out, and later on, Rosalía went to her dressmaker's house to begin the economic study required in order to procure a pretty ballgown for herself. Even though she could count on little presents from the Queen, who might send her some skirt or other still in good condition, to alter it always incurred expenses and it was essential to reduce these as much as possible for the sake of that epitome of fusspots, Saint Francisco Bringas.

Caballero returned to the house in the afternoon, when he trusted he would find it free of importunate witnesses. And it was as he thought, for the children were not yet back from school, the maid had gone out, and the little orators were so engrossed in their rhetorical game inside Paquito's tiny assembly, that they were not in the way. So Agustín went into the sewing room, sure of finding what he was looking for there. So it was. Silent and as if fearful, Amparo turned pale when she saw him come in. He smiled and also paled. It was quite late now and they could not see one another well enough to observe their respective emotion. She was thinking that she must not waste such a good opportunity to say thank you for the merciful aid received; but she could not find a way of doing so. If she found it though, what things she would say! All that her mind could come up with, ruthlessly dredged by her will, sounded cold, trivial, silly and vulgar. When he said:

'I didn't think you were here', all that occurred to her was, 'Yes, sir. I was here.'

'What are you still sewing for? There's not enough light to see now.'

'There's still a little bit of light . . .'

These sublime rhetorical conceits were the sole product of those two brains swollen with ideas and those hearts overflowing with sentiment. But Caballero, spurred on by impatience, thought: 'Now or never', and a phrase lit up in his mind, one of those phrases that one either says or they smash the tight mould enclosing them. The concept contained was stronger than the shy container and out of that discreet mouth came these words, like a shot from a gun barrel.

'I have to talk to you . . .'

'Yes, yes, I'm so grateful . . .', she faltered, with a lump in her throat.

'No, that's not it. It's that this morning, Rosalía and I spoke about you, and about whether or not you're to enter a convent. I'm ready to provide the dowry; but let this be understood, on one condition; that you must not marry Jesus Christ, but me.'

Ah! You rogue! You came with it well prepared; if not, how would it have come out so neatly! Caballero, in a horrible battle with his own shyness, had thought as he came in: 'Either I say it word for word, or I open the window and throw myself down to the courtyard.' The triumphal phrase was followed by a silence ... Snap! Amparo's needle broke. The gaze of the man from the Indies watching the outline of his beloved in the penumbra would suffice to substitute for the rapidly fading sunlight. The bell rang.

'Excuse me, sir,' said she, almost jumping to her feet. 'I'll go and open the door ... It's Prudencia, who went out for some coal.'

But Agustín intercepted her at the door and, taking her hands and squeezing them tight ...

'Are you giving me no answer at all?'

'Excuse me for a moment ... They're ringing again.'

Our Emperine went to open the door. Prudencia charged down to the kitchen with the heavy tread of an unbroken horse. Shortly afterwards Amparo and Caballero found themselves in the corridor, next to the corner of the entrance hall, as dark as a cave. The shy man's hands stumbled upon the timid woman's hands in the gloom, and he caught them again in flight. Leaning against the wall, she said nothing.

'What's all this? ... Are you crying?' asked the American, hearing her breathing heavily. 'Aren't you giving me an answer to what I said?'

Not a word, just wailing.

'Doesn't my proposal please you?'

Caballero heard the following words which were uttered with increasing speed and sounded like the first drops of rain that threatens to grow heavy:

'Yes ... I ... I ... yes ... no ... I'll see ... you ...'

'Be completely frank with me. If it displeases you ...'

'No ... no ... I'll say ... You're very good ... I gratefully.'

'But this crying, what's it for?'

She seemed to be calming down somewhat, quickly drying her tears with her handkerchief. Then she turned towards the sewing room and signalled to the man from the Indies to follow her.

'If Rosalía comes in and sees me crying ...!' declared the girl with great fear, once they were in the room.

'Don't worry about Rosalía and answer.'

'You're very good: you're a saint.'

'But one can be a saint and not be attractive ...'

'Oh! no ... yes ... I'm very grateful ... But I have to think it over ... Of course I ...'

'Come on,' said Agustín with some bitterness, 'I'm not attractive to you ...'

'Oh! you are, very much so, very very much so,' she rejoined in an expansive outburst. 'But ...'

'But what ...? You have no relations who might oppose ...'

'No ... but ...'

'You're free. Now if you have some kind of commitment ...'

'I ... yes ... no ... no ... that's not it. I have no objection,' she replied vehemently. 'I'm a poor woman, I'm free, and you're the most generous man in the world, for having noticed me, I who have no standing nor family, I who am a nobody ... This seems like a dream. I don't want to believe in it ... I wonder if you have taken leave of your senses, if you will regret it when you reflect upon it ...'

The respectful, introverted Caballero would have answered her with an embrace, expressing in this way, better than with cold words, the tenderness of his affection and how contrary it was to the regret she imagined. But at that moment an indiscreet witness entered the room. It was a movable brightness coming from the corridor. Prudencia was passing with the hall light in her hand, to put it in its place. They both waited. The brightness entered, grew and then faded until it was quite extinguished, mimicking a thirty-second day bounded by its two twilights. The lovers were silent, waiting for night to fall once more; but as Amparo suspected that the lass had looked into the dark room, she went out and said:

'Isn't Madam late!'

'Shall I light the dining room?' asked the harpy.

'Already? ... It's very early.'

When Prudencia returned to the kitchen, our Emperine went over to the door of the sewing room, and the shy man heard this whisper, which had the timbre of a sweet confidence:

'Pst ... Come along here, gentleman Caballero ...'

One behind the other, they reached the dining room, faintly lit by two patches of light, one from the kitchen nearby and one shining through the fanlight of the children's parliamentary assembly. The voice of Joaquinito Pez could clearly be heard proffering this precocious piffle: 'What I say to the honourable gentlemen is that the revolution is approaching with its flaming torch and axe of destruction.'

'Balderdash!' murmured Agustín.

'Sit down here; said Amparo, indicating a chair and opening the drawers of the dresser to take out the wherewithal to set the table.

'Once I decide on something, I'm a man who likes to carry it out come what may.'

'Well, what I say is that you shouldn't be so precipitous and you should give much thought to such a serious matter,' replied the timid girl in a quiet voice, so that the maid should not hear. The jubilant happiness that filled her soul was not clouded at that moment by any painful thought.

'Much thought has been given to it all,' he affirmed, delighting in looking at her over and over again. 'And furthermore, feelings cannot be the subject of calculation, for feeling and calculation are not good friends. Some time ago I said: "This woman will be for me, and over and above everything else, she will be." Those of us who are truly in love have second sight; and without having known you before, I know for certain, yes, for certain, that I'm talking now to the purest virtue, and as for loyalty, the most . . . And you don't speak only to my heart and my head, but also to my eyes, for you're lovelier than a goddess.'

This was the first gallant flower that the hermit had ever thrown at the feet of an honest woman in his whole life. He said it so easily and was so satisfied with it, that he enjoyed keeping the conceit that he had just uttered in his memory.

'For goodness' sake, Don Agustín!' observed Amparo, disguising her delight as joviality. 'I shall break the plates if you go on saying such things . . .'

'You'll break all the crockery, because I still have much to say.'

The tired doorbell rang again.

'It must be Don Francisco,' said the girl, leaving the room to open the door to him.

It was indeed he, and he could be recognised by his way of ringing, for his thrifty spirit went so far as to make him economise even on the sound of the bell. Bringas went into his room and was changing his clothes in the dark, when his other half, having rung loudly, came in. She was very upset, for she had gone from the dressmaker's workroom to the Palace, but had not managed to see Her Majesty, as it was a day on which there were audiences and a Cabinet meeting. No sooner had she set foot in the dining room than she began scolding left, right, and centre: the hall light was smoking, the dining room was pitch dark and there was a smell of burning in the kitchen. Amparo lit the lamp in the dining room. Setting eyes on her cousin Rosalía's anger vanished forthwith.

'I didn't know you were here. You're always to be found emerging from the darkness like a weasel. Tell me something. Why don't you come tonight? It's a gathering of close friends ... few people, Doña Cándida, the young misses Pez ... Will you come? Don't be so retiring, for Heaven's sake. Let yourself go for once. I guarantee you that with hardly any effort you're bound to make a conquest. The Pez girls never stop asking after you ... what are you doing ... how do you live ... why don't you marry ... how well you ride ... It's what I keep saying: you have your admirers, you do and you won't believe it.'

'Well tell Pez's little girls not to hold their breath waiting for me. They're very disagreeable, very ill-bred, very stuck-up, and I for one pity the unfortunate men who'll marry them.

'You're talkative tonight, I do declare! The turtle wants to come out from under his shell, it seems. Good, Agustín, good.'

'Greetings,' said Bringas, coming in unexpectedly, swathed in his smoking jacket dating from 1840, which one could not have given away in the flea market, let alone sold.

Caballero said goodbye with a warm handshake for his cousin and pulled his muffler up over his mouth.

'But are you leaving so soon?'

'Oh ... I forgot. The piano for the little girl will be brought tomorrow. I'll pay the music master. Her and her little brother's school fees are also to be at my expense.'

'There's no one like you in the whole world ...' declared Bringas, embracing his cousin with feeling. 'God grant you all the life and health you deserve ...'

Rosalía sighed as she tenderly embraced her daughter, who had just come in from school.

'Are you leaving so soon?' repeated Don Francisco.

'I have some letters to write.'

'By the way: look, Agustín, don't spend money on ink. The day after tomorrow, that is on Sunday, I'm going to make a couple of gallons for myself and the office. I'll send you a large bottle. I have the best recipe ever and I've already got the ingredients . . . So don't buy any more ink, will you? Now then, bye-bye . . . and thank you, thank you.'

With these affectionate words and the offer that he had made, a sincere expression, albeit black, of his immense gratitude, Mr Bringas saw off his cousin at the door. When he returned to the dining room, rubbing his hands so hard that they were virtually sending sparks flying, his wife, pensive, staring vacantly at the floor, appeared to be in ecstasy. To her husband's enthusiastic observations she only replied in a transport of admiration:

'What a man . . . but what a man! . . .'

A short while later, Amparo was saying goodbye, and taking the following orders from Rosalía:

'Tomorrow I want you to bring me half a dozen lamp glasses. The one in the hall has just broken. Go past the Cava Baja and leave a message for the egg-man. Bring two dozen buttons like this one, and come early so you can do my hair, because I have to go to the Palace before one.'

In the street, Amparo saw that a body came over to her, a person, a muffled spectre. Her heart leapt as she recognised the red and grey trimmings of the cloak.

'You shan't escape me,' said Agustín, letting his muffler slip down to show his face.

'Oh!'

'There's no need to be afraid. We must conclude this matter without delay. We must be able to speak whenever we please. Watching for the brief moments when you're alone at my cousin's place, waiting for you at the door, as one would for a dressmaker, are not to my taste.'

'You're absolutely right,' said she, carried away by her feelings.

'Consequently, you'll give me permission to come to your home. From today onwards you're starting a new life. She who is to be my wife . . . and up to now you've said nothing against it . . .'

In the pause that he left, Amparo, confused, searched for the most appropriate phrases for a reply; but that smooth balm that was covering the wounds in her heart, dulled her wits.

'She who is to be my wife,' continued Caballero, 'can't live like this, a servant in a household . . . because this is worse than being a servant . . . Besides, it's high time that you began to put your affairs in order . . .'

This was heavenly music to Amparo's ears. Her ecstasy was such that she knew neither where she was walking nor how to express her feelings. The roundly affirmative answer stumbled on her lips against something choking, bitter and obstructive that emerged from her conscience when she was least expecting it. But so weak was her character, that neither her conscience nor her affection managed to declare themselves, and the *yes* and the *no*, after a period of painful stammering, went back inside her ... To turn down flatly so much happiness was impossible for her; to accept it seemed somewhat indelicate. She thought she could get out of trouble by expressing her gratitude, which, as she saw it, was like a conditional acquiescence.

'I don't know how to thank you ... Don Agustín. My worth is not what you believe it to be.'

Paying no heed to this, Caballero went on:

'From tomorrow, your life is changing. That's at my expense. Bringas and Rosalía must know about it, because mystery is pointless.'

They were going down Ancha Street, not separating to let anyone past. From time to time they looked at one another and smiled. A more innocent and mundane idyll is not to be seen by gaslight and in the crowded solitude of an ugly street, where all those who pass by are strangers. In the following ups and downs of that conversation, which held so little dramatic interest and whose flavour could only be savoured by themselves, Amparo's voice was heard saying:

'Yes ... I had realised; but I was afraid you would say something to me. My worth is not so great as you imagine.'

'But you, who are modesty itself, are bound to say that.'

They were walking slowly and at each phrase they would stop, wishing to make the journey very long. Her eyes shone in the dark with a sweet, poetic light, and Caballero was so proud and so moved looking at them, that he would not have changed places with the angels playing harps on the steps of the Creator's throne ...

'Another thing ...' he said, trembling under his cloak. 'Don't you think we could use the familiar?'

This sudden proposal of closeness took our Emperine so much by surprise that she burst out laughing.

'I think,' she observed, 'it'll be hard for me to get used to.'

'Well, for my part ...' declared the shy man, 'I think I shan't have any difficulty. The truth is that for me this is a long-standing passion and I've grown so used to the idea, that when

I'm alone and bored at home, I imagine that I see you entering; I imagine that I see you entering, and that I hear you giving instructions to the servants and running the household ... If these hopes that I have held for so long were now to vanish, believe me, they would send me to my grave.'

Amparito, confused, allowed her friend's vigorous, ardent hand to squeeze her own. She averted her eyes, staring into space. Her eyesight was troubled. She had seen a black shadow pass.

'That great sigh,' asked Caballero in childish tones, 'is it because of me?'

She looked at him. She was going to say yes, but all she actually said was:

'If I had a hundred thousand lives, I still couldn't repay you . . .'

'I don't want a hundred thousand lives; I'm happy with one, in return for the one I'm giving. What I'm offering isn't much. Everyone says I'm a brute, a savage. I understand well enough that I'm unattractive, that my manners are somewhat rough and my conversation dull. Solitude has raised me and it isn't strange that that I should take after this second mother of mine a little. In private life, perhaps those that label me as boring in company would find me acceptable; but those who see me from afar don't know this . . .'

'What the others don't like,' affirmed the girl resolutely, inspired, 'I do.'

She was such a pretty little thing, that even a man made of the sternest stuff could be forgiven for falling madly in love with her on first sight. The expression in her eyes was like a gentle caress, a little sad and with a glow like the evening twilight; her complexion was beautifully delicate and pale; her chestnut hair, abundant and curly, with soft natural waves; her figure slender and shapely; her mouth a delight and incomparable teeth, like even little pieces of well-polished white marble; goodness and modesty somehow emanated from her, and plenty, plenty more charms made of her the most perfect picture of a woman that could be imagined. What a great pity that her only finery was cleanliness and that her dress was so ancient! Her veil was pleading for a substitute, as was her shawl; and her boots, by dint of mending, feigned a youthfulness they did not have. But all of those imperfections and even other less visible ones, would soon be remedied. Then, what would compare with how she looked? As this thought crossed her mind, her whole being throbbed with the sharpest pangs of yearning. For Amparito, let it be made clear, had no ambition for luxury, but for decency; she aspired to an ordered, comfortable life without ostentation, and that fortune which was drawing close to her saying 'Here I am, take me,' drove her wild with happiness. And yet, she lacked the courage to take it, because from the turmoil within her came terrible reservations which clamoured: 'Stop . . . that's not for you.'

They spoke a little more than what has been transcribed, empty phrases for others, of the utmost interest for them. At the door, when they were both taking pleasure in gazing at each other, drinking in and returning their stares in a pleasant game, Caballero slipped in these words:

'Shall I come up?'

'I don't think it prudent.'

They were both serious.

'That's fine with me,' said Agustín, who was always reasonable. 'Tomorrow . . . I'm so happy! And you?'

'I am too.'

'Go up. I'll wait until I see you go round the first bend in the staircase.'

CHAPTER 21

That good man, who had devoted the best part of his life to arid work, in which he combined the trader and the adventurer in his single person, had a passion, when he gave himself up to rest, for order, a mania for comfort and everything that could make life pleasant and give it an even, leisurely pace. Anything erratic, anything that was out of tune with the routine habits that he so easily acquired, upset him greatly. He had established a regime in his house, whereby everything happened at a fixed time. His meals had to be served on the dot and even things of very little importance were subject to his methodical rigour. To see any object out of place in the study or the small parlour upset him greatly. If he noticed dust on any of the furniture, or if Felipe's negligence was detectable anywhere, he would be cross, but keep his temper: 'Felipe, look at the state of that candlestick ... Felipe, is that where you think the cigar boxes belong? Felipe, I notice that you're rather preoccupied ... You've left your class notes here. Do be good enough not to put papers other than my own here.'

This obsession for method and regularity was made even more manifest in matters of greater importance. Precisely because he had spent the best part of his life amidst disorder, he felt a vehement yearning, on reaching middle age, to surround himself with peace and to secure it by clinging to the institutions and ideas that go along with it. This is why he aspired to a family, to marriage, and he wanted his house to be the most solid seat of moral law. Religion, as an element of order, also attracted him, and a man who had not remembered to worship God in any rite when in America, declared himself a sincere Catholic in Spain, went to mass and found the democrats' attacks on the faith of our forefathers most improper. Politics, another cornerstone of social permanence, penetrated his soul likewise, and he was to be seen applauding those who wished to reconcile historic institutions with revolutionary novelties. Caballero was greatly upset by anything that constituted an exception to calm and routine in the world, any discordant voice, anything out of place, any protest against the foundations of society and the family, anything that heralded discord and violence, in the private just as much as in the public sphere. He was a weary traveller who wants to be allowed to rest where he has found tranquillity, peace, and quiet.

He had bought a new, extremely beautiful house in Arenal Street, the entire first floor of which he occupied. Part of it was already furnished, more importance being accorded to finding a comfortable disposition of things, as in the English style, than in that luxury of the Latins, who sacrifice their own wellbeing to stupid appearances. There, without its being devoid of visual attractions, all that was necessary to good, comfortable living prevailed. The decoration of all the rooms was not yet complete, particularly those destined for the lady of the house and the future Caballero offspring; but new prodigies arrived every day. Such was the house that only a few families of recognised opulence could have competed with it in those times when a modern capital city was beginning to dawn over the vulgarity of the sprawling town of Madrid. This was thanks not only to the wide thoroughfares and spacious neighbourhoods, but also, and even more importantly, to the comfort and cleanliness of people's homes. Caballero's friends looked in wonder upon the magnificent bathroom that the extraordinary man back from America had been able to install; they were dumbstruck at that gigantic kitchen stove, which as well as cooking to feed an army, provided hot water for the whole house; they marvelled at the spacious bedrooms, moved out of the poky nooks to a position where they received light and fresh air direct from the street; they noticed that the purely ceremonial rooms did not steal the south-facing aspect of the living rooms, and they were shocked to see that there was a gas supply in the corridors, the kitchen, the bathroom, the billiard room, and the dining room; and they saw and praised many other things that we omit here to avoid prolixity.

The study was not furnished according to conventional standards of elegance, which can so easily become vulgar. Scorning the professionals' routine furnishings, Agustín gave his office a rich trader's style, and the first thing to be seen upon entering the room, was the letter-copier with its iron press and other devices. Inside a luxurious glass display case, there was a pretty collection of Mexican figurines, typical folk portrayed with veracity and admirable grace in wax and cloth. There is nothing more charming than these creations born of an unschooled art, in which the imitation of Nature goes to incredible extremes, demonstrating the Indians' aptitude for observation and the skill of their fingers to imbue form with spirit. Only in Japanese art can one find something of a value similar to the Aztec sculptors' patience and taste.

Two shelves, one filled with books about trade and another with literature, went with the exhibition of the figurines; but the works of literature were only there for decorative purposes, even though amongst them there were some as notable for their content as for their bindings. An American calendar, at that time a novelty item, took up one of the most prominent places. The clock on the chimneypiece was a beautiful Parisian bronze one in the Egyptian style, with gold and pale green chimes; and upon the same chimneypiece, as well as on the table, there was a great variety of objects fashioned from that Mexican jasper, unrivalled the world over for the vividness of its colours and the transparency of its veins. There were little jugs and paper-weights, the majority of which last were made to look like fruit, and in some of these pieces, the illusion came so close to perfection that mineral passed itself off as vegetable. The decor of the study was completed by seating in studded green rep, which Caballero found to be in execrable taste; but he had resolved to give it to his cousins when the furniture consignment he was awaiting arrived.

Agustín worked in there for two or three hours every day. He wrote terribly long letters to his cousin, who had remained in charge of the business in Brownsville, and he also had a drawn-out correspondence with his agents in Bordeaux, London, Paris, and New York. His clear, commercial hand was a delight, with its good, clean flourishes; but his style, a stranger to all literary pretensions and sometimes even divorced from grammatical obligations, certainly does not merit that the respectable confi-dentiality of the post should be breached. That day, however, he put into his epistle news that was so foreign to the subject of trade, that it is not possible to fail to attract attention to it. In one paragraph he was saying: 'I have fallen in love with a penniless girl', and further on: 'If you saw her you would envy me. I met her at my cousin Bringas's. Her beauty, which is great, is not the main thing that captivated me, but her virtues and her innocence ... Dear Claudio, I must apprise you of the fact that the ladies and gentlemen of this land drive me mad. The poorer the girls are here, the more arrogant they are. They have no breeding; they are chattering spendthrifts who think of nothing but enjoying themselves and wearing frills and furbelows. In the theatres you see ladies who look like duchesses, and it turns out that they are the wives of miserable office workers who hardly earn enough for their shoe leather. Pretty women there are; but many whiten their skin with all sorts of potions, they eat badly and they are all pale and half-consumptive; but before they go to the ball they slap themselves to bring out some colour ... These feather-headed creatures can talk of nothing but betrothals, their strutting male counterparts, their frippery, the tenor H., ball X, the scrapbooks they keep, this, that or the other hat ... One young lady who has been at the best school here for six years, told me a few days ago that Mexico is beside the Philippines. They don't know how to make a pot of soup, or sew on a mere button, or add up two amounts, although there are exceptions, Claudio, there are exceptions . . .'

And in another letter: 'Mine is a gem. I met her working day and night, her head bowed, her tongue still ... I met her with torn boots, she who is so utterly ravishing, she who by just looking at any man would have had millions thrown at her feet! ... But she is an innocent and as retiring as I am. We are made for one another, and a better couple I do not believe could exist. Anyway, Claudio, I am as happy as can be, and I now turn to saying that you should keep the batch of hides until the summer is over and the deliveries from Buenos Aires are scarcer. I have received news of the payment transferred to Bordeaux and of another smaller one to Santander. I am crediting both to your account.'

It is worth noting that the desire for order and legality that had dominated good Caballero since his arrival in Europe, extended, in order to cover everything, even to the domain of language. Wishing not to break any rule, he had bought himself the Academia Grammar and Dictionary and he kept them close by as he was writing, so as to manage to defeat, by dint of timely consultations, the spelling problems that assailed him at every turn. He struggled so much, that his epistles were growing clearer and clearer of the rambling that disfigured them formerly, when he used to scribble them at the filthy, messy desk in his Brownsville house.

Every evening, he would go out on horseback. He was a skilful and safe rider, of that unique Mexican school that seems to fuse into a single entity the man and his mount. In his wanderings around the city outskirts, just as in the solitude and peace of his house, he never belied his enamoured state; that is to say, he never for an instant stopped thinking about his idol, contemplating her image in the mirror of his mind and caressing it, now this way, now that. Sometimes he could see her so clearly, as if she stood alive before him. At other times, his imagination became strangely blurred, and he had to make an effort to know what she was like and reconstruct those pretty features. What a strange phenomenon, this vanishing of the image in the very brain that honours it! Luckily, it was not long before she would present herself once more to him as clear and alive as she was in reality. Those dimples, when she laughed, were they not pretty! That particular way of saying *thank you*, how could it be erased from the fantasy of the man who loved her? And how could he forget that sweet expression that crossed her face before saying *no*, that sudden and graceful nod of the head in agreement, the good company that her hair provided for her eyes, that tone of innocence, of simplicity, of insignificance that she used to talk about herself? Ah, the way she looked at him when he was saying something serious! And then that way of wrapping her shawl around her, with her right hand inside it and covering her mouth . . .?

The day after the conversation in the cold street (and it was in that conversation that Caballero observed the detail of the hand in the shawl, so well preserved in his memory), he wrote her a long letter. In it, more than amorous words, the coldly positive abounded. Starting with allotting her a substantial monthly allowance, until the happy day of the marriage, he suggested she should live at the Bringases'. If the cousins refused this, he would visit her at her home. Amparo should prepare her trousseau without delay, so as to enter into her new status in triumph but with decorum.

CHAPTER 22

Only to his few, well-chosen friends had Caballero announced in a vague sort of way his matrimonial plans. But as he was not known to have a fiancée, it all became a game of guesswork, conjecture and speculation. They were well aware that Caballero did not frequent social gatherings. Never did they see him flirtatiously parading up and down the avenues, only on the rarest occasions at the theatre, and he did not frequent meetings of ladies, other than those of dear Mrs Bringas, where he shone for his frostiness and the aridity and evasiveness of his conversation. All were in agreement that Agustín was the strangest of men; but they were so happy with his kind friendship and were so fond of him, that they respected him notwithstanding their innocent criticism of his oddness.

Among these friends, three stood out, who were properly speaking the close ones. Here they are: Arnáiz, now old, the proprietor of a long-established and accredited wholesale cloth business; he imported merchandise from Nottingham and honoured bills of exchange drawn on London. With his honest constancy, he had amassed a nice fortune and by that time, removed from active dealings, he had handed the business over to his brother's sons, which kept it going under the famed name of *Arnáiz Nephews*. Trujillo y Fernández, who had married the only daughter of Sampelayo, was in charge of the long-established and respectable banking house of Madrid G. *de Sampelayo Fernández and Company*, which dates back to the last century. Mompous y Bruil, at first a broker in exchange bills, had subsequently made a large fortune buying tracts of land to resell in plots. The three were people of the most flawless integrity, of excellent habits, and boasted rock-solid creditworthiness in the market-place.

Trujillo, who had several pretty and marriageable daughters, tried to woo Caballero from the time that he met him, and the lengths to which he went in order to have him frequent his home were indescribable. One night he finally did go; but he did not cross the threshold again except to make the statutory quarterly visit, which lasted fifteen minutes and at which Agustín was extremely embarrassed and inhibited, talking about the weather and counting the minutes that separated him from the blessed moment when he could get out into the street. Trujillo, clinging stubbornly to his idea, kept inviting him for a meal on such and such day; but Caballero always looked for a way to excuse himself and dodge the issue, using illness or engagements as a pretext. At length, the honest banker had to give up on having him for a son-in-law, but this did not diminish the noble affection that united the two of them. For his part, Mompous had cherished identical plans in his fanciful schemer's mind. He had one plot, which is to say a beautiful only daughter, and on her he planned to erect, with Agustín's help, the fine edifice of perpetuity for his race . . . 'Caballero, my wife has told me to invite you over to eat on Sunday.' The ambitious Catalan repeated this so much, that one day Caballero had no choice but to go. What a dreadful time the poor man spent there, wishing time would fly! For the girl, who was vaporous and pretty, he had no liking at all; but there was no feminine accomplishment that she did not have, including singing and playing the piano in self-accompaniment. She showed off the varied multiplicity of her talents to him, whilst her Mama praised the priceless good nature of that model of girls. But Agustín could not or would not address to her any other gallantries than those which are such commonplaces that they fall from all lips and are neither heartfelt nor true. 'The man is a boor.' That opinion became proverbial in Mompous's house. The boor, or whatever he was, did not appear there again despite his friend's passionate hinting. Caballero cared so little for his wife, what with her syrupy tongue and her far-fetched naturalness of expression, that he would give anything not to see her. So, when he used to go to the house to talk business with Mompous, he would swiftly ensconce himself in the study and stay as short a time as possible. If he heard the rustle of skirts, he would suddenly be in a great hurry and go, leaving the business half done.

Speaking of the mystery surrounding Caballero's matrimonial plans, Trujillo used to say:

'The man will bring a harpy into the house, you'll see.'

Mompous was of the same opinion; but Arnáiz, who had a

clearer view since he had no little sweetheart available apart
from the one beating in his own breast, leapt to the defence of
his friend.

'You're wrong, gentlemen. This man of few words has a great
deal of sense. He speaks little and knows what he's doing.'

On Sundays, this illustrious trinity would meet without fail at
the house of the rich man from the Indies for coffee, because
there really was no coffee in Madrid like it. That gaping,
interfering Torres whom we saw at the Bringases' was also wont
to poke his nose in. He had been made redundant and Mompous
occasionally gave him little brokering jobs and commissions
from buying or selling property. On working days, the three
friends used to go over in the evening to play billiards with
Caballero, and to chat, milking the usually burning political
issues of the moment. Arnáiz and Trujillo were moderate
progressives; Mompous and Caballero were defenders of the
Liberal Union, seeing it as the most practical and efficient
government, and all inveighed against the prevailing situation,
which with its imprudence was driving the country to seek a
solution in revolution. But the discussions only grew heated
when they came to touch upon the subject of trade policy, for
Caballero was a furious supporter of free trade and Mompous,
as a faithful Catalan, favoured prohibitive tariff barriers, so they
could never reach agreement. Arnáiz and Trujillo tended
towards Agustín's ideas, but protested that in practice they
needed to be introduced gradually. These disputes never overstepped the mark of courtesy. Caballero always kept his voice
right down, as though he were afraid of his own accent, and his
concepts were always very moderate. His listeners, not hearing
his words clearly, often had to say 'What?' and then he would
slightly raise his voice, which quavered somewhat through
timidity. Arnáiz on the other hand, a corpulent, ruddy-faced
man, used to make the most trivial points in a voice like thunder,
preceded by violent coughing. *Jupiter with his thunderbolts* is
what Trujillo called him, and it was enough to make you plug
your ears when he said: 'Today I've paid London at a rate of
47.9.'

On Sundays, when evening fell, Caballero would receive a
welcome visit from his cousin, for she always used to take the
children back that way from their walk.

One evening, she observed that the house had been enriched

by valuable ornamental items and some extremely elegant
furniture that Agustín, an insatiable shopper, had acquired some
days before. Mirrors with bevelled edges, bronzes, porcelains
and little pictures, not to mention a tasteful set of chairs
upholstered in pink satin, embellished what was to be the
boudoir of the unknown and mythological Mrs Caballero. Our
dear Mrs Bringas was stunned by these delights and could find
no better way to sweeten her bitter displeasure than to try out a
beautiful armchair, whose comfort and ample proportions were
beyond the realm of her experience. Sinking down into it, with
both hands in her muff, the cashmere wrap given by Her Majesty
the year before thrown back, she shot inquisitorial glances at
her cousin. Agustín was seated opposite her, with Isabelita on
his knee.

'This is profligate, Agustín,' she began. 'The luxury you have
here is insulting and revolutionary ... I'm no longer in any
doubt that you plan to marry. But whom? You're as furtive as a
mole and you will do everything on the sly. Arnáiz told Bringas
yesterday that you were indeed to be married, but that nobody
knows to whom. For goodness' sake!' she ended with ill-
concealed anger, 'be frank, be communicative, be civilised.'

While waiting for her cousin's reply, which was bound to be
slow in coming and obscure, Rosalía contemplated the little girl,
still so small. Oh! Bringas be cursed, why had Isabel not been
born five years sooner!

'Well, yes,' declared Caballero; 'I'm getting married.'

On hearing such terrifying words, Her Ladyship looked like
someone having hallucinations.

'Hit him, child, hit him, yes,' she said to the little girl. 'Pull on
that beard of his. He's very, very bad.'

Isabelita, far from doing as her mother commanded, looked
at him doubtfully and as if disconcerted. She held him in terribly
high esteem; she considered him a being superior to all others,
and the accusation of badness hurled by her mama confused her
greatly. She put her arms round Agustín's neck and whispered
secrets in his ear.

'Your daughter is paying no heed to you,' remarked Caballero
laughing. 'She says she loves me very much and I'm not bad.'

'Stop clinging, child ... Off you go with your brother, who's
playing with Felipe ... Now then, my good man, explain
yourself. You go nowhere, you're not known to have relations

with anyone ... Where the devil have you gone to find this woman? Have you ordered her from a doll factory? Are you going to have a savage brought over from America, with her arms painted and a ring in her nose? Because I wouldn't put anything past you.'

As she said this, a suspicion went through the lady's mind, an idea that made her hair stand on end, auguring death and tragedy. That livid flash was soon gone, like a flash of lightning, leaving the aforementioned Pipaonic mind in the darkness of her former doubts.

'Stop clinging, child . . .'

'Isabel says she doesn't want to go and play with Felipe; that she prefers to play with me.'

'So is the masked man going to reveal himself or not? I don't know what the point is of all this subterfuge . . .'

'I'll tell you soon.'

'Well, I don't know . . . You'd think it was a crime,' declared Mrs Bringas with sudden vehemence as she stood up. 'I've seen furtive men, I've seen tedious men, insufferable men; but none, not one like you. Let's go, child; call your brother. This house sickens me with so much useless bric-à-brac. No, something here smells no good to me. And when it comes to it, what do I care? You can marry a streetwalker from Fuencarral or import one from Paris . . . I'll leave you to it. That's it, that's it; keep the secret well, don't let anyone rob you of it. That's the way to do it, hush-hush.'

And the most reserved of men, as he said goodbye at the door, said two or three times:

'I'll tell you tomorrow, I promise!'

And indeed, he did tell her the following morning.

For a space of some minutes Rosalía looked as if she had been showered by Niagara Falls.

'To Amp . . .!'

She had no breath to finish pronouncing the word. She visualised the Sánchez Emperador girl enjoying the treasures of that unrivalled house and considered this as absurd as if oxen were flying in flocks over the rooftops and the sparrows, yoked in pairs, were pulling the carts. Her confusion did not dissipate for the whole of that day; she was flushed as if she had come out in a severe rash, and she kept putting her hand to her head and saying: 'I feel as though I have the two of them here turned to lead.' But reflecting on the extraordinary case, she could not find an explanation for her despair. 'For what have I got to gain or lose by this? . . . He wasn't to marry me, for I'm married; nor Isabelita either, for she's too young.'

She could not wait for the time when Bringas would return, to fire the tremendous news at him at point-blank range. Great too was the astonishment of Don Francisco. His wife, in a temper, addressed him rudely, as though that saint were to blame, saying: 'But can't you see . . . can't you see how shocking?'

'But, my dear woman, what . . .?'

'The truth is, I was counting on Agustín's waiting a mere six years . . . Isabel is ten . . . you see . . . But you never think of anything.'

'God in Heaven! . . .'

'And he suggests we bring her here until the day of the ill-fated wedding . . . Oh yes, here we are to cover things up . . .'

Bringas, a man of sound judgement, who always tried to take things calmly and see them for what they really were, endeavoured to placate his excited consort, with the most philosophical reasoning that could come from human lips. According to him, far from being offended, they should rejoice at their cousin's choice, because Amparo was a good girl, whose only defect was to be poor. Agustín wanted a modest, virtuous, unpretentious wife . . . He was no fool and knew well enough how to run his life. So the right thing was to celebrate the choice as a happy event and not show any annoyance, still less anger. If Agustín wanted his intended to live with them for a short while, it should be fine by them. 'Because, look here,' he added, perspicacity sparkling in his eyes, 'there's more in it for us to be on good terms with our cousin and his wife than bad. If we upset them now, perhaps they'll bear a grudge against us after they're married and . . . I needn't tell you who'll come off worst. He's very good to us, and I don't think Amparo will be against his continuing to be so. We owe him innumerable presents and favours, and what about us, what have we given him? One miserable bottle of ink, dear . . . Let's keep calm, keep calm and praise him now as always. I'll probably be his best man, and we'll have to run to a good present. No matter; we'll get by as best we can. You know yourself that he's never slow to come forward. Our situation today, my dearest, is rather tight. If I

order the coat, which I need so much; if we go to the ball at the
Palace, we'll have to deprive ourselves cruelly; and that's always
counting on Ma'am giving you the peach-coloured dress she's
offered you, for if not, where will we end! ... But economy and
hard times inside the house will work that miracle and the one
for Agustín's present. So the order of the day is much prudence
and put a brave face on it.'

This juicy little speech resounded so loudly in Rosalía's
selfishness, that her anger was tamed and she realised how out
of place her opposition to the marriage had been. She wished
Amparo would arrive so she could talk to her about the matter
and know more than she did. The little monkey hadn't been
since Saturday! ... She'd grown vain. She wanted to play the
role of humiliator now, to take revenge for having been so often
humiliated.

CHAPTER 23

Her incredible luck did not bring frank happiness to Amparo's heart, but the torture of alternating hope and fear. Because if to refuse was very sad and painful, to consent was a crime. Fear of betrayal made her shudder; the idea of deceiving such a generous and loyal man drove her to the brink of madness; but to renounce the crown being offered to her took virtue superior to her feeble strength. Oh selfishness, root of life, how you ache when the hand of duty tries to tear you out! . . . She had not the perversity of character to commit the fraud, nor sufficient self-sacrifice to avoid it. It did not seem right to disregard everything and let oneself be carried along by events; but neither did her weak willpower give her the courage to say: 'Mr Caballero, I can't marry you . . . for this, this, and this reason.'

She spent the hours of the day and night thinking about the bald terms of her problem, persecuted by the image of her generous suitor, in whom she saw a man without rival, his worth enhanced by merits of the greatest rarity in the world. Even before she had suspected Caballero of being in love with her, Amparo had felt extremely well-disposed towards him. What others took to be defects in the character of the man from the Indies, she perceived as contributing to its perfection. She guessed a certain harmony and kinship between her own character and that of the gentleman, so quiet and fearful of everything; and when Agustín came close to her, moved by his amorous affection, she was waiting for him, also prepared with similar affection.

As soon as they began to speak to one another a little, the fearful woman saw in the shy man, just as one sees one's own image in a mirror, feelings and tastes that were also hers. Yes, they both were, as they say, cast in the same mould. Agustín, like her, passionately wanted peaceful, quiet wellbeing; like her, he detested idle chatter, the empty words and vanity of the present generation; like her, he had a strong sense of family, an ambition for comfort in obscurity and without ostentation, tranquil affection and an ordered, law-abiding life. He had undoubtedly been able to read her perfectly; But God decreed that when he turned over the pages of her soul, he should see only the pure, white ones and not the black one. It was so well hidden, that only she could and should show it, realising an act of sublime valour. The only way to tear out the page was to go to Caballero and say: 'I can't marry you ... for this, this, and this reason.'

When the poor woman came to this conclusion, which, although tardy, gave her some rest from her tortures, simply because it was a conclusion, it seemed as though a serpent hissed these ideas into her ear:

'Listen here, miss, if you're determined not to accept this character's hand, what role are you playing taking his money? The day after that night when your fiancé walked you to the door, you received a letter containing banknotes. They weren't the first to come, but they were the most compromising. In that letter he said, oh foolish child, that he already considered you his wife, and therefore there must be openness and community of interests. He was sending you a quantity of money and announcing that he would repeat the gift every month until you were married. And the object of this aid was that his betrothed might prepare herself with dignity for marriage. If you intended to refuse, why didn't you return the money in the same envelope in which it had been brought? ...'

Oh, that voice! The argument hurt like an open sore, for which there could be no answer to provide relief! The poor woman, on receiving the monies, did not see how accepting them would compromise her; she was in a sort of stupor, drunk with the excitement of the splendid luck that God had bestowed upon her, with the idea of his magnificent house and of that heaven-blessed family she would found.

By the time she came to see the great impropriety of accepting the money, part of it had already gone in pursuit of paying some old debts, the poverty-stricken fiancée had already ordered herself two pairs of boots and two dresses. Oh goodness! What an equivocal situation! Whom could she go to for advice? What should she do?

Wakening frightened from her soundest sleep, Amparo turned this idea over in her mind: 'The best is to let time pass, let it run,

keep quiet, however repugnant this silence is to my conscience.'
... Then the viper, slipping between the pillows, hissed in her
ear thus: 'If you keep quiet, there will be no shortage of others
who'll talk. If you don't tell him, someone else will. If he finds
out before the wedding, he'll push you away with derision, and
if he finds out afterwards, imagine the to-do ...' Hearing this,
she cried silently, wetting her pillows with her tears, and fell
asleep on the warm dampness of them ... Three or four hours
later she awoke once more as if she had heard a shout. It was a
shout, yes, that was coming from within her, saying: 'If he finds
out, before or afterwards, he'll forgive me ... Just as he has
understood other things about me, he'll understand my
repentance.'

She rose quickly. Daylight was now coming in through the
windows. She dressed and the fresh water cleared her ideas ...
Shivering with cold and then comforted by the reaction, she told
herself: 'He'll forgive me ... I can see it.'

She set to work tidying up with nervous energy. Her domestic
aptitudes had doubled and she felt a real frenzy for cleanliness,
for putting everything in its proper place. Taking up the broom,
the way she wielded it was almost inspirational. There was
something about her hands that recalled the convulsive strength
of the violinist with his bow. Little clouds of dust were pushed
across the floor. Going to the window next, which looked onto
a panorama of rooftops, the girl took pleasure inhaling the icy
morning air ...

Then she thought about the dresses the dressmaker was going
to bring. In addition she had another, not new, but adapted by
herself, and she planned to give it its first wearing the next day.
This was not vanity, but the burning desire for decency that was
so strongly rooted in her soul. Her passion for a regular life also
manifested itself in her preference for utility over glitter, and in
the due importance she accorded to people's keeping up
appearances ...

She made a little chocolate and drank it with stale bread. The
house needed to shine like a new pin, for that day Caballero
would come to visit her. She would have given anything to
possess the art of enchantment in order to mend the ancient
furniture, to put varnish on it, patch the holes in the upholstery,
and make everything, not luxurious, but presentable. With the
visit fixed in her mind, she gave consideration to the dangers

that surrounded it, and it was out of this thought that the great, dynamic idea re-emerged in triumph: the need to open her soul to the man who was so worthy of seeing it in its entirety.

As she was preparing her food, she took to considering the terms best suited to making the hair-raising declaration. First she thought she needed many, many words, to be talking for a whole day ... Then she imagined it would be better to use few. But which would those few words be? When she made her confession tears would certainly well up in her eyes. She would say, for example: 'Look here, Caballero, before we go any further, I must reveal a secret ... My worth is not what you believe, I'm an infamous woman, I've committed...' No, no, not that, that was nonsense. Better to say: 'I've been a victim...' this struck her as pretentious. Don José Ido's novels came back to her. She would say: 'I've had the misfortune ... Those things that happen, one knows not how, those delusions, those errors, those inexplicable things...' On hearing this, he would be consumed with curiosity. He would ask her so many questions, he would be so keen to know even the most well-hidden details, the things one tells even one's own conscience with some apprehension! ... The great difficulty was in getting started. Would she have the courage for the beginning? Yes, she would, she was determined to, even if she died of the anguish brought about by that revelation akin to suicide.

She heard her sister rising. Refugio joined her in the kitchen and after exchanging insignificant words with Amparo, went into her room to dress and beautify herself, an operation over which she took much time. Amparo wished her little sister would go out soon, so as not to be there when *he* arrived. Refugio was irritable and was quickly transforming herself, through the frivolity of her habits, into a scandal-mongering, envious gossip of a woman. Amparo feared some indiscretion from her. She was always scolding her for being out in the street and for her dislike of work. That day she did not say a word to her. After they had eaten, seeing that the other was staying in, she spoke to her thus:

'If you're going out, go once and for all, because I'm also going and I want to take the key with me.'

The younger sister was impertinent that day. Realising that she would be placated with a certain kind of talisman, Amparo gave her money.

'You're rich . . .'

'Go away once and for all and leave me in peace.'

Once she was alone, she had another go at cleaning the furniture and made herself look as best she could with the very little she had. She could not get the idea of the confession out of her mind . . . She felt herself soothed inside by a powerful force born in the heat of her conscience and fortified thereafter by an indefinable religious, sublime feeling that filled her soul. She imagined herself with the man who was to be her companion for life before her, and her, brave, not getting upset, tackling the sacred task of confessing the greatest error which any woman could commit. And she was not upset by the looks he was giving her, on the contrary it seemed as though the honesty painted on Agustín's austere countenance gave her more courage . . .

But, alas! This heroic ardour was extinguished when the lover presented himself before her in reality. Amparo went out to open the door and upon seeing him – oh my goodness! – the most frightful cowardice took possession of her spirit. Before the gaze of those loyal eyes, the penitent woman was rigid and the confession was as impossible as stabbing herself . . . She forgot the words that she had practised for the beginning. Agustín spoke about commonplaces; she answered him in a distraught fashion. She had even forgotten how to breathe. And how slow-witted she was! To answer several of Caballero's questions, she had to think for a long time.

Slowly her upset state began to dissipate. The conversation was discreet, maybe too discreet and cold to be amorous. Caballero was also inhibited on finding himself alone with his loved one. He recounted dramatic episodes of his life; he made an ingenious and delicate critique of the Bringases. Then they turned to speaking about themselves. He was terribly happy; he was going to realise his greatest desire. He loved her with a tranquil love, the eyes of his soul dwelling more on the charms of a homely life, ever busy and affectionate, than in passion's uneven disquiet. He was a man of more than forty summers and as a settled person, his greatest desire was to have a family and live a completely law-abiding life, surrounded by honourableness, comfort, peace, savouring the fulfilment of his duties in the company of people who loved and honoured him. God had bestowed upon him the woman best suited to him and he found her so perfect that if he had ordered her from Heaven, she would not have come any better ... She, for her part, looked upon him like Providence made flesh. Without knowing why, as soon as she first saw him, she considered him a model of men and if there were not a thousand other reasons to love him, the generous kindness he had shown, stooping as low as a poor, humble orphan-girl would suffice ...

Whilst such dull exchanges were taking place, Amparo was reasoning otherwise within herself, if not with these, with equivalent words:

'Goodness, I don't know where this is going to take me ... I'm letting myself go, and I'm more and more of a criminal keeping quiet what I'm keeping quiet. The longer I take to confess it, the less right I'll have to be forgiven.'

'Tell me about your childhood, about your past life.'

On hearing this, the fiancée went from doubt to fright. Might Caballero have guessed something?

'Oh! I've been very unfortunate.'

'But now you'll be happy. Tell me something about it.'

She recalled then some of the words she had thought up and with an effort of the utmost will, as though she were yielding to irresistible force, she let herself say:

'Before we go any further ...'

'What?'

'I mean ... Nothing ... It's just that I was remembering when my poor father died ...'

'Is this his portrait?' asked Caballero, standing up to have a closer look.

Meanwhile, Amparo was saying: 'They'll have to cut my throat first. I'll die, but I'll keep quiet.'

The afternoon was getting on. Agustín spent two hours there, and on saying goodbye, he permitted himself to be carried away by his love no more than to kiss his fiancée's hand. He was a man to whom the toughness of a hard fight for survival had given great self-control. But even with the willpower he had, from time to time some effort was necessary in order to sustain the austere role of a person of irreproachable integrity, a perfect, clean, fully paid-up cog in the triple mechanism of State, Religion, and Family. That proprietor who had lost his temper with Mompous because the latter wanted to put him down in his tax return for a little less than he ought; that man who had given money to the Pope so as not to stand out from the religious conformity of his time, could not on any account set out to take possession of his amorous asset by less than straight means. 'Everything must be orderly,' he used to say; 'either I live by my principles or I don't live at all.'

After an absence of three days, excused on the pretext of serious occupations at home, Amparo went to the Bringases'. As she climbed the stairs she was dreading reaching the top. How would Rosalía greet her, knowing of her engagement now? Because the orphan did not love her illustrious friend, and that respect which she had for her might more accurately be described as fear. Now Don Francisco did inspire her affection and thinking about the two of them and what they would say, she entered their abode. She did not know why, but she was embarrassed to find herself there with her recently adapted dress, her new boots, and also her new veil. She thought she was flouting the modesty of her poverty.

Rosalía came out to meet her in the corridor, laughing, and then embraced her with a great fuss of studied affection. Such vehemence must be suspect for its excessive degree; but Amparo, abashed like a schoolgirl caught in a sergeant's arms, accepted it as a good thing. After the vehemence came ironical remarks in extremely poor taste.

'Well, well, my girl, thank heavens you've turned up here. Since you're so exalted, you don't remember us poor people any more ... You've certainly won the sweepstake! No, you don't deserve it, although I admit you're a good girl ... Lucky, lucky thing ...! Sit down ... Agustín wants you to live with us, and we're not against it ... On the contrary, we're delighted. I don't know if you'll be able to make do with these cramped conditions, because now you've got the idea of living in that palatial residence, this is going to seem like a hovel.'

Recovering, the fiancée answered that she was very grateful; but that not being able to leave her sister on her own, she would go on living in her own house, not that that would prevent her from going to Rosalía's as usual, to help her in any way she could.

'Well I never, that Agustín, and didn't he keep it quiet! The man is such a mystery. Listen, I should be quite wary . . . Yes, of course, you can stay here the whole day; you'll eat with us, what little there may be. Then you'll go off to your castle and we'll stay in our hut. I expect we're bothering you . . . Here I am mothering you . . .! But what wouldn't I do for Agustín and for you? Sit down . . . You can sew these sleeves for me . . . Oh! no, what audacity! Sorry.'

'Yes, yes, give them to me . . . That's the least . . .'

Bringas, who had just had a shave in his room, came out into the dining room without his glasses, drying his little pink and very shiny face.

Amparito, how are you? I'm fine. Ah! You little rascal! What luck you've had! . . . You owe it all to me. The good things I've said to my cousin about you . . . You can just imagine how black a picture I've painted of you. The truth is, he's under your spell . . . This might be called *Virtue's Prize*. That's what I say, merit always finds its reward.'

Soon after this, Bringas and his wife met in secret session in the study.

'Agustín's going to have a carriage. He's already ordered it from Paris.'

'Oh! . . .' exclaimed the lady, mopping her brow, for she could already see herself cosily ensconced in the softly upholstered coach of her friends.

'You must be sure to treat her very well. They will hold seats at all the theatres.'

'Amparo,' Mrs Pipaón said to her protégée soon afterwards; 'look; don't strain your eyes with those tiny stitches. Tomorrow or the day after you must come to the shops with me. Agustín has charged me with making several purchases for him and of course . . . it's only right that you should give your opinion and choose whatever you like best, since it's all for you. I also have to buy some trifles for myself, because it's essential that we go to the Palace ball . . . Come to my room; you shall see the peach-coloured dress that Her Majesty has sent me.'

This matter of the indispensability of attending the ball was giving Thiers much cause for thought, since although the costs were not great, the figure exceeded the whole column for extras over a three-month period. But with courageous rigour Bringas brought down entries attached to the very necessities of life and the family was sentenced to one month of starvation rations.

And as he could no longer present himself decorously in his six-year-old coat, another had to be ordered, calling upon a tailor who owed him some favours and who was making it for the cost of the cloth. Orders were issued for the children to make the shoes they had last until February; the light in the hall, the tip for the night watchman, and other things were eliminated. Rosalía, always tortured by the growing scarcity, saw the future as black, darkened still more by the predictions of revolution on everyone's lips. One thing consoled her. Her daughter now had a piano and a music master, and would receive that part of her education that was so necessary to a young girl from a good family. The child was so assiduous that the whole blessed afternoon and part of the evening she was tinkling out her easy exercises; a novelty discovered by Amparo in the house that day. The tiresome music and Mr Torres's soporific conversation led to tremendous boredom settling upon her spirits. Caballero came as evening fell and after chatting agreeably for a while, walked her home. This time Rosalía no longer charged her with purchasing lamp glasses, cotton reels, buttons or yards of ribbon, and saw her off, as did Bringas, with honeyed goodbyes.

In the solitude and seclusion of her house, Amparo had a happy thought that night. She did not know how something so right had occurred to her and decided that the Holy Spirit itself had taken the trouble to inspire her with it. The happy idea was to call upon religion for help. If she confessed her sin before God, wouldn't He give her sufficient courage to declare it to a man? Of course He would. She had never unburdened her conscience of that weight as Jesus Christ commands. Her piety was lukewarm and routine. She only went to church to hear mass, and even though it did occur to her more than once that she ought to approach the tribunal of penitence, she was terribly frightened to do so. Her sin was enormous and did not fit through the little holes of the confessional grille, which were big enough for the human voice, but too small, in her opinion, to allow the passage of certain crimes.

'That's it, that's it,' she thought, taking great comfort from it and bubbling with joy; 'any day now, once I've prepared myself well, I confess to God, and afterwards . . . I'm bound to have tremendous courage.'

That was the right plan! . . . Take refuge in religion, which would be nothing if it were not the bread of the afflicted, of sinners, of those who hunger for peace! And it hadn't crossed her mind, silly goose that she was, to proceed so simply, so naturally . . .! She would go, she would, resolute and with heart, to the divine tribunal. If she already felt strong in spirit just from planning it, what would she be when she followed up the plan with its realisation? The fear that she had always had of such a grave act, dissipated; and if the priest, seeing her deeply repentant, forgave her, then she had in her soul sufficient fortitude to present herself to the man she loved and say: 'I committed an enormous sin; but I have repented. God has forgiven me. If you forgive me, fine. If not, farewell . . . let us go our separate ways.'

Everything she saw, everything, supported her Christian idea; the heavens and the earth, and even the objects most resistent to personification changed into animate beings to applaud and fête her. The portrait of her father congratulated her with its honest gaze, saying: 'But, you silly girl, it's what I've been telling you for so long and you wouldn't listen . . .!'

She spent the night feeling exuberant. Oh, the benefits of a good intention! In the sicknesses of the conscience, the desire for medicine is in itself half of the cure. During the night, she thought a great deal about what the priest would be like, about what he would look and sound like. However great her shame before God might be, it would be easier to pour her sin through every confessional in Christendom than into the ears of her trusting lover. But she was sure that once she had taken that step, the rest would be made a great deal easier.

She allowed three days to go by, and on the fourth, she rose very early and went to Buena Dicha church. She entered trembling. She imagined that they already had news in there of what she was going to tell them and that someone would say to her: 'We know all about it already, child.' But with the peaceful solemnity of the church, her calm returned and she could take proper stock of the act she was going to carry out. And good heavens it lasted long enough. The pious women waiting on their knees at an appropriate distance – they were the kind who go every day to discuss their every scruple until the confessors' heads are spinning – grew impatient with the delay, grumbling about how tiresome that lady was; she must be up to her ears in sins.

When she withdrew from the confessional, she had a feeling

of great relief and spiritual fortitude hitherto unknown to her. How her faint words had slipped through the little spaces in the grille, even she herself did not know. It was magic, or to speak in Christian terms, it was a miracle. She was astonished that her lips had said what they did say and even after the confession was made, she felt as though expressions that were not slim enough, that did not bear enough compunction to be able to get through, had got stuck in the grille. That priest, whom the sinner did not see, was very kindly; he had said some terrible things, followed by other sweet, consoling ones. Oh penitence, bitter balsam, curative pain! It was like a suicide when the sinner tore open her breast and bared her conscience so that all that was in it could be seen. Showing what was corrupt, she was also showing what was sound. The priest had promised to pardon her; but postponed the absolution until the penitent had revealed her sin to the man who wanted to take her as his wife. Amparo found this as reasonable as if it had been said by God Himself, and promised with all her soul to obey blindly.

Before leaving the church a disagreeable vision troubled the peace of her spirit. There at the end of the nave, sitting in a pew, she saw a woman dressed in black, who was looking fixedly at her. It was Doña Marcelina Polo. The penitent covered her face with the veil of her mantilla, wanting to pass unrecognised; no such luck ... The other woman gave her not a moment's rest from the torture of her staring. To shorten it, Amparo, who had intended to hear two masses, left after hearing one.

When she was home, she took the measure of the strength that had been born within her and was astonished by how great it was.

'Now I will tell him,' she thought; 'now I really will. I'm not short of words, nor courage either. It's as clear as daylight that I'll talk ... Let's see; I start like this: "I went to confession today. ..." From this to the rest the path is smooth. I'll say: "I had a great sin." "What is it? Can I know what it is?" "Not only can you, but you must know, because before you do, I mustn't consider marrying." Word by word, out will come the thing as it came out in the confessional. If after knowing about my repentance, he persists, I'll set a condition that we go and live in a foreign country to avoid complications.'

Feeling sure of herself and courageous, she ardently wished Caballero would come soon so that she could raise the matter as soon as he walked in. He could not fail to appear that day. They had agreed that she would not go out on Tuesdays and Fridays and that Caballero would visit her on those days so as to be able to talk more freely than at the Bringases'. It was Friday.

Refugio was full of smiles that day.

'I know you receive visits,' she said. 'Doña Nicanora told me about it. You're onto a good thing, dearest.'

Amparo did not pursue this dangerous conversation. As she did not want to give explanations yet to her indiscreet sister, she asked her to go out once and for all. Refugio did not have to be begged. Her painter was waiting for her to model the figure of a Callipygian woman of the people helping bury the victims of the 2nd May uprising. Bolting her light breakfast in great haste, she went out.

Shortly afterwards, there was a ring at the door. Would it be him? It was still early ... Sweet Jesus, the postman! ... From that man's hands Amparo received a letter and the sight of it made her instantly start shaking from head to toe. She stood looking at it without daring to open it. She knew the hateful handwriting on the envelope. Via Celedonia, who had come begging for alms some days before, she knew her enemy was out in the country; but the unfortunate girl had not suspected that he would take it into his head to write to her. Would she open the epistle or throw it into the fire unread? Satan had chosen a fine time to come and disturb her spirits, when she had made her peace with God, and fortified her conscience!

'But I shall read it,' she said; 'I'll read it because whatever it says will increase my sacred horror and give me even greater strength. God cannot send me a new source of misery today, but rather some relief for all the old ones.'

CHAPTER 25

The letter was written in pencil and said this:

                    El Castañar, 19 December 1867.

'My own Inferno, Scaffold, my own Inquisition,

'Even if you do not wish to know about this poor man, I want news of me to reach you. That old saint de Nones ordered me here to lead a rustic and penitent life, and even though he banned me, amongst other things, from playing the little letters game, I cannot resist the temptation of writing you this one, which will surely be the last. And God knows my friend was quite right! I am so well that I do not know myself. Exercise, hunting, the pure air, the continual walking, healthy toil have made me as good as new in ten days. I have become a savage, a real primitive man, a caveman without a cave and a hermit without a hair-shirt. I live amongst oxen, dogs, rabbits, partridges, ravens, pigs, mules, hens, and the occasional being in human form, who reminds me even more of the innocence and roughness of the times of the patriarchs. I imagine myself as Papa Adam, alone in the middle of Paradise, before Eve was brought to him or was taken out of his rib, as Mr Moses says. I wear a kerchief on my head, a fur cap, and a long dun-coloured cloth jacket lent to me by the woodcutter. I have recovered my agility of former times and a voracious appetite that tells me I am still a man and will be for quite some time. What does not return is happiness, or peace of mind. I am banished from life and confined to a rustic limbo, from which I believe I shall emerge healthy, but an idiot. The beast is alive, the delicate being is dying; but what does it matter – oh rabid irony! – if principles have been salvaged?

'I am writing to you with a stump of blunt pencil, seated on a pile of stable straw and golden compost, which in the sunlight looks – do not laugh – like a mound of spun gold. A movable court of hens surround me, whose red crests, as they jump on the straw compost, resemble coral dancing on a carpet of sunbeams.

Do not laugh ... What nonsense! ... Two lordly peacocks are also walking around here, constantly spreading their tails, as if they wanted to express the lofty disdain they feel for me. A piglet is rootling behind me and a country dog is taking a melancholy stroll in front of me, thinking perhaps about the instability of things canine.

There are no men nearby at the moment. The local ones, with their ingenuous simplicity, are a living, permanent lesson demonstrating the superiority of Nature over all things. Accursed people who have dethroned Nature in the artificial labyrinth of society only to put pedantry in her place, and who have built the citadel of falsehood upon a pile of books chock-full of rubbish! ... Do not laugh.'

'He's mad,' thought Amparo, and she went on reading:

'My good friend has made up his mind to cure me completely. The first part of the medicine has not been inefficacious; but now the second is coming, my own Inferno, the second and the fiercest and most bitter part. But I have sworn to obey and the plan will not fail on my account. I am resolved to go through with this until the end, to cross my arms and give myself up to idiocy, to see if, as Nones says, my social and spiritual salvation is born of it. Pay attention to what follows and rejoice, since you want to lose sight of me. Nones writes that he has already got me a humble position in the Philippines and tells me to prepare for the lengthy voyage, which seems to me like a journey to the other world. If I were travelling with company, how happy I would be! But I am going alone, so let me die once and for all.

'I do not know yet when I shall be leaving, but it will be soon. Between my sister and Nones, they can manage the cost of the passage and anything else I may need. From here, I go to Alicante and from there on to Marseilles. This is necessary, definitive, irrevocable. It is also like driving a dagger into oneself; but I am doing it, and we shall see where and how I come back to life. I commit the imprudence of disobeying my friend in this farewell. Do not say anything to him if you see him, and here is my last goodbye. Have compassion for me, in the absence of any other sentiment. If you take the veil, pray for me; dedicate two or three tears to me, counting me among the dead, and ask God to forgive me.'

The letter said no more. Among that disordered farrago of ideas, appropriate to a madman, with its mixture of buffoonery and the occasional sensible point, one happy fact stood out. Amparo ignored everything so as not to see more than that fact. He was going, going forever! 'Pray for me, counting me among the dead,' said the letter. This phrase declared that horrible past broken off and buried forever, and the serious problem was resolved smoothly and naturally, without any scandal . . . Intense joy flooded our Emperine's soul. She thanked God for that unexpected event, saying to herself: 'He's going, it's all over! God is smoothing the path, and I haven't to do anything for myself.'

The idea of the danger receding into the distance cooled her spirit, which had been emboldened by the confession and ready to make a new one. Weakness, regaining the supremacy it had momentarily lost, proudly settled itself in that ingenuous being, not born to tackle life, but rather to take it as it came with the circumstances.

The deferral of the danger brought the non-urgency of the remedy and, perhaps, its pointlessness. The integrity of the penitent faltered and the unpalatability and difficulties of making the declaration to her intended embittered her spirit. She accepted the restful solution afforded to her by Providence as transitory, refusing to make it final and certain on its own.

'That I must tell him is beyond doubt,' she thought; 'but I no longer think it's so urgent. I must reflect calmly on the terms I should use to tell him.'

She was delivering the letter into the embers of the stove when the doorbell announced the arrival of Caballero. He came in and they sat down opposite each other. Our Emperine looked at her lover and at the mere thought that she had to make her confession to him, she was blushing. She was so ashamed! What had become of the plucky determination she had felt that morning?

Letting herself be carried along by the easy course of a dull, amorous conversation, she gradually forgot about the good priest's orders. At times, her conscience would stir; but soon the same conscience, grown lazy, would curl up in its bed of roses. It is worth noting that in keeping with the temperament of both lovers, their dialogue interlaced the spiritual element appropriate to such an occasion with practical ideas and comments on the most ordinary aspects of life.

The greatest happiness in the world, according to Caballero, consisted of two characters savouring their own harmony, and each being able to, say: 'How like you I am!...' When he (Agustín) had met her, he had experienced tremendous sadness, thinking that such a beautiful treasure wouldn't be for him ... When she had met him, she had felt like crying at the thought that a man with such qualities couldn't be her master ... Because she (Amparo) was of no worth; she was a poor girl whose only merit, if she had any, was to possess a heart inclined towards all that was good and a great love for work ... The things of this world, which sometimes seem disposed so that everything comes out the reverse of what is natural and against what hearts desire, had that time worked out for the good, for harmony ... Wasn't God good! He also liked work and if he weren't preoccupied by love and the preparations for the wedding, he'd be terribly bored. As soon as he was married, he'd have to undertake some business. He couldn't live without his desk, and his ledger and day-book were the best comfort he could fancy ... With this and the love of the family, he'd be the happiest of men ... They'd have few friends, but they'd be good ones; they wouldn't give great gluttonous feasts. Let people eat in their own homes. But they would give a warm welcome to the needy and aid them with many necessities ... What he liked was for everything to be done in an orderly way, everything at the right time; that way the house would never become chaotic ... She was a dab hand at that sort of thing; she was good at planning, and had everything ready with sufficient notice for it not to be lacking at the right time. And wouldn't the servants have to be on their mettle, wouldn't they just! ... She wouldn't pardon the slightest carelessness ... What he liked a great deal were eggs with rice and beans in the morning. American beans were very scarce here, but Cipérez usually had them ... What she'd have to get used to doing was keeping his accounts book, where she would note down the household expenses. When this is not done, everything is chaotic, and one is groping in the dark ... They would go to the theatre when there was something good playing; but they wouldn't take a season ticket, because the idea that the theatre should be an obligation did not appeal to either of them. Such an obligation only existed in Madrid, a town of gadabouts and vice, with an industry manufacturing time to waste. In London, in New York, there isn't a soul to be seen in the streets at ten o'clock at night, apart from drunkards and immoral people. Here, night is day, and everyone leads a life of idleness or play-acting. Theatre season tickets, as a necessity for families, are immoral, the negation of home life . . . No indeed, they would take a season ticket for seats in their own little house. Another thing: she didn't like to pay fortunes to dressmakers, and even if she had all Rothschild's millions, she would only use a prudent amount on frippery. Moreover, she knew how to make up her own dresses . . . Another thing: they'd have a carriage, since it was already ordered from Binder's; an unostentatious landau to be able to go for a comfortable ride, not for parading up and down the Paseo de la Castellana, like so many other fools. Whenever they went out in their coach, they'd invite Rosalía, who yearned to show herself off. They both agreed on the expansive thought of helping Don Francisco's honest family, continually giving presents to husband and wife and discussing a delicate way to help them in the poverty they concealed beneath a shiny veneer . . . He was thinking of granting them an allowance for the children's clothes, shoes, school fees and salutory seaside trips. But how to suggest it to them? Oh! She'd take responsibility for carrying out such a pleasant mission. In the first instance, they'd invite them for a meal twice a week . . . He fancied keeping a good wine cellar. Above all, he wouldn't miss a single one of the famous clarets. And was Bordeaux pretty? Oh! Lovely. (Description of the *Quiconces*, the port, the *Allée de l'Intendence*, the *Croix Blanche*, and the pleasant surrounding areas full of beautiful vineyards.) That tranquil city, which seems like a royal capital for the sumptuousness of its buildings, but without the tumult or the madness of Paris, was where the couple would go for a spell. Another thing: he didn't dislike French food . . . Good, good, because she had learnt how to make *beefsteak* and other foreign delicacies from her aunt Saturna . . . As for Spanish foods, some he didn't care for, others he did . . . Fortunately, she would learn diverse new ways of cooking, because as they were to go to London too . . . When years and years had gone by, they'd love each other just the same as then, because their affection wasn't one of those whirlwind passions which within their very intensity carry the seed of their short duration; it wasn't the work of fantasy, nor a caprice of the senses; it was all sentiment, and as such, it would grow more robust in the course of time. It was an English kind of love, deep, secure and unshakeable, firmly established on the basis of domestic ideas . . .

This music, which flowed from the lips of each in alternate stanzas, sometimes calmly, sometimes joining together and going over one other as in a duo, made Amparo forget everything. Unexpectedly coming to her senses, she felt some pangs from the old wound, and the sharp pain forced her to contain the flights of fancy to those regions of bliss . . . but she herself tried to soothe the sore with remedies taken from her imagination. She saw a barbarous man, going swiftly by canoe with other savages along a river in distant and unexplored lands, like those pictured in the plates of the book *Around the World*. He was a missionary, who had gone to christen heathens in those lands that are in the other part of the world, round like an orange, over where it is night when it is day here.

Towards the end of the visit, by now around six o'clock, Refugio came in, setting Amparo on edge, for fear that her sister would not be sufficiently decorous in Caballero's presence. Refugio had become quite brazen and with one word could make the difference between herself and a decent young lady obvious. To give truth its due, the girl behaved herself well and as she did not lack certain principles, she managed to appear sensible even though she was not so. But her sister could not relax and wished Caballero would leave. Whenever she saw anyone who knew her secrets together with her friend, she quaked with dread, and the alarm brought now fire, now a deathly pallor to her cheeks. In the end Agustín withdrew and his intended breathed again.

Refugio knew! . . . Refugio, because of her lack of discretion, was a constant danger . . . Dreadfully upset by this idea, the fiancée made up her mind to incline her husband, once he was her husband, to settle in a place far distant from Madrid. She wanted to leave everything here: relationships, kinship, memories, the past and the present. Even the air she breathed in Madrid seemed to hold something in its vague substance that betrayed her, something indiscreet and revealing, and she yearned to inhale a new atmosphere in a world and under heavens distinct from these, to which she could say: 'Neither do you know me, air; nor have you ever seen me, heavens; nor do you know who I am, earth.'

CHAPTER 26

Her sister teased her that night.

'You've netted a fine bird. Keep him under lock and key as long as you can, dearest, for ones like him aren't to be caught every day. But God made you so dull-witted that you'll let him escape ... If he were my prey, they'd have to flay me alive before I'd let him out of my clutches. But you, I can just see it, you're such a silly goose, you've got your head so high in the clouds, that for one word here or there you'll let him leave you. If you do let him go, he's for me.'

This brazenness and common turn of phrase mortified the elder Emperine so much that she harshly admonished her sister.

'So we're having a little lecture, are we?' the other one riposted. 'Stop your squawking, if you don't want me to leave and not turn up again round here. For what you give me ...'

She went on chattering like a parrot that has been fed wine sops. Amparo, terribly annoyed, calmed down enough to realise that she would keep control of her termagant more easily with kindness than cruelty, and chose not to respond to such nonsense. They retired and from one bed to the other, launched into easy chat, the elder revealing to the younger the true situation. That gentleman was not her lover, he was her fiancé, and he was going to marry her. The other was laughing; but in the end, she had to believe what she heard. And didn't Amparito explain herself well! ... If Refugio mended her ways, if she were sensible, if she didn't wear her down with her witticisms, her sister would give her however much she needed ... But one thing was clear: it was essential that she put an end to her little follies. The sister-in-law of such an important personality had to be absolutely impeccable ... Of course! If not, she wouldn't recognise her as her sister. A radiant future lay ahead for the two of them. It was right and proper that they should both make themselves worthy of the great fortune that the Lord was bestowing upon them.

These revelations had an effect on Refugio's spirits; she fell asleep happy and dreamt that she was living in a palace, along with other absurdities galore. The following day she was very reasonable and docile.

'Virtue,' thought Amparo with innate philosophy, 'depends upon having the means to preserve it. All it took was for me to say to that madcap "we'll have enough to eat" and she's beginning to reform.'

She gave her a reasonable amount of money to keep her happy and took her leave.

'Today I'll go to the Hill. He wanted me to live there and so did Rosalía; but I can't desert you. I'll come home every night and give you whatever you need as long as you promise to make an absolutely clean break with the Rufete girls and not to be a painters' model ... That life has ended, and so have the little outings at night time, the trips to the stage door and the café. From tomorrow onwards I'll give you work ... Why shouldn't you earn what a dressmaker would have? You'll see, you'll see ... Piles of linen, some wraps and some alterations to your dresses and mine. You can count on a new one for yourself ... But keep it well in mind, Refugio, if you don't work, if you go back to your old ways, you can expect nothing from me ... Oh! I forgot something else important: I forbid you to go downstairs to chat to Ido and his wife; she's too loose-tongued. I don't like certain of our neighbours. Reserve, seriousness, virtue, good conduct is what I desire.'

'Yes, yes,' the other one answered, with an obvious desire to obey then, for the benefit which it brought her.

Refugio left and Amparo went, as usual, to the Hill. The days that followed were devoted to shopping, of which Rosalía was in charge, with plenipotentiary authorisation from her cousin. I think it pointless to declare how much Lady Pipaón relished these things and how self-important she was in the shops. Amparo, despite being the interested party, could not overcome her unhappiness and her conscience stirred within her every time that Rosalía, after haggling over the richest fabrics, lace, fans and jewels, struck a bargain with the traders, telling them to send the bill to Mr Caballero. When it came to selecting a colour or a design, the fiancée would be completely bewildered, and her spirit, attentive to graver concerns, could not make the right choice. Our dear Mrs Bringas always chose with as much certainty and aplomb as if the items bought were for her.

'You have no taste,' she would say. 'Leave it to me, I'll be able to fit you out elegantly. Anyone would think you were not all there, the way you look at things with those great big eyes ... Why are you so dead set against the colour black, and all you notice are gaudy colours? Anyone would think you were from the provinces. If it weren't for me, you'd be a laughing stock. If this is how good you're going to be at running your household, poor Agustín is going to have a fine old time.'

Some afternoons, if the weather was fine, Caballero would bring a closed calash and the three of them would have a ride along the Paseo de la Castellana. Rosalía accepted this gift with a satisfaction verging on jubilation; but the fiancée found little amusement in that self-exhibition in the streets. She thought all the passers-by were noticing her, making saucy comments. While Rosalía was trying to be seen and was busily calling out greetings at the top of her voice to anyone she knew who passed in their carriage, Amparo ardently wished the shadows of night would fall upon Madrid, the avenue, and the carriage. When she withdrew to her own home, at the usual hour, Caballero would accompany her as far as her door, speaking about the eternal subject and the endless series of domestic plans. A happier man had never existed.

The fiancée, on the other hand, had to labour at dissimulation so that she would be believed happy; but inside her the lugubrious procession of doubts and fears marched on; she was afraid of everything, and even the most trivial incidents were a source of anguished worry for her. Whenever someone came into the Bringases' abode, the hapless girl suspected that that person, whoever it might be, was coming to tell something. If she heard whispering in the drawing room, she thought it was about her. In any of Rosalía's or her husband's idle phrases, she believed she could discern suspicion or a sly allusion to things that only she could think. She found Caballero a little sad at times; had they said something to him? ... Even the postman's arrival at the house made her shudder. Would he bring some anonymous letter? This idea of anonymous letters took root in her mind to such an extent, that merely seeing a postman in the street made her tremble and the sight of any letter in a sealed envelope addressed to Don Francisco made her quake. That unpleasant Mr Torres, who came over some afternoons, frightened her without her knowing why. The wretched man never tired of looking at her with a malicious smile, endlessly fondling his beard; and under that gaze she felt an immense dread, just as if a fierce Jarama bull had loomed up as she stood in some deserted spot threatening her with its horrible horns.

The nervous susceptibility of our Emperine went to such an extreme that even when she heard a newspaper being read, she thought that those printed lines would mention her name. If Paquito came in saying: 'Haven't you heard what's going on?' that phrase alone would make her heart give a terrible thump. What else? The very maid, harmless Prudencia, sometimes looked at her with a smile, as if she possessed a dreadful secret.

When she and Agustín billed and cooed in their virtuous dialogues, she found some rest from that torture. But perhaps Rosalía would unexpectedly walk in, a person recognised as one born to hamper the happiness of others, and casting inquisitorial looks at her would say:

'And yet, Agustín, your fiancée's not content . . . Look what a miserable face she pulls when she hears me say it . . . There's something the matter, but if she isn't honest with you, with whom will she be so?'

Such jokes, which did not seem like jokes, tortured the fiancée more than if they put her on the rack to tear her limb from limb. At home she never stopped thinking about these things, repeating them and making comments to herself about them to discover what hidden meaning they might contain; and as nothing happened around her which did not constitute a new agony for her, behold an insignificant incident that increased her suffering:

The simplest of mortals, Don José Ido del Sagrario, visited her one night. Although Amparo's opinion of him could not have been better, his presence always inspired her with repugnance and fear. Upon seeing him, she suddenly felt a chill, as if she had been wrapped in blankets of ice. That man doubtless refreshed the unhappy woman's memory, bringing back to her scenes and episodes that she wished not to remember. For that reason, the former writing teacher's woebegone countenance looked to her as though its features were the terrifying, hideous ones of an emissary from Satan.

What did good old Ido desire? What could she do for him? It was a simple enough matter. The illustrious novelist had quarrelled with his publisher, who no longer wished to take his manuscripts from him even if he gave them for free and paid money on top. Seeing himself about to fall back into wretchedness, that man, with all his diverse talents, was considering seeking a stable little position at the side of someone influential and distinguished. Through his friend Felipe, he knew that Don Agustín Caballero was thinking of taking on an employee to keep his books and deal with his correspondence . . .

'No one's better placed than you,' said the calligrapher, with a face as sweet as sugar, 'to get me that position, if you take up my cause, if you take pity upon this poor paterfamilias. With just two words from you to Mr Caballero my happiness will be sealed, because I know that you're the apple of the gentleman's eye, and quite right too, he couldn't be more right, because you . . . (*sweetening to an incredible extreme*) are an angel, an angel, yes you are, of beauty and goodness.'

Amparo cut short the panegyric. She wished to conclude and for that monster to leave. She could not stand the sight of him, whilst recognising his absolute innocence. To testify to his aptitude for the duties that he sought, Ido del Sagrario was carrying on him that night a sheet of paper.

'You can show him this sheet,' said he, holding it timidly out to her; 'and there he'll see my handwriting, which, although it's not for me to say, is such that he surely won't find better. I wrote that *calamo currente*; it's part of the latest novel . . .'

To get him out of her sight, she offered to support his application, and the poor man left so grateful and satisfied, threatening to return for the answer within a couple of days. Amparo, on finding herself alone, cast her eye swiftly over the page of the novel and read odd words that terrified her: *crime . . . inferno . . . sacrilege . . . deception*; and other hair-raising terms jumped out at her and reverberated horribly in her brain. Tearing up the page, she threw the pieces into the fire.

The fright that the man caused her increased with the recollections that came to her of the few occasions that she had seen him in earlier times. Good old *Simple Cerate* had once come to the School of Pharmacy to bring a letter for her . . . They had spoken about the school, the mischief the boys got up to, the sermon . . . What sharp thorns were these! . . . Ido del Sagrario knew! And a man like that was trying for a position in her future household! . . . God was abandoning her, without a doubt, handing her over to Satan.

CHAPTER 27

Ruminating on and tortured by these and other thoughts all night long, she resolved to go back to the confessional at Buena Dicha the following morning. She did so. She was not going to confess, but simply to say: 'I didn't have enough courage, Father, to do what you ordered me.' The priest preached a very stern sermon at her and then encouraged her and assured her that if she made up her mind, happy success would be hers. On that day too, she saw Doña Marcelina Polo from afar, all black, her face the colour of mahogany, stock still in her pew as if she were a carved part of it. The penitent went back home feeling calmer; but looking within herself she did not find the fortitude that the priest had meant to instil in her.

'If I dared,' she was thinking afterwards at Bringas's. 'But I don't; I'm certain that I shan't dare. I know now what I have to tell him, and when I see him before me, goodbye idea, goodbye, intention. I'm so weak that God undoubtedly made me out of something completely useless.'

And it was late to confess now! Caballero would accuse her with reason of having deceived him. Didn't she already enjoy the position of a married woman? Wasn't she living at his expense? Hadn't the groom spent sizeable sums of money in preparing her for the wedding? He could justly call it deceit, accuse her of disloyalty and see in her the greatest perversion there was, a fraud of a woman, an impostor, a crook, a . . .

And through his contact with her, Agustín had come to form such a lofty idea of his fiancée, that the confession would be like a bombshell for the poor man. He looked upon her as a superior being, of matchless purity and virtue. How had she permitted her intended to have such a false opinion? What expression would she wear to say to him now: 'No, I'm not like that, I have a horrendous stain, I did this, this, and this . . .?' Caballero would die of a broken heart when he heard it, because such a frightful declaration was enough to kill the toughest of men, and he would have only scorn for her; he would cast her away, far from him, in horror, in disgust.

Several times had he said: 'The best part of my happiness is in knowing you have never loved anybody before me . . .'

And she, foolishly, without weighing her words, had answered him: 'Nobody, nobody, nobody.' It was true, no doubt, in the sphere of sentiment, because the old story was pure lunacy, delirium, something unconscious, irresponsible and stupid, like a thing one does while sleepwalking or under the influence of a narcotic . . . But such arguments, piled up until they made a sort of tower, did not take away the fact, and the fact came, brutal and terrible, to light the lamp of its clear logic at the apex of that obelisk of subtle distinctions . . . Dreadful lighthouse that illuminated her every step! . . . Oblivion, oblivion was what was needed; that earth, much earth should fall upon all that, so that it would be buried forever and eradicated from human memory.

That afternoon Caballero found her very much wrapped in her own thoughts and asked her the reason several times.

'My sister has upset me,' she answered.

And she visualised the expression on Agustín's face if she began to tell him . . . and the sound her words would have, and a dread so great came over her that she said to herself: 'I'll kill myself before I confess.'

Furthermore, neither he nor anyone else would understand her if she did talk. Only God could decipher such a great mystery. She did believe that purity and rectitude were still preserved in her heart; but how to make others understand that, let alone a jealous man? Out of the question; there was nothing for it but to keep quiet. God would find her a way forward.

It was true that her sister was upsetting her. Ido, who often came upstairs to find out about the course of his aspirations to the position of book-keeper, told her that a man had come twice in succession; that Refugio brought back food and drink from the inn and that they had scandalised the building. This upset her enormously. At night the two sisters quarrelled. Proud Refugio accused her sister with insolent words. Amparo still tried to use her wits to control her, offering her money. But Refugio had bolted off downhill unbridled and it was no longer possible to hold her back.

'I want nothing to do with you,' she said. 'You go your way and I'll go mine. I shan't be short of a gentleman as you will be.

But I won't be taken in by the offer of a daft and impossible marriage. You, getting married! Very likely. To a blind man it'll be. Don't turn pale. I shan't say a word. I'm not a great hypocrite and I don't like making accusations either. It's your funeral. I'm off.'

She picked up her clothes and left without another word. When she was left alone, Amparito's weary spirit divided itself between two modes of equally painful suffering. One was her sister's dishonour, the other this tenacious consideration, lodged like a red-hot thorn in her brain, where there were already others: 'Refugio knows!'

In the small hours of the morning, in a terribly agitated dream, the fiancée confessed all to her lover, who, on hearing her words, had taken out a knife and cut off her head . . . Where did the head come to rest? Over there, in a land of savages, a tanned man was holding it in his hands, kissing it.

Awake and out of bed, she did not know what to do or think. As a nightmare comes, so Ido del Sagrario came on the dot of nine o'clock.

'Miss . . .'

'What is it, Don José?'

'Yesterday, seeing that you had forgotten about me, I decided to present myself to the gentleman, who, as soon as I told him that I knew you, looked very kindly upon me. He liked my handwriting very much. He instructed me to come back. I think I have the position.'

That dolt also looked at her in an odd way. Was it simplicity or malice, was it kindness or treachery that shone out of those watery eyes? Amparo wished the earth would swallow up that Don José.

'What a house you're going to have, miss! When I went there, the gentleman was not at home and Felipe showed me everything. It's a palace. But frankly, you deserve it . . . There were the carpenters nailing up embroidered curtains. Then they brought some chairs that look as if they're made of pure gold . . .'

'Don José,' said she, humbly lowering her eyes under the gaze of that wretch, which to her was like that of an inexorable judge. 'If you behave yourself, I'll look after you.'

Poor Ido's eyes filled with tears.

'Oh, miss, can we hope for . . .? Will you be so kind as to . . .?

I dared not importune you; but seeing that you take an interest in our welfare, dare I say it . . .? Oh! Miss. Few can iron as well as Nicanora. She wishes you would give her the ironing in your new house.'

'We'll see . . .'

'And our eldest boy . . . You know him, Jaimito, our dear eldest . . . Now if you wanted to take him on as a young footman . . . He couldn't be more ideal for dressing up in livery with lots of buttons on the front and a little gold-braided cap.'

'We'll see, we'll see . . .'

'I don't know if you know that my wife is one of the best hairdressers in Madrid. The wife of the Minister for Promotion of the Biennial has a head of hair that speaks for her, and so do many other heads, miss, many others. I met Nicanora in the minister's house. I was giving the children lessons. One of them has now been elected. But that's beside the point . . . Will you keep us in mind . . .? Our eldest girl, Rosa, sews marvellously . . .'

'Very well; we'll see, we'll see . . .' repeated Amparo, harassed.

So that he would soon leave, she chose not to destroy his bright hopes of placing the whole family.

In these and other things not worth recounting, the few days that were left of '67 went by. I do not wish to speak about the nativity scene that Bringas *rigged up* for the children nor of the din Alfonsito made with the drum his uncle gave him. There was a dinner, which we must perforce call sumptuous, out of sheer routine, and Caballero and his fiancée attended it. The wedding had been set for the end of February or beginning of March. The preparations and other events took up almost the whole of January '68. The newly-weds would go to Bordeaux for a spell.

When Rosalía and Amparo were alone, the former never missed an opportunity to make her ex-protégée see what favours she deserved from her generous cousin.

'Agustín has given me this fan,' said she one day, showing her one of the best buys they had made. 'It hasn't all got to be for you, dear. We poor people can have an occasional trifle. And it seems that one of the two mantelets is also to be for my humble person. Yesterday he said: "You can keep it if you like it so very much" and I answered: "Oh no, under no circumstances!" But maybe I will take it. And why not? Isn't the work I'm doing worth something? ... All day long in the street, ignoring my own concerns! ... There are some things, dear, which simply don't suit you, because you can't carry them off; let's be honest, the little merino wool dress is all that looks good on you. What a pity: all that fortune of money Agustín's spent, for you not to show things off. As far as the navy blue poplin dress is concerned, believe you me, I'd willingly keep it, even if it meant giving my cousin the money it's cost him. I must suggest it to him ... You don't look good in that colour, and you don't know how to wear those things either. You'll look as though they have brought you here from a village and put you in what's not fitting for you. Habit, dear, habit is all when it comes to dressing. Put a fine satin skirt on a peasant and she won't know how to move her feet under it ... After you're married, you must swap this diamond pin for the one I've got with two little corals and eight little pearls. It's less valuable than yours, but it'll suit you better. Leave it to me, I'll fix you up so that you don't look too bad and I'll make the best I can of your plainness.'

The girl agreed to everything; but inside herself she resolved that after she was married, she would keep in check Her Ladyship's meddling and despotic airs and graces. Amparo had observed certain new developments in Rosalía's character: her taste for finery had developed, and coquettishness and a mania for beautifying herself were now discernible when before they had been limited to when she presented herself in public. Inside her home, the vain lady was now never as dishevelled nor as shabbily dressed as before. She had made two quite pretty wraps for herself; she nearly always wore a corset, and it was plain to see that she did not want to look disagreeable. But the fiancée took pains not to make manifest her observations, even jokingly, due to the great fear she felt of her protector, a fear that increased with the lady's insinuations and that way of looking, that expression of brooding suspicion.

'If Rosalía knows nothing,' Amparo used to think, 'she wants to know, and she cherishes her suspicions as one cherishes a hope. She's relishing the prospect of a stain on my honour. I'm asking God for oblivion and she's asking for discovery ...'

'Do you know where Doña Marcelina Polo lives?' asked Rosalía abruptly one day. 'She's been to see me several times and I must repay her visit.'

Amparo became so alarmed that she was unable to give her

address. To cover it up, she named several streets, finally blurting out the real one. Afterwards, having told weighed so heavily upon her! But how to lie, if our dear Mrs Bringas's gaze went right to the bottom of her soul and like a fishing-line, had a hook on the end to pull out whatever it found?

'You're so agitated,' she said on another occasion, 'with your fairy-tale marriage, that you look as though you've got electricity going through you. I can imagine your suddenly giving a jump and maybe taking right off. Is it that my cousin isn't pleasing to you? Do you find him old? Hell is full of ungrateful people, dear. At all events, don't marry against your inclinations. If you prefer a worthy twenty-year-old barber or a distinguished shop assistant, a shoemaker or something of that ilk, speak out honestly.'

Amparo could not respond to this nonsense except to take it as a joke. And how hard it was for her to laugh! To change the direction of the conversation she would speak about the approaching Palace ball, and the Pipaóns' descendant would take pleasure in expounding at length on this subject. The alterations to her dress, the skirt of which came from the inexhaustibly merciful Queen, took up all her available time. The two women were working on decorating it with flowers, lace and ribbons that belonged to what had been bought for the fiancée's presents. On the night of the ball, Rosalía planned to put on the great set of jewels from Samper's that Agustín had acquired for his intended and was saying in this regard:

'I suppose you'll give your permission for the poor jewels to be shown off occasionally.'

To such a solemn function, Don Francisco would wear his Charles III cross, an insignia given to him by Agustín. The new overcoat would also be worn for the first time the same night, for although this garment was not to be shown off at the ball, it was worth exhibiting it on the stairs and in the vestibule, where the lighting would be bright. And what hardship it entailed for the economical Thiers to cope with the overcoat, the patent leather boots, the two wraps that Rosalía had made herself, the Christmas dinner, the children's footwear, which was a pitiful sight by now, and other trifles! Luckily there was a double salary in December, which is to say an official gratuity; for if not...! Even so, the Bringuistic treasury was in danger of falling into the horrific abyss of insolvency. To avoid it, Don Francisco had begun by cutting out coffee and ended by dispensing with wine at meal-times. And helpful people come in for such let-downs! Our dear Don Francisco was hoping that the Marchioness de Tellería, for whom he had done the favour of repairing an antique chest, leaving it as good as new, would send him a good Christmas present. So confident of this was he that every time the doorbell rang those days, he would say: 'There it is now', going out with a peseta in his hand to give to the servant bringing the present. But the Marchioness did not care to do any such thing. 'Work, work for the powerful . . .' Thiers would say, pushing his glasses up his Roman nose.

Caballero wanted to show his house, now almost completely done up, to his cousins and fiancée and one evening they all went there. This must have been around the last days of January. García Grande's wife joined the party, eager to give her verdict on the marvels of that enchanting abode. On the way, Bringas said to his wife: 'It seems he's giving her a dowry of fifty thousand duros.' On hearing this, Rosalía scowled just as if she were the one who had to give the money.

'I've told you,' she answered her husband crossly, 'that the follies committed by the poor man ought not to concern us. We wash our hands of it all.'

Amparo and Doña Cándida were ahead, at quite some distance, and could not hear.

Bursting with pride, Caballero showed them round his house, in which he had brought together comforts little known in Madrid until then. Doña Cándida, being an intelligent person, was the one who led the song of praise. Rosalía, downcast and sad, regretted with all her soul that courtesy prevented her from picking faults. Well, it was all pretty overelaborate! The fiancée walked around the exquisite rooms, doubting the reality of what she was seeing a little and sometimes taking it to be the creation of her fevered brain. Because to think all that was going to be hers within a few days and she would rule such a beautiful roost was more likely to drive her to madness than happiness. A kind of dizziness came over her from seeing so many good things so appropriate to their purpose, and she thought how great human needs are and to what lengths industry has gone to respond to them. She considered that man's inventions, producing objects with various useful applications, create and increase need, whiling life away and making it more pleasant. The delight she felt upon beholding so much wealth, almost in her hand, upon seeing herself envied and elevated, and above all on considering herself loved so tenderly by the lord and master of it all, weighed upon her breast terribly heavily, so that only by crying a little could she have calmed herself.

They saw the nuptial bedroom, the dressing room, which according to Doña Cándida's opinion, was an *adorable little museum*; they delighted in the pink small parlour, that looked like one big open flower; they saw the dining room with walnut chairs and dressers in the classical style; they wondered at the glass cabinets in whose dark depths gleamed the Christofle plate and silverware glinting softly. But what entertained the ladies most of all was the kitchen range, a huge iron contraption, product of pure English industry, with various hotplates, doors and compartments. It was an extraordinary item. 'All it needs are the wheels and it would look like a locomotive,' said the well-informed Bringas opening one door after another to see inside that marvel.

Then García Grande's wife made an extremely sharp critique of the old system of our charcoal-burning stoves, and spoke about the little pots crowded together as though they were sharing secrets, about ladling, about pot-roasting, about grates and other things. Rosalía defended, not only eloquently but angrily, the primitive system; but Doña Cándida burst into gales of laughter, comparing our native stoves with the tripod and pan used by shepherds to fry up a few crumbs. Then they went to the bathroom, another wonder of the house, with its beautiful marble basin and its round sprinkler shower head. Rosalía shrieked at the very thought that an unclothed person would stand under that grater and that water would come out forthwith. When Caballero turned it on and the many threads of water gushed out, all the women, even Doña Cándida, and also Bringas, shouted in unison.

'Stop, stop,' said Rosalía, 'that's terrible.'

'It's a shocking thing, a shocking thing,' García Grande's wife kept repeating.

In the sitting room there was also much to applaud. All that could be heard were the words: 'pretty, lovely, tasteful'. More than pictures, bronzes, and furniture, Amparo admired the grave figure of her future husband, on whose face the light shone full as he held it up to illuminate the objects. In his black beard, the grey patches shone out like threads of silver and his sallow complexion, bathed in bright light, took on a warm *terracotta* tone, comparable to Indian, Egyptian, or Aztec things. She did not know how to complete the comparison; but it certainly did give a characteristic effect. On reflection, Agustín was a handsome man, with his noble, loyal eyes and that expression so typical of him, like someone concealing a pain. Amparo never tired of looking at him, and considered him the most ideal, the most kindly, and the most perfect of men in every way. She would gladly have flung her arms round his neck, expressing with a very tight squeeze the admiration, affection and gratitude she felt for him. But this was still impossible and she contented herself with adding to the general chorus of praise the cold words: 'Isn't it pretty! Isn't it tasteful! Isn't it all well chosen!'

At last the tour ended and the visitors withdrew. Rosalía was complaining of an aching head and bones. She was afraid she would break out in a nasty hot rash. When Amparo left for home, in a state resembling intoxication, Caballero showed her to the street door. The visit to her future abode had had the virtue of clearing her mind, sweeping away doubts and fears. She was astonished to be so happy and she delighted in that forgetting of her troubles which had seeped slowly into her heart like celestial balsam. But this repose was merely a horrific trick of destiny, as it scornfully prepared its rude blow for her. Doña Nicanora handed her a letter posted in Madrid.

CHAPTER 28

Another letter! Amparo felt as though she was falling from the top of a great tower, on seeing the handwriting she loathed on the envelope. Looking at the name over and over again, she could scarcely believe her eyes. Her spirit was suffering such extraordinary upheavals that it was easy to suspect that it was giving her waking nightmares. Would she read the letter? Yes, yes, because it might well announce something good like the definitive distancing of the enemy; and if it brought bad news ... she should read that too to avoid danger and parry the blows! The letter was brief:

'Oh Inferno you rogue, so you are to be married? ... My sister wrote to me in El Castañar telling me so. The instant I found out, I lost all that I had gained in health and sense. If I tell you that the sky fell in on me, that is putting it mildly. I forgot everything, and without commending myself either to God or the devil, I came to Madrid, where I am prepared to be entirely rash and barbarous ...'

She was unable to finish reading and fell into a long paroxysm of rage and terror, from which she was to emerge with no ideas other than suicide. 'I'll kill myself,' she thought, 'and that will be the way to end this torture.' Then, trying to strike a spark of hope in her breast, as one tries to revive a moribund fire by blowing on the embers to blaze it up, she began to think through favourable arguments and take away as much importance as she could from the fact. 'Who knows,' she said; 'maybe I can manage to find an amicable way of getting him to leave me in peace.' With the idea that her enemy would come and see her at home, she fell once more into despair. What a horrible predicament! ... Him coming through the door and her throwing herself out of the window ... She'd move, she would hide in the most remote corner of Madrid ... How naïve could she get! If he didn't find her there; if Don José Ido didn't inform him of her whereabouts, he would look for her at the Bringases' ...

The thought of seeing him walk in at Los Angeles Hill was a thousand times worse than the thought of Hell with all its horrors . . . What would she do then? Well, it was very simple: she would go and confront him, she would go looking for him, determined to win out or die. Either she would succeed in making him let her go free or she would take her own life. This resolution, bravely made, calmed her somewhat, although the idea of going to the unpleasant abode in Fe Street disgusted her, like the recollection of drinking a very bitter draught. But there was nothing for it, was there . . .? She would go, yes, she would take that dangerous step, the last step to salvation or death. Her heart told her: 'You yourself, if you are skilful and artful, can make him understand his stupid stubbornness and deflect him from the path of rash and barbarous acts. You, if you keep your head, will defeat the monster, because you're the only being on earth with the power to do it. But you need to study your role; it's essential that you know the measure of your strength and how to use it at the right moment. That animal, whom no one can chain up, will succumb to your skilled handling; you'll tie him up with a silken thread and you'll make him yield to the point when he submits to your will in everything and for everything.' Even though her heart had said these consoling things to her, she still doubted whether to go and confront the beast or not. She looked at the portrait of her father, whose eyes seemed to say: 'Silly girl, ever since you came in, I've been advising you to go, and you refuse to understand . . .' The faces of all the Pharmacy students portrayed in the large picture were saying the same thing.

Other solutions occurred to her: to inform the authorities, to flee from Madrid, to tell Caballero everything . . . Oh, if she had the guts for this last . . .! The rest was nonsense. Among all the solutions, killing herself stood out: that really was a good one; but before tackling it, wouldn't it be best to try to tame the dragon and get him, with kind words and some astuteness, to go to other lands and leave her in peace?

Once this was decided, the question of choosing the right time remained. Would she go that very night or on the following day, which was Sunday? The second prevailed, and she took to thinking about the lie she would use to excuse her absence from the Bringases'. She could not talk about illness, because then Caballero would come and see her. It occurred to her to say that her sister had disappeared ... And how could she not seek to ascertain her whereabouts? The first was true, the second, a lie. However long the visit lasted, she would be back by evening, for she had to dress to go to the theatre. Caballero had arranged to come and collect her at eight o'clock.

In the end, the fearful morning came and she set off after breakfast, dressed in poor but decent style, with a veil and gloves. She wanted to look neither rich nor destitute. In order to be quick and avoid being seen, she took a cab. On the way, she studied her difficult part and the pleas and reasoning with which she intended to tame the untamable man and convince him of the extremely grave harm he was doing her. The basis of her argument was: 'Either this ends forever, or I kill myself this very night ... I have taken an oath ... It's done ... Peace or death.'

She arrived. Who would have known that she was to see once more the horrible wire screen and the yard furrowed with green and red streams! ... As she was going up the stairs, two women were coming down saying: '... won't get through the night. No hope, dying ...' About whom were they speaking? Could it be him on his deathbed? There are deaths that resemble resurrections because of the hope they embrace within their funereal horror ... The door was open. Amparo entered cautiously, fearing that she would meet foreign faces, and she reached that parlour, formerly crowded with furniture and now almost empty ... One could see at a glance that the rag-and-bone men had passed through.

The girl took a few steps into the room and stopped, waiting for someone to come in. She could hear sounds of movement and voices within. Suddenly he appeared. He was so transformed that she almost failed to recognise him on first laying eyes on him, for he had grown a beard, which was thick, strong and curly, and country life had been an efficacious and swift curative agent acting upon that rude nature. His appearance was bursting with vigour, and his gaze had all the gleam of his best days. He was wearing a long dun-coloured cloth jacket and on his head he had a fur cap. Both garments suited him so well, that they almost made him handsome. He was not a man in disguise, but a man who had removed his disguise, appearing in his own, fitting form. He was delighted to see Amparo; but no doubt something was going on that prevented him from expressing his happiness.

'Are you here at last?' he said in a low voice. 'I was expecting you ... Very happy I am ... You're to blame. We'll talk presently and you'll explain ... What? Are you shocked by the look of me? I have the most horrifically barbarous appearance you've ever seen. Are you afraid of me?'

'Not exactly afraid ... but ...'

'You're trembling, though ... Calm yourself; I don't eat people ... Sit down and wait for me.'

He rushed out of the room and came back a short while later to rummage in one of the drawers of the chest. Three or four times did Amparo see him coming and going, fetching or carrying something or other, and she could not find an explanation for these trips.

'Forgive me,' he said in the course of one of those appearances, taking out a sheet and tearing it into strips. 'When I came here I found poor Celedonia so bad with her rheumatism that I think we're losing her ...'

Then the sound of human groans were heard, announcing acute pains.

'Poor woman!' said Polo. 'I didn't want to send her to hospital. Who's to care for her if I don't?'

During the time that she was alone, Amparo decided it was wise to close the front door, for with it open, she considered herself betrayed in that mansion of sadness, fear and pain.

'Here I am again,' said the fellow, reappearing in the parlour with a handful of cotton wool that he left on the chest. 'She can't move. I've had to turn her over in bed. I give her the medicines ... She refuses to take anything at all unless I give it to her. I also put the bandages round her knees and apply the ointments and poultices. I didn't sleep a wink last night. She never stopped shouting and calling me for one moment. It's two days since I arrived and here I am without a moment's rest. But I'm strong, very strong ... You shall see ...'

To demonstrate his strength, he took Amparo round the waist, before she could prevent it, and raised her aloft like a feather.

'Ooh!' she cried upon seeing herself nearer the ceiling than the floor.

The athlete, with a graceful movement of his herculean arms, sat her on his right shoulder and took a few steps round the room bearing that precious cargo.

'Don't shriek, don't fuss now, for it's not the first time . . .'

'But I'm falling! . . .'

'Silly goose, not falling . . .' said the brute, carefully depositing her upon the sofa. 'Now let's hear the explanations. I'm angry, furious. When I found out, I felt like coming and . . . I can't explain it, coming and devouring you. Afterwards, I calmed down a little and last night friend Nones gave me a sermon so profound, and reasoned with me in such a way that I'm almost, almost inclined to resign myself to this horrible lesson that divine Providence is teaching me.'

On hearing this, Amparo felt enormous solace in her soul. The thing was on the right path.

'I must confess,' added the brute, sitting down next to her, 'even though it shatters my soul to say it, that the match you have on offer is such that to spurn it . . . well, I won't say any more.'

How flustered she was! She felt that everything she had to say would come out inappropriately. She was no diplomat; she was not sufficiently skilled at conversation to know how to say what was to her advantage and keep quiet about what could be harmful. Polo continued thus:

'When that first fit of anger passed, I had a thought concerning you and your wedding, which serves to console me and at the same time let me forgive you. I'll explain. I identify with you so much that I have had the same thought as you on accepting this good match. You'll judge how right I am. A man who's a gentleman and extremely wealthy presents himself to you, and you, evaluating the matter by a common and vulgar criterion, said: "What can I expect of the world? Wretchedness and slavery. So I'll marry and have wellbeing and freedom." Caballero, because of what he has and what he has not, because of his wealth and his gentlemanliness, for his kindliness and his candidness, is all you could have wished for. You're marrying him without loving him.'

Inferno already had the words on her lips to protest with all her soul; but fear struck her dumb and she swallowed the protest.

'This is my idea,' he proceeded, 'an idea that consoles me and exonerates you in my eyes. Speak frankly. Isn't it true that you don't love him one iota?'

Indignant, she would have vehemently answered him what

her heart dictated; but her panic increased to such a degree that it hampered her and flattened her; transferred to the material sphere, it was as if an enormous load of iron had been placed upon her body. At the same time her reasoning was this: 'If I tell the truth, if I say I love the man who's to be my husband very much, this barbarian will fly into a fury. I know his bad temper and the danger of hurting his pride. The most prudent thing will be to tell him a whopping great lie, a lie that tears me to shreds inside, but which may save me.'

'Do you love him, yes or no?' asked the wild beast impatiently and with brutal curiosity.

Inferno said: *No*. And she said it with her mouth and her head, emphatically, like children who are making their first attempts at the human farce. As she said it, her whole being was rebelling against such dreadful falsity and the lips that pronounced the word were left feeling decidedly bitter. The brute moved his chair closer. She could not move back, because she was on the sofa, sitting with her back to the window. She would willingly have incrusted herself in the wall or partition to flee from the threat of that rural creature's affection, who was now so repulsive to her. The sight of the dun-coloured cloth, the rough beard and the rabbit-fur cap coming closer was like the sight of the devil descending upon her.

'Just as I thought,' observed Polo, taking her hand, which she wanted to, but could not withdraw. 'I know the individual in question; I've seen him once. He's an unfortunate man, of good character, but short of brains. You'll manipulate him at your will, if you're clever, you'll rule him as one rules a child and you'll do whatever the devil you wish.'

The meaning behind these words was perfectly clear to the unhappy girl, who was now more afraid. But when human nature is subjected to the greatest of trials, the terrible fear – in keeping with the law of reaction – engenders a surge of valour and the peril suggests the way to salvation. So understanding from that indication of her enemy's words and ideas that he wanted to lead her to a criminal and repugnant solution, the innate virtue of Inferno's soul protested and she felt her dignity shaken. She looked at the brute and so odious did he seem to her that between dying in a struggle and the torture of seeing him and having dealings with him, she preferred the first.

Wounded in her own instinct as if by a whiplash, she abruptly rose to her feet and spoke without hiding her anger.

'Well now . . . Is there an end to this or not? I came to find out if you will leave me alone or if you want to finish me off.'

'Calm down, calm down, child,' murmured Polo, turning pale. 'You know you'll get nothing out of me by being nasty. By being nice, anything you like . . .'

Inferno made an effort to be prudent, tactful, skilful. Drying the tears that came to her eyes, she said:

'You can't want me to be unhappy; you must wish me to be a good, honest woman with dignity. You've done bad things; but you haven't got a bad heart; you must leave me in peace, not pursue me any more, leave for the Philippines as you planned and forget you ever heard of me.'

'Oh! Poor Inferno,' he exclaimed with profound bitterness. 'If that could be as easy as you say . . . You've said I'm not perverse. How wrong you are! There in that wilderness, several times I was tempted to hang myself from a tree, like Judas, because I've also betrayed Christ. Sometimes I despise myself so much that I say: "Won't somebody, some unknown person, some passer-by hit me as he goes past?" And I'll speak frankly to you. While I was a hypocrite and play-acting at religion, I didn't have one iota of faith. Since throwing off the mask, I believe in God more, because my disturbed conscience reveals Him more to me than my conscience at peace. Before, I used to preach about hell without believing in it; now that I don't name it, I think that if it doesn't exist God needs to make it especially for me. No, no, I'm not a good man. You don't know me well. And what are you asking of me now? To leave you in peace . . . What were you after, when you were after me?'

Confronted by this question, the timid woman's alarm increased by one more degree. The things going through her mind would have made her drop dead as if struck by lightning were it not for the fact that the human brain is built to be proof against explosions, just as the heart is proof against remorse.

'What were you after, when you were after me?' repeated the brute with the forcefulness of passion sustained by logic. 'Your lovely mouth, what did it say to me? Don't you recall? I do. What were you after when you said it?'

Confronted by this bloodthirsty, brutal logic, the spineless woman was succumbing.

'The things I heard are not to be heard without the soul being turned upside down. And now, what *you* turned upside down, you want me to put back to how it was? . . .'

She burst into tears like a child given a beating. For a while all that was to be heard were her sobs and the distant groans of Celedonia. Polo ran to the ailing woman's side.

'But,' he said as he hurried back in shortly afterwards, 'I take all the blame upon myself. I undoubtedly have the worse part; but I'll take it all. I sinned more than you, because I deceived men and God.'

Inferno looked at him, not with annoyance, but pleadingly, as the lamb looks at the butcher armed with his knife, and in mute language, with her eyes alone, she said to him, 'Let me go, slaughterer.'

And he, interpreting this language rapidly and exactly, responded, not with looks alone, but with forceful words: 'No, I'm not letting you go.'

Now feeling dizzy, the hapless woman threw herself out into the passage to look for the door and flee. What a dreadful panic she was in! But if she ran like the wind, Polo ran faster, and before she could escape, he locked the door and put the key away.

Amparo screamed.

'Let me go, let me go,' she cried, pressing herself against the wall, as if she wanted to make a hole in it with the pressure of her body and escape through it.

Polo took her by the arm to lead her back inside. Freeing herself, she ran towards the parlour. Blind and in despair, she was going straight towards the half-open window to throw herself down into the yard. He closed the window.

'Here . . . prisoner!' he growled.

Amparito let herself drop onto the sofa, and burying her face in a little cushion on it, she clamped the fingers of both hands to her head.

CHAPTER 29

A long while passed before she moved. Suddenly she heard these
words, uttered very close to her ear:

'You know only too well that by being nasty you'll get
nothing, by being nice, everything. You want to treat me like a
stray dog and that's not fair . . . Even if I try to contain myself,
I shan't be able to avoid being carried away and doing something
rash and barbarous.'

The deplorable position in which the girl found herself and
her fear of catastrophe worked away at her spirit, instilling in it
something that it did not have, namely: deviousness, tact. Life
forms character with its laborious action and also modifies it
temporarily or disfigures it with the explosive action of a
terrible, abnormal situation. A coward may become heroic at
certain moments and a miser generous. In the same way, that
timorous woman, spurred on by the compromising situation in
which she found herself, acquired for a brief spell a certain
flexibility of ideas and some astuteness that did not exist
beforehand in her frank and truthful character. 'This way,' she
thought, 'I won't get anywhere . . . If I knew what other women
know, if I could manage to trick him, promising without giving
and beguiling him until he gives in . . . Let's have a try.'

'That's a strange way to love someone!' she said, sitting up.
'It seems natural that what we should want for those we love is
to see them happy . . . I mean with peace of mind. I fail to
understand how I can be loved like this, making me unhappy,
wretched, taking away my dignity, so that everyone despises me.
Poor me! . . . I can't raise my downcast eyes to people because I
think they're all going to say: "I know you and what you've
done". I want to get out of such a situation and this selfish man
won't let me.'

Don Pedro heaved a great sigh.

'Me, selfish? And what you're doing is self-sacrifice, is it? I'm
poor, he's rich. Isn't that the same as saying: "Me, me, and

always me"? It's fine if we both sacrifice ourselves, but that I alone should sacrifice myself and you triumph . . .! I can see well enough what you want: to marry and be powerful and on the very day of the wedding, for me to shoot myself so that everything remains a secret.'

'No, I don't want that.'

Amparo felt her wits sharpening as an actress's expertise slipped over her. She realised that a slightly affectionate turn of phrase would be just right for the situation.

'No, I don't want you to kill yourself. That would make me very sad . . . But I do want you to go far away, as you were planning and as Father Nones advised you. There can be nothing between us, not even friendship. If you go far away, time will gradually heal you, you'll experience sincere repentance and God will forgive you, He'll forgive us both.'

Profoundly moved, the brute looked down at the floor. Believing in the likelihood of triumph, the troubled, timid woman reinforced her argument . . . she even went so far as to put her hand on his shoulder, something she would not have done just before.

'Do it for my sake, for God's sake, for the sake of your soul,' she said pleadingly.

'That's it, that's it,' mumbled Polo gloomily without looking at her. 'All the sacrifices for me, all the triumphs for you . . . You know what I say to you? That that man poisons my blood . . . he sticks in my throat. I can imagine you're going to love him a great deal as soon as you're living with him; and that makes my spirit rebel, it takes away my courage to leave; it makes me furious and incites me to be more wicked still.'

He stood up and paced from one corner of the room to the other, then burst out in an anguished voice:

'God, God, why did you give me the strength of a giant and refuse me the fortitude of a man? I'm an ignoble puppet padded out with the muscles of a Hercules.'

And stopping before her, he said in a more familiar tone:

'I swear to you, my little Inferno, that if I leave, as you wish, for the Philippines, and I go without wringing the neck of that husband of yours, you must take me to be a saint, for a greater victory over himself has never been achieved by any man. And I should like to please you in this, I should like to leave you with your freedom; but neither you with your requests, nor Nones with his advice will get that from me. It's a long path to tread from a barbarian to a saint and I . . . start off well, but halfway along my strength fails me and . . . Get thee behind me, barbarian, get thee behind me!'

Amparo felt a cold sweat breaking out on her face. There was no alternative for her and the negative and conclusive solution took possession of her mind.

'I'm resolved . . . I know what I have to do.'

'What?'

'I cannot marry . . . Impossible, impossible! How could I? Does one simply pass over such a grave sin like this? My conscience doesn't permit me to deceive that good man . . . I know what I have to do. I'm going home right now; I'll write him a letter, a very carefully planned letter saying: "I cannot marry you, sir, because of this, this, and this".'

'You always think the worst,' observed Polo with apparent indifference. 'Your plan sounds quite absurd to me . . . No, you have no choice any more but to put up with him. To refuse now, after having consented and kept quiet about your scruples for so long, would be a dishonour. No, no, get married . . . We mustn't cause a scandal.'

The moral laxity suggested by that plural *we mustn't* wounded the girl so much that she was transfixed with horror and knew not what to say. He gave her no time to reflect on that ill-concealed suggestion, but continued:

'I understand that this has to end; I understand that I must sacrifice myself . . . because I'm the more criminal. But won't you sacrifice yourself a little bit too?'

'Me, how?' she asked uncomprehendingly.

'By not bidding me farewell as you would to a dog. Just before you said you don't love your fiancé. If you wish me to obey you in the sense of getting out of the way, don't make me believe you don't love me either, because then I'll ruin everything. If it suits you for me to have the strength for this heroic act you're demanding of me, give it to me yourself.'

'Me? How?'

Amparo would gladly have slapped him.

'Like this! . . .' shouted the brute with a savage amorous impulse, wrapping his arms tightly around her. 'If you tell me you love that boneless fool more than me . . . right now, right now, you see? I'm going to squeeze you, more and more, until I choke you. I shall wrench your last gasp from you and drink it.'

He suited his actions to his words, squeezing harder and harder until Inferno, suffocating and breathless, cried out: 'Ow ... You're choking me! ...'

'Concede one day to me, one day and no more. I'll give you a whole life of peace and I'm only asking one day of you.'

But she, terribly breathless, found a last gasp to say 'No'.

'Yes!' he shouted with brutal longing.

'No, I say.'

'One day!'

'Not one minute.'

'Oh ... you bitch!'

Furious, he loosened his grip ... His attack had shown an insane, spasmodic fury ... Amparo jumped back, terrified, and ran to look for the way out again. Not finding it and running through the whole place, she came upon the room where the patient was lying. That seemed like a sacrosanct place, where she could enjoy a right of asylum. She cowered in the only free corner that there was in the room and waited. Something between a mumbled complaint and a sound of curiosity issued from the patient's lips. But Inferno was not uttering a word; she was dumbfounded. Soon afterwards, he came in.

'How goes it, Celedonia?'

'I was just sleeping a little but you two woke me up with the noise ... The very idea! Having your romp here! ...' faltered the patient, livening up and looking at the two people in her presence. 'Having your romp here! ... The times and places you choose to sin! ... at a dying woman's bedside ...!'

'But we're not sinning, silly old girl,' said Polo affectionately. 'Would you like something to eat or drink?'

'I want to think about my salvation ... You be damned if you wish; but I'm going to be saved ... I'm dying, I'm dying ... Send word to Father Nones and leave off romping.'

'Nones will come in good time, he'll come in good time. But you're not so bad. This afternoon the doctor said this would wear off.'

'The doctor's as daft as you ... You're a hopeless good-for-nothing ... keep away; don't touch me ... I think I see the devil coming to take me away ...'

'So we're making little jokes are we?' said Polo, arranging the covers. 'Now, I'm going to put the hot flannels on you again. Are you in pain?'

'Horr..rribly . . .'

'My dear little Inferno, go to the kitchen and warm the flannels. The fire must be lit. Old girl, don't be ungrateful, this poor thing is here to care for you, don't you see? See what an angel she is?'

'Angel?' muttered the old woman, looking at both of them with rolling eyes. 'Of darkness, yes. You're a fine pair. But you shan't take me with you, you shan't take me with you . . . Get Father Nones to come, get him to come soon.'

Amparo went to the kitchen. She could not refuse to do such a simple and at the same time so Christian a service. Meanwhile, the brute saw to turning the patient's aching body over, changing the rags and bandages round her swollen legs for her. In this he displayed a delicacy and skill only possessed by mothers and nurses accustomed to such a worthy job.

'Now I'm going to give you a cup of broth,' he said; and running to the kitchen, he ordered Inferno to warm it up.

Once the flannels had been applied to that poor body, not to mention various ointments and wads of cotton wool, the barbarian gave her the broth and along with it he spoke to her most tenderly: 'Come, come, you're not that bad even though you complain enough. Now you're going to sleep just beautifully. I know you don't feel like food, but make an effort; you're very weak. Drink this broth to our health, to my and Miss Amparo's health, who came to care for you. So . . . be brave! . . . Good, good. Now rest; I'm not going to give you any more chloral tonight, because it may harm you.'

The old woman, delirious, was laughing and moaning by turns, and stroking a cross hanging round her neck with her clumsy hands. 'Oh! . . . Oh! . . . Have you come to take me away? . . . Yes, it was indeed for you. This man, this man who is on the cross will defend me.'

When the patient grew drowsy, Polo signalled to Amparo to leave the room. They both went back to the parlour. During that sad parenthesis, which had so strangely interrupted her frightful struggle with the monster, the timid woman had thought that she must expect nothing of him from discussion and explanations. How terribly stupid to have gone to visit him. She had no diplomacy, nor any idea of how to avoid difficulty by means of clever words. The only recourse left to her now was to escape from the house as best she might and submit to her wretched fate. She now saw the wedding as impossible; she could no longer doubt that that savage would cause a scandal ... Dishonour was inevitable. She would have to choose between killing herself or putting up with the ignominy that was going to cover her like a moral leprosy, incurable and revolting. Anything was preferable to dealing with a beast like him and suffering his barbaric beatings or his repugnant caresses. In despair, once they were in the parlour, she calmly said:

'We have nothing more to talk about. Will you let me leave?'

'First we'll have a light lit. It's almost dark. Be good enough to ...'

He pointed out the tallow candle standing on the chest next to the box of matches.

'The key of the door, the key,' cried Inferno once she had lit the light. I want to go out, I'm suffocating.'

'Keep calm, keep calm. Be good enough to close the shutters ... And it wouldn't do any harm if you took a needle now and put a stitch or two in this waistcoat ... Lazybones! I want to create the illusion for a moment that you're keeping house for me. You ought to make my dinner and eat with me.'

'I'm in no mood for jokes ... The key!'

His reply was an embrace, squeezing, squeezing ...

'Tell me you love me as before and I'll let you go,' he declared, still holding her in that infernal grip. 'Otherwise, I'll strangle you ...'

'All the better ... I prefer you to kill me,' murmured the wretched woman, beginning to have an idea of the horrible contractions of the boa constrictor.

'So we're making little jokes are we? ... So I should kill you, queen and empress of the world? ... Go on, say you love me ...'

'All right, I do,' answered the fearful woman, once more feeling the necessity to be diplomatic.

'Say it clearer.'

'I ... love you,' she declared, closing her eyes.

'No, you said that reluctantly. Say it with warmth and looking at me.'

Inferno had no patience left for more. She was going to give a spirited shout: 'I detest you, you ferocious beast'; but she just managed to contain herself, weighing up the consequences of such a damning phrase. She made a superhuman effort and managed to say this:

'How can you expect me to ... love you with all this brutality? ... For me to love you you'd have to ... behave otherwise.'

'You tell me how.'

At this he let her go.

'First, by not strangling me, and treating me reasonably.'

'Stay with me tonight,' said Polo brutally.

'No, a thousand times no,' countered Inferno with all her soul.

'Let me finish ... I swear to you that tomorrow you're free and I'll bother you no more.'

Amparo thought this over for a while. Things had reached a point of such extreme gravity that she was in the unfortunate position of having to consider the infernal proposition. But her conscience triumphed over her vacillating weakness, inspiring her with these words that revealed disgust and courage in equal measure.

'On no account. I prefer to die right here.'

'Tomorrow you'll be free.'

'I'd rather be stone dead.'

Her doubts returning, she weighed the abominable deal in the balance of reason, then said:

'And what guarantee have I that you'll keep your word . . .?'

But triumphing over her doubts once more, she emphatically exclaimed:

'Oh! No and a thousand times no. It's a worse shame than the one I have hanging over me already. I won't, I won't. I have no other way out than death, and I'm resolved to kill myself, me myself, with my own hands. Yes, you savage, you demon from hell . . .!'

Transfigured, the lamb was taking on the aspect of a lioness. Never had Polo seen anything like this sublime rage from she who was all peace, meekness, and cowardice.

'Yes, you haven't even a scrap of a conscience any more. I'm not like that,' she added ardently. 'I'm a Christian, I know what repentance is and I know how to die of a broken heart, dishonoured, before falling into the quagmire where you want to drag me.'

The barbarian was blinking like someone who is sleeping and suddenly has a very bright light shone into his eyes. One of those fits of expansiveness swept over his soul, the sort that occasionally fired him, now in the direction of goodness, now in that of evil, and handing the key to his victim, he said in a hollow voice:

'You can leave whenever you want.'

The prisoner's first impulse was to start running and after a moment's hesitation, she did so. But she hadn't taken one step on the stairs when the voice of expediency stopped her once more. It was hesitation itself. The thought came to her that that dash of generosity from her enemy did not suffice to resolve the fearful issue. She did not want to leave without receiving an assurance that everything had ended and she was recovering the peace she longed for. Moved by these selfish scruples, she went back in, carelessly leaving the door open.

'But you won't persecute me, you won't create a scandal, you won't do anything against me?'

Polo, on his feet, turned his back on her; but she walked round until she had him in front of her. In her delirium, she went so far as to take his hand, bending over it . . .

'For God and the Virgin's sake . . . don't dishonour me, don't damn me, don't reveal any of this secret, which is my death; don't see anyone . . . Let the past be as though it had happened a thousand years ago; let no living soul know about it . . . You're not wicked; you're not capable of committing an infamy . . . What you must do . . .'

'Yes, I know, I know,' he muttered, turning round again to hide his face. 'What I have to do is . . . go and roam around far, far away . . .'

With a quick movement, he separated himself from her and went into the bedroom. Amparo decided not to follow him. From the drawing room she saw a shape in there throwing itself into a black armchair, head hidden between arms that were resting on an unmade bed; and she heard a bellowing sound, like an injured beast taking refuge in its den.

CHAPTER 30

Inferno was in doubt as to whether to go in or withdraw. 'I think I've defeated him,' she thought, 'but I'm not sure yet. What gives me hope is that he never does things by halves. If he does evil, he stops at nothing until he reaches the ultimate extreme; if the idea of doing good comes over him, he's capable of going further than most.' The beast suddenly reappeared, looking haggard and with shaky hands.

'Oh! You bitch!' he said. 'If I didn't love you as I do . . . I'm made of better stuff than you, indeed I am, I am, and I can go further than you ever will. You talk of killing yourself! . . . What do you know about that, silly goose, you who recoil in fright at a pin-prick?'

At this point, they heard noise on the stairs and afterwards the grating squeak of the door opening. Both stopped to listen. Amparo, fearful, noted that the people who had walked in were now coming along the passage.

'My sister!' murmured Don Pedro.

Upon hearing this word, the timid woman did not know what had come over her. In her alarm and consternation, all she had time to do was rush into the bedroom and hide. Oh! If it had taken her two seconds longer to flee, she would have been caught right there. The visitors were Doña Marcelina and Father Nones. Amparo heard that lady's voice with terror, and fearing that she might also come into the bedroom, she planned to hide in a cupboard. Luckily, there was a very narrow, little triangular room, cluttered with old things, at the back of the bedroom, in which she would hide if need be.

The lean, wiry cleric, the lady with the mahogany face and the black dress, both took a seat in the parlour. The former looked as though he had escaped from a painting by El Greco. The latter was akin to Goya's *Caprichos*.

'But tell me, you savage, haven't you taken off that monstrous

Simon of Cyrene beard?' said the sister to her brother. 'Aren't you ashamed to be seen looking such a fright?'

'You see, he's readying himself to be a missionary, Madam,' observed the indulgent and jovial Father Nones, taking out his tobacco pouch. 'And how's the poor woman?'

'Very bad. Now it seems she's getting a little sleep.'

'Let's come to the point,' said Marcelina, slotting herself into her seat at one end of the sofa. Don Juan Manuel and I have arranged everything. This blessed man was saying as we were coming along the street: "Much care is needed with that brute. He escaped from the estate to return to his bad old ways. With every day that passes without our packing him off to the antipodes, he's in greater danger of perdition for himself and a great deal of upset for the rest of us." Isn't that true, Father?'

'It's Gospel,' answered Nones, smiling.

'Right then, right then,' added the former. 'We have now arranged your voyage. Thanks to a lady who lives with me, I've got together what's needed for the ticket. With what the rag-and-bone men gave you this morning for that junk and what this Mr Nones is letting you have . . . as an advance on what the Town Hall owes you . . . – thank him, man – with all that, as I say, you have enough to deal with anything that comes up on the way. I've got you letters of recommendation.'

'And I'm giving him one that's a rare privilege,' interrupted Don Juan Manuel.

'As soon as you arrive, you take up your position, which is a gift, so they say. Now, answer. Have you made up your mind to leave?'

'Yes,' affirmed Polo resolutely.

'The steamship sails from Marseilles on the eighth, mark you, so if you want to catch it you had better make haste and set off no later than tomorrow. '

'Well, tomorrow it is then.'

'That's the kind of man I like to see,' declared Nones, affectionately slapping his friend on the back.

'Thank the Lord, I thank Him eternally,' uttered the pious sister vehemently, 'for this resolution of yours. Let's hope that once you're out there you'll go back to being what you used to be, and mend your ways and purify yourself. You won't be short of ways to make yourself good and meritorious for there are plenty of savages to convert over there.'

'The first thing we need,' said Nones dryly, 'is that he may convert and straighten himself out; the other savages, my dear lady, aren't short of people to bring them to heel.'

'So, my dear unfortunate brother, I shall see you no more,' she declared, moved and raising her hand a little in the direction of her eyes, which certainly would have cried if they were not made of wood. 'Oh! It's all over for me. Thankfully, I console myself with my ideas. I imagine that I'm in a very large convent, that the streets of Madrid are the cloisters, that my house is my cell . . . I come and go, in and out, all on my very own amidst the tumult, silent in so much din . . . In this solitary life family affections are still alive within me . . . However much I think of God, I can't stop loving my brother and the idea of the toil awaiting him in those lands will give me some very bad nights . . . During mass this morning, I was saying to myself: "But Lord, can't this man correct his passions, can't he restrain himself as others have done who have come to be saints? Is he so weak, so spineless, that he'll let himself be ruled by a disgusting vice?" Oh! Brother, there is no room for hatred in my heart; but there are times, Lord forgive me, there are times when I sin and can't help it; I sin when I remember the rogue who turned your head, taking you away from your duty; yes, I sin, I sin . . . I sin because I fly into a rage . . .'

'Madam,' said kindly Nones, 'don't upset us now with your feelings, for we have reasons enough to be melancholy. My friend Perico is leaving us tomorrow. Let's use the time we have left in his company to be good to him and show him our affection.'

'But I don't trust him, I don't,' added the virtuous lady, looking at him as one looks at a child suspected of naughtiness. 'You know him as well as I do and you're not ignorant of his vices. I found out through Celedonia that before he went to El Castañar, he had that . . . woman here. Mr de Nones, don't be such a saint, don't play the simpleton. You're well aware that just before, when we were coming up those tiring stairs, I said I thought I'd heard a woman's voice and you burst out laughing and . . . recall your words well: "Anything's possible . . . There's nothing new under the sun . . . You're right, I smell a female rat."'

'What nonsense!' stammered Polo, who was breaking out in one sweat after another.

'It may well be nonsense; but you give grounds for making people always think the worst of you. Oh! My dear brother, the possibility of your perdition is an idea that makes me ill. A few nights ago I dreamt you'd gone away, and there in lands of Indians, where there are very big trees and the smell of cinnamon, cloves and camphor, there you were, alas, in a hut, and you were dying, yes, dying of a horrible fever. But what terrified me was that you were dying thinking of that accursed woman, which is the same as saying that God couldn't forgive you ... Believe me, brother, I awoke grief-stricken, in a cold sweat ... Never ever have I suffered greater anguish.'

'What nonsense!' said Polo again, in a state of utter exhaustion and consternation.

'Madam,' observed the kindly Nones, 'you're going to make us cry.'

'Well, if this sinner did cry for three days together, it would do him no harm ... To return to what I was saying ... Oh! You must know that the girl is getting married next month. The wicked are all lucky. That fool is coming in for a let-down the like of which ...!'

'Madam, we don't speak ill of our neighbour.'

'Let me continue ... And the presents! Rosalía Bringas has shown me them all. This morning I met her at Buena Dicha church and she insisted that I go back to her place with her. I couldn't snub her by refusing, and there we were chatting and chatting for at least two hours. She entertained me with a little tipple and sponge cakes ...'

'Madam, I find the part about the little tipples dangerous and liable to make one say more than one should.'

'I greatly regret,' said Polo, 'that you and that lady should have spoken about what's of no concern to you ...'

At this point, Marcelina, who was staring at the floor, bent over and without registering any great surprise, picked up an object that had been dropped as if lost on the matting. It was a glove. Taking it with one finger, she showed it to her brother and said with inquisitorial iciness:

'Whose is this glove?'

Polo became alarmed.

'Oh! ... I don't know ... it must be ... It must undoubtedly belong to someone who was here this morning, the sister of Francisco Rosales the dyer.'

'That was a good one!' exclaimed Nones, clapping his friend hard on the back.

'I know this hand,' affirmed Marcelina, examining the corpus delicti as it hung from one finger.

Then she blew into it to inflate it and see the shape of the hand.

'Take it, keep it: I don't want this sort of material proof of your infamy, because I shan't use it for any purpose. Now if I were wicked, if I wished to harm that young woman . . .'

'Enough, Madam,' said Don Juan Manuel expansively, 'we all know you're an angel.'

'Indeed I am,' she rejoined, hitting the cleric on the knee with her fan. 'Not all occasions are right for little jokes, Mr de Nones. I'm neither an angel nor a seraph; but I'm better than many . . . If I wanted to harm . . .! Hah! In my possession I have two letters from that hussy, two little pieces of paper she sent you and I took away when we quarrelled and separated. I treasure them like gold, but whilst I'm living and breathing, no human being shall set eyes on them. For if I chose to give them to Rosalía Bringas, what damage couldn't I cause . . .? But I'm not spiteful; you and the lucky girl can have your peace of mind.'

'That's how I like people to be,' said Nones. 'That's the road to heaven, Madam.'

'But there's a great difference between that and being stupid,' continued the lady, confronting her brother furiously. 'You don't fool me any more than anyone else does. That . . . I don't want to say a bad word, she's been here today.'

'Don't be absurd,' replied Polo in a terrible state of nerves.

'Madam, Madam,' cried Nones, 'you're putting us all in a compromising position.'

'And furthermore, I say further,' added the sister, extremely irritated, sniffing the air, 'I contend that she's still here.'

So saying she fixed her dull eyes on the bedroom door.

'I would swear I heard the rustle of skirts there making a dash for it.'

'You're delirious, woman.'

'Well open up then.'

Nones marched towards the bedroom and opened the door, saying:

'We'll soon resolve our doubts.'

Polo held the light and took a few steps inside the room. Marcelina looked all around with eager curiosity. She went as far as lowering herself to let her gaze slip under the bed, behind the furniture, behind the stand full of clothes.

'There's a door there,' she said, pointing to that of the little room . . . 'I would swear I heard . . .'

'That door is disused. It gives access to next door.'

Marcelina looked at her brother with grim incredulity.

'Open it.'

'But, Madam, it's nailed up,' said Nones, crossing his arms. 'Do you want to knock the building down too?'

'If you wish to search the whole house . . .' said Don Pedro.

They returned to the parlour.

'Aren't you going to look in on Celedonia? The poor woman will be happy to see you.'

'Yes, I'll go in for a moment, but not for long, because I haven't the heart to see anyone suffering.'

'I think she's getting some rest now.'

'Your charity towards that woman is really meritorious . . . But don't think you're going to cancel out your sins; small merits don't wipe out great faults . . . For my part, I'd like to care for the sick very much, to turn over people covered in sores or pox, to clean wounds . . . but I haven't the stomach. When I've tried, I've become ill. The unfortunate are also helped by prayer.'

Polo said nothing about this view. They heard the groans of Celedonia. The three of them went to her.

When they entered the cramped room, the poor woman was suffering horribly. In the flickering light from the small lamp, her livid complexion, kissed by death, was a cold mask of pain that almost instilled more fright than compassion. Her brain was addled.

'What's the matter with the old girl?' said the barbarian to her, showing affectionate pity. 'Do you want a little chloral?'

'Oh! . . .' she cried, looking at all of them with rolling eyes; 'I can hardly believe that here, in this hospital . . . But are the two love-birds still romping . . .? What a way to sin! . . . I'm dying; but you won't take me with you, you won't. Get Nones.'

'But here he is, can't you see him?'

'Is it really Father Nones?' stammered the patient, opening her eyes wide.

'Yes it's I, you malingerer . . . So you want to die?' said the good cleric. 'That's not allowed without my permission.'

'Romping . . .' repeated Marcelina, tormented by her obsession.

'Is that Don Juan Manuel . . .? Now I see you . . . Now I see you . . .' faltered the patient, suddenly lucid. 'Thank God you've come to see me. Will you hear my confession?'

'Now? Leave it until tomorrow.'

'Right now . . .'

'You are in a hurry, aren't you! It makes no difference whether it's one day or another.'

The wretched woman seemed to have found some relief in her happiness at seeing the priest.

'Shoo,' said Nones wittily to the brother and sister, 'you two go and romp out there, for Celedonia and I have some talking to do. Her head has cleared; let's take advantage of it.'

The two siblings went out and returned to the parlour. When they entered, the lady in front, him behind, mute and with his hands behind his back, the mahogany woman started with fright and surprise, saying in the harshest tone possible:

'Don't deny it to me now. I quite clearly heard the rustle of skirts, like a woman running to hide.'

'Hey, I'm not in the mood to listen to this ... Leave me in peace ...'

Now that Father Nones, who inhibited him so much, was not present, the ex-chaplain answered his sister with scornful gestures and words.

'I tell you she's here.'

'All right, let her be here then ... You're insufferable ... You try the patience of a saint.'

Seeing that Marcelina was calmly sitting down on the sofa, like someone ready to stay there a long time, Don Pedro lost that diabolical temper of his and with the hot-headedness that had been so harmful to him in his life, he seized the lady by the arm and shook her, shouting:

'Look here, sister, stand up and clear off ... Get out, my blood's boiling and I can't bear you any longer.'

'Stand, I certainly will, I'll stand,' replied the mahogany figure, rising stiffly to her feet. 'I'll stand guard until I see her leave and have your sins confirmed.'

Don Pedro had turned his back on her. She followed him with her gaze. Her face, that roughly hewn block, that bas-relief devoid of both art and grace, did not wear an expression of hatred, or affection, or anything at all, when her wooden lips terminated the visit with these words:

'I shall not withdraw and go home until I know for certain whether you're really wicked or I've been mistaken. I'm after the truth, you brute, and for the sake of the truth, what wouldn't I do? I don't want to live in error. Since you're throwing me out of here, I'll have to station myself in the street and one of two things will happen: either she comes out, in which case I'll see her, or she doesn't come out, in which case she won't be home at eight o'clock, the time when I happen to know a certain person is to visit her . . . Since you always think ill of people, you think I intend to tell tales . . . Oh! How little you know me! Not one word will come out of this mouth that could offend anybody, not even the most unworthy, sinful and heartless. I say neither yes nor no; I neither make nor break anyone's good name. But I want to know, I want to know, I want to know . . .'

Repeating this last phrase twelve times or more, which constituted a synthesis of her ferocious curiosity, a sort of concupiscence compatible with her pious habits, she left at a slow, deliberate pace.

When the door was heard to close, slammed behind her, Amparo came out of her hiding place. Her eyes were wild and her pallor was sepulchral.

'There's no salvation for me,' she murmured, dropping onto the sofa.

The barbarian looked at her sympathetically.

'Did you hear the last thing she said?'

'Yes . . . either I don't go out, or she'll see me go out.'

'Marcelina is capable of standing guard the whole night. I know her. She's made of wood, you see . . .! There's no soul there, you see, all there is is rabid curiosity. She'd give her right hand to see you come out. Neither cold, nor rain, nor your despair, nor my shame will put her off.'

That irregularly shaped abode had just one room that over-looked Fe Street. It was a poky little one, situated at the end of the zigzagging passage. This room served as a dining room for Polo during the summer, because it was the coolest in the place. In winter it was forlorn and empty. They both went there, creeping down the passage so that Nones should not hear them; and through the narrow window they looked out to the street. The panes were misted over by the cold and Amparo cleaned them with her handkerchief. On the opposite pavement and in a doorway with a locked door behind her, next to the apothecary, Marcelina was seated, like the beggars who wait to ambush the passer-by.

'What a horrible sentinel!'

'There she'll stay until tomorrow,' said Polo. 'That's the way God made her.'

They returned to the parlour. As they stole along the passage like thieves, they heard Don Juan Manuel's hushed voice and the patient's muffled monosyllables. They passed by with extreme caution so as not to make any noise, him trying to prevent his boots from squeaking, her picking up her skirts to avoid the slightest rustle.

In the parlour, they sat down facing one another, equally disheartened and dejected. She could not manage to make a decision, nor could he suggest one. So many contretemps had rained down upon her in succession that she had become almost idiotic and as far as Polo was concerned, he only gave signs of life through the tenacity of his gaze upon her ... So beautiful and lost to him! The thoughts of the unfortunate fellow oscillated, like a pendulum swinging between the good that he was losing and that long journey that he was irrevocably to undertake.

'What time is it?' asked Amparo, breaking that utterly miserable silence.

'Half past seven ... almost twenty to eight. You're a prisoner.'

'No, for goodness' sake!' she exclaimed, standing up anxiously. 'I'm going. Let her see me ... My conscience is clear.'

But she sat down again. Her irresoluteness had never manifested itself so clearly as it did then. More time passed, all silence and mute anxiety. When they least feared it, an extremely tall and venerable figure, swathed in black, with white hair and gimlet eyes, appeared framed in the doorway ... It was Father Nones, whose footsteps could not be heard when he walked because he wore rope-soled shoes. The sight of this apparition did not make much of an impression upon them. She was so overwhelmed that she nearly, nearly glimpsed in the presence of the good priest, a means of salvation. The brute made no movement whatsoever and waited for his friend's attack. The friend went slowly over to him, put his hand on his shoulder and squeezed it. There was no telling if these words from Nones were terribly severe or familiar and jesting: 'You villain, so this is how you behave ...!'

The cleric's flexible spirit permits us to have doubts about the meaning of his phrases. Without waiting for a reply, he added: 'You won't trick me again.'

But the most curious part was that, letting go of his friend's collar, he went and stood in front of him and making a threatening movement with his two arms, rather like a boxer, he snapped:

'Even at my age, old as I am, and with you looking like a ruffian . . . I can still cut you down to size, my friend.'

Whatever one says about good old Nones, his eccentric ways and idiosyncratic impulses, none of it can be too far-fetched to credit. Those fortunate enough to have known him are well aware of his capabilities. It was upon seeing him do such strange things and hearing his words that Amparo had the worst fright of her life, thinking: 'Now he'll turn against me and give me a sermon that will kill me.'

But Nones contented himself by looking at her, as they say Martínez de la Rosa used to look, but with the difference that Nones did not wear spectacles.

Polo wordlessly took his friend by the arm and led him away to the inner part of the house. Amparo realised they were going to look out to the street. Following them down the passage at a distance, she heard Don Juan Manuel laughing. Then the two chatted together for a long while. The one doing most of the talking was Polo, in a sad, droning voice; but the girl could not hear what they were saying. The dialogue lasted close to half an hour and she, choked with impatience, felt unhappy staying there but could not make up her mind to leave. In that long interval, there was a knock at the door and Amparo, whose fear of great evils had stifled her fear of little ones, opened it. It was two women who lived nearby coming to see Celedonia. They went into the patient's room, making a great commotion.

From the parlour, Amparo then heard Nones's voice. He had gone back into Celedonia's room and was saying: 'I wonder if you could set up a little altar in here, for we're going to bring God over tonight . . . Even though she's not going to die, far from it, she wants to receive God and that never goes amiss.'

When the cleric and his colleague came back into the drawing room, the latter said that the sentinel had not moved from her post.

Inferno looked at both of them, revealing in her eyes all the irresoluteness, all the timidity, all the weakness in her soul, which had not come into the world to face difficulties.

'Out, out!' said Nones, picking up his enormous hat. 'I'm blowed if you're needed here. We shall go out together; have no fear.'

He said this in the most natural tone imaginable and turning to Polo:

'Keep in mind, you old rake, what's going to enter this house tonight. Great sobriety, all right? I'll be back in half an hour. And you . . .!'

When he said *and you* in such a rough voice, confronting the timorous woman, she thought the sky was falling in on her; she burst out crying like a fool.

'Well anyway, I shan't say anything for now either,' added the cleric calmly and deliberately. 'I'll deal with *you*, Pedro, myself . . . Let's go.'

Nones and Amparo went in front, with Polo behind lighting their way, for the stairs were pitch dark. The idea that he would never see her again made the barbarian come within inches of doing or saying something rash. But he found the strength to contain himself. The timorous woman did not turn round even once to see what she was leaving behind. When they reached the first step, Nones looked apprehensively at the steep staircase. Seeing that the girl wanted to go ahead to support him, he said to her:

'No, you can take hold of my arm if you wish . . . I'm frightened at nothing.'

But she, attentive and respectful of the elderly, positioned herself next to him saying:

'No, you will lean on me . . . Careful.'

And Nones, turning to see his friend holding the light, burst out laughing and did not hesitate to make this observation:

'What a picture we make! . . . Aren't we a fine pair? . . . As though we were just off to Capellanes dance hall.'

The hollow, sarcastic chuckle could be heard all the way down the stairs.

When they reached the doorway, Don Juan Manuel whispered to Amparo: 'There she is; take no notice, don't look. If you're with me, she won't dare say a word.'

And he was right: the fearful watch did not stir; all she did was look.

When they took their first steps into the street, Nones, at the top of his rough, rasping voice, first gave a great, artificial cough and then exclaimed: 'What extraordinary bollards they have these days . . .!'

In spite of her terrible state of alarm, Amparo could not help but smile. She gave the cleric the pavement; but he gallantly refused to take it. Then he spoke in an absolutely natural tone about things also very natural, as if the company he was keeping were the most normal in the world.

'That poor Celedonia, how poorly she is! . . . At seventy-eight, evidently . . . I'm also starting to prepare myself and I think every day that dawns is to be my last . . . Happy is he who sees death approach with equanimity and doesn't have either in his soul or in his business affairs any loose ends for that rogue Satan to seize hold of! Do try to organise your life with death in mind . . . Wrap up well, it's cold . . . I'll walk with you until we find a carriage. Yes, you'd better take a cab . . . Have you any money? Because if not, I can offer you one peseta that I have on me . . .'

'Oh! Many thanks, I have some money. There's a carriage over there.'

'Driver! . . . Off you go. God be with you. Health, wealth, and good behaviour. I'm going to the church to take the Viaticum to that poor woman . . . Good night.'

When Amparo got home, Doña Nicanora told her that a gentleman had called at eight o'clock ... that gentleman, and that tiring of ringing the bell, he had gone away. This came as no surprise to the girl; she feared it; but she was no less upset for all that. What would her fiancé think of her? At that moment perhaps he and Rosalía would be talking about her in the box at the theatre. What would they say? Luckily she could explain her absence with the lie about tirelessly pursuing her sister to bring her back to the path of righteousness. She spent the whole night in a state of agitation the like of which can only be appreciated by those who have been in a similar predicament. She was no longer in any doubt that catastrophes would overtake her and that the matter of the marriage would turn out badly. But she could not think of any way of avoiding this. The great recourse of the frank discussion with Caballero seemed to her, not only harder and harder, but also belated, and as such, likely to bring derision upon her sooner than forgiveness. What she had heard Doña Marcelina saying was enough to drive her to madness. In her delirium, she thought that the said wooden lady would go out into the streets calling out like a town-crier with Amparito's whole story on paper, as the blind do when they sing their wares of stories of crimes and robberies.

It was day by the time her tiredness overwhelmed her. She slept for a few hours, and once she had tidied up and made herself ready to go out, the clock had struck eleven in the morning. She had resolved to go to Los Angeles Hill, because if she did not go, Mrs Pipaón's suspicions would be greater ... Would she find Caballero there? ... Would she find Doña Marcelina, who had already been eating cakes and drinking wine there the previous day? These thoughts took away her desire to go; but Lord above! If she didn't go ... Be brave and forward march.

When she went in she was like a sleepwalker, due to the upset and the lack of sleep. She did not take in what she heard; her movements were like those of an automaton.

'Well, dearest,' said the lady. 'You're as solemn as a man condemned today. You look as though you haven't slept all night. So? . . . Did you find that villain of a sister of yours in the end? As you weren't at home when Agustín went to collect you, I suppose last night's wandering was on the long side.'

These words might have been said without being ill-intentioned; but to the girl they seemed astute and cheeky. She apologised as best she could, getting muddled and explaining her uneasiness and the reasons for her sleeplessness in the most incoherent way. What attracted her attention most was that the lady was not angry, but on the contrary, in excellent humour and almost exultant.

'Well I rose very early,' said Rosalía with an inner smugness rather like someone with good news to report. 'I've been at Buena Dicha church all morning . . . Look, do be good enough to go to the kitchen and wash me these two handkerchiefs.'

It had been some time since our Emperine had been ordered to do such things. When she came back having carried out that job, Mrs Bringas said to her:

'I have a lot of sewing to do today. I'm determined to alter the skirt of the ballgown . . . I can see you're acting frightened . . . Calm yourself, girl; it won't be the end of the world.'

Each of these obscure phrases was like a dagger thrust into the nervous woman. They ate in silence, for although Rosalía tried to make the event more pleasant with the witticisms inspired by her inexplicable gleefulness, Don Francisco was as solemn as a pallbearer. Amparo observed in her kindly protector's physiognomy, a sadness that terrified her. Several times did she address her words to him, but she obtained no reply from Don Francisco. He did not even look at her once. This cut her to the quick, confirming her suspicion that the hour of her undoing was nigh.

'The time has come,' said Rosalía when they were left alone, 'for us to step up the pressure. The whole skirt has to be decorated by tomorrow . . . Don't get distracted, there's no time for airs and graces. Agustín isn't coming today. Well dear, as he believes you to be so busy out in the streets looking for your sister in every nook and cranny, he's also going for a walk. It's natural.'

Later on she ordered her back to the kitchen, and she, with exemplary and extreme humility and submission, obeyed without a murmur. Among the many commands she gave her was this one:

'Make a cup of lime-blossom tea and bring it here.'

When Amparo brought the cup and presented it to the lady, the latter, smiling maliciously, said:

'But it's for you . . .'

'For me!'

'Yes, drink it up to calm those nerves . . . I don't think you should be all mysterious with me . . . We'll do everything possible so that Agustín, that good soul, doesn't find out anything. It's a thing of the past and very shameful, so it must remain a secret within the family.'

'What?' murmured our Emperine like a cadaver that can speak . . .

'You won't want *me* to tell you the story, blockhead . . . But if you insist . . .'

Thereupon, Amparo dropped to the floor out cold, as if she had been shot in the temple by a revolver. The cup was smashed, the lime tea spilt on Rosalía's wrap.

'What's this, a little nervous breakdown?' she said. 'Look what you've done to my wrap. But come now, are you really in a faint or is this play-acting? . . . Amparo, Amparito, for goodness' sake, dear, don't alarm us . . . I shan't say anything. For goodness' sake, child!'

Recovering her senses, the girl sat up. Her tribulations resolved themselves in dry, convulsive weeping. Sobs and groans choked her; but her eyes remained dry.

'You'll get over it by crying. Let yourself go, have a good cry,' said Rosalía. 'You had better get up, dear, and go into the small parlour. You can stretch out on the sofa.'

She helped her up and they both went into the small parlour.

'Lie down, rest for a little while and cry as much as you want. I'll put this towel on the headrest of my sofa so you don't wet it with your tears . . . How do you feel? Any better? . . . Fainting fits are outmoded now. It's in poor taste . . . Would you like to be left on your own for a moment? Would you like some water?'

She lavished upon her, it is fair to say, the best care. Then she left her on her own, because somebody had come in. What Amparo thought and felt during that time when she was on her own, is indescribable. Her whole soul was shame; shame was her mind, and the horrible heat in her skin and her face, shame as well. From the small parlour she could hear the confused voices of Mrs Bringas and the visitor in the next room. It was Mr Torres. What would they be talking about? Maybe her.

When the lady returned, Amparo's morale was in the same state. She gave the impression that after that crisis, she had gone paralytic, her mind clouded. She did not move from the sofa, she gave no sign of understanding what was being said to her, and only answered with anguished looks.

'Are you over your embarrassment yet?' said Rosalía, bending down to her. 'Mind you, given the magnitude of the thing, I quite understand. You should have had the courage to tell that angel the truth right from the outset and disabuse him. Now it would be extremely dangerous for you to talk to him about those horrors. You don't really know him. He's the most rigorous man, the greatest enemy of any kind of messy business . . . For him, everything has to be in order, everything in absolute conformity with morality. And as he loves you so blindly, if you talk to him and remove his blindfold, I believe it would be like shooting him down with a pistol . . .'

No answer, apart from with her eyes.

'Why are you looking at me like that? . . . Have you lost your tongue? Are you feeling better? . . . Well, pay close attention to what I'm telling you. The best you can do now is keep quiet, and we shall try to ensure that that Simple Simon finds nothing out . . . What will be remedied by a scandal? . . . And have no fear that Doña Marcelina will sell you out. She's an excellent lady and very pious, incapable of harming anyone, not even her enemies. And if she wanted, dear, she could certainly sink you . . . because . . . don't get upset again; if you're getting worked up, I'll say no more.'

Amparo's eyes revealed a dread similar to that of a person with a gun pointing at him.

'Don't look at me like that, you're frightening me . . . Do you want the cup of lime tea now? . . . Well, as I was saying, Doña Marcelina has two letters, two scrappy sheets of paper that you wrote to a certain person . . . But you may be sure she won't show them to anyone. She's a lady of great delicacy. Why are you closing your eyes, screwing up your eyelids like that? . . . Don't be like that; have no fear. For your information, the same

Miss Polo has told me that they will have to chop her as fine as mincemeat before she'll show anyone those little documents . . . And I believe her. She doesn't like making trouble for people . . . What? . . . You've decided to cry now? That's right, that's right, it will do you good.'

The hapless woman was shedding a few burning tears, which struggled to come out of her reddened eyes. Rosalía's kindness went as far as taking her hand and stroking it. At that hour of anguish, the sinner had moments of cruel despair and others in which, as if distracted from her suffering, she noticed things alien to her, or things related to her by only very remote and confused ties. This lack of continuity in strength or vehemence is a condition of human pain, for if it were not, no temperament could cope. Amparo observed at times how pretty and well dressed Rosalía was at home. This phenomenon was increasing with every day that passed and on that one, her hairstyle, her wrap, the fit of her bodice and all the rest revealed a care and attention verging on vanity. Since one always lets oneself wander far in this observation game, without meaning to, the unfortu-nate woman also noted, through that thick, burning veil of her affliction, that Rosalía was sporting on her person certain objects acquired for her, for the fiancée.

'What are you looking at?' said our dear Mrs Bringas; 'have you noticed this ring that Agustín bought for you? Don't go thinking that I'm the sort who appropriates other people's things. Cousin told me yesterday that I could take it for myself . . .'

The fiancée made no reply at all. Mishaps of such minor importance only attracted her attention for the most fleeting moments. The lady was not leaving her side, fearful that she might be overtaken by another faint. When she was least expecting it, Amparo sat up and said:

'I want to go home.'

'Thank the Lord you've found your tongue. I thought you'd been struck dumb . . . Believe you me, there have been cases of people losing their voice, if not their mind, through a great dishonour. Do you really want to leave? . . . I don't think it's a bad idea. That is, you go on home and you get into bed and try to rest. You may have a slight temperature.'

Amparo stood up with difficulty.

'Do you want Prudencia to go with you?'

'No . . . I can walk alone '

'Bah! There's not much the matter with you apart from over-indulgence . . . Do you need anything?'

'No, thank you.'

'Agustín is bound to go and see you as soon as he finds out you're unwell . . . I'll find a way of managing to finish off my dress on my own. Don't worry about that, and don't force yourself to come tomorrow if you don't feel well. I'll get a seamstress in . . .'

She helped her to put on her shawl and her veil and seemed to be pushing her out as though she wished to see her leave as soon as possible.

'Leave by the drawing room,' she said affectionately. 'You won't want to be seen by Prudencia, or Paquito and Joaquín, who are wandering about in the passages . . . Goodbye.'

Amparo went downstairs step by step. She did not lack the strength to walk, but she was afraid she might fall down in the street, and she hugged the buildings so as to be able to lean against the walls if her head began to spin.

'If this indisposition that I'm experiencing,' she was thinking, 'if this horrible coldness, if this gall that I have in my mouth, were the beginning of an illness from which I died, I'd be glad . . . But I don't want to die without being able to say to him: "I'm not as wicked as I seem".' Shut in her house, she went to bed fully clothed and piled on all the covers she could find. How cold and how hot she was at the same time! . . . She was in no doubt that Rosalía, one way or another, would make sure the story reached Caballero. Though simple and fairly ingenuous, she was not so much so that she believed the hypocritical words of the proud lady. That the ignominious scandal was on its way was plain to see. But if he visited her, if he asked her to explain herself, if she did so and her pained repentance was matched by an indulgence preceding forgiveness . . . Oh! How difficult this was! That man, good as he was, could not read her soul, because for that sort of reading matter, the only eyes that are not myopic are God's.

Amparo had little hope of a solution now; but she was still counting on Caballero coming to see her . . . Surely, in that predicament, she would not be able to dissimulate further and the truth would issue from her lips. If on the contrary, Agustín did not come, it was a sign that he had been told something shocking and ... All that afternoon, the hapless Emperine waited, counting the minutes. But night fell and Agustín did not come.

'He has undoubtedly been at Rosalía's this afternoon,' she kept thinking, shivering and faint. 'If he doesn't come, it's because he doesn't want to see me any more.'

'Because he doesn't want to see me any more,' she kept repeating in terrible distress. 'I'm so ashamed! There's nothing left for me but to die. How shall I have the courage to mix with people?'

She spent the night in feverish insomnia, without eating, crying at times for a spell, launching her imagination on the wildest wanderings at other times. The following day, her soul once more cherished hopes that Agustín would come. Counting the hours, she made ready to receive him. But the hours did not let up and plodded by gloomily, without anyone coming to the wretched house. Not the gentleman with his respectful affection, nor the servant with some message or note; nobody, not even a message from Rosalía to see how she was! . . . Every time she heard a noise on the stairs, she trembled with hope. But her funereal solitude was uninterrupted during that horribly sad day. To make it even sadder, it did not stop raining for a moment. Amparo thought that the sun had clouded over forever and that the liquid shroud in which Nature was wrapped was like an extension of the same gloom she felt in her soul.

In the afternoon, she was no longer thinking but delirious. She no longer felt cold, but had an extremely uncomfortable burning sensation in her whole body. She went from one end of her home to the other in a state of morbid disquiet and on occasion saw objects upside down, inverted. Even her father's portrait was standing on its head. Lines all wavered before her sore, dry eyes and the very rain was like threads of water ascending to the sky. Then she put on her best clothes, ate some dry bread and repeatedly wet her head to calm that fire. All hope lost and certain of her shame, she decided it was a great folly to preserve her life and there was no better solution than to tear herself away from it by any of the means known for this purpose. She reviewed the different kinds of suicide; knife, poison, charcoal asphyxiation, throwing oneself out of the window. Oh! She was not brave enough to stab herself and see

her own blood run out. Nor did she have the strength to shoot
herself in the temple with a pistol. The certain and painless
effects of charcoal attracted her more. She had heard that the
person who submitted to its poisonous action, locking himself
in with an unraked brazier and making sure air could not get in,
fell into a sweet sleep, and stayed in that delightful sleep with
no death throes . . . Fine; she definitely chose charcoal . . . But
her thoughts very soon took a different direction. The desperate
woman had an efficacious weapon that was also easy to use . . .
She remembered about it as she looked at her father's portrait,
which was now the right way up again. When the good
Pharmacy doorman was terminally ill, he was afflicted by a
tenacious neuralgia that did not yield to belladonna, or mor-
phine. To soothe his horrible pain and give him some rest,
Moreno Rubio had prescribed a very powerful medicament, for
external use, which was administered by placing cloths soaked
in it on the patient's forehead. When he gave the prescription,
the doctor had said Amparo: 'Very careful with this. Anyone
who drinks a fraction of the contents of the phial, will go
straight to the other world without a murmur within five
minutes.' The orphan had not kept any of this terrible drug; but
she did have the prescription and as soon as she remembered it,
she fetched it from a drawer in the chest where she had various
mementoes of her father. As she unfolded the paper, she could
not help taking fright somewhat. The most determined suicide
does not look with absolute calm at the scissors stolen from the
Fates. The prescription said: *Potassium cyanide – two grammes
. . . Distilled water – two hundred grammes . . . External use.*

'Within five minutes . . . without a murmur . . . that's to say,
without any pain,' thought Amparo, so crazed as to look upon
the paper as a sad friend. Before tomorrow's out.'

She put it away in the pocket of her outfit, resolving to go to
the apothecary herself in quest of her remedy. But when? . . .
Not that afternoon; nor in the night. It would be premature.
The next day . . . without fixing a time . . .

The solitude in which she found herself continued all afternoon, more sinister and dreadful with every hour that passed.
Night came and that damp sky darkened to look like mud. One
might have thought that grass was going to sprout from the
rooftops, and from above one could hear the splashing of
passing feet in the muddy streets.

It struck six, seven, eight. Not a living soul came to the door to pull the green bellrope. Nine o'clock and no one was coming! At ten, footsteps; but the footsteps disappeared on another floor. At eleven, doubts, disquiet, delirium. Twelve chimed twelve times on the University clock, and the ultimatum for hope that she had given herself was reached. One o'clock passed briefly and slunk off, getting muddled with half past twelve. On hearing two o'clock, our Emperine's deranged mind repeated the idea of that drunkard who said: *One o'clock twice? There's something wrong with that clock.* Three o'clock was accompanied by distant cockcrows, and four followed so close on three o'clock's heels that both seemed an oversight by time or else twin hours. A brief period of lethargy concealed the sound of five o'clock from Amparo. But suddenly she could see the ceiling of her home. Day was beginning to come in, that is to say, another day, the one following the one that had passed. What a silly thing . . .! For on that day, she was to kill herself without fail. The day dawned raining again, the earth drinking the tears of the heavens.

Amparo did not have to dress because she had spent the night fully clothed on the sofa. She herself noticed that she could not do a single thing right. To pick up a towel, she picked up the candlestick. She went to make chocolate and could not remember how it was done. Instead of going into the kitchen, she went into the bedroom, and wanting to put on her pretty boots, with pearl grey legs, she only noticed after much walking around the place looking for them that she had them on already.

In the end she breakfasted on raw chocolate and water. She had no matches, because she had thrown them out of the window, thinking she was throwing away the empty box.

'Now,' she thought, recalling the events she had once read in *la Correspondencia*, 'when the neighbours see that days are going by and the door isn't opened, they'll inform the authorities . . . lots of people will come here, they'll break the lock and find me . . . there . . . stretched out on the sofa . . . white as a sheet . . . rigid.'

Looking at herself in the mirror, she added:

'I'll put on the black silk dress . . . which I've never worn yet.'

Eight o'clock, nine o'clock! . . . That wretched University clock would not let one hour go by . . . At ten the suicide had put on her black silk dress, after having tidied her hair a little ... although on reflection, what for? ...

'I'll go to the apothecary in Ancha Street ... No; it had better be the one in Pez Street.'

Lord above! ... She thought she would jump as high as the ceiling with the fright ... The doorbell had rung! ... Open it, open it at once. It was Don Francisco Bringas. The great Thiers had never been there and as he was so good, when Amparo saw him, her heart told her that he could not come for ill. Unable to contain her joy, she ran to embrace him. She felt as though years had gone by without her having seen a friendly face. Something terribly important was happening when Don Francisco came to visit her.

'My child,' said the dear gentleman, letting himself be embraced, 'I maintain that it's all slander ... Why at first sheer surprise disconcerted me, but then I said, "Lies, lies" ... Some things are so horrible that they cannot be believed ...'

'They cannot be believed,' repeated Amparo, becoming sad again.

'And as you haven't appeared at home, I've come to tell you to make haste to vindicate yourself, to exonerate yourself, to prove your innocence. Oh, my child, you can't imagine the state poor Agustín is in!'

Amparo was as if dead ... With a groan she uttered the two words: 'He knows! ...'

'Yes ... He believes ... They've made him believe ... What an infamous story! Rosalía, as she's so credulous, so naïve, also accuses you, although she exonerates you; but I'm not giving in to this, I believe none of it, I reject it all, absolutely all of it.'

He underlined his words with his finger in the air. How grateful the sinner was for his indulgent stubbornness!

'Well yes, poor Agustín looks like you could knock him down with a feather ... Between them all, they've filled his head with hot air. I believe it was Torres who took the gossip to Mompous, and Mompous must have told my cousin, claiming he was doing him a favour. I assure you that this makes me furious. Rosalía denies that she had any part in it and I believe it: she's incapable ... Agustín was at our place all day yesterday ... insisting that Rosalía tell him ... My wife couldn't say anything against you ... On the contrary, she was defending you ... The poor man's a pitiful sight. I've just come from his place now and if you go there straight away, if you don't waste time, you can clear his head of what's tormenting him . . . Come along.'

'I!' murmured Amparo like an idiot, resisting Bringas's affectionate effort to take her with him by pulling her arm.

'Won't you come? . . . Where does that leave us? Will you let yourself be slandered like this? . . . And you as cool as a cucumber!'

'Not cool . . .'

'Because it's slander . . . slander! . . .' exclaimed Thiers, his gimlet eyes upon her, their gaze seeming to sharpen as they passed through his glasses.

'Yes . . . slander . . . I mean . . . no . . . I must explain . . . it seems . . .'

Amparo was getting tangled in her own words.

'Are you coming or not?' fretted Bringas, trying to take her almost by force.

'Now?' she replied, turning the colour of the whitest wax. 'I have to go to the apothecary . . .'

'It's true you're ill . . . You'll have your cure afterwards, dear . . . You look pale to me . . . You must make an effort. What, doesn't your dishonour affect you? You can look on calmly as people say such horrors about you?'

'Oh, no . . .! If they're horrors, they're not true.'

'Well come along . . . For your own sake, for my cousin's sake, I want this cleared up. If you don't come soon, the thing might get complicated. There's trouble brewing, my dear child. If you don't go soon, Agustín, who's half-crazed, will go and talk to your enemy, and just imagine what hot air that individual will fill his head with . . . There's still time . . . Hurry, go there at once. Agustín's at home. I left him there in such a state of despondency that he looks like a schoolboy who's failed his exams. You get there, you throw yourself at his feet, you weep, you beg him to listen to you and not to pay any heed to evil tongues, you tell him whatever there is to tell, if there actually is some slight, unusually liberal trifle . . . Anything's possible, the ways of the world . . . Listen carefully; you tell him whatever things come straight from your heart, tender things, truly felt; and that's how you'll capture him and keep him . . .'

Amparo was looking at her protector like someone who has no ideas favourable or in opposition to what she is hearing.

'But have you turned into an idiot?' he cried, bursting with impatience and raising his voice as one does when speaking to a deaf person. 'Look; you're going to lose him . . . I've told you that only you can capture and keep him, giving him explanations, if there are any, caressing him and putting your pretty face before him so that his passion is stirred . . . If you don't make your mind up to it, I don't know what will happen. They've told him and Rosalía swears it wasn't her; they've told him that Doña Marcelina Polo possesses two letters of yours, addressed to I don't know whom; there you have the man desperate to see them, to have some proof of your . . . I maintain it's slander . . . But, alas, Lord knows if that blessed lady, who's not fond of you, won't make him see white as black.'

Mechanically, Amparo said these words:

'He's been to see Doña Marcelina . . .'

'No, woman, no, no,' shouted Bringas, still thinking he was speaking to someone deaf; 'but he will go. He sent a message with Felipe this morning, asking at what time he could see that lady, and they answered saying twelve o'clock . . . It's a quarter past eleven already. Put your shawl on, there's not a minute to lose. I breakfasted with him. The poor soul was eating nothing . . .'

Without waiting to reason any more, Bringas took the veil and the shawl that were on a chair and put them on her. Amparo, more and more devoid of a will of her own, of any discernment or decisiveness, let Don Francisco do it. He took her by the arm and led her to the door. They went out; they locked the door.

'Because it's nonsense,' said Bringas going down the stairs, 'that you should allow yourself to be intimidated like this, when with just one word maybe . . . You'll still find him there, if we're careful . . . So you know, you speak to his heart. If there is anything, if there's some ancient little hindrance, the truth, Amparo, always put the truth first. Take good account of Agustín's character, his rectitude, his abhorrence for a messy business. The idea of being deceived drives him into a fury . . . He'll forgive the greatest crime if it's confessed, rather than a trivial slip that's concealed. Take good account of it, and have some guts, have some dash . . .'

The girl was hearing this as one hears the drone of a distant storm. She was going along the street like an automaton. She thought that all the people she saw participated in that anxiety of hers, which was so excessive as to verge upon imbecility.

'Hurry up a bit, dear, hurry . . .' Thiers was saying. 'It's twenty to twelve. We'll take a carriage. I'll drop you at the door. I'm not coming up with you, because for this delicate encounter, it's right that the two of you should be all on your own . . . I'm going to my office.'

During the brief trip in the carriage, he repeated to her the same exhortations over and over again. 'Careful, dear, careful . . . sentiment and sincerity . . . Don't get muddled . . . don't contradict yourself. If there's anything to tell, face up to it. If there's nothing, have no mercy on the slanderers, be hard on them, pummel them, don't waver . . .!'

They reached Arenal Street and both alighted from the carriage. At the door, Bringas thought it inopportune to admonish her again and when he had seen her go up, he left for the Ministry.

CHAPTER 34

Amparo went up and when she saw that exquisitely beautiful, wide, varnished, mahogany door, she imagined the scene that was going to take place on the other side of it and the things she was going to say. Never had she seen a more venerable door. Neither a holy cathedral's, nor even those of the Pope's palace, nor, she could almost say, those of heaven were its equal. Merciful God! Would that eventually be the door of her house?

She placed her hand on the shiny metal bell pull. 'Will this be,' she thought, 'the first and last time I ring here?'

She had no time for further reflection. Felipe opened the door.

'Your master . . .?'

'He's not here . . . But do come in . . .'

Amparo entered. And he was not there! . . . Fate was frowning, foretelling disaster.

These jokes played on us by time are so tiresome! These apparent discrepancies of the eternal clock, sometimes making people's steps coincide, sometimes not, forever thwarting human desires, now for our benefit, now to our detriment, are the most readily visible part of the grand reality of time. We should not properly appreciate the idea of continuity without this frequency with which our steps get out of gear with that infinite cog that never wears down. Art, abusing Perchance for its own ends, has not managed to discredit this hidden logic, upon whose terms the machinery of public and private events rests, just as these come to be the pedestal for the organism we call History.

'Do you know where he's gone?' said our Emperine, going through the sitting room.

'To Doña Marcelina Polo's in Estrella Street. I went there this morning to make an appointment and it was set for twelve o'clock.'

'Twelve o'clock! . . .'

'Yes, miss . . . I don't know how you missed him. He hasn't

been gone ten minutes. He must be going along Hita Street or Perro alley by now. Did you come via the Hill?'

'Yes, and in a carriage.'

'Wait for him . . . he'll be back before long.'

She went from the sitting room to the small parlour and then to another one that was . . . hers. Ironies of destiny!

Centeno was moving away . . .

'Felipe.'

'Miss . . .'

'Nothing, nothing. It's just . . .'

She had an impulse to go out again and run home. In her bewildered mind, she suddenly saw two documents written by her long since, two short letters, full of foolishness and the most shameful things conceivable . . . Her heart was not a heart, it was a crazy little machine that was racing madly and was going to break at any moment . . . Farewell hope! At that moment Caballero was entering the lodgings of the mahogany woman; both were talking . . .

'Felipe.'

'Miss . . .'

'I'm leaving . . . Show me the way out. I can't find my way around this labyrinth.'

She took a few steps. Her strength failed her and she dropped into an armchair. She feared she would lose consciousness.

'Are you unwell? . . . Shall I call Doña Marta?'

'No, for goodness' sake, don't call anyone. Look, would you be good enough to bring me a small glass of water?'

'Right away.'

In the brief while that Felipe was out of the room, Amparo allowed her gaze to wander around the luxurious room in which she found herself. 'This is where I was going to live, I,' she thought, whilst the fierce disappointment in the bottom of her soul repulsed the savage delight that wanted to come in. 'This is where I was going to live . . . well, this is where I want to end my life.'

'Thank you,' she said to Felipe, taking the glass of water and putting it on the table. 'Now you're going to do me another favour.'

'Anything you say.'

'Will you be good enough,' said Amparo slowly, searching in her pocket and taking out a piece of paper, 'to go to the

apothecary, which is in this very street, two doors down . . .
Take the prescription; bring me this medicine . . . It's something
I take every day for my nerves, you know . . . Wait, take the
money . . . On the double, I'll be waiting here . . .'

'I'm going right away.'

From the passage, Centeno returned and said somewhat
awkwardly:

'So you don't get bored . . .'

'What?'

'I'm just going to wind up the musical box with the funny
birds. That way you'll be entertained while you're alone.'

The miniature orchestra began to sound and the birds,
opening their little beaks and flapping their wings, seemed to be
singing in that glade enclosed within a bell glass. Very proud of
his idea, Felipe went out.

The hapless woman scarcely fixed her attention on the little
birds for a split second. Then she took to thinking about her
resolve, which was unshakeable. In five minutes it would all be
over. When he returned he would find her dead. What would he
say? What would he do? . . . Because he would be furious when
he came home, determined to kill her or to say terrible things to
her, which was far worse than death. How could she tolerate
such a great dishonour? . . . Impossible, impossible. By killing
herself, it was all swiftly brought to an end. In her preoccupation
with suicide, the similarity between this and episodes in plays
and novels did not fail to occur to her. This momentarily cooled
her homicidal enthusiasm. She abhorred affectation. But remembering the letters, her horror for existence was such that all she
desired was for Felipe to return swiftly so as to have done with
it.

'When Agustín comes in, he'll find me dead.' This idea gave
her a certain mysterious, inner pleasure. It was the last piece of
excitement that, arising from life, was going to blossom and
come to an end in the dark realms of death, like the rockets that
go off, sparks flying, from earth and explode in the heavens.

'And what will he say, what will he think when he sees me
dead? . . . Will he cry, will he be sorry, will he be glad? . . .
Because by this time he's bound to know everything, and he
must despise me as one despises a disgusting worm when one
puts one's foot upon it to squash it . . . He must be seeing it now
. . . Virgin of Sorrow, forgive me for what I'm going to do!'

The cardboard birds, animated by a diabolical mechanism, were giving a deafening commentary to this with their metallic singing and their flapping on the cloth branches. It was like the vibration of a thousand steel needles, shrill music that scratched the brain, leaving it giddy. Amparo felt she had all the birds inside her head.

For an instant, the monomania of the suicide softened, allowing her to contemplate the pretty room. Those chairs, those mirrors, that carpet! ... To die there was a delight ... relatively speaking ... Oh, Holy Mary, if it weren't for those two letters ...! Why didn't she die before writing them? ...

At this point Felipe arrived. He was carrying a small phial containing whitish, slightly milky-looking water. He put it on the table, where the glass of water still stood with some meringue sweetener and a silver spoon.

'Anything else I can do for you?' he asked, raising his voice a little, because the din from the little birds forced him to do so.

'Be so kind as to bring me paper and an envelope. I have to write a letter.'

'And ink?'

'Or if not, a pencil: it doesn't matter.'

'Do you want anything else?' asked Centeno when he brought what she had asked of him.

'Nothing else. Thank you.'

Wise Aristotle left.

When she found herself alone, Amparo had moments of vacillation; but the idea of the suicide assailed her so strongly after one of these, that she decided to put death between her life and her shame. Doña Marcelina ... the letters! ... This time, she was overtaken by a kind of delirium, and she paced up and down the room in a state of agitation, covering now her eyes, now her ears. She could not see anything; she lost consciousness of everything that was not her perverse idea; there was suddenly a cataclysm in her brain. Over the uproar of her disconcerted reason, the monomania of dying fluttered triumphantly, mistress at last of her spirit and her nerves.

A moment of solemn stupor sprinkled with those piercing notes from the songbirds! The demented woman poured out the water in the glass and added half of the contents of the phial; she drank it down ... What a strange taste! It seemed like ... just like brandy ...! Within five minutes she would be in the kingdom of eternal shades, with a new life, unshackled from the rack of her troubles, with all dishonour behind her, cast down to the world she was abandoning as one casts down a dress on getting into bed.

It occurs to her to go into the adjacent room. It is her bedroom. Proud and almost enchanted marriage bed! There is also a comfortable, wide sofa. She has hardly taken four steps in that room when she notices inside herself a sort of trouble, like a general decomposition. She believes she is fainting; that she is losing consciousness; but no, she doesn't lose it. One minute has passed, no, more ... But then she feels a horrible fear, nature's defence, the potent instinct for self-preservation. To cheer herself she says: 'But I had no choice; I just couldn't live.' The weakness and disconcertedness of her body are increasing so much, that she collapses onto the sofa face down. She notes a great oppression, a desire to weep ... She presses her handkerchief to her mouth and closes her eyes tightly. But she is astonished not to feel sharp pains or nausea. Oh! yes, now she can feel a kind of tickling in her stomach ... Will she suffer great pain? The indisposition is beginning, but it is a slight indisposition. What very good poison this is, it kills peacefully! Suddenly, it seems to her that her vision is clouding over. She opens her eyes and everything looks black. She cannot hear either, and the birds are singing far away, as if they were at the Puerta del Sol ... And then panic grips her so tightly that she sits up and says, 'Shall I ring? Shall I ask for help? It's horrible ... to die like this! What a pity! And also a sin! ...' Hiding her face in her hands, she resolves firmly not to ring. What then, is this the theatre, pray? Afterwards, she feels herself fainting ... her ideas leave her, all of her thoughts leave her, the pulse of her blood leaves her, her entire life, pain and consciousness, sensation and fear, she is fainting, falling asleep, dying ... 'Sweet Virgin,' she thinks with the last thought that escapes, 'take me unto you ...!'

The route by which the suspicions entered the spirit of good Caballero, and after the suspicions, something to confirm them – news, information, and references – is not known for certain. It is believed that that man going by the name of Torres was the one who took the story from the Hill to Mompous's office, and that old Mompous then transported it with his Catalan accent to the ears of Caballero himself, justifying his actions with reasoning appropriate to the situation ... In doing it he was moved by friendship, to put him on his guard. Perhaps it was slander; but as the merchandise was circulating, it was only right and proper to notify the person with the greatest stake in it, for the sake of the honour of his name, etc ... The impression that these revelations made upon the trusting lover, can be imagined by any who know him from these pages, or because they really have had dealings with him. That man of such peaceable appearance could move easily from sombre despondency to puerile fury. Rosalía was afraid of him when she saw him come in that afternoon, three hours after Amparo had gone home after the fainting scene was over. It was Monday afternoon.

Agustín briefly told his cousin what had been said to him and turning an incredible colour, gritting his teeth and clenching his fists, he said: 'If it's a lie, I'll make the swine who invented it pay.'

'Come along, come along, calm down, for Heavens' sake,' said Rosalía. If you take it like that ... if you let yourself be blinded by anger, maybe you'll see things blacker than they are. In these serious situations everyone involved must behave in accordance with their station, and you're a decent, sensible gentleman.'

'By the way you're talking,' said Agustín, his anger unabated, 'I gather you knew about it too ... and until now neither you nor Bringas said a single word to me about it, at least to warn me.'

'We,' rejoined the lady with haughty dignity, 'are not in the habit of talking about what does not concern us, or of giving advice to those who do not ask us for any. How could you expect us to risk discrediting someone in our own family, when by doing so we would give you a lethal blow and when we had no certainty about the fact, nor were able to provide you with any proof? . . . This is a serious matter, dear boy . . . And tell me something: when you noticed her and picked her out to be your wife, did you consult us on such a delicate point, as would have seemed natural? You certainly did not. Off you went to do it all on your own and when we found out you already had it signed, sealed, and delivered.'

As she was saying this and what followed, anyone who had observed Rosalía closely, could have surprised in her, along with the desire to convince her cousin, the no less strongly felt one to display her beauty, set off on this occasion by her smart attire and by well-chosen embellishments and adornments. How she showed her white teeth, how she arched her neck, how she drew herself up to give her well-corseted body a momentary slenderness, were details that you and I, friend reader, would have noticed, but not Caballero, because of the state of his spirit.

'And don't think,' added Rosalía sadly, 'we weren't hurt that you didn't consult us on a matter in which your honour could be compromised . . . You didn't take into account how much we love you, how much we care about you.'

'I'm going to see her,' said Agustín on a sudden impulse and taking no notice of his cousin's tender words. 'The first thing is to hear what she has to say . . .'

'I think you're wasting your time if you go to her house,' declared Rosalía, hastening diligently to contain that natural impulse. 'You won't find her there. I know you won't find her there . . .'

Caballero looked at her as if he had taken leave of his senses.

'I have reasons for knowing and I'll say no more,' added Bringas's wife with studied coldness. 'Go home and don't move from there, for Amparo herself will come to see you and apologise . . . That's what she's promised me at least. She was here this morning the poor thing and I swear I've never been through anything worse in my entire life. It was pitiable to see and hear her. Goodness me, the tears, the sighs! She fainted clean away in my sewing room and I had to bring her in here. She was a veritable Mary Magdalene the way the tears were streaming, a wretched penitent woman ... What pains her the most, my dear, is having deceived you. You mustn't treat her badly; you mustn't be cruel to her, because her pain is very great ... she thinks you're going to kill her ... I've told her you're not an Othello and you won't take it so hard. She's promised me to go to your house and give you the fairest of explanations. The poor girl is well aware that she can no longer be your wife, but that you should despise her drives her to distraction ... She's an unfortunate, who amidst all that, retains a certain sense of decency ...'

Agustín turned full circle twice, a sign of horrible despair, as it also is of drunkenness. He left without adding another word and retreated into his house. Arnáiz and Mompous went there that night to play billiards and during the game, the man from the Indies affected absolute peace of mind. He even seemed more communicative than usual.

The next day, Tuesday, a sad rainy day, Agustín spent the whole morning pacing up and down in his study. He was certainly expecting a visit of significance; but the one he received was from Rosalía, looking very spruce, very youthful, very fresh and as well turned out as when she went to the theatre.

'You're not well,' she said with affectionate frankness. 'I understand why, because these things make their mark. I think you must calm down and try to forget all about it ... A man like you ...! Yes, you'll find women by the thousand ... and a thousand times prettier, a thousand times more interesting ... And anyway: has she been here? I assume not, because I sent word to her house and she isn't there and nobody knows her whereabouts. I swear that it grieves me ... poor girl! After all, she's not bad at heart. Amongst these unfortunates, there are some who have an excellent disposition and even traces of dignity. When it comes to keeping up appearances, she's second to none.'

As he made no answer whatsoever, seeming to pay more attention to the flowers on the carpet than his cousin's words, she was forced to take a new tack with her affectionateness.

'I repeat that you're not well. You're the colour of verdigris. Let me feel your pulse. You're burning. Rest, my dear boy, rest is what you need. Don't admit any visitors, don't talk, don't write. Stretch out on the sofa and wrap up warm with the travel rug. I'll care for you, since I can certainly drop all my duties for the sake of your health. I'll make you drinks; I'll stay all day, and if you get really ill, I'll stay all night too.'

Agustín rejected the idea of illness. Between one pause and the next, Rosalía slipped in advice and admonitions brimming with sweetness and kindness ... 'Don't take it so hard ... If you'd consulted me at the right time ... You'd better lie down ... you're cold.'

Later, much later, Agustín, expressing without reserve what was most spontaneous and natural in his soul, let himself say these grave words:

'That woman has pierced my heart and I cannot pluck her out.'

On hearing this, Rosalía took off her cashmere wrap, leaving her in her bodice. It was hot. To console her cousin she came out with the occasional phrase, full of affectionate and thoughtful sentiments. In the middle of these, Doña Marcelina Polo suddenly emerged, the only person who could give unimpeachable information about the fact, because she possessed written testimony.

'Where does that lady live?' said Caballero forcefully. 'I'll go there right away.'

'It's very late. For goodness' sake, don't get like that. You're like a character in a novel. That lady and those that live with her are real early birds. You can go tomorrow; but not very early, because at dawn the three of them go to church. The best idea is to send a message with Felipe and make an appointment.'

Don Francisco came in, returning from his walk.

'How's it going? . . .'

'I'm telling him to get into bed and he won't listen.'

'Don't we bet it's all slander?' said kindly Thiers.

Agustín asked them to stay to lunch, which they were glad to accept. Centeno went to the Hill to tell Prudencia (alias That Hopeless Girl) to feed the little ones, because Mama and Papa would not be home until very late.

CHAPTER 36

Wednesday! ... A worthy successor of the previous day, it was all damp and dark, the sky crying, the earth transformed into a lake of thick, dirty water. One might have thought that a great mass of grey melted chocolate had been spilt onto the streets. The moving flocks of umbrellas went along the pavements, giving way to others with difficulty and covering people inefficiently. The water streaming from the gutters overhead played drumrolls on them and people charged into one another, jabbed one another, scratched one another. Hats were to be seen looking like waterfalls and faces like those of the marble tritons and naiads who play the dampest roles in public fountains.

Agustín looked at this through the glass of his bedroom balcony and to the beat of that sad weather he sang to himself this unmusical elegy:

'Why didn't you stay in Brownsville, idiot? Who would put you of all people in the civilised world? Now you see ... At the very start you've been tricked. They're all playing with you, as they might with a child or a savage. When you're suspicious, you're wrong. When you're credulous, you're also wrong. This world is not for you. Your world is the Rio Grande and the Sierra Madre; your society the mobs of Indian braves and fierce adventurers; your social contacts the revolver, your ideal, money. Who would put you in these parts? Some by hook and others by crook, they're all laughing at you and deceiving you and exploiting you.'

'Sir,' said Felipe coming into the room. 'Doña Marcelina is at church. Another lady I know who lives with her, has said you can go at twelve o'clock.'

Don Francisco was not long in coming over with his face full of smiles and his greatcoat wet. His wife was terribly busy with her ballgown, and could not come until after midday. Then they spoke about what was perturbing the man from the Indies so much and Thiers brought out the most extenuating and conciliatory points that his kindliness suggested to him. It was all slander, and Agustín would be best advised not to get involved in further investigations. He was greatly saddened by what his cousin told him: 'One of two things: either I take myself back to Brownsville, or I cock a snook at the world.'

They ate together and before the meal was over, Bringas got up from the table, impatient and anxious. He had an idea, and hastened to realise it, confident of the certainty of its success. He went out hurriedly to go to we know where. Even though Rosalía was assuring everyone that Amparito was not at home, she could well have returned by now. Maybe the neighbours knew the whereabouts of the two sisters. Forward noble heart and have no fear.

Caballero went out later on, and via Descalzas, Postigo, Hita Street, Perro alley, etc . . . he made his way to Estrella Street. It is easy to imagine that he was in infernal humour and could not choose between doubt and certainty as to his misfortune. That individual called Doña Marcelina, what species of animal would she be?

This is what he was thinking as he went up the stairs of that house, which was older than evil talk. He rang and a maid told him that Madam was not back yet but she wouldn't be five minutes. He was shown into the drawing room, and when he was waiting there, a lady of singular appearance presented herself to him. She was pale-skinned, refined, clean and almost diaphanous, an elderly woman who looked like a kitten, with two emeralds for eyes and steps that padded silently as if her feet were made of wool.

'Caballero,' said that human relic looking sweetly at him. 'Are you by any chance from El Toboso?'

'No, madam,' he replied, 'I'm not from El Toboso, nor indeed La Mancha.'

'Oh! Forgive me . . .'

And she darted off, glaring at the slightly muddy marks the visitor had left on the matting. Agustín looked around the room, which contained some seven chests of drawers and other truly ancient pieces, that were, however, very well preserved, four crucifixes, two Baby Jesuses and something of the order of four dozen pictures of saints, decorated with houseleeks, ribbons and bows. Before long, a likeness to a mahogany carving under a black veil appeared.

'Are you Mr Caballero?'

'At your service . . . I wished . . .'

Doña Marcelina ushered Agustín into an adjacent small parlour. After seeing the drawing room, it seemed as though there were no more chests of drawers left in the world. However, in that room there were three. A brazier burning brightly warmed the forlorn parlour. The visitor and Polo's sister took an armchair each.

'Have you seen what a day?' observed the lady, lifting her veil and displaying the bas-relief of her face, which no Christian could fathom.

'Yes, madam, a very bad day . . . Well, I'm coming to beg you to be good enough to give me details . . .'

'I know, I know,' replied Polo's sister sharply. 'You're asking me for information, the past history of that unfortunate woman? By your leave, I shall exercise the greatest reserve, because it is against my principles to tell tales and concern myself with the actions of others. I – even if it's not for me to say – am not accustomed to harming even my greatest enemies . . . It's not to praise myself; but I have heaped benefits on many who have detested me . . .'

'In the present case,' said Caballero eagerly, 'you can make an exception in my favour, by telling me . . .'

'Whoa there,' interrupted the austere lady. 'I tell no stories, I know nothing, I've seen nothing, absolutely nothing. Somebody comes along and says Amparo's a saint? Not a word from me. You come along and tell me you want to marry her? Not a word from me. Not a word, not a word, that's my hallmark . . . Today I received God, and if I hadn't enough strength to stick to my guns, that alone would give me it.'

'But madam, for the love of God!' exclaimed Agustín in the greatest confusion. 'Truth comes before all else.'

'That's the point: there are truths which are not for telling . . . Don't ask me anything . . . my lips are sealed . . . All I'll tell you – and this is not because it's of interest to you, but for my own satisfaction – is that my brother has been saved; my brother is now on his way to Marseilles, whence he sails in three days' time for the Philippines; my brother isn't bad at heart, and over there in that land of savages, my brother will come to his senses. Do you know where the island of Zamboanga is? Because I've been told that you also come from lands of primitive people.

Well there, in that blessed Zamboanga, my brother will disembark in two months' time and there he'll have the opportunity to christen heretics and do work of great merit. This is not to say that I trust completely in his salvation, because just as leopards don't change their spots, so the man of vice doesn't change . . . what he doesn't change. Oh! The effort we had to make at the last minute! If you'd seen . . .! What a brute of a man! At the station he was telling us that he's going to be a Nebuchadnezzar in a soutane over there. He can be whatever he pleases as long as he doesn't go back to his bad old ways, nor turn up back here . . . And mark my words . . . I'm so scared . . .! I imagine that from Barcelona or Marseilles he'll return to Madrid and walk through the door when I'm least expecting it . . . You don't really know him. And those who suppose he's naturally wicked are lying; for if he hadn't been bewitched, if his head hadn't been completely turned, it would be quite another story.'

In a state of indescribable irritation and vexation, Caballero had to restrain himself from doing something silly. The truth was that he felt inclined to thump her a couple of times.

'Ah!' exclaimed the wooden woman. Did you know that poor Celedonia hasn't died? We took her to hospital the day after the scandal . . . And even if they tell you otherwise, I saw nothing, I know nothing.'

'Madam, I don't know who Celedonia is, nor do I care. Let's turn to what concerns me. I know, I have evidence that you possess two letters . . .'

His irritation impelled him to dispense with all circumspection and delicacy. He put the matter in discourteous terms, saying:

'I need you to hand those two letters over to me. I'll buy them. Do you hear? I'll buy them. Name your price.'

'Oh, I'd forgotten about them,' declared Marcelina, going to one of the chests.

'I'll buy them,' repeated Agustín, savouring the bitterness of his satisfied curiosity.

Polo's sister rummaged in the top drawer for a moment. She had her back to Caballero, at a considerable distance from him. Agustín could hear papers rustling. After a pause, Marcelina spoke.

'Well, I'll have you know that there's nothing here, nothing that you desire . . . Try your luck elsewhere, for here we don't compromise the reputation of anyone, good or bad. If a line or two turns up in these nooks and crannies, I'll follow the advice of Father Nones who's said to me: "Either you give them to their owner or to the fire", and I . . .'

She turned to face Caballero with her hands behind her back.

'There's nothing, sir, there's nothing. I'm sticking to my guns. I do no harm to anyone; not even my greatest enemies. I'll die before failing to carry out Don Juan Manuel's orders, and as I shall not see the woman involved, nor am I inclined to do so, wait . . .'

With a swift movement, she uncovered the brazier and threw into it what she held in her hand. Caballero ran to save from the flames what that devil of a woman had cast into them; but he was too late. The embers were glowing, and the curious man only saw a piece of paper twisting and charring and giving off a thin flame . . . Nothing could he read but a name which was the signature and said: *Inferno*. With the final 'o', there was a little squirl . . . Yes, it was her little squirl, her autograph in that feature which resembled a lock of curly hair.

Furious and unable to keep up the appearances that good breeding required, being a creature more of Nature than Society, where he was as if on loan, he squared up to the wooden effigy and said with maximum brutality:

'You have annoyed me . . . God keep you, or the Devil, who's already inside you, and I'll be glad if you meet your end sooner rather than later . . .'

He stormed out, furious . . . He headed towards his house; but he had hardly taken twenty paces, when he had an inspiration, a veritable thunderbolt from the blue that entered his mind. Beatas Street was just nearby . . . A secret instinct told him that there the burning fever of his doubts could find a better remedy than anywhere else. 'Who knows!' he thought, his spirit careering from one confusion to another, 'when everyone deceives me and toys with me, maybe she'll be the very person to tell me the truth . . . I do declare, if it turned out now that she was innocent . . . But where is she? Why is she hiding? . . . They must be hiding her from me so that I don't see her . . . A curse on this blindness of mine, my inexperience in the world! Rosalía is tricking me, my friends are tricking me and all are playing with this poor man, who has no understanding of riddles . . . Who's telling me the truth? . . . Which of the voices in my soul shall I listen to? The one that says: *kill her* or the one that says: *forgive her*? Brute, unhappy man, savage, you shouldn't have left your woods; swear to yourself that if she tells you the truth, you'll forgive her ... Yes, indeed I will forgive her ... I feel inclined to forgive her, Madam Society ... If she's guilty and repentant, I'll forgive her, Madam Society: devil take you, I don't care a tinker's curse for you.'

'Miss Amparo,' the concierge's wife told him, 'went out half an hour ago with a gentleman.'

'With a gentleman?'

'Yes, wearing glasses ... somewhat short, with a greatcoat the colour of dried figs.'

'Ah! My cousin ... farewell ...'

It seemed to be the devil's doing. Never had he walked the streets in such haste and never had he been thwarted so much. His umbrella became entangled at every turn with those of the people going the opposite way. One might have thought they wanted to bite each other and throw at each other the water that cascaded down on them. Then he never stopped meeting people he knew at every turn, who detained him to ask after his health and say to him: 'Have you ever seen such frightful weather?' He reached the point of thinking that they had made appointments to be in his path so as to torment him. And notwithstanding, Good Lord, the pains he had taken to limit the number of his friends!

'Don Agustín, frightful weather! There's a new moon tomorrow; it might change,' said one of Trujillo's assistants in Perro alley.

'Goodbye, goodbye ...'

At length he arrived home ... On opening the door to him, Felipe said:

'Miss Amparo is waiting for you ...'

And he, hearing this, started to tremble with alarm and grief, with curiosity and fear of satisfying it ... What expression would she wear? What would she say to him?

'And my cousin Bringas: is he here too?'

'No, sir; the young lady came alone.'

Caballero walked through the rooms. In the first she was not to be found, nor in the second. What surprised him most was to hear the chirruping birds. But as he set foot in the second small parlour, the music suddenly ceased. It had wound down. The

silence which followed the suspended symphony was so respectful and lugubrious that fear now took hold of Agustín ... Well,
she was not in there either. He saw a glass, a small phial on the
table. Then our illustrious friend lifted the curtain to the
bedroom with some dread and saw a foot ... He stopped short,
horrified, squinting, because the bedroom balcony was closed
and there was very little light ... He saw a black skirt ... an
arm dangling, its hand touching the floor ... a pink ear ... a
handkerchief covering a face ... He drew near, harbouring the
horrible suspicion that there would be no signs of life in that
body; it was so still ... He looked from close to ... He touched
her, he called her ... Yes, she was alive ... her breathing was
laboured as if she were suffering a severe asthma attack. Her
eyes were closed, dry ...

Going back out to the small parlour, Caballero saw the
prescription ... He read it for a moment, ran out ... Felipe
came to meet him in the sitting room ...

'Get a doctor,' said the master. 'Tell me, did the young lady
come alone? Did *you* see her take ...?'

'A medicine: yes, sir. She sent me to the apothecary to fetch
it.'

'You! Damn you!' exclaimed Agustín, laying into the servant
with such fury that he thought it was the end of him.

'Sir,' stammered Felipe, in tears. 'I made the medicine
myself ...'

'What with? ... Swine ... murderer.'

'Don't worry ... The apothecary told me it was poison and
then I ... ow, don't hit me! ... I came home, I took an empty
phial, I filled it with tap water ... and into the water I
poured ...'

'What did you pour in, assassin?'

'I poured in a little tincture of guaiacum ... from what Doña
Marta got for her toothache.'

'Call Doña Marta ... Don't send word to the doctor yet.'

Caballero returned to the small parlour. There was also a
letter on the table. Tearing open the envelope, he read these
tortured letters written in pencil: *It is all true. I do not deserve
pardon, but pity.* Then followed the name *Amparo* and after the
'o', the little squirl ... Confounded little squirl! ... He ran
towards her because he had heard her moan ... The suicide

looked at him with rolling eyes and began to utter half words, very incoherently and making no sense.

'She's delirious ... Her mind is affected,' said Doña Marta, who had hastened there ...

'Get a doctor – no, no, don't. Wait, wait ...'

And he returned to the small parlour. Either Sir was demented or he was very nearly so.

'Doña Marta.'

'Sir ...'

'What shall we do?'

'This is serious. She's talking nonsense and her head is burning hot ...'

'Take her home ... take her home immediately, to her own little home,' said Caballero, extracting one clear plan from his confusion. 'You be in charge, Doña Marta, of her safety and go with her. You, Felipe, fetch a carriage; but a decent carriage, a good carriage ... No, you'd better fetch the first one you find ... Doña Marta, you're in charge of taking her and making sure that she's in need of nothing ... Then, Felipe, send word to the doctor, a good doctor, is that clear? And tell him to go there, to her place ... Wrap my Amparo up, I mean, wrap her up well ... Don't let her get cold ... Make haste; get ready ... This won't be anything bad.'

Having given these orders, he looked again, from the small parlour, at the pitiful but lovely picture: the foot uncovered, the dangling arm, the oval face drained of colour, the parted lips ... Her pretty looks have been mine enemies ...! His heart crushed, our man shut himself into his study ... If he was not crying it was because he could not, for the desire to do so was not lacking.

CHAPTER 37

Four days later, according to reliable information supplied by Centeno's diligent observation, Don Agustín Cahallero was in the condition and state appropriate to someone convalescing from a serious illness. His poor colour betrayed insomnia and inadequate sustenance, and bad temper his tortured spirits, symptomatic of a liver disorder perhaps, complicated by melancholia or feelings of depression. And it is well worth noting that our good friend had rarely been so talkative, except that the wonderful things he said were spoken to himself. In the casting of that play, a long speech or monologue had fallen to him; it had already been running for four days without a break, and showed no signs of reaching a conclusion; so that if such a monologue could be heard, the audience would be, as it were, pelting him with stones. Owing to the feverish repetition of ideas and concepts, this soliloquy was unworthy of reproduction. From time to time one idea separated itself from that inner discourse and burst out, condensing itself into a sentence spoken out loud. This sentence, when it resounded in the study, had an echo which issued from the authoritative lips of Rosalía Bringas.

'You're right; I think that very sensible. The idea of leaving for America is a gesture of puerile nonsense. Take yourself off to Bordeaux for a few days and there you'll find some diversion. Then you must come back here, where you have so many friends, where you're so well loved and respected . . . and we'll see to it that you don't slip up again.'

They were in the study with the song-birds, who had not opened their beaks again since that sad episode. Rosalía had ventured to alter the place and position of some objects purely out of her love of meddling. Perhaps thoughtlessly, she took on certain airs of being the mistress of the house, and superciliously issued instructions. The previous night, Caballero, whose irritated disposition manifested itself in the most trivial things, had decreed: 'I don't want anything touched . . . Everything's to stay

where it is . . .' On hearing this, the lady had responded somewhat disconcertedly: 'All right, man . . . don't think I'm going
to dismantle your little altar . . . There it all is . . . I'm not taking
anything with me.'

That day, after wholeheartedly approving the resolution of
the little trip to Bordeaux, the lady gave a verbal chronicle of
the celebration at the Palace the night before. As she had just
come in from the street, she was sitting on the sofa in her
cashmere wrap, with her muff and veil. Lying indolently in an
armchair was that sagacious being, the great Thiers, mute and
melancholy, unlike his normal self, because of a mishap of the
greatest gravity that had occurred at the ball and which he could
not, alas, dispel from his mind for a single second.

Caballero was pacing to and fro with his hands in his pockets.
Not hearing the eulogistic descriptions of the do given by his
cousin, he stopped in front of a mirror and looked at himself
. . . Listen to a snatch taken at random from his interminable
speech, translated rather freely:

'Brute, idiot, simpleton, or I don't know what name to call
you . . . what were you after when you thrust yourself into the
civilised world? Who told you to leave your own terrain, which
is the frontier zone, where men live chained to the oars of rough
work? Your outlandish yearning to settle in the middle of an
ordered world, to be a perfect cog in these clockwork mechan-
isms of Europe, makes me laugh . . . Well, what a fiasco, my
good friend! . . . Pontificate about the family, sing the praises of
the State; wallow in Religion . . . At the very outset, civilisation,
resting on these foundations like a cauldron on its tripod, falls
down and smashes you on the nose, and breaks your head open
and blackens you all over, leaving you covered in shame and
ridicule . . . A regular lifestyle, law, order, method, concert,
harmony . . . you don't exist for a boor. The boor goes back to
his wilderness; the boor cannot be a paterfamilias; the boor
cannot be a citizen; the boor cannot be a Catholic; the boor
cannot be anything and he recovers his savage free will . . . Yes,
rustic adventurer, don't you see how lamentable and foolish
your attempt has been? Don't you see everyone laughing at you?
Don't you know that every step you take you stumble? You're
like someone who has never walked on a marble floor and falls
at the first step. You're like a labourer who dons gloves and
once they are on loses all sense of touch and is as if without

hands ... Go away, flee, clear off soon, saying: "Society shoe, you pinch, so I'm taking you off. Order, Politics, Religion, Morality, Family, fiddlesticks, you irritate me; I burst out of you like a tight garment ... I throw you far from me and tell you to go to the devil, indeed I do, confound you ..." '

Don Francisco heaved a great sigh, in which his soul seemed to be torn asunder. His wife said things to console him; but he, like those who suffer a great tribulation, knew no relief from his pain other than pain itself, and fed his soul on the recollection of his misfortune. What was it? Let us tell without further ado. His overcoat had been stolen from the Palace cloakroom!!! ... This sinister, hair-raising incident was nothing new at Palace occasions; there never was a ball at which three or four capes or overcoats did not disappear ... The wicked soul who had purloined that fine garment left in its place a tattered, grimy one that did not bear looking at. In the overheated imagination of Don Francisco, the image of his brand-new overcoat could not be dispelled, with that light, clean cloth that resembled the purest downy skin of an apricot, with that silk lining that was a dream ... In his despair, the worthy civil servant considered reporting it to the courts, telling Her Majesty about the incident, taking the matter to the press; but Palace decorum restrained him. If he caught the rogue, the scoundrel, who ...! It was hard to believe that people of the sort were admitted to those august ceremonies! ... A country where such things went on, where such misdemeanours were committed at the very foot of the throne, was a country lost to hope. To take his mind off it he picked up a newspaper.

'There can be no doubt any more,' he said in funereal tones after reading a little; 'revolution is on its way; on its way is revolution.'

'I'm glad! ... Let it happen!' exclaimed Agustín, stopping in front of his cousin.

'No one can stop this now ... The spirit of demagogy has broken loose ... the nation is breaking up, smashing itself to bits. Poor Spain! ... God save the country, God save the Queen!'

'I'm glad ...'

'Because it suffices to read any rag of a paper to see that this is getting unhinged ... Ideas are so disordered, there's such boldness, such lack of propriety, such shamefulness ...!

Nothing is respected any more, not the sacredness of the home, nor the family. Religion is made mock of and the rights of the State are laughed at. The mob is looming, the disgusting rabble is poking its nose out . . .'

'I'm glad . . .'

'Underground noises are to be heard; the throne is tottering . . . Catastrophe will soon be here . . . The sans-culottes will turn Madrid into a bloodbath, and what happened in France in '93 will be a picnic compared with what we'll have here . . . Farewell property, farewell family, farewell religion of our ancestors. The axe of destruction, the flaming torch . . . Oh, communism, atheism, the Goddess Reason, free love will come too . . .'

'I'm glad.'

'It's hard to believe,' said Don Francisco suddenly, unable to conceal the anger that he felt in spite of his bland nature; 'it's hard to believe that you of all people should talk like that, Agustín. It's hard to believe that a man like you, affiliated to the party of order, a wealthy proprietor, a citizen of integrity, who was cross because he was not asked to pay much tax; a Catholic who has given aid to the Pope in his penury; a subject who paid his respects to the Queen, a man, in short, who boasted that he was all law, all order, all precision in the social mechanism, that such a man should say *I'm glad* . . . You'll see . . . when the day dawns and that lot come in here and strip you of your property and chop off your head with the guillotine they'll set up in the Puerta del Sol; you'll see if you say *I'm glad* then . . . I want to see the look on your face when we see the throne and the altar trampled underfoot . . . when we see . . . Oh good God!'

Such eloquence was not suited to the mean humanity of Don Francisco. Perhaps he choked and had to save the rest for a better occasion. But he became more nettled still when Agustín answered him with a loud guffaw, the most spontaneous and frank one he had heard in his entire life.

'As I'll be far away then . . .' said the cousin. 'I'm going back over there to my frontiers, where gunpowder and doing exactly as one pleases are king. A pupil of anarchy, I was raised by her and to her must I return.'

'No, no, no,' declared Rosalía vehemently, standing up and putting a protective hand on her cousin's shoulder. 'Don't speak about returning to those foreign climes. Here you must live, here with us, we who love you so much. Take no notice of my husband, who's agitated today because of the theft of his overcoat and sees the black side of everything. Nothing will happen here. Those horrors are only inside my poor Bringas's head.'

'Look, Francisco,' rejoined Agustín, bursting into laughter again; 'don't distress yourself over such a little thing. I'll buy you four overcoats. Order them and tell your tailor to send me the bill. You'd better order them from my own tailor.'

Rosalía began to clap her hands, as if she were at the theatre, and her delight was so great that she could find no other way to express her jubilation. Later, on their way to their humble abode, she was daydreaming along the streets. 'He's ours,' she was thinking, 'he's ours . . .' And after feasting her imagination on the beauty of that house in Arenal Street, the home of a wealthy bachelor, she could see mountains of satins, velvets, silks, lace, furs, endless jewels, a thousand charming colours, the most elegant hats, the latest Paris fashions, all well displayed at the theatre, in the avenues, at social gatherings. And this grandiose vision, stimulating dormant appetites for luxury, letting them grow until they became completely unbridled, made her head whirl and turned her into a different woman, the same Mrs Bringas retouched and adulterated, but consoled over her falsification by the ardent intoxication of triumph.

CHAPTER 38

The master was unrecognisable; he was another man, according to Felipe. In the wake of sweetness had come peevishness. He would scold for any reason and there was no talking to him, because he would come out with all kinds of nonsense. One morning when it occurred to good old Ido to address him whilst he was pacing up and down in his study, and ask him for instructions about some entries in the large ledger, the master turned to him in a fury and . . .

'I do believe,' Don José would say when he told the story, 'I do believe that if I hadn't run for it, he would have thrown me over the balcony.'

He pulled Felipe up a few times too. But he knew how to handle him and when he was in one of those sulky moods, he kept his distance. One night Centeno came home more pleased than usual and fearlessly went running to his master to give him the following information:

'The doctor says that the young lady is out of danger . . . that it was nothing serious, and that he has ordered her to get up today.'

'Fine,' snapped the master. And a moment later: 'Felipillo . . . listen . . . You may go to the theatre this afternoon as it's Sunday. I don't need you . . . Listen, listen. If the coachman comes for the order, don't send him away as before . . . but let me know he's here.'

Monologue.

'She's pierced my heart and I can't pull her out. Accursed thorn, how soft your caress inside and how painfully you prick when pulled out! You've excelled yourself, unsociable man, you mole who can only see in the gloom of barbary, bedazzled by the bright light of civilisation so you can't see where you're going. The apple I picked seemed good to me. Cut open I find it damaged. How it enrages me to think that the part that's still good is to be for someone else . . . Because she's finished for me and I for her. Her conduct has been so dishonourable that I cannot pardon her ... I'm leaving, fleeing from her and my own shadow, from this counterfeit, this false self that wished to fit into the vice-ridden culture over here ... Marriage nauseates me. I abhor it as one abhors the tank into which one was on the verge of falling ... I shall take to my heels and leave this land, this atmosphere; but I shall not depart without seeing with my own eyes the rotten apple and having a long look at those good parts which another man will bite into, not I, unfortunate and wretched I, who always arrives too late through not knowing how to walk on these fine floors ... And if social decorum prohibits me from seeing her, I say to Society that I don't give tuppence for all its frills and furbelows, and I'll go and stand right in the middle of the street, if necessary, shouting: "Long live immorality, long live anarchy, long live folly!"'

And it was on the seventh day, according to Felipe, that the master made himself all ready to leave for France on the evening express train. His cousins had stayed with him since very early, and Rosalía went to the greatest lengths to be useful, looking for opportunities to display her activeness. She was dressed exceedingly ostentatiously that day and had certainly given her all to creating the most showy image.

'Agustín,' she repeated in a tone that lay somewhere between sentimentality and jocularity, 'mind you write to us at least once a week. Remember we can't live without hearing from you regularly. We're inconsolable. I shall reply to all your letters, because Bringas is very busy and can't do so ... And don't you stay away from us for long out there; back you come as soon as can be. Don't leave us for long in this sad state ... A fortnight of rest is quite enough.'

At about one o'clock the arrival of the carriage was announced and Agustín went out without saying where. In the room that led into the study, Ido and Centeno conveyed their impressions of events to one another.

IDO [*the pen between his teeth, while he drew lines on some paper with a pencil and ruler*]: Thank Heavens the master's happy. Do you know what he told me? That all I've to do for now is put the Bordeaux address on any letters that come in.

CENTENO [*cupping his hands round his mouth so as to say secret words into Don José's ear*]: I know where the master's gone. I was coming in when he was getting into the carriage and he said to the coachman: *four Beatas Street*.

IDO [*surprised*]: He's going to take his leave of her . . . Between ourselves, Felipe, I think the master is not considering his decorum in taking such a step. Because, frankly my friend, naturally, honour . . .

CENTENO: The doctor has said she's out of danger . . .

IDO: Not so fast . . . Nicanora, who's attending her on Sir's orders (and I suppose he'll pay well for the attendance); Nicanora maintains . . .

CENTENO [*impatiently*]: What does she say?

IDO: Let me do these lines in ink . . . Well, she says . . . First I'll tell you what I think.

CENTENO: What have you been thinking?

IDO: I shall trust it to you . . . discreetly. Well, I think that there's only one solution if Miss Amparo is to find regeneration . . . What is it? I shall convey it to you . . . but with the greatest discretion. Great was the sin . . . so the expiation, my lad, the expiation . . .

CENTENO: Come to the point, will you? . . .

IDO [*presumptuously smug*]: In short, she has no option but to become a Sister of Charity . . . That, on top of being poetic, is a means to regeneration . . . Mark my words . . . Curing the sick and wounded in hospitals and camps . . . To labour and toil . . . ! Just imagine how pretty she'll be with that white veil . . .

CENTENO [*spellbound*]: She'll look delicious.

IDO: Ha, ha . . . Sister of Charity. She has no other choice.

CENTENO [*mockingly perceptive*]: Don José . . . you never do stop being a novelist . . .

IDO: The truth is that over these lazy days I will write one entitled: *From the Whore-House to the Cloister* . . . It came to me now, witnessing these unlikely events . . . Ah! I was forgetting to tell you that according to Nicanora, the girl seems cured by now of that mishap, but she isn't. She gets up, she eats; but her soul is deeply wounded, and when we are least expecting it she's going to give us a fright . . . Who knows, my lad; maybe when the master gets there, he'll find her dead.

CENTENO: Sweet Jesus!

IDO: I'm saying it may be . . . It would be a poetical end for her, and if on seeing him enter, she had a shred of life left to recognise him and be able to say a couple of tender words of repentance, of love, an *Oh, Sweet Jesus*, an *I love you* or something of the kind, I believe that she would die happy . . .

CENTENO: You think things have to go the way you imagine them . . . Don't be stupid . . . Everything turns out the opposite of how one thinks . . .

IDO [*with vanity*]: As far as I'm concerned, my lad, reality always proves me right . . . But don't delay . . . I think Doña Rosalía is calling you.

CENTENO: Let the stuck-up braggart wait. She's unbearable . . . And how she enjoys giving us orders, as if she were the mistress of the house. Her airs and graces are so infuriating! Yesterday she pulled this ear of mine . . . I was all but bleeding . . . she called me *good-for-nothing* and said: 'You're getting to think yourself quite a gentleman. And I'm going to put you in your place . . .' To call her a busybody is to put it mildly; and *en plus*, friend Ido, last night she took the two fine little vases with china flowers top and bottom, you know? And she went off with them, the great . . . She said there was no need at all for them here. The day before yesterday she made off with a dozen napkins that had never been used and three tablecloths . . . In sum, this is a thief's paradise. It makes me feel like calling a halt when I see such cheek.

IDO [*maliciously*]: Don't get involved in that, friend Aristotle, the master is the master and he sees well enough what's going on with that woman . . . and if he's seeing and saying nothing, there'll be a reason . . . This morning she came into the study saying: 'Is there a *scrap* of paper around here?' And she made off with three reams of letterheads and some three hundred envelopes. So much for the scraps the lady uses . . . Quiet; I think . . .

ROSALIA [*from the door, extremely angry and in a very despotic tone*]: Felipe! I've been calling you for an hour . . . You're the most hopeless case I've ever seen. I don't know how Agustín puts up with you, you great lazybones . . . Let's see . . . your master's shirts, you good-for-nothing, where have you put them?

CHAPTER 39

Striding up the stairs to Amparito's lofty dwelling, Agustín was near the top when he met Nicanora coming down.

'Ah! Is it you?' said Ido's wife, surprised. 'She's better. Yesterday she got up. She ate very well just before . . . The gentleman has no need to ring. I've left the door open, because I'm coming straight back.'

Amparo was sitting in an armchair, well wrapped up, her mouth covered by her right hand which was itself inside a fold of her shawl. Through the glass in the narrow window she was watching the sparrows on the next-door rooftop, now frolicking, now flying off in groups to be lost from sight in the blue sky. It was a splendid day; the sight of that sky made the phenomenon of rain's existence seem incomprehensible. When she heard the door creak and she looked round and saw who was coming in, she was on the verge of losing consciousness. She did not utter a word; that idiocy from which she had suffered days back came over her. Agustín smiled very courteously and, transfixed with emotion, asked her how she was. She knew not whether she said *well* or *ill*, or even if she said anything at all. He who had been her betrothed took a chair and sat down beside her.

'How are things?' he said, after a pause, devouring her with his eyes. 'Have you had some food? Are we getting our strength back?'

'A moment ago . . . all right . . . well.'

Judge the one, delinquent the other, both seemed like criminals.

'I've come to say goodbye,' remarked Agustín, after another long pause. 'This evening I'm leaving for France.'

Amparo looked at him, blinking. Her eyelids were in continuous motion . . .

'Don't cry, don't upset yourself,' said the ex-fiancé. 'It's all over between us; but I don't bear you any grudge. Your lack of sincerity has wounded me as much as your misdemeanour, of which I still know nothing concrete, because no one has given me the proof I desire ... But be that as it may, you yourself have said enough for you not to be able to be my wife. I don't need to know any more, I don't wish to know any more ... You're not worthy of me. Recognise that you're not worthy of me. When I depart, I'll leave you safe from destitution for some time ... for I must go far and you certainly won't see me again, nor I you either.'

The fortitude that he was showing was going to fail him; for which reason he judged it prudent to withdraw, in order that his dignity should not suffer. He rose to his feet to go out, when he suddenly felt a hand detain him. He pulled hard, but it did not let go. This foreign hand that clutched his had supernatural strength. And truly, how could he be allowed to leave without even an explanation? That really was the right moment. Once the initial embarrassment was past, the confession came out of her mouth, free, fluent, unfaltering, with her very soul in it, all truth and sentiment.

Doña Nicanora says that when she opened the door of the room, she saw them sitting there right next to one another, their faces quite close, her whispering, him listening with every fibre of his being, like priests in the confessional. The wise neighbour, seeing that that hushed talk deserved the greatest respect, preferred not to enter, and leaving the door ajar, remained in the corridor. Much as she wanted to catch something of what the penitent was saying, she spoke so quietly that not a single word reached Mrs Ido's eager ears.

When that mysterious dialogue had concluded, Amparo's face was radiant, her eyes sparkling, her cheeks flushed, and in her look and her whole being there was an intangible air of triumph and inspiration that made her look extraordinarily beautiful.

'Never have I seen her looking so pretty,' that wise neighbour used to say.

Our respectable friend, sighing deeply two or three times, paced up and down the room looking at the floor.

Monologue.

'Not my wife ... But time will pass, indulgent time, and she'll be another man's wife. Another will bite into the good part of the fruit, for there is still plenty of good, plenty that's appetizing, plenty that's saying: *eat me* ... It's done, onward, and let them say of me what they will. Scandal! So what? Immorality! What's it to me? When one reaches the age of forty-five, has one to look upon old age from so near without being able to live a little before entering it? To die knowing nought but a dog's life is a sad thing! . . . Don't you realise, fool, that you're doing just the opposite of what you planned when you began your life in Europe? Exult, unworldly man, in the horrible contradiction that is yours, and don't call it an outrage but natural law, because life is imposing it upon you, and we don't make life, but it's life that makes us . . . And you, what do you care for what the neighbours will say, that you've been enslaved? You were bred in anarchy and to it your fatal destiny makes you return. It's an end of artifice. What do you care for the social order, for Religion, or any of all that? You sought to be the most orderly of citizens and it was all a lie. You sought to be a conventional Christian; a lie too, for you have no faith. You sought to take as a wife virtue itself; lie, lie, lie. Come out now and tread the broad path of your instinct, commend your spirit to the great, free God of circumstance. Put not your trust in the conventional majesty of principle and kneel before the shining altar of fact . . . If this is folly, let it be.'

Ending this soliloquy with another great sigh, Agustín went over to the young woman and placed his hand upon her head in a gesture akin to that of stage priests when they are supposed to bring heaven's blessing upon some virtuous character: martyr, neophyte or such like. And his initiative did not stop here, for he said to his ex-fiancée:

'Have you by any chance a small trunk? . . .'

'A small trunk!' repeated Amparo, like an idiot.

'Yes; I need one, you see. I'm carrying so many things . . .'

'There's quite a large one in that room,' interfered Doña Nicanora, who was present.

'Bring it here, madam.'

No sooner said than done. A moment later a trunk of middling size, lined with green paper, was in the middle of the room displaying its capacity. Agustín looked at his watch.

It's half past two,' he said gravely. 'Well now, Amparito, you should start putting all your clothes in here.'

Incredulous, the young woman was looking at her ex-fiancé, who was finally going to be her . . .

'There's no time to lose. I have to talk to you; but as I can't delay my journey, you're going to be good enough to come to Bordeaux with me. Pay attention to what I'm telling you. Try to be ready by a quarter to four or four sharp at the latest. At that hour Felipe will come in my carriage or another. He'll take you to the station.'

At a quarter to five, Don Francisco was looking for his cousin on the North platform to bid him an affectionate goodbye and embrace him warmly half a dozen times.

'There they are, in that reserved carriage,' said Felipe, whom he found with a basket, a hatbox, and various other small items appropriate for a journey.

The *they* surprised the illustrious Thiers somewhat; but Agustín gave him little time to dwell upon that strange plural.

'Look who I'm taking with me,' he said, indicating the back of the carriage.

Thiers, disconcerted, mumbled a few words; but then he recovered and as it was not in his nature to find anything that his powerful cousin did worthy of censure, he ended by smiling and regarding the matter through indulgently tinted spectacles.

'How are you, dear; do you feel better? Are you well? . . . Mind you wrap up well, because you haven't got your full strength back. There's a great deal of snow in the port. For goodness' sake, Agustín, make sure she wraps up well. And you take care, for you're not well either. I believe you will be provided with heaters . . . Amparito, muffle yourself up, dear.'

'No need to worry. She'll make the journey quite happily,' said Caballero, 'and the change of air will do her a world of good.'

'I think so too. Have you got a picnic? If you'd said, we'd have made you a bottle of good broth at home.'

Afterwards, the two cousins spoke a little, but no one discovered what they were saying. In the opposite corner of the carriage, Amparito was directing her attention to the activity in the station and silently observing the harassed travellers who were rushing to find seats; the drinks, books, and newspaper vendors, the little barrows that carried luggage and the hurried coming and going of the station master and his underlings. She desired that the train should soon set off at speed. The immense

CHAPTER 41

Small parlour in the Bringas household. Nightfall.

ROSALÍA: [*with consternation, fanning herself with a fan, a handkerchief, a newspaper, and anything she finds to hand*]: I'm going to come over queer. My blood feels as though it were boiling and all rising to my head ... Tell me no more, man; for the love of God, tell me no more ... Such shocking immorality bewilders me, overwhelms me, drives me to distraction ... And you saw her yourself? Could it have been an illusion of yours ...?

THIERS: How could I not see her! There she was in the reserved car, nice and snug, not saying a word, and so happy that her eyes were literally sparkling ...

ROSALÍA: And you had the forbearance to witness such a scandal? ... So he can't make her his wife because she's a ... and he makes her his mistress ...! I'm shaken ... Such terrible ignominy, in our family, in this family of more exemplary decency than most, infuriates me ... [*Looking at him fiercely.*] And you, you said nothing? You put up with having right under your nose ...?

THIERS [*preparing to tell a fib*]: Such was my indignation when Agustín declared to me ... because he was shameless enough to confess his weakness to me ... well, I was so indignant that I said what I thought and turned my back upon him and left the station.

ROSALÍA [*satisfied*]: You did that? Of course; you were unable to restrain your anger. You turned your back on him, you left him with words upon his lips ...

THIERS [*mentally begging God's forgiveness for his dishonesty*]: Just as I say. The truth is that we shall no longer be able to have dealings with my cousin. Who would have thought it! A man of moderation, who wanted to be so punctilious about everything, to fall short of good principled behaviour in this way, to give joy that she felt seemed like a provisional happiness, as long as the engine was stationary.

'Goodbye ... goodbye ... do enjoy yourselves ... mind you write, Agustín ... Close the door, close it ... Don't you both stay over there for long ... Goodbye ... bon voyage. Woe betide you if you fail to write. We'll be distraught until we hear ... Goodbye, goodbye.'

A train departing is the most similar thing in the world to a book ending. When the trains return, new pages: open up.

society, religion, the family, everything we venerate in short, a slap in the face! ... Well, it's what I keep saying: this way madness lies. This is disastrous. Revolution is not far behind; we shall see the rich stripped, atheism, free love ...

ROSALÍA: We shall, we shall; I do believe we shall see that and more ... When such incredible horrors are witnessed, anything may be expected. [*Extremely upset.*] There's not a cataclysm left that could take me by surprise.

THIERS [*melancholic*]: You'd have to be blind not to see that this society is rapidly losing respect for everything. The throne and the altar are held up to public ridicule; the gangrene of demoralisation spreads, and when I see that my own are clear of the rot, it seems like a miracle to me.

ROSALÍA [*pensive*]: And didn't he say whether he would return with the precious cargo of his lover?

THIERS: Yes. They'll be back, they'll be back ...

ROSALÍA [*her nostrils dilating extraordinarily*]: Because I don't want to bottle up the thing or two I intend to tell him and her. Oh no! I shan't bottle it up. I would go to France, to Peking, to get this anger off my chest ...

THIERS: Here we'll have them one fine day as large as life ... and they'll live as man and wife, an insult to decency, to virtue ... such horrors will be there for us to see ...! Joaquín and Paquito were saying it quite clearly the other evening: *The axe of destruction, the flaming torch stand in wait. Demagogy ...!* Oh! I was forgetting one important thing. We do gain something. That fool told me you could have everything that was bought for the wedding.

PRUDENCIA [*from the door*]: Madam, the soup.

ROSALÍA [*aside, her gaze lost in contemplation of the portrait of Don Juan de Pipaón, depicted with a roll of papers in his hand*]: They'll be back ... Here; I want to get you both, here ...! Bloodsucker of that saint, we shall come face to face.

NOTE ON THE TRANSLATOR

ABIGAIL LEE SIX M.A., Ph.D. (Cantab.) is Chairman of the Department of Hispanic Studies and Italian at Queen Mary and Westfield College, University of London. Her research field is nineteenth- and twentieth-century Spanish fiction.